EXECUTIVE ORDER 14900

GARY A. KEEL

Aperture Press

Hardcover ISBN: 978-0-9995158-8-4
Paperback ISBN: 978-1-7329329-1-3
Library of Congress Control Number: 2018961887

First Edition: October 2018

Cover photo © aheflin / stock.adobe.com.

ACKNOWLEDGMENTS

—

Getting a first book published is a formidable undertaking. Hours at the computer, mountains of work, and learning the ins and outs of publishing do not guarantee success. The support of good people does increase one's chances. For that reason, I want to acknowledge those who played key roles in this wonderful adventure.

In addition to serving as the inspiration for my lead heroine, my beautiful wife Caroline stood with me throughout this daunting process. Besides providing valuable insight, she sacrificed holiday road trips so I could write. More importantly, she gave me the emotional and psychological support needed to get through the low points every author faces. Her pep talks were invaluable.

I'm grateful to my Cherokee grandmother who taught me that there's a story teller in all of us. As a youngster, I spent many sleepless nights after hearing her stories about wild animals, shamans, and evil spirits.

Kudos to my writing group, Diane Berry, Mildred Farrior, and Barbara Wiggins, plus my editor, Naomi Dixon, who helped me turn lemons into lemonade.

To my beta readers who trudged through tangled early drafts and still encouraged me to proceed, God bless you! They are Tina Cowell, Henri McClees, and June Nichols.

Many thanks to an eclectic group of authors who contributed to my evolution from story teller to author. Steven James taught me the value of organic writing and the difference between drama and narration. He also called for trusting one's instincts. Les Pendleton pointed out several land mines one should avoid as an aspiring author. Danny Ferguson encouraged me to keep editing because my manuscript "wasn't ready for prime time." Nevertheless, he nudged me forward with Winston Churchill's immortal words, "Never, never give up." Lisa Wingate showed me smooth flowing prose. Phil Bowie's novels made me appreciate that heroes can be common people facing uncommon situations. I even picked up some valuable catches while avoiding fouls from Jim Sargent, who writes about baseball, among other things!

Woe to those who call evil good
And good evil;
Who substitute darkness for light
And light for darkness;
Who substitute bitter for sweet
And sweet for bitter!
Woe to those who are wise
In their own eyes
And clever in their own sight!

Isaiah 5:20–21

When people fear their government,
You get Tyranny

When government fears its people,
You get liberty

Thomas Jefferson

CHAPTER 1

—

Private Denny Lang sat behind his M240 machine gun on high alert. He and fellow members of the Georgia National Guard were dug in along a desolate strand of Interstate 20 near Madison, Georgia. They were the first line of defense against a rogue government, a government laying siege to its own citizens.

Though a relatively new guardsman, Lang's prior training in the Marine Corps qualified him as a proficient gunner. The Bronze Star in his breast pocket served as a testament to darker days in Iraq and Afghanistan, experience that would serve him well on this mission. He reached for the medal, kissed it for good luck, and reverently placed it back in his pocket, close to his heart.

Colonel Jeffrey Ames, the Guard's executive officer, ambled down the line on his last inspection of their defenses. His notable frame cast a long shadow over the sand-bagged emplacements. "At ease, Private," he barked before Lang could snap to attention. Eyeing the stockpile of ammo, he added, "Think five crates is enough, Soldier?"

Lang's last engagement in Iraq flashed through his memory. Pinned down by mortars and rocket propelled grenades, or RPGs, his squad had exhausted their ammo. The feeling of helplessness changed him forever. He peered up at the colonel. "I don't want to go down for lack of shooting, sir." He patted the closest crate for effect.

Ames circled the emplacement, running his hand along the gun's smooth barrel as if he were stroking a beautiful woman. "That's good, private. But remember to let your barrel cool. If it fails, you're out of business. And so are those depending on you for cover."

"Don't worry, sir. If I go down, a bunch of them are going with me."

The colonel smiled and flashed a thumbs up. "I'm just glad you're on our side, Son." He walked away to inspect positions farther down the interstate.

Machine gun nests were set up on both sides of the roadway to sweep any advancement from the east. Lang manned the most strategic position in front of a ramshackle barricade.

Another gunner asked, "Where are you from, Lang?"

Lang beamed with hometown pride. "I'm from Albany."

The other soldier removed his helmet and scratched his head. "Where the heck is Albany? I'm from a town in the mountains. Local Cherokees named it Dahlonega when gold was found there in 1828. Dahlonega is Cherokee for yellow money."

Leaning on his machine gun, Lang glared. "We don't call it Albany. That place is in New York. We call it Albany, like Jack Benny, with oomph on the last part."

The soldier cast a sarcastic smirk. "I got it. We'll be sure to ship your body to the right place when this fracas is over."

The sight of Colonel Ames leaving the area meant the squad had passed muster. With time to relax, Lang started boiling water for a helping of MREs, meals ready to eat, as the military calls its rations. A packet of beef ravioli, his favorite, sat on a sandbag next to him. The soothing gurgle of boiling water was drowned out by the distinctive crack of a high-powered rifle. Lang instinctively ducked behind the sandbags, knocking scalding water everywhere. "Crap," he mumbled, wincing from the hot water seeping into his boot webbing.

Peering over a sandbag, he saw Dahlonega, who'd been walking from the latrine to his gun emplacement, stagger then crumple to the pavement. He jerked spasmodically with his arm pinned under him. Blood gushed from a gaping wound in his chest, pooling near his shoulder.

He knew from his training that Dahlonega's heart would be racing to compensate for his plummeting blood pressure. That would speed up his bleeding, reducing the time to save him. It pained Lang to see Dahlonega's eyes pleading for help, knowing his torn lungs couldn't power words. With hope fading, he prayed, *God, please help me save him.* He could see Dahlonega's eyes widen in terror as blood oozed past his cheek. There was no mystery where it came from.

To a sniper, a horizontal target is harder to hit than a standing one. With adjustments for range and windage, deadly rounds inched closer and closer to Dahlonega's head. Fragments of lead and asphalt blasted all around him. The final shot sent a chunk of pavement the size of a golf ball smashing into his face.

Lang gazed in horror at Dahlonega's teeth scattered among the debris like oddly-shaped pearls resting on the ocean bottom.

"Ah," Dahlonega moaned in a weak, trailing breath. Everything turned to darkness, then nothing. He lay motionless until a jagged bolt of pain made him writhe like an injured snake. His contorted arm looked out of place. *Help me,* his mind screamed, even as his voice remained muted. The pain faded as he slipped back into unconsciousness.

Dahlonega's sarcastic remark about shipping his body to the right place blared in Lang's ears. Their predicament defied all human reasoning. Dahlonega was shot by another American soldier. A soldier of the 82nd Airborne Division under orders from a deranged President, but an American soldier nevertheless. How were they going to explain to his father and mother, or his wife and kids, that he was killed by another American soldier? They would never understand, nor did he.

"Not on my watch," he swore. From previous firefights he knew he had less than five minutes to save Dahlonega before he bled out, if he were still alive. He focused his binoculars intently on the woods, eyes straining for signs of a sniper in a camouflaged ghillie suit. He scanned heavy underbrush that could serve as cover. Fragments of foliage drifted to the ground as he unleashed his gun. He desperately searched the tree line to stop the sniper before he could zero in. His eyes focused and re-focused while Dahlonega's body lay on open ground, the perfect kill zone for a marksman. Regrettably, Dahlonega now served as Lang's bait, just like Lang and his men had served as bait for the air strike in Mosul.

Seconds seemed like eternity. Another shot ricocheted off the pavement two inches from Dahlonega's right ear. Fragments of lead and asphalt peppered his cheek and forehead, adding puncture wounds to his torment. A heartbeat later the report of the shot echoed from a canopy of kudzu. Dahlonega drifted back to consciousness with his eyes darting from side to side in a desperate search for help. Pink bubbles spewed from his shredded mouth as he attempted to cry out, but no words came. The slightest movement brought excruciating pain.

"Thank God, he's still alive," Lang muttered. He knew 82nd reinforcements were probably moving toward the gunfire. Dahlonega had to be rescued now. Time was running out as his lifeblood turned the asphalt bright red.

Dahlonega inched toward Lang, clawing at the ground until pain paralyzed him. Alone, vulnerable, and injured, he still showed the will to live.

Lang hung onto hope. He was tempted to bolt to his downed brother, but leaving his fortified emplacement would be suicide. Torn by untenable choices, he released another burst of fire to keep the sniper off balance.

With each passing second, Dahlonega slipped closer to death.

Catching a glimpse of movement behind some kudzu, Lang delivered another devastating burst. Obliterated greenery covered the ground. As soon as the gun fell silent, he heard Lieutenant Sparks barking orders behind him as his squad advanced. Fire from the sniper's backup had them pinned down, leaving the rescue solely up to him. He searched for signs of movement from his wounded comrade and was relieved to see him strain to free his pinned arm. Beneath his blood-soaked shirt, his wound oozed with each heartbeat. His eyes were now glassy and empty, his breathing labored.

"Gotta move," Lang seethed. He raised slightly, then dropped down just as a deadly round struck a sandbag next to his head. Cool moist sand drifted down his collar. He blasted the tree line again, firing directly over his dying comrade. "Sniper in the trees," he screamed to his squad hunkered down behind him. "LT, what can we do? We can't just leave him there."

Sparks cupped his hands and yelled over the barricade, "Maintain your position, Lang. They're trying to flank us. B-Company's holding them off, but they're counting on us to block the interstate."

Lang knew his strategic position had to be defended, but if Dahlonega wasn't rescued quickly, he would perish. Abandoning a brother simply was not in the former Marine's playbook. He had to make his move, and he had to do it now. Clutching the bronze star in his breast pocket, he remembered something he saw in a movie. He removed his helmet, then focused his binoculars on the far tree line. While scanning for movement, he slid his helmet on top of the sandbags. The helmet jerked backward as if shot from a cannon. It spun upside down on the ground with fingers of light shining through two gaping holes. The location of the muzzle blast was seared in his mind's eye. Pivoting his gun to the exact location, he fired another long burst into the spot. Trees burst into splinters while shreds of leaves floated in the breeze. Once the smoke cleared, his binoculars picked up the unmistakable image of a Remington M24 sniper rifle with a shattered buttstock. A lifeless arm clutching the rifle signaled an opening.

"Sorry, LT!" he yelled, scrambling over the sandbags. "Cover me." He weaved toward his downed brother in a crouched position. A wall of automatic fire rained from behind him.

Dahlonega couldn't make out the blurry image rushing toward him. Like every other bodily function, his vision was failing.

The weaving and ducking Lang had perfected in Iraq made him nearly impossible to hit. Bullets ricocheted off the asphalt, sending fragments in every direction. With total disregard for his own safety, he slid into the kill zone like a New York Yankee stealing second base. The painful abrasions to his hands didn't deter him as he flattened on the roadway beside Dahlonega. "Come on, pal, we're outta here," he yelled while trying to ignore Dahlonega's grotesque facial wounds. They could be fixed, but his death couldn't.

Flaps of torn flesh mouthed a thank you, but only blood gurgled out. His look screamed with gratitude.

With no time for niceties, Lang draped him over his shoulder like a sack of rice, ignoring his tortured groans. Precious blood trickled down his back. "Hang on, partner," Lang grunted. He had about three minutes left.

As Dahlonega's life slipped away, his arms fell limp. Warm blood dripped from his fingertips down Lang's backside.

To Lang it was just another distraction to be ignored. The former Marine ran like a scared jackrabbit, conscious of the weight. He wouldn't lose his brother now. Two minutes left to save him. Lang's lungs burned. *God, give me strength*, he prayed silently.

"Run, Lang, run," his squad yelled above the ear-piercing gunfire. Bullets whizzed around him in both directions. He relied on his squad's friendly fire to be safe and true.

Dahlonega's dead weight was Lang's imperative. He pushed on toward the barricade, trying to block out the rest of the world. "Gotta keep going," he mumbled. "So tired, so heavy." Just 15 more feet, now 10. With a few steps to go he stumbled and fell to one knee. Pain shot through his downed leg to his lower back. Momentum carried Dahlonega forward, pressing the bronze star into Lang's sternum. *Is this it*, he wondered. *Is this how it ends?*

"Get up, Lang," his squad yelled.

"Move it, Private," Lieutenant Sparks screamed.

His squad knew the shooters would zero in on the now stationary target.

Lang knew it, too. With a fear-induced adrenaline rush, he pushed upward with every ounce of strength. His downed knee sprang up, allowing him to race the remaining distance to the barricade. Safe but exhausted, he dropped to the ground with the limp, lifeless body on top of him. His chest heaved with every breath. He looked up at a medic who had joined them from another position. "Patch him up, Doc," he whispered.

After a couple more deep breaths, he rolled Dahlonega onto the ground next to him and raised up on one elbow. Pointing a bloody finger to his emplacement, he said, "Have to get back to my position, right, LT?"

"Hold it," Sparks said as a bullet slammed into a nearby sandbag. "Hang tight for a minute."

The medic watched the brief exchange between Lang and the Lieutenant before turning back to Dahlonega. "One casualty is enough," he mumbled with wishful thinking. His first attempt to insert an IV plasma line missed. On the second try the cannula slid effortlessly into a thirsty vessel. Dahlonega didn't flinch.

Meanwhile, Sparks applied a QuikClot dressing to the chest wound, but it continued to ooze. He looked up to the medic for guidance, but got an alarmed look instead. "Oh hell," he mumbled, thrusting his index finger into the wound. Dahlonega writhed in pain, but the bleeding stopped.

"His vitals are stabilizing," the medic said. "I think he's gonna make it." Their triage had worked.

Dahlonega's blood-shot eyes crept open, searching for Lang. The movement drew attention to his mangled face, making it difficult to tell what he looked like before. He inhaled deeply, but still no words. A cough from aspirating his own blood brought another painful spasm. He closed his eyes and thought of the Georgia mountains. Thanks to Lang he would see them again.

While everyone stood in silence, Lang felt a weak tug. He gazed down at two nearly lifeless eyes. "I know, Dahlonega, you owe me," he said, as only a soldier would understand.

The battle had just begun and Private Denny Lang had proven again that he was worthy of the medal in his pocket. But he wasn't finished yet.

"Hang in there, pal," he said turning toward his emplacement. An eerie silence swept over Sparks's men. The 82nd patrol had withdrawn to probe for a weaker position. Their search would be as futile as their attempt to take out Dahlonega.

I hope they took the sniper with them, Sparks thought. *I can't afford a burial detail.*

"Hey, LT, what's that above the trees?" a sentry yelled.

Sparks raised his binoculars, focusing on the unmistakable profile of an MQ-9 Reaper drone heading straight toward them, its camera focused and scanning to relay the Guard's strength and position back to the 82nd.

Sparks twirled toward his gunners. "Take it out! Now!"

Back at his post, Lang had already taken aim. Without hesitation he gently squeezed the trigger, just like he'd been taught in gunnery school. Three rapid bursts sent the drone into a spiral, crashing into the trees less than two hundred yards to the east. Private Denny Lang from Albany, Georgia had become the first person in history to shoot down a military drone in United States airspace.

A buzzer sounded on the central communication panel at Guard headquarters. The communications officer held the headset out to Martinez. "Major Simms is on the horn, sir."

Martinez grappled with the springy headset, making a couple of adjustments. "Major."

"Sir, one of Lieutenant Sparks's guys just downed a Reaper flying west along I-20."

Martinez peered out the window toward the interstate. "I see the smoke from here. Double your patrols, Major."

"We'll be ready, sir."

CHAPTER 2

—

Just a few hours earlier, Adjutant General Rudy Martinez, Commander of the Georgia National Guard, relaxed in the Calabash Café near downtown Madison. Thoughts of the impending battle had ruined his appetite. A tasty-looking gyro, the specialty of the house, lay untouched on his plate.

Colonel Jeffrey Ames, his Executive Officer, burst into the room. His deliberate gait conveyed a sense of urgency. Towering over the general's table, he leaned down to whisper, "Sorry for interrupting, sir, but the 82nd just crossed over near Augusta."

Stone-faced, the general jumped up, sending his chair skidding backward. Ames stepped aside as it settled against the wall. Martinez threw a twenty on the table, then broke for the door. "Let's do this, Colonel."

The Guard's temporary headquarters in the historic James Madison Hotel stood just beyond a serene town park. The sculptured water fountain, colorful playground equipment, and an open stage for local concerts were typical of so many small town parks. As Martinez and Ames strolled by, the general shuddered at the prospect of armed conflict in a place where families and children gathered to play. He silently cursed President Elliott for placing so many innocent civilians, as well as loyal soldiers, in harm's way.

Ames leaned heavily on the hotel's mammoth double doors. Their heavy iron hinges resisted, then yielded. "After you, General," he said. The two men entered the historic icon of a bygone era. Two-hundred-year-old planks creaked in protest as the burly officers strode through the majestic lobby. Soldiers moving an ornate secretary desk to make room for military equipment snapped to attention.

"Careful, men. We're here to preserve, not to damage," Martinez said while returning their salute.

"Yes, sir," the soldiers replied in unison. Once their commanders had passed, they gingerly lifted the secretary and carried it across the glossy heart of pine floor.

Martinez led Ames to a temporary office provided by the manager. He reached into a canvas pouch and handed Ames a copy of Governor Spivey's order to block the 82nd's advance without collateral damage. Ames slumped into the nearest chair from the weight of the order. His downcast gaze expressed more than words. He knew the dangers faced by innocent civilians during combat. He had learned through too many bloody engagements that bullets and artillery shells are indiscriminate killers without a conscience.

Martinez noticed Ames's distress. "This downtown is in harm's way as long as we're headquartered here," he barked. "Let's get everything moved to the County Building near the interstate before things heat up. Hopefully, that will put enough distance between civilians and the point of engagement." As an added precaution, he ordered an evacuation of the business corridor along Eatonton Road, the main thoroughfare from I-20 into Madison. He preferred some higher ground for a tactical advantage, but such terrain simply wasn't available in middle Georgia. His men did hold the moral high ground, however, as citizen soldiers protecting their families from an invading force.

Driven by discipline, Ames refocused. "I'll have the headquarters moved before evening, sir."

Martinez casually glanced out the window. The park was now occupied by a young couple pushing a child in a swing. They seemed frozen in time, oblivious to the juggernaut closing in on them. As the child giggled and kicked her feet, Martinez thought of his own children who were safe in Douglasville. "Governor Spivey insists we take the high road in this mess, even if the President won't," he said.

"In my humble opinion, this President couldn't find the high road with a map and a GPS," Ames scoffed. He turned toward the window. "I'll send someone to warn that family."

Before retiring that evening, Martinez wrote in his journal, *I think I know how these folks felt when William Tecumseh Sherman stormed through during his legendary "March to the Sea."*

Martinez would need every tactical advantage and a heroic effort to stop the 82nd. He called on Madison's able bodied men to help build a barricade across I-20 at exit 114. Heavy farm equipment, junk automobiles, and a couple of semi-trailers were piled across the interstate to block the 82nd's advance. Martinez watched his guardsmen working alongside townspeople, while military policemen detoured civilian traffic away from the combat zone. *Why can't the politicians work together like this?* he wondered.

The Central Georgia State Militia, self-appointed guardians of the people, yearned to join the Guard's ranks. Their commander challenged Martinez. "We suspect you're gonna be outnumbered, General, and we'd like to even up the fight. Most of us are seasoned hunters who can drop a buck deer at three hundred yards."

Martinez saw an aged Vietnam veteran through the checkered hunting jacket, faded jeans, and snake-proof boots. "God knows we could use your help," he said. "Since you're unfamiliar with our equipment and tactics, it'd be nearly impossible to coordinate. Could you guard the townspeople and serve as a reserve unit instead?"

Content with his important backup role, the Commander shouldered his rifle. "Consider it done, General," he said. On his way out, he spied some communication equipment on a nearby table. "Can you spare one of those walkie-talkies so we can stay in touch?"

"We have new technology now, Commander," Martinez said. "They're called land mobile radios, or LMRs. Lieutenant, give him a couple and show him how they work." Watching his lieutenant instruct the Commander, he was relieved that he wouldn't have to divert guardsmen to deal with emergencies in town. He sensed he could count on his determined but unconventional allies.

Mindful of their assignment, the militiamen boarded their pickup trucks and headed for town. Mayor Seth Edmonson had already set up an emergency operations center in the municipal building on the northeast corner of the square. The Commander delivered one of the LMRs to Edmonson so they could stay in touch with each other and Martinez.

The Mayor's first order of business, an evacuation order for the townspeople, was already being circulated by militiamen. Some residents showed their appreciation with hot coffee and donuts. Others posed for pictures, creating a surreal carnival-like atmosphere. Meanwhile, the most combat savvy militiamen fanned out to guard entry points into Madison.

"Daddy, can I borrow your gun?" a small boy asked.

"Why?" the father asked.

"So I can guard our house," the boy said.

"Sorry, Son. You're way too young to handle a gun safely. Besides, I'm sure these men will protect our house."

Shuffling his feet, the boy frowned. "Then what are *we* going to do?"

"We're going to follow Mayor Edmonson's instructions and go to Aunt Betty's for a while."

The little boy twirled, casting a left-handed salute to a nearby militia-man. The militiaman smiled and winked. "Safe travels, soldier," he said, to the little boy's glee.

Private vehicles overloaded with personal belongings resembled Conestoga wagons heading west as they followed designated evacuation routes. Mayor Edmonson was relieved that most residents took his order seriously as they scurried out of harm's way. Evacuees maneuvered around news satellite trucks parked along the streets in anticipation of an historic battle.

As the Mayor feared, they didn't have long to wait.

CHAPTER 3

—

Seventy-two hours before the Georgia Guard bivouacked in Madison, Major General Patrick "Bo" Graham, Commander of the 82nd Airborne at Fort Bragg, had received a fateful phone call. His office was already abuzz when he arrived at his usual time. Tall and trim with a pencil-thin mustache, he always wore the standard 82nd Airborne uniform consisting of camouflage fatigues decorated with insignia and an impressive plank of medals, camouflage jump boots, and a burgundy beret. G.I. Joe never looked more prepared for battle.

On this inauspicious morning he sported a fresh Monte Christo cigar. Considered the ultimate smoke by tobacco aficionados, they were supplied by pilots flying the milk run to and from Guantanamo Bay, or Gitmo, as the pilots referred to the U.S. joint command base in Cuba. "There's nothing like a good Cuban with your first cup of joe to get your blood flowing early in the morning," he was fond of saying, especially to those who seemed squeamish about such things.

Before Graham could get settled, a sergeant entered his office and announced, "You have an urgent call from the White House, sir, and they seem to have their knickers in a wad."

"Make my coffee extra strong. Got a feeling today's gonna be a meat grinder."

The general took a breath, then punched the blinking button on his phone. A chorus of voices in the background reminded him of cackling hens. *Which birdbrain is calling from the chicken coop this time*, he wondered. "General Graham here," he answered in his most authoritative voice. He continued to roll the large cigar in his mouth, savoring Cuba's finest leaf tobacco.

Mitch Brady, President Elliott's Chief of Staff, invoked the President's name in an attempt to establish parity with the decorated combat general. "This is Mitch Brady calling on behalf of President Elliott. I hope we're not interrupting your first cup."

Before the general could answer, Brady continued. "As you know, General, the 1st Armored Division out of Fort Bliss, the 1st Calvary Division out of Fort Hood, and the 1st Infantry Division out of Fort Riley are all currently deployed. That makes you our general du jour."

Graham bristled, his teeth impaling his cigar.

Brady didn't pause. "We just want to make sure you are clear on your latest orders from the Joint Chiefs. President Elliott is counting on you to shut down the illegal Constitutional Convention in Austin and round up the insurrectionists. We can't allow them to interfere with the government's business any longer."

Graham bit off the end of his cigar and spit the plug into his trash can, causing a loud ping. "I'm anything *but* clear," he bellowed in a deep voice befitting a combat flag officer. "Admiral Latham expressed concern about the Posse Comitatus Act when he called last night. As you know, it's intended to prevent the military from performing any police action, especially against civilians within the confines of the United States."

During the ensuing pause, Graham could hear muffled voices on the line. The cackle rose to a crescendo, then went silent.

"That issue has been cleared up," Brady said. "And it's no longer Latham's concern. Bill Ziegler is now the Chairman of the Joint Chiefs. He and Attorney General Oliver are convinced the Patriot Act trumps Posse Comitatus."

Graham bristled again. "Let me guess. The Attorney General wrote the opinion himself."

"That's right," Brady said. "And White House Counsel concurred."

"You know, Mr. Brady, the Army Adjutant has to concur as well."

"No problem. Bill cleared it with him last night."

The general rolled his cigar in an ashtray. "Did the Adjutant sign off after Ziegler explained how Latham was replaced for objecting to the mission?"

With Brady thrown off guard, another awkward pause ensued.

Sensing a break, the sergeant re-entered the office. He handed the general a mammoth coffee cup inscribed with a quote from John Wayne that read, "A Man's Got To Have a Code, A Creed To Live By." More than a mere token, the cup had been given to Graham's father by General George Marshall during World War II. Graham took a quick sip and even though the coffee was strong enough to strip bark from a tree, it didn't wash the sour taste from his mouth. "I suppose you've already figured out what to do with all the conventioneers," he finally growled, breaking the silence.

"We *have* thought of that," Brady boasted. "The Department of Homeland Security will coordinate with local law enforcement to transport the agitators to FEMA Camp Bravo-6 in Waco. DHS is prepared to nationalize the local bus system under the Patriot Act to transport them."

Graham drove his cigar into the ashtray, sending sparks and ashes flying. "These agitators, as you call them, are legally elected governors, legislators, county commissioners, and judges. All of them have authority granted under the law and that pesky thing called the Constitution. They just might not cooperate with your plan to tread on that authority."

Known as a strong opponent of states' rights, Brady countered. "That's exactly why we have you and the Department of Homeland Security, General. I've seen their hokey banners with the snake and the 'Don't Tread on Me' slogan. They don't mean a thing."

"They didn't mean much to the British either, right up to Cornwallis's surrender at Yorktown," Graham said. "And what do you mean, that's why you have me and DHS? How many armies do you need to protect the country from itself?"

"DHS has been activated for this mission to back you up, General," Brady said.

Graham snorted, wishing he had his cigar back in one piece. "I have the Air Force, the Navy, and the Marines to back me up, Mr. Brady. I don't need a bunch of retrained security guards to help me do my job."

"Your Commander in Chief is calling the shots personally on this mission," Brady said, his voice cracking. "I'll be reporting that you understand what is expected, and you'll be moving right away to shut down the Convention. Goodbye, General."

Graham slammed his receiver home and yelled for his staff assistant. "Hanson!"

Major Hanson hustled in to face the general. "Yes, sir."

Checking his watch, Graham barked, "Have the Strike Force Commanders assembled in the squad room at 0-eight-thirty."

Hanson saluted and rushed back to his desk.

Graham stared at the imposing photo of General Dwight D. Eisenhower on the opposite wall. "We sure could use the old war horse right now," he mumbled.

Anxious to report on his conversation with Graham, Mitch Brady strolled into the Oval Office.

President Elliott was immersed in an animated telephone conversation, but motioned for him to take a seat. "I've signed the executive order mobilizing all National Guard units," the President said into the receiver. "Copies will be delivered to the governors later today. If you get any flak, remind them that under Title 10 and Title 32 of the Federal Code I have full authority to call those units up, with or without their approval."

The President rubbed his forehead during a brief pause, then said, "No, don't worry about Congress, Alex. Only the libertarian kooks are giving us any trouble so far. They're on their usual rant about upholding the Constitution and protecting the rights of the people. What about protecting their President? Excuse me, Alex, Mitch just walked in. I have to sign off."

"Morning, Mr. President," Brady said.

Elliott shook his head to clear his irritation with Secretary of Defense Harrison. "Is the good general on board?" he asked.

"I have to say, Mr. President, Truman had MacArthur to deal with, and you have General Graham."

"I should have appointed him Academy Superintendent instead of Commander of the 82nd. His father and grandfather were such strong supporters, I assumed I could count on him, too. There's nothing more annoying than a flag officer with a conscience."

"I made it clear that you expect him to carry out his mission," Brady said. "If he doesn't, he's forewarned."

"Make sure Secretary Harrison and Secretary Massey are up to speed. I don't want anyone off cue on this. And make sure the Press Office has a plan to keep the media at bay."

"Right away, Mr. President."

Reflecting on his conversation with Harrison, Elliott asked, "What are the chances the convention states will resist us with force?"

Brady knew this wasn't the first time Elliott had considered the possibility. As he gazed out the window behind the President's desk, Brady answered, "I think we can count on it once we move on the Convention, but without their National Guard units they'll have to rely on their state militias."

"What can you tell me about these militias Ziegler seems so worried about?"

Brady reluctantly opened another can of worms. "DHS was making headway identifying their leaders when we turned our attention elsewhere."

Elliott tapped his fingers in agitation. "Are you suggesting we'd already have them in custody if the Political Office hadn't insisted we focus on the Freedom Caucus?"

Brady saw the opportunity to give the President a reality check. "Some of the more sophisticated militias have already gone underground. Ziegler is convinced their numbers in states like North Carolina and Wyoming are way underestimated. He also believes that unlike the Civil War, when the home guard was made up of old men and undesirables, most of today's members are veterans, ex-policemen, and experienced hunters, all with capabilities comparable to the military."

The President pushed some papers out of the way and folded his hands in their place. "How quickly can they mobilize?"

Brady knew his answer would further enrage the President. "Some already have," he said. "DHS shut down a couple of detention centers in Connecticut and Pennsylvania because of threats from local militias."

Elliott contorted his face in anger. "Are you telling me we ran from a bunch of measly armed citizens?"

"Actually, Mr. President, DHS Secretary Massey feared heavy casualties if they clashed with the formidable militias in those areas. He didn't want the compounds rendered inoperable if they were overrun. We need them to house dissidents later on."

"It sounds like we need to up our game against these domestic terrorists," Elliott said.

"I'll schedule a meeting with the Domestic Terrorism Task Force in the morning, Mr. President." Brady shuffled back to his office wondering if their plan would work. He worried that Secretary Massey, known for being a maverick, might stray on this critical mission.

CHAPTER 4

—

While the White House grappled with the evolving political crisis, Colonel Wayne "Bull" Perkins, General Graham's best field commander, made preparations to carry out President Elliott's orders. Nicknamed by his championship wrestling team at Notre Dame, Bull Perkins was undefeated as a junior and won the NCAA Heavyweight title the following year. He attained legendary status when he wrestled a year-old Angus bull to the ground during a beer bash on the farm of a teammate. On this day, he would rather face that bull again than carry out his orders to march against fellow Americans.

Plumes of acrid gray smoke spewed from diesel engines as the column rumbled onto Bragg Boulevard. A military policeman's shrill whistle pierced the roar of engines to direct the column forward along highway 87 south from Fayetteville, North Carolina to I-95. A detour for bridge construction on Grove Street would add thirty minutes to their exit from the base. Within forty-five minutes of clearing the ramp onto the interstate, civilian traffic was backed up fifty miles, all the way to Selma.

By the time the column crossed the South Carolina border near Florence, several trucks were already low on fuel. Tankers rolled past the stalled column to refuel the thirstiest vehicles. With the logistical skill of UPS, they were refueled and underway within the hour. Perkins called Captain Barry Anderson to congratulate his men on their efficiency. "Remember, Captain, contrary to popular belief, the army runs on a timetable, not its stomach."

"Yes, sir," Anderson replied, reaching down to pull a fist-sized sausage biscuit from a yellow takeout bag.

The column merged onto I-20 west from I-95 and proceeded through the night. Perkins called Graham to report civilians photographing the column from a Columbia overpass.

Graham offered an assessment based on late breaking news alerts. "Reporters are already speculating about military action against the

Constitutional Convention, despite the Administration's denials. An impassioned speech by the President against states' rights in Chicago two days ago is fueling the speculation."

Perkins craned his neck to check the column in the mirror of his Humvee. "How can we stop the media from spying on us, General? They'll broadcast our every move."

"The last time I checked we were still a Constitutional Democracy," Graham said. "The President seems hell bent on changing that single handedly, but the people haven't signed off yet. As a matter of fact, we've received intelligence reports that forty states have called up their Guard units, and state militias are mobilizing. Some libertarian talk show hosts are actually calling on the citizenry to take up arms to protect the Convention."

"Are you saying there's an insurrection brewing, sir?"

"What I'm saying, Colonel, is the American people are not going to accept from our Imperial President what they refused to accept from the King of England. What you saw on that overpass was a group of modern day Paul Reveres equipped with digital cameras and cell phones instead of lanterns."

Perkins expressed overconfidence. "Even with the media shadowing us, our drones will let us know what's ahead."

Graham nodded as if Perkins could see him. "You raise an important point, Colonel. The world is watching and everything's being recorded. Make sure the men don't violate our rules of engagement."

"You can count on it, sir."

After a sleepless night due to his tortured conscience, Graham called Perkins to check on his progress. "Are you going to make it to Atlanta by nightfall and Birmingham by tomorrow morning?" he asked. "Central Command is on my butt like a duck on a June bug."

Perkins fingered the mike. "Not sure, sir. We lost our signal from Speed Bird 6 an hour ago. That probably means there's resistance up ahead."

"Do you have any other birds in the air?"

"Yes, sir. We put another one up right after we lost the first one."

Despite the setback, the general remained confident. "Stay frisky, Colonel. You have a brigade of armed escorts to clear the way to Austin. Keep me posted."

"Will do, sir."

Later that morning, a second lieutenant, known as a shave tail in the ranks, walked out of the 82nd's drone control trailer fifty kilometers from Madison. He approached Colonel Perkins standing next to his Humvee. "I thought you'd want to know, sir. Our second drone picked up images of debris across the interstate at exit 114."

Deep in thought, Perkins looked straight ahead. "What kind of debris, Lieutenant?"

"It looks like a pile of wrecked cars and farm equipment, sir."

Perkins's stern look forced the lieutenant back a step. "Well, it's not likely a traffic accident, Lieutenant. Even in Georgia folks don't drive farm equipment on the interstate. Drop the bird down for a better look."

The lieutenant stuttered and looked away. "Y-yes, sir, but it looks like troops are in the area, too."

The spotty intelligence tested Perkins's patience. "What kind of troops?"

"All I can tell, sir, is they look like us."

"Of course they look like us, Lieutenant. We are in the United States. Any signs of artillery?"

The lieutenant's eyes darted nervously. "I don't think so, sir, but there's a line of trees blocking our view."

"Like I said before, guide the bird to the other side of the trees and take another look."

"Uh, yes, sir. I'll get back to you, sir."

Ted Johnson's farm stood twenty clicks, or kilometers, from the 82nd Airborne's location. Johnson, a Madison farmer and decorated Vietnam War veteran, sat in his study following the 82nd's advance on cable news. Every channel offered the same disturbing report that the column was closing in on Madison.

As he often did when he needed to blow off steam, he grabbed his rifle and headed to his private target range behind his barn. Since the range was far enough away and in the opposite direction from the interstate, he could shoot at will without posing any danger. His Ruger Mini-14 Ranch Carbine, his weapon of choice, offered pin-point accuracy and superior ballistics. As a former Army Ranger with two purple hearts, and a silver star, he appreciated a good rifle.

While organizing his gear on the shooting bench, he caught sight of the MQ-9 Reaper swooping down on his side of the woods. He instantly recognized the military reconnaissance drone and realized it was collecting intelligence on the guardsmen. Hair stood up on the back of his neck as an automatic reflex kicked him into combat mode.

The drone buzzed low and steady along the tree line. *Perfect,* he thought. The rifle came up with its sights on the engine above the fuselage, leading just a tad. He gently squeezed the trigger, confident of a perfect trajectory. The .223 caliber round ripped through the drone at four-thousand feet per second, shattering key engine components. Another round through the camera turret ensured that no images of him or his farm would be captured before the drone crashed.

At the end of a steep dive, the Reaper tumbled into a neighboring pond, sending waves of muddy water cascading over a freshly mowed field. A trail of smoke drifted in the breeze. Ted symbolically kissed his trusty carbine as a sobering thought crossed his mind. *Will I have to pay for that darn thing when this is over?*

B ack at Guard headquarters, a sergeant handed General Martinez a headset. "It's Major Simms again, General."

"Simms, what's up?"

"A second drone went down near the woods on the south side of the interstate."

Martinez peered out the window. "Did the sharpshooter from Albany get that one, too?"

"Can't say for sure, sir. Didn't even know it was there until we heard shots and saw it nosedive behind some trees."

Martinez rubbed his throbbing temples. "Get some men over there and find out what's going on, Major."

"Right away, sir."

Simms dropped the headset and motioned to Lieutenant Arnold "Arnie" Hicks. "Take a couple of Humvees with some men to check out the downed drone and report back. And, Lieutenant, stay on your toes."

"Right, sir."

Back at the 82nd, bad news kept mounting. The Drone Flight Control Officer walked up to his superior. "Major Sanders, we've lost the signal from our other drone."

Sanders frowned, then scratched his five-o'clock shadow. "It's a good thing you aren't directing the entire column, Lieutenant, or we'd all be in a ditch."

"Sorry, sir, we can't figure out what went wrong. Our remote diagnostics show there weren't any mechanical malfunctions. We were about to swing around to the debris across the interstate when everything went dead."

Sanders pressed his inexperienced young officer. "What was the fuel reading?"

"We were right at 63 percent, sir, so that's not it. The control signal was normal, as were the gyros. I'm thinking it was taken out, sir."

"Why is that?"

"There were a couple seconds of data sent after the engine stopped, which tells me it was still flying."

"What about a bird strike?"

"Doubt it, sir. The camera is low and forward, so a bird strike would have taken it out before the engine."

"Okay, Lieutenant, I'll call it in." Sanders called Perkins to report the latest setback. "We've lost our other recon drone, sir. It went down on a run to check out the roadblock on the interstate. We're sure it was shot down based on our remote diagnostics."

"I don't know anything about remote diagnostics, Major, but I do know we're approaching resistance of unknown strength. I want some solid intelligence if we have to crawl through a mine field on our bellies to get it."

"I'll get you what you need, Colonel," Sanders said. He keyed the mike through the open window of his Humvee. "Captain Baker, come in."

"Baker here. Over."

"Captain, take Sergeant Dawson and a couple of men to check the area south of the woods where our drone went down. Find out what we're facing up ahead and report back."

"Right away, sir. Out."

Baker walked up to his best squad. "Sergeant, grab Helms and Ingram and saddle up. We're pulling out in ten."

"Beggin' the Captain's pardon," Dawson said. "Ingram's been acting squirrely this whole trip. He's talking about taking out civilians who are undermining the President, and crazy stuff like that."

"Settle down, Sarge," Baker said. "He's just talking trash to take the edge off. We're all jumpy right now."

"I think he's itching for a fight and might get reckless," Dawson said.

"Let me worry about the men," Baker said. "You make sure we're combat ready."

Being overruled by an inexperienced officer was a bitter pill for the battle-tested sergeant. Nevertheless, he pulled the Humvee up to the supply truck so each man could grab a bandolier of ammo and other supplies.

Captain Baker swapped out the batteries in his GPS and slipped into a shoulder holster housing a Beretta nine-millimeter. "Let's go, Sarge. We don't have all day."

Helms and Ingram loaded and locked their M-16s just as their Humvee sped away from the column. "Time to rock and roll!" Ingram shouted.

The speeding Humvee rumbled off the pavement on its way to the line of trees bordering Ted Johnson's pasture. Sergeant Dawson ignored the "NO TRESPASSING" sign on a fence post as he forged through the fence line. They lunged and lurched out of the edge of the woods just as Johnson pulled off a round that sent a rusty bucket careening into their path.

Before the bucket stopped rolling, Ingram unleashed a volley of fire that missed Johnson's head by inches. He dove behind the barn just as another burst peppered it. With the agility of a cat that belied his years, he sprang away, firing the semi-automatic carbine as he fled. One round shattered the mirror of the Humvee and another struck the ground between Ingram's feet.

"Get your finger off that trigger and get your butt in the vehicle," Dawson ordered. Ingram scrambled inside just as the Humvee darted after the fleeing civilian.

Fearing for his life, Johnson jumped into his 4x4 pickup and tore down his lane toward the interstate, spraying rocks and dirt from all four tires. A speeding Humvee cut him off just before he reached the end of his lane. *How'd he get in front of me?* he wondered. Skidding to a halt, he braced himself for another hail of bullets. When Lieutenant Hicks jumped out, he recognized the Georgia National Guard insignia and realized these were not the same soldiers he was evading.

Before he could exit his truck, and just when he thought he was in the clear, the first Humvee skidded to a halt behind him.

Captain Baker and his men emerged with guns drawn, provoking

Lieutenant Hicks's men to do the same.

Caught in a potential crossfire, Johnson prayed, *Lord, I know you didn't bring me back from the swamps of Vietnam to be shot by American soldiers in my own driveway.*

Like Custer facing the Sioux at the Little Big Horn, Baker and his men challenged the larger contingent. "Stand down!" he ordered.

"No, you stand down," Hicks answered, prompting one of his men to pull the .50 caliber M2 machine gun around on the roof of his Humvee. Nothing gets the attention of a combat soldier like the sound of a machine gun's receiver ramming a round home, especially if the business end of the barrel is pointed directly at his head.

"I'm ordering you to stand down," Baker repeated.

Hicks didn't budge. "As an officer of the Georgia National Guard standing on good ole Georgia red clay, I refuse your order and give you formal notice that the Girl Scouts of America have more authority around here than you do. Tell your men to drop their weapons or you'll see what happens when a wide open Ma Deuce smokes a Humvee and everything around it."

"I'll see you court martialed and hanged, Lieutenant," Baker vowed.

"Maybe so," Hicks replied. "Until then, you're far outnumbered and outgunned, so I'd do the smart thing and drop those weapons."

Mindful of the devastating firepower of an M2 machine gun, or Ma Deuce, as grunts call the mainstay of the U.S. Army, Baker relented. "You heard the man. Dawson, Helms, Ingram, put 'em in the dirt."

Johnson breathed a long sigh of relief until he noticed Ingram flick off his safety while raising his M-16 in Hicks's direction. In half a heartbeat he put a round in Ingram's right leg just above the knee. "I know *that* hurt," he mumbled to himself.

Crumpling to the ground, Ingram let loose a burst of fire intended for Hicks. The errant rounds slammed harmlessly into the red Georgia clay. Before the smoke had cleared, two of Hicks's men disarmed him before dragging him to their Humvee.

Both sides thought the rust-colored trail in the dirt symbolized the first blood spilled in the conflict. Neither knew yet that the machine gunner from Dahlonega had already fallen.

Once secured, a guardsman grabbed a first aid kit to attend to Ingram's blood-soaked leg. Nerves near the wound were awakening, bringing unbearable pain to life. With fists raised, he cried out in anguish, "Easy,

Private. You're killing me!"

"Sorry, bud." The guardsman scowled as he tightened the tourniquet. "I know it hurts, but we can't let you bleed out." One more turn and the bleeding stopped.

Ingram turned his head toward the open door to hide his tears.

Hicks' men dragged Captain Baker, kicking and swearing, into Guard headquarters. Military gear interspersed throughout the county offices gave the appearance of disorder. But that was not the case, and Baker knew it. He could tell that this was a modern, fully functional command and control center. He took one more crack at his captors. "You have no authority over us," he screamed, sending spittle spraying outward. "Release us or face the consequences." The threat fell on deaf ears as the guardsmen went about their duties.

"I'd say you have things upside down, Captain," Hicks replied with confidence. "Someone will explain the facts of life to you, shortly. Meantime, you'd better settle down before we hog tie you."

For the next thirty minutes Baker stonewalled his interrogators. "Willie J. Baker, Captain, United States Army, serial number 314-82-6697," he repeated in accordance with the Geneva Convention. Eventually, his parched throat reduced his voice to a mere whisper, making him appear small and feeble.

The Guard's chief interrogator, a tall muscle-bound major, placed his cigarette in an ashtray and walked directly in front of Baker. "I can't hear you, Captain. Is this how you speak to your men so you don't intimidate them?"

Spontaneous chuckles from the interrogation team was more than Baker could take. His brief swearing tirade ended when General Martinez walked in. He froze from the general's menacing presence.

"Relax, Captain. Can I get you anything?" Martinez asked while rifling through Baker's field pouch.

"I could use some water," Baker whispered.

"Get this man some water, Sergeant," Martinez ordered. He pitched the field pouch on the table, satisfied it contained nothing useful. The general glared at Baker as if comparing him to his own officers. He wasn't particularly impressed. "Is it your practice to fire on civilians, Captain?"

"I'm not following you, sir," Baker said. "My unit was just doing some recon when we started taking fire from that crazy civilian. We returned fire in self-defense."

Martinez stood erect, his six-foot, five-inch frame towering over Baker. "That crazy civilian, as you call him, is named Ted Johnson. He's a local hero around these parts."

Baker rolled his eyes, clearly unimpressed.

Though Martinez tried to ignore Baker's disrespect, his anger swelled. "If you had been more astute, Captain, you'd have realized that you were trespassing on Johnson's private property, and his target was a rusty bucket, not you. Otherwise, you would no longer be with us. Do you follow me, Captain?"

Baker envisioned Ingram's shattered leg. He gulped, then stared at the floor without responding. A moment passed before he timidly reached around Martinez to hand his empty glass back to the sergeant.

Martinez stepped backward for better eye contact. "You should also know that Ted's father is a Superior Court judge over the judicial district you are unfortunately standing in. By the way, the distinguished looking fellow in the corner is Fred Stone. He's the Morgan County Prosecuting Attorney. He has something to say that's going to give new meaning to the term *bad day*."

Baker raised his head, showing they now had his attention. The corners of his mouth turned up in amusement at Prosecutor Stone's appearance. Stone's blue-and-white-striped seersucker suit with a red bow tie and matching suspenders was right out of *Andy of Mayberry*. His wispy white hair and neatly trimmed goatee rivaled Colonel Sanders. *Why is this clown wasting my time?* Baker wondered. His amusement was short lived.

Stone rose slowly, checking Baker up and down as if he were inspecting a side of beef in a meat locker. Placing his thumbs in his pockets and leaning backward to balance himself, he rocked the captain. "We don't take kindly to people driving through the woods taking pot shots at residents. Under the authority vested in me by the State of Georgia, I hereby charge you with criminal trespass and attempted murder. Excuse the short notice, but your probable cause hearing is scheduled for nine o'clock tomorrow morning in Judge Johnson's courtroom."

Perspiration glistened on Baker's forehead and his cheeks flushed, then flinched. His amusement turned to confusion, followed by terror. His eyes darted toward the doorway as if he were going to bolt. Two guards holding M-16s blocked his escape.

Martinez noticed Baker's sudden interest in the exit. He secretly hoped for an opportunity to vent his anger. *Go for it, Baker. Make my day*, he thought.

Stone continued, studying the captive while stroking his chin whiskers. "Don't you have anything to say for yourself, Captain?"

Baker squinted at the hardened prosecutor, then stuttered, "Y-you can't try me in civilian court for something I've done in combat."

Stone continued stroking his goatee. "And who exactly are you in combat against?"

"We're putting down an insurrection," he said. "Don't you people follow the news in this hick town?"

Stone stood unmoved by Baker's contempt. "Are you familiar with something called the Posse Comitatus Act, Captain?"

"I think we studied it at the War College, but I'm afraid I don't recall it now," Baker said.

"That's unfortunate, young man, because your ignorance has gotten you into a world of trouble today. I spent a lot of my daddy's money when I left this hick town to attend the Columbia University School of Law. I learned a good bit about jurisprudence in spite of my backward upbringing."

Baker stared at Stone like a bored grade school student, then glanced again at the exit.

Martinez clenched his fists. *Do it; run for it.*

Stone again ignored Baker's insolence. "The Posse Comitatus Law prohibits the military from engaging in any police action against American citizens within the confines of the United States. In short, it allows you to shoot foreign enemies, but prevents you from shooting the very people you are sworn to protect. That includes Ted Johnson. Does any of this strike a chord with you?"

With unabashed arrogance, Baker put the prosecutor on notice. "I hate to rain on your parade, but there is an entire brigade of the best-trained soldiers in the world fifty miles from here who will be looking for me shortly. Neither you nor the ragtag Georgia National Guard will be able to stop them."

With his patience exhausted and his hot-button tripped, Martinez moved as close to Baker as he could get without jumping into his pocket. "My men fought two wars in Iraq and Afghanistan, sacrificing their lives and their livelihoods to defend the very principles you are now treading upon. No one parading around as an officer and a gentleman is going to dishonor their service or their sacrifices while I'm around." His eyes flashed with rage, as he shoved Baker toward the Morgan County sheriff in the back of the room. "He's all yours, Sheriff."

Baker's cockiness evaporated when a deputy wrapped cold steel handcuffs around his wrists while the sheriff recited his Miranda rights. "Here are your charges," the sheriff said, stuffing some paperwork in Baker's pocket. Baker's eyes locked onto Martinez's in a desperate plea for help. Martinez's cold, unsympathetic stare made it clear that he was on his own and out of luck.

Stone extended his foot to block Baker's forward movement. "Since you're so sure your buddies are going to rescue you, you won't mind signing a couple of waivers for me. Stone extended a waiver for Ted Johnson to serve as a witness in his father's court and a waiver of discovery.

Baker grabbed the pen and scribbled his signature on the forms. "Your kangaroo court has no jurisdiction over me," he sneered. "Why should I worry about legal technicalities?"

Stone retrieved his pen and tapped it on Baker's nose. "A word of caution, Captain," he said. "I'd work on that attitude before you face Judge Johnson. Ted's a pussycat compared to his old man."

The prospect of facing trial for attempted murder was starting to sink in. Judgement by the very people he had marched against meant he could take the rap for those up the line, far beyond the military chain of command. His only hope was a rescue by the advancing 82nd, but they were still miles away. Besides, a foreboding Georgia National Guard backed by a seasoned militia stood between him and any rescue.

Within the hour Baker, Dawson, and Helms were incarcerated in the Morgan County Jail, nibbling on bologna sandwiches and boiled potatoes mixed with rutabagas. Helms asked the guard what was in his potatoes.

"Don't you know a *rutabagy* when you see one, son?" the guard asked. "Where are you boys from, anyway?"

Perched comfortably on their cots, Dawson and Helms tried to figure out where rutabagas come from.

It's a common root, originally from Scandinavia," Baker said. "They're a cross between cabbage and yellow turnips."

No wonder I can't stand 'em," Helms said. "I hate cabbage and turnips. How do you know so much about veggies, Cap?"

My ex-girlfriend watched a lot of cooking shows," Baker said. "I had to watch them with her so she would watch football with me. Our relationship went to hell when she started keeping score during the playoffs." Baker washed down some bologna with a sip of his watered-down fruit drink. "I thought everyone in the South drinks sweet tea," he said. "How did we end up with this crap?"

While his fellow squad members honed their culinary knowledge, Ingram underwent surgery at the Morgan County Hospital. Fortunately, Johnson's shot missed all the major arteries and only grazed his thigh bone. But the exit wound, the size of a lemon, was severe enough that Ingram no longer represented a threat to anyone.

The high drama of U.S. soldiers being prosecuted for assaulting a civilian on their way to raid the Convention captured everyone's attention. Reporters and spectators flocked to the courthouse. The next morning, with an overflow crowd lined along the outside wall of the courtroom, the bailiff reached for a seldom-used sound system to call the proceeding to order. "Oyez, Oyez, Oyez. All rise. The Honorable Judge Miles Johnson presiding."

Judge Johnson commanded everyone's attention as he swept into the courtroom, his long black robe streaming behind him. Settling at the bench as if it were his throne, he addressed the courtroom with complete authority. "This court is now in session. Mr. Bailiff, please proceed."

The bailiff peered through wire-rimmed spectacles at the court docket. "This is the case of Georgia versus Captain Jeffrey Baker, Sergeant Lloyd Dawson, Private Thad Ingram, and Private Mark Helms, docket number 255-1017. Each defendant is charged with trespassing, felony destruction of property, and attempted murder."

"Defense Counsel, how do the defendants plead?" Johnson asked.

"Not guilty, by virtue of federal sovereignty, Your Honor," the public defender said.

"Defense Counsel is reminded that this trial is proceeding under state law," Johnson said.

"Prosecutor Stone, please present your opening statement."

Stone cast his usual pose with his thumbs in his suspenders and his back arched. "Thank you, Your Honor. Ladies and gentlemen, there has never been a case like this in the history of our country. A military attack against innocent citizens cannot be tolerated, regardless of the reason. Congress forestalled this danger by passing a law called—" Stone's voice was drowned out by distant gunfire echoing through the courtroom.

"The 82nd is here," a reporter blurted out. He and his cameraman scampered out to cover the action. Others in the press section stirred, wondering if they should follow.

As the firing intensified, fear gripped the courtroom. Nervous chatter turned to near panic. Judge Johnson motioned for opposing counsel to approach the bench. Bailiff Parker nudged the defendants' attorney who stood frozen by fear. Johnson's sleeves fluttered as he waved for them to hurry. He leaned over the bench. "Gentlemen, for obvious reasons this trial is recessed until further notice. Bailiff Parker, return the accused to their cells and assign the usual guards." He peered out the window for signs of immediate danger. *Wham, wham, wham*, the gavel sounded.

All chatter ceased as frightened spectators looked to the judge for guidance. "This trial is recessed until further notice," he bellowed. "Everyone is advised to evacuate or seek safe shelter."

Unfortunately, like the trial, safety was now suspended in Madison.

Reporters and correspondents on location to cover Johnson's one-of-a-kind trial turned their attention and cameras to the inexplicable battle between the United States Army and the Georgia National Guard. True to a previous era, this battle pitted American against American, and neighbor against neighbor.

CHAPTER 5

—

Residents who had remained in Madison prayed for protection as the battle raged near exit 114. Artillery shells whistled overhead like Hitler's V-2s that terrified London during World War II. When shells began landing closer and closer to downtown, everyone assumed they were misdirected fire from the 82nd Airborne. Horror overtook them when plumes of smoke and debris rose from the Morgan Memorial Hospital just blocks from downtown. Madison's civil defense siren wailed as militiamen and local policemen raced frantically to direct residents into basements. The unthinkable was happening.

The warnings were too late for several occupants of the hospital. Mayor Seth Edmonson arrived just in time to see four deceased nurses and three deceased patients rolled out on gurneys covered with blood-soaked sheets. The mayor had commandeered school buses to transport the bodies along with surviving patients and staff to St. Mary's Good Samaritan Hospital in Greensboro. "God save us," he cried out.

Pandemonium gripped downtown as a policeman ushered Mary Baxter and her family into the basement of a local thrift store. Though old clothing and broken furniture littered the musty-smelling shelter, it appeared to be safe. Mary nestled five-year-old Brittany and eight-year-old Max under a soiled utility sink in a far corner. Streams of dust drifted from old brick walls, while ancient windows rattled from each explosion.

Max wrapped his arms around his little sister. "It's going to be all right, Brit. We're safe here. Mommy and the militia will take care of us."

Brittany's lips quivered behind strands of flaxen hair that had jostled from her ponytail.

"But I'm scared, Max. The noise hurts my ears." Dirt stained tears streaked down her rosy cheeks. She tightened her frail arms around Max's neck. Max endured the pain for her sake, while the words of his grandpa echoed in his ears. *Always take care of your little sister.*

When everything went quiet, Mary peered out the closest window, hoping the nightmare was over. An unexpected blast shattered the temporary lull, sending a shower of fire, bricks, and glass from the chocolate shop across the street. Militiamen scampered for cover with their hands over their heads to ward off flying debris. Mary screamed as she staggered backward into a rusty post in the middle of the basement that saved her from falling. She hugged the post, whimpering like a frightened puppy. Dusty, willowy cobwebs clung to her hair creating a *Lady Frankenstein* look. Brittany closed her eyes and burrowed her face into Max's heaving chest. Still huddled under the sink, their shaking bodies caused glassware in the basin to rattle in sync with their mother's whimpering. Brittany burrowed deeper to block out the cacophony.

Time faltered as the nightmare drifted into slow motion. Across the street young Heath Andrews stumbled from the rubble, his arms waving madly to avoid his blazing apron. He shrieked as flames lapped at his nose and ears, crackling as it singed his hair. An acid-like burn tortured him where nerve endings lay exposed by blistered and charred flesh. He gagged grotesquely from a jagged shard of glass protruding from his throat. Its clear transparency disappeared beneath a torrent of red.

Springing from a nearby portico, an alert militiaman tackled Andrews, then rolled him on the ground to smother the flames.

Flailing arms, still smoking and charred, pummeled the militiaman as Andrews tried to pull free. "Don't touch me!" he screamed. Third degree burns rubbing against the ground created unbearable pain. Clear fluid and blood oozed through the remnants of his clothing.

"Sorry, son," the militiaman called out as he struggled to snuff the flames. He succeeded on the third roll, but Andrews continued to smolder from head to foot. "Medic! I need help!" the militiaman screamed.

Another militiaman staggered from an adjacent bakery, unhurt but covered in white confectionary flour. He dashed toward Andrews with white flour trailing behind him like an apparition whisking across the landscape.

"What's happening, Mommy?" Brittany called out, her voice barely audible. She and Max scrambled to their mother, each one grabbing a leg. Brittany sobbed freely, while Max remained strong.

Mary held on tightly, wondering how she could protect her children from this hell on earth. With the stench of burning flesh seeping into the basement, she stammered, "Why is this happening? How could our government do this to us?" Hopelessness and helplessness engulfed her like the flames consuming the chocolate shop. She gazed at the destruction through tears, thinking how the chocolates littering the landscape symbolized the affront to humanity unfolding before her. She cursed President Elliott for his wanton act of barbarism.

For a brief moment her thoughts drifted to Mark Helms, her sister's son, currently serving with the 82nd at Fort Bragg. Mary had taken him into her home while her sister worked nights following a contentious divorce. Mark had become like a brother to Brittany and Max. *Surely, he's not part of this insanity,* she prayed.

The Georgia National Guard fought valiantly, despite the 82nd Airborne's superiority. When reports of indiscriminate shelling reached General Martinez, he called Governor Spivey. "I have bad news, Governor. They're shelling the town and we're taking civilian causalities. The local hospital was hit this afternoon, killing medical personnel and patients. Surviving staff and patients have been moved by bus to St. Mary's in Greensboro. So far thirty civilians have been killed and I've lost nearly seventy men."

Spivey's rage crackled through the phone line. "I've protested to the barbarians in the White House, but they insist it's a national security issue."

"National security?" Martinez roared. "They're murdering innocent women and children! This happens elsewhere in the world, but no one ever expected it here." He took a deep breath and refocused. "An officer captured by the militia let it slip that they plan to round us up and hold us in some kind of FEMA camp."

"We can't let that happen," Spivey said. "What do you recommend, General?"

Drawing on his training at West Point, the general offered a baneful assessment. "We can fight on, but there'll be heavy casualties on both sides, including more civilians. For their sake, I recommend we fall back and regroup to fight another day."

Spivey hesitated briefly. "I agree. Meanwhile, reinforcements from Alabama and Tennessee militias are on the way to Atlanta. Godspeed, General."

As TV coverage of the Madison attack filled the airwaves, public anger boiled over. Fearing they could be next, cities and towns erupted into demonstrations against the federal government's brutality. The entire city of Atlanta was mobilized along I-20 by the time Perkins arrived. Armed citizens, interspersed with uniformed members of the Georgia State Defense Force, displayed banners with an ominous message: "GOVERNMENT ASSASSINS, LEAVE OUR STATE VOLUNTARILY OR LEAVE IN A BODY BAG."

General Graham sat in his Fort Bragg office with Major Hanson watching news from Atlanta. "I've had divisions of troops under my command, Major, but never a whole city. If those defensemen and angry civilians are anything like Martinez's guardsmen, we'll never get past them." With grim resignation, he barked, "Get Perkins on the horn!"

Hanson got through to Perkins in less than two minutes. "Hanson here, Colonel. General Graham wants to chat."

Perkins commenced to ramble from fatigue and lack of sleep. "Is he going to pull us out of this pressure cooker, Major? I've never seen anything like it. Even the women are carrying AK-47s, and they know how to use them. Martinez had this one wild-eyed machine gunner who took out two or three squads before he either ran out of ammo or his gun melted down."

Graham bit into his Cuban and snatched the phone. "Bull, this fool's mission is over. I should have resisted more when the order came down."

"Excuse me for interrupting, General, but some of our men were captured in Madison and are being tried in state court. There's no way we can rescue them as long as the entire state is mobilized against us."

"I saw that on the news," Graham huffed. "We have people working through official channels to get them back, but given public sentiment it doesn't look good. By the way, how did you overshoot Martinez's position by five miles?"

"No way, General," Perkins scoffed. "You know my guys can shoot a gnat's ass off from that distance. Our scouts reported a Department of Homeland Security special operations unit tailing our column, toting some M777s. At the time Madison was being hit, our sentries reported fire coming from their position."

"DHS needs artillery like a schoolboy needs nitroglycerin in his chemistry set," Graham said.

"The Secretary and our oversight committees in Congress would agree with you," Perkins said. "They have disagreed with the White House on that issue for several years now. Congress defunded the purchase of armored vehicles, artillery, and other heavy weapons, but Massey convinced the President to siphon funds from other departments so DHS could arm up for moments like this. Here's the squirrely part, sir. Before we left Madison, their local militia captured the DHS commander and marched him before the same hard-boiled judge who's trying my guys. There are rumors he might be turned over to the International Criminal Court."

"That's not our problem," Graham said. "The White House can deal with the political fallout. My job is to get you back to base before this harebrained scheme spirals further out of control."

"You'll get no argument from me, General. We'll be heading back to base within the hour. Is there any way you can arrange safe passage? We're pretty beat up from our skirmish with Martinez and the entire state's crawling with heavily armed militias. I'm sure they're looking for payback. The last thing we need is another butt kicking."

"I'll make some calls," Graham said. "See you shortly, Colonel." He slammed the receiver home. "Major, notify base ops that Perkins is on his way back. Put the hospital on alert with the number of casualties. Do you think you can reach Martinez?"

"Probably not, sir. He's on the move, and after the confrontation in Madison, I'm sure he'll avoid us like the plague. I might be able to get you through to Governor Spivey's office."

"Do it."

Graham braced himself for the Governor's wrath. When Hanson again handed him the phone in record time, he spoke with deference. "Governor Spivey, this is Graham at Fort Bragg. Five minutes, please, that's all I ask."

"I have my hands full with a disaster of your making, General, so five minutes is all you get."

"I'm profoundly sorry that I was in command of such a despicable attack against your citizens, Governor. Let me assure you that I feel no honor or satisfaction in what happened."

"Is that because Martinez disrupted your invasion and you were about to lose your entire column in Atlanta?" Spivey asked. "The Georgia Defense Force was sitting at key exits with rocket propelled grenades to take out your trucks, one by one. More good soldiers would have fallen on both sides, and who knows how many civilians."

"Losing is never acceptable to a soldier, Governor. I should have fought harder to prevent the mission in the first place. When I realized the White House would simply replace me with a military hack if I didn't follow orders, I chose to limit losses as much as possible."

"That might be the way you see it, General, but thirty civilians including eleven children are now dead," Spivey said. "The cowardly shelling of the regional hospital killed several nurses. Those are not what I would call limited losses."

Graham cringed at the grim report. "I swear that fire didn't come from us, Governor. We followed strict rules of engagement that prohibit us from intentionally firing on unarmed civilians or a hospital."

Governor Spivey grunted. "I'm inclined to believe you because local militiamen captured a DHS official named Hank Applegate and some M777s. When their camp was overrun, they were firing on downtown. You can count on one thing, General. The higher-ups who are responsible for those murders will be held accountable."

"As it should be," Graham said. "I have an urgent request, Governor. I ordered my men to disengage and return to base. Once I notify the Pentagon and the White House, I will be relieved of command. Could you guarantee safe passage for my men out of Georgia?"

"That's a bold request, considering you invaded us," Spivey said.

Graham softened some more. "I totally understand your position, Governor. But I implore you to consider that those men simply followed orders. You probably think I'm unworthy of their trust and confidence, but they believed I would do the right thing. Regrettably, I didn't. Please don't punish them for my mistake."

"It might come as a surprise, but I do think you and your men are honorable patriots caught in the grip of a corrupt administration," Spivey said. "On that basis, you can count on safe passage as long as you remain in retreat. One more thing, General. I fear that if left to this administration's devices, the country will suffer far more than it already has."

Graham's feelings burst through. "For that reason, I don't regret that I will be relieved of my commission and my command. Good night, Governor."

"Good night, General."

Graham turned back to Hanson. "Major, report to Perkins that Governor Spivey has guaranteed safe passage, then ring up the Pentagon and the White House, in that order."

As he waited, Graham recalled how President Truman had relieved General Patton of command of the Third Army during World War II. Like Patton, he would find redemption.

After notifying Perkins, Hanson dialed the Pentagon and asked for the Chairman of the Joint Chiefs.

Graham sucked up his pride in anticipation of his detestable fate. "Admiral Ziegler, Graham here."

"I understand we have an uprising in Atlanta and a public relations nightmare in Madison," Ziegler said.

"With all due respect, sir, what we have is a self-inflicted crisis of unprecedented proportions."

"Let's not get hysterical," Ziegler said. "We have a uniformed force of over two million men to get the situation under control."

Graham could imagine Ziegler puffing up like a toad with self-importance. "Admiral, in case you didn't notice, there was an entire army of angry citizens mobilized in Atlanta alone. It's a documented fact that there are fifty million licensed hunters in this country and all of them are armed. The largest army in the world is dwarfed by comparison. Many of those citizens are former military who know how to fight. The DHS unit you people value so highly encountered some of them in Madison and won't be coming home as a result."

There was a brief pause. "We can talk statistics another time," Ziegler said. "Right now we have to deal with your failure to carry out the President's orders. I regret to inform you that I've been instructed to relieve you of command."

"I can honestly say that I'm neither surprised nor disappointed," Graham said. "You and I are sworn to uphold the Constitution and to protect our citizens. We have no authority under the law to kill those we are sworn to protect. We certainly have no moral authority to kill innocent civilians."

The Admiral's voice became loud and preachy. "As soldiers, our job is to follow orders. We don't set policy, and we don't question our civilian leadership."

Graham bit off his cigar and spit the end on the floor before lashing out. "I disagree, Admiral. When our civilian leaders lose their moral and legal compass, it's our solemn duty to question them or get out of their way."

"That, General, is precisely why we're instructing you to get out of the way!" Ziegler said.

"Understood," Graham said, "but let me give you the benefit of my thirty years as a professional soldier. When you accepted your job as Chairman of the Joint Chiefs, you started viewing the world through an ideological spectrum. Soldiers, on the other hand, see the world through the lens of what's good for their fellow countrymen. We love this country enough to give our lives for it, and we'll not stand idly by and let a bunch of radical ideologues flush everything down the toilet."

"Careful, General. You're sounding like an insurrectionist."

"Jefferson, Madison, and Hamilton were called just that in their day," Graham said. "The American people will not accept from this self-perceived imperial president what they would not accept from King George. If I were you, Admiral, I'd start preparing for the wrath of Hell. Good day, sir."

Graham's conversation with the White House was just as contentious. Mitch Brady, President Elliott's Chief of Staff, admonished the stalwart general. "The President is furious with your failure. He has sworn to punish anyone disloyal to his administration."

"I hate to be the bearer of bad news, Mitch, but all of the polls show support for the administration has evaporated, while support for the Convention is skyrocketing. Even your media puppets are outraged by the incident in Madison."

"You can rest assured that as soon as we get resisters like you out of the way and deliver the proper messaging, things will turn around," Brady said.

"So you think that while the 82nd Airborne is marching on American cities and DHS is murdering innocent women and children, the public is going to tune in to cable news to hear your propaganda on why it was justified? You don't know the American people very well."

With nothing more to lose, Graham continued to wire-brush the President's Chief of Staff. "The problem with people like you is your radical ideology has blinded you to reality. President Elliott's tirade on TNN about punishing political opponents will prove to be the final nail in the administration's coffin. It was your paramilitary unit that murdered thirty civilians in Madison, assuring the standoff in Atlanta. Who would have guessed that the President's comment about the need for a civilian security force referred to the establishment of an American Gestapo?"

"You are now spouting treason, General," Brady said.

"The truth and treason will never be the same thing," Graham said. "Remember, Mitch, the International Criminal Court investigates crimes against humanity. By any standard, when a government drops artillery shells on the heads of small children, it qualifies as such a crime."

"We're through here, General, and you can forget about a pension."

"You're a real piece of work, Mitch."

Brady fumed as he tossed his phone onto the Oval Office sofa. President Elliott grossly underestimated the unanimity of the military in placing loyalty to country before loyalty to its political leadership. "Mr. President, we're suffering another unintended consequence of the attack on Madison," Brady explained. "Soldiers at Fort Bragg, as well as other bases around the country, are deserting to join state militias and Guard units. Some have stated openly that their motive is to protect their families and neighborhoods from what they're calling a government no longer guided by allegiance to its people."

President Elliott kicked his trash can across the Oval Office. Its contents spewed over the Presidential seal in his royal blue rug, an indignity emblematic of his presidency.

CHAPTER 6

—

Even the most prosaic government officials became ensnarled in the tentacles of President Elliott's overreach. Lonnie Bell, coordinator of the Small Business Administration's disaster loan program, was destined to become such a pawn.

Bell caught the attention of high level administration officials while supporting the Federal Emergency Management Administration's response to Hurricane Sandy. Known as a smart, hardworking employee with the unique capacity to engage people at all levels, he ranked high on FEMA's recruitment list when congress moved FEMA under the Department of Homeland Security. That realignment gave President Elliott a golden opportunity to advance his agenda.

As a rookie FEMA executive, Bell was assigned to a new department responsible for building and managing disaster relief centers around the country. His excitement over being part of a well-funded program soon turned to suspicion over its true purpose. The agency's reliance on executive privilege to deflect congressional oversight triggered his alarm.

Soon after his appointment, he was invited to a high level, strategic planning session in Silver Springs, Maryland. As the meeting progressed and attendees became more comfortable with each other, FEMA's senior staffers began referring to their centers as camps. The opaque references resonated with conspiracy theories Bell had heard regarding covert government internment camps.

Well into the meeting, he mustered enough courage to step out of his bureaucratic comfort zone. "Mr. Chairman, how would you describe the specific purpose of our centers?"

The chairman's response was far from reassuring. "I think our mission is clearly stated on our website, Mr. Bell."

Despite his temptation to challenge the answer, years of government service had taught him to choose his battles wisely. His acquiescence didn't go unnoticed. Within six months he was summoned to Washington, DC by the meeting chairman, who also served as the Deputy Director and Chief Operating Officer of FEMA. No reason was given for the meeting.

Bell waited patiently outside the Deputy Director's office wondering why he was there. His speculation was interrupted.

"Mr. Bell, Deputy Director Lucas will see you now," the receptionist said. Her upbeat, almost giddy demeanor suggested that he was in for some good news.

Skipping all formalities and introductions, Lucas didn't disappoint him. "Bell, we would like you to run the most advanced center in our system. You have the attributes to make Waco a model center. The appointment would make you the youngest center director in the agency."

Bell's pride and ambition surged. "I'd be happy to step up," he replied, a little giddy himself.

Lucas sized him up, searching for signs of reticence. "I like your attitude, Bell. Current events have accelerated our schedule. When can you start?"

Bell presumed Lucas's urgency was being driven by the likelihood of future budget cuts. "I can start in a couple of weeks," he said. "I just need to give notice."

Lucas said, "We'll take care of that. You need to focus on getting a higher security clearance."

Bell looked confused. "I don't think so, sir. I already have a Top Secret."

"That's not high enough for what you'll be doing," Lucas said. "The White House wants center directors to have a compartmentalized clearance to handle intelligence related to domestic terrorism."

The statement struck Bell as odd. A higher clearance made sense, but involvement in the decision by the White house didn't. Once again, his bureaucratic discretion prevailed, and he let the issue slide.

Following the meeting, he stopped in the FEMA cafeteria to call his wife, Cathy. "It's the opportunity I've been hoping for," he said. "I'll be the youngest director in the entire agency."

"I know you've worked hard for this, but why did they pick you over your more experienced colleagues?" she asked.

"They seemed more interested in attributes than experience," he replied. "I got the sense they were looking for a strong team player."

Based on her husband's exuberance and convincing appeal, Cathy agreed to pull up roots and move to Waco. "When are you coming home?" she asked.

"I'll be back in a couple of days," he said. "I have another call, sweetie. Gotta run."

"Director Bell, this is John Moran, your new deputy. I understand you'll be reporting to the camp on the 19th of this month."

There's that freaky reference to camp again, he thought. He assumed Lucas had already notified Moran that he was on board, another sign of urgency. "That's right, John," he said. "The agency is lining up a house for us, so we're moving right away."

"That's great," Moran said. "We'll be able to go ahead with our schedule. Just so you know, you'll have an orientation on Monday and Tuesday. People from the Civil Unrest and Domestic Terrorism Unit of DHS will lead off on Monday. Greg Olson, the Director of Camp Bravo-8 in Grand Junction, will cover operational procedures on Tuesday."

Bell hesitated with a sip of coffee. "Why is DHS leading off when this is a FEMA operation?"

"You work for DHS now, Mr. Bell. FEMA camps fall under the Civil Unrest and Domestic Terrorism Unit of DHS."

"Bear with me, John," Bell said. "I assumed I would be working for Lucas since he hired me."

"Not to put too fine a point on things," Moran said, "Lucas recommended you, but you work for the special ops guys at DHS. Now, back to scheduling. After your orientation we'll have a full alert to test our readiness."

Bell's warning sirens wailed. "Our readiness for what? Is there some impending disaster I don't know about?"

Moran's answer gave him goose bumps. "The emergency drill is on civil unrest and insurrection."

His instincts now screaming, he walked into the hallway beyond earshot of other people. The hidden risk of *going along to get ahead* was becoming clearer. "Are there things you aren't telling me, John?" he asked, clenching his fists.

"You'll get filled in on all the particulars during your orientation, sir. All I can say is we need to be prepared in light of current events."

Moran's evasiveness reinforced Bell's worst suspicions. The rumors he'd been hearing took on an eerie ring of possibility. He decided to keep Cathy in Portland until he knew exactly what he was getting into.

Bell relived the day's events during the cab ride from FEMA headquarters to his motel at 13th and Wisconsin in Georgetown. When he kissed Cathy goodbye he had promised not to drink on this trip. His reliance on red wine to soften the edge of job-related stress, drowning the demons as he called it, had contributed to his rising blood pressure. Nevertheless, his promotion called for a special celebration. "Is there a minimart near my motel?" he asked the cabbie.

"There's one three blocks down Wisconsin toward the river," the driver said.

"Drop me off there, please."

Bell paid the cabbie and entered the minimart so typical of those in Washington, DC. Usually run by an Asian or Middle Eastern proprietor, it offered a limited choice of food staples, but an ample selection of alcohol, cigarettes, and lottery tickets.

An all-time favorite beckoned from the wine shelf: Fog Bank Select Merlot, a smooth light wine with no sulfites from an organic vineyard in Oregon. Without hesitation, he placed two bottles in his basket before grabbing a couple of bananas and a jar of unsalted peanuts. He carried his groceries to the counter where the clerk was busy restocking cigarettes. "A corkscrew?" he asked.

The clerk pointed down toward his knees. "Front of the counter," he answered with a thick accent.

Bell bent down to retrieve a fifteen dollar corkscrew that would have cost five bucks back home. He paid without hesitation. His raise would cover lots of excesses.

A full moon lit the three-block walk from the minimart to his motel. His Burberry trench coat blocked out the crisp autumn air. Comfortable row houses lining the street were models of peace and tranquility. His casual glance through a glass door caught a family sitting together watching TV. Noticing Bell through the door, a barking terrier alerted the father who closed the inner door to block out further distractions. Bell felt a twinge of guilt for interrupting the Norman Rockwell setting.

Another block of sidewalk riddled with cracks and protruding roots brought him to his destination. Autumn leaves swirled in the blustery wind as he searched for his key. Once inside, he shed his Burberry and wingtips. Two hours and two bottles later, his reservations about his new job had dissipated like smoke wafting from a snuffed-out candle.

CHAPTER 7

——

Lonnie Bell set out on his sojourn from Portland to Waco. Someone else would have to deal with the problems in Georgia while he prepared for his new job in Texas. But no amount of preparation could prepare him for what he was about to encounter.

He had reviewed travel brochures to learn the topography and demographics of northern Texas. To his dismay, one of them pointed out that the location of Camp Bravo-6 was less than three miles from the infamous Branch Davidian compound. In 1993 a confrontation between the Davidians and agents from the Federal Bureau of Investigation and the Bureau of Alcohol, Tobacco, and Firearms left four agents dead. The Davidians weren't so fortunate. All survivors of the of 84 member sect, including an aborted newborn, perished during the standoff.

Now open prairie with an active Davidian church, the site houses a memorial listing the names of those killed. While driving by the site Bell remembered reading somewhere that governments have killed more civilians in the past two hundred years than all the soldiers killed in battle combined. The thought made him shudder and amplified his qualms about his new job.

The first thing he noticed about the Waco Center, or Camp Bravo-6 as DHS called his facility, was its ominous appearance. He wasn't prepared for the guard towers on each corner with smaller ones along a perimeter wall topped with concertina wire. *This place looks like a Russian gulag,* he thought.

Catching Moran just inside the administration building, Bell muscled him into a side hallway. "You've got a lot of explaining to do, John," he said. "No more evasion. No more half answers. Your job is to cover my back."

Moran pulled free of Bell's adrenaline-fueled grip. "Everything will be crystal clear by the end of the day, Mr. Bell. You know the saying, 'God works in mysterious ways.' Well, DHS works in more mysterious ways, and even God wonders what they're up to sometimes." He adjusted his tie while regaining his composure. "We're in the conference room on the right. Can I bring you some coffee?"

Bell's disillusionment brought a sigh. "Please do. Make it dark and deep, just like this job I've stepped into."

Moran guided Bell into the conference room where an officious-looking man at the table spoke up. "Welcome to Camp Bravo-6, Director Bell."

This guy in the tactical uniform and knee-high boots must be in charge since he spoke first, he thought. "And who might you be, sir?"

"I'm Duane Walker, Regional Director for DHS in Dallas. And this is Justin Brooks, head of the Civil Unrest and Domestic Terrorism unit out of Washington," he said, pointing to a man across the table. "Mr. Brooks will conduct most of your orientation today."

"Hello, Bell," Brooks said without looking up. "Welcome to the front line in maintaining order in times of civil unrest."

Bell's worst suspicions seemed to be materializing. "Hello, Mr. Brooks. Excuse me if I look puzzled, but I was under the assumption I was going to manage a disaster relief center."

"Officially, you are correct," he said. "If we ever encounter a typhoon or a tsunami in Waco, you will be called upon. Meantime, we face a disaster with clear political origins that threatens our national security."

"What do you mean?" Bell asked.

"We have seventeen hundred delusional Convention delegates in Austin who are talking insurrection and treason. President Elliott and the Department of Homeland Security are determined to prevent them from disrupting the government. And as the newest member of our team, you're going to help us carry out that mission."

Brooks seemed to relish the chance to bash the conventioneers while projecting his own self-importance. His message seemed to be *either you are on our team, or you are an insurrectionist.*

Bell slid further into disbelief as Brooks and Walker outlined a plan to storm the Convention with federal agents and intern the delegates in Camp Bravo-6. Over a thousand captives would be his responsibility, with no indication of how long they would be in his custody.

Stupefied by the plan, Bell pushed for clarity. "Let me fully understand what you are telling me, Mr. Brooks. You and your band of merry men are going to arrest thirty-four governors, their respective attorneys general, plus over sixteen hundred more delegates made up of legislators, mayors, judges, and county commissioners from all over the country and intern them here in my facility?"

"*Correctamundo*," Brooks said with a satanic smile.

"Under what authority are you going to carry out this plan?" Bell asked.

Brooks propped his boot on a chair while chewing on a toothpick. "That's above my pay grade, Bell. President Elliott, Attorney General Oliver, and DHS Secretary Massey have worked that out. As I understand it, they are relying on the Patriot Act."

"And once the delegates are moved here, what am I supposed to do with them?"

"Hold them until we can try them for treason."

"How long might that take?"

Brooks rubbed a scuff from his spit-shined boot. "Who knows? We're plowing new ground here. That, too, is the Attorney General's concern. Our mission is to get them here and hold them."

"You expect the public to sit idly by while we incarcerate their local leaders?" Bell asked.

Brooks's smile turned from sinister to fiendish. "What are they going to do about it? Most of our fine citizens don't care what goes on as long as they have their beer, sports, and social media."

Bell reeled from what he was hearing. Instead of helping fellow Americans displaced by national disasters, he would serve as a prison warden in charge of political detainees who disagree with an increasingly-delusional President. "This is not what I expected based on my conversation with Lucas," he said.

Walker mirrored Brooks's sinister smile. "Was Lucas unclear or did you just hear what you wanted to?"

Bell realized Walker was right. He also realized he didn't particularly like any of his new partners, including his own deputy. As the meeting progressed, he felt more isolated from reality. "Can either of you gentlemen tell me when all of this is going down?"

Brooks's tenor changed dramatically. "I don't need to remind you that every detail of our plan is highly classified and should be discussed only with those who have a need to know."

"Understood," Bell said.

"DHS has been making preparations since Texas passed the first Article V bill calling for a Convention," Brooks continued. "There will be over a thousand DHS agents arriving in Dallas shortly to carry out Walker's plan. As a matter of fact, Walker is driving to Dallas after this orientation to meet his squad leaders who are arriving with the first wave of special ops troops."

"Meantime, Moran has been bringing the camp up to speed in preparation for your arrival," Walker added.

That's a great comfort, Bell thought before throwing out a thorny factoid. "I understand there are several companies of National Guard troops protecting the Convention."

"We know that," Walker said. "Those weekend warriors won't be much of a match for my Special Operation guys."

"I understand another group of weekend warriors gave the 82nd Airborne all it could handle in Georgia," Bell said.

Undeterred by reality, Brooks pushed on. "President Elliott said the 82nd was led by poor commanders who undermined their mission."

Brooks was unaware that Bell was a former Army Ranger who kept up on the latest military news in *Stars and Stripes*.

Bell's eyes narrowed. "If I remember correctly, President Elliott appointed General Graham to command the 82nd Airborne."

"That might be the case," Brooks said. He tossed his toothpick toward the trash can. It fell short, just like his reasoning. "But I can assure you that command and control won't be a problem as long as DHS is heading up this operation."

"You can say that again," Walker said.

My new colleagues are as crazy as they are arrogant, Bell thought. He suspected they were grossly underestimating the resolve of the Convention delegates. A more fateful error was underestimating the will and capabilities of Texas law enforcement.

CHAPTER 8

—

Seventeen-hundred delegates from thirty-four states streamed into the Moncrief-Neuhaus Events Center in Austin, Texas. Multiple admission points were slowed by officials scanning credentials for authenticity. Select members of the press were admitted, but passes for White House observers had been summarily denied. While credentials were checked, undercover officers scrutinized the crowd for insurgents bent on sabotaging the proceedings. Dale Perez, Commander of the Texas Rangers, the longest-standing law enforcement agency in the country, headed up security. He had the Convention locked down as tight as a nuclear missile site.

Around midmorning, a state patrol officer sped through the security checkpoint with an emergency message. The former wide receiver for Texas A&M University offered his hand. "Officer Lance Taylor, sir. I have a message for you."

"What's up, Taylor?" Perez asked, wincing slightly from the iron grip.

"I was in the area so Superintendent Meeks asked me to brief you on a situation," he said. "Abilene officers picked up a guy for speeding in a federal SUV. The driver was uncooperative and when they searched the vehicle they found fully automatic assault rifles and grenades, all military issue, in a secret compartment."

Perez's expression turned grave. "What did the Abilene officers learn from the guy?"

Taylor shifted nervously before replying, "Before they could even ask for his name, he pulled out one of those 'get out of jail free' national security cards. When Abilene asked us to help in the investigation, Superintendent Meeks called the Attorney General who claimed that under the state's agreement with Homeland Security we had to turn him loose. When we cut him loose, Meeks told him we'd need a court order to give his weapons back. I've never seen anyone curse the Super and get away with it."

"How long ago was that, Taylor?"

"I'd say less than an hour."

"Excuse me a minute," Perez said. He walked a few steps away, pulled out his phone, and hit speed dial. "Meeks, this is Perez. Did you get any info on the guy with the stash of weapons?"

"I was expecting your call," Meeks said. "He wouldn't answer any questions, so we did some checking. Turns out he's a bigshot named Walker, assigned last week to head up the Department of Homeland Security in Dallas. I remember getting a notice from Washington. Yours is probably in your circular file."

Perez sensed a likely connection between the stop and the Convention. Given the failed raid by the 82nd, he wasn't taking any chances. "We need to put out an APB on this guy, so we can find out why he's so heavily armed in our backyard."

"We can't do that, Commander," Meeks replied. "He had one of those federal immunity cards."

Perez chuckled. "If this Convention goes the way I expect it to, those cards won't be worth the paper they're printed on."

"Can't wait for that day." Meeks said.

"None of us can," Perez agreed. "Besides, fragmentation grenades are classified as weapons of mass destruction in Texas so no civilian should have them in public no matter who they are. When you pick him up, bring him to me personally. We'll find out what he's up to."

"Guess we should have held him on the WMD violation in spite of the AG's reluctance," Meeks said. "We'll bring him to you as soon as we track him down."

"Thanks, Meeks," Perez said. He stowed his phone and walked back to Taylor, who was patiently waiting. "If you want to be a hero, jump in your cruiser and collar that guy. He's probably heading toward Dallas on I-10. Meeks is running an APB as we speak. Step on it, Taylor, this is urgent."

"My pleasure, Commander," Taylor yelled over his shoulder while hustling to his patrol car.

Before Perez could get back to his office, he heard Taylor's tires squeal onto San Jacinto Street as if he were in contention at Daytona.

Twenty minutes later, Officer Taylor flipped on his blue lights as he pulled in behind a black Suburban parked on an I-10 rest area entrance ramp.

He approached the unmistakable profile of Officer Tess Grissom—Big Tess as she was tagged at the police academy—kneeling over a captive with her firearm drawn and her knee firmly planted on the nape of his neck. The captive squirmed under the crushing weight. Holstering her firearm, she dangled her handcuffs and yelled, "A little help, Taylor."

Taylor reached down and grabbed their captive by the thumbs to minimize resistance. Squealing in pain, he complied.

With the agility of a person half her size, Tess flipped her cuffs open then latched them firmly on each wrist. Each click brought a wince from the prisoner. He swore profusely, insisting they had no jurisdiction over him.

Taylor dragged the prisoner to Grissom's cruiser and shoved him into the back seat. When he reached in to connect Walker's seat belt, he noticed two shiny darts imbedded in his neck. With his prisoner secured, he walked back to Grissom. "Good grief, Tess," he said. "Did you have to use your Taser?"

"Absolutely," she said. "All standard procedure. He kept reaching inside his jacket and I thought he was going for a piece. Turns out he was actually going for this national security card." She pulled the laminated card from her shirt pocket and waved it. "He insists he's a federal something or other, and this card keeps us from arresting him."

"I saw that card a couple of hours ago when we picked him up the first time," Taylor said.

Big Tess shook her head in confusion. "You mean you had this guy and let him go?" she asked. "I don't get it."

"That card spooked the AG into advising the Super to let him go," Taylor said. "Perez convinced Meeks otherwise, and the APB was issued. I'll fill you in over a beer after we drop him off."

"Make that two beers, Taylor. I'm real thirsty from wrestling with this guy, especially when he insists he's in charge of us."

"Let him try to convince Perez that he's in charge of the Rangers," Taylor said. "That will be a show. Meantime, let's get him to the Travis Building before my shift ends."

The two officers delivered Walker to Ranger headquarters, where he was processed then placed in a holding cell. On their way out of the building, they bumped into Perez.

"Hello again, Taylor. Who's your intimidating partner?"

"This is Officer Tess Grissom, Commander," Taylor said. "She collared

Walker single-handedly and had him on the ground before I even got there."

"Good work, Grissom." Perez said.

"Call me Big Tess, Commander. Everyone else does, even my kids."

"Okay, Big Tess. Thanks for the collar. Any idea why he's driving around Texas with an arsenal in his trunk?"

"He said he's on official business and we'd be wise to cooperate with him," she said.

"So we should be taking advice from a man who's under arrest and in handcuffs?"

Big Tess shrugged. "That's the way *he* sees it, Commander. You have to admire his bravado."

Taylor laughed. "On the other hand, you have to wonder about a person who resists when you're pointing a fifty-thousand-volt Taser at him."

"One thing's for sure," Grissom said. "His cockiness melted away once he got struck by lightning. He started pleading for mercy while he was rolling on the ground kicking his shoes off!"

Perez glanced down the hallway toward the cell blocks. "I think I know how to find out what he's up to. We've got Ricardo Rodriguez and Carlos Sanchez on ice over at the detention center. Maybe we'll let Mr. Walker hang out in their cell for a while and see what brews."

"Didn't the feds deport both of their families a while back?" Taylor asked.

Grissom broke in. "I read in the paper how they issued a warrant in the middle of the night, scaring the daylights out of their kids. Both vowed to get even with the government for messing with their families."

"We picked them up on weapons charges shortly after that," Perez said. "Seems they might be looking for a little payback. Could be our local deportation chief turned up in the wrong place at the wrong time."

Perez bid the officers goodbye then retrieved Walker to escort him to the detention center. Pinning Walker against the bars, he called out, "Hola Ricardo, Carlos, meet Mr. Walker, your new cellmate. He's in charge of Homeland Security. You know, border patrol, immigration, deportation, and stuff like that. I want you to take special care of him because he's real important. If you don't believe it, just ask him."

Carlos peered at Walker with a venomous grin. "Hola, Gringo. Mi Casa, su Casa."

"What is that supposed to mean?" Walker asked, oozing with contempt.

"It means, Señor, you are on our turf now. Comprendes?"

The veiled threat washed over Walker like a voodoo curse. "Hey guard, I need to be moved."

"Does this look like a Holiday Inn, and do I look like a reservations clerk?" the guard asked, walking away.

Neither Ricardo nor Carlos had any formal education, but both were brimming with street smarts. They knew, for example, that a federal official like Walker had no authority to offer immunity from local prosecution. At the same time, they knew any information that was useful to Perez might mitigate their local charges. With that in mind, they played Walker for all he was worth. Before the night was over, Walker had struck a deal with the devil. In an effort to ingratiate himself to his threatening new cell mates, he outlined every detail of DHS's plan to raid the Convention.

CHAPTER 9

—

Mitch Brady needed a temporary respite from the mountain of bad news, especially that coming out of Georgia and Texas. He quietly slipped out of the West Wing to visit Julio's coffee shop two blocks down Pennsylvania Avenue. His usual order, a double espresso with two creams and two sugars, would hone his wits to guide the President through another day of harsh criticism.

The heart of the political universe teemed with activity as he wound his way back to the White House. Instead of the expected energy boost, his potent coffee and mounting anxiety ignited a case of heartburn with the intensity of a blowtorch. Wilting from internal combustion, he pitched the high octane espresso into the closest trash receptacle. Like Pavlov's dog, he reached for his constant companion these days, a nearly empty pack of antacids.

Another loop around the block to clear his mind brought him back to the West Wing where his secretary hovered over his desk like a mother hen. "POTUS needs you right now, sir." The use of POTUS, an acronym used by insiders for President of the United States, meant something urgent was afoot.

The chill in the Oval Office was a stark contrast to the inferno raging within his gut. The President glared from behind his desk. "What's going on, Mitch? Most news reports sound like I'm finished and the Convention is going to save the country. Are things really that bad?"

Mitch had never seen the President in such a frenzy. With another surge of indigestion, he popped his last two antacids. "Well, sir, I've had feelers out to both detractors and allies. I fear we've pushed the envelope too far. Allies in Congress who lost their seats last November feel like we placed our agenda ahead of them and the party. Then we assured them that we were going to work with both sides of the aisle on immigration reform. When opposition leaders reached out to us, we mocked their proposals and their intentions."

"Come on, Mitch. No pain, no gain."

"Sometimes, Mr. President, when you inflict pain you get payback."

"We should have declared martial law before the off-year elections," Elliott snarled.

Incensed by the President's political ineptitude, Mitch responded with an unfortunate choice of words. "That would have amounted to throwing gasoline on a fire." Reminded of his own misery, he reached for another antacid and came up empty-handed. "The public was already starting to question our motives," he said. "Declaring martial law would have convinced progressives and libertarians alike that we don't care about civil rights. And it certainly wouldn't have passed the smell test with those who are looking for excuses to impeach you."

"I'm not going to roll over and play dead from empty threats," the President said. "Congress doesn't have the kahunas to go after me."

"Some things are worse than impeachment, Mr. President. The Constitutional Convention is one of those things. The delegates in Austin are determined to rein in the government and limit your executive power. Their reforms could bring our agenda to a standstill."

"I know you've tried to be a moderating force around here," Elliott said in a mildly conciliatory tone. "I should have consulted with you before I gave Secretary Massey the green light to shut down the Convention, but he convinced me that DHS could do what the Army couldn't. I'm determined to put this ordeal behind us and get our agenda back on track."

Disappointed by the President's unilateral decision, and pained by a resurgence of fire in his gut, Brady pushed back. "I wish you had discussed this with me before making your decision, Mr. President. Despite all our efforts, we have not been able to overcome public backlash to the Madison fiasco. Our political office fears that another major setback could throw us into a political death spiral."

"I disagree," Elliott argued. "It's time to squeeze those traitors and galvanize our support."

Mitch shuddered at the President's myopia. They'd lost both houses of Congress and there were thirty-four opposition governors assembled against them in Austin. The President's approval rating hovered around thirty percent. *Where exactly is all this support we're supposed to galvanize?* he wondered. His empty pocket was an unwelcome reminder that his antacids had run out just like their options.

Just then the President's buzzer sounded. "Secretary Massey is on the line, sir."

Elliott dove for the phone. "Just the man I need. Have a seat, Mitch, I'll put him on speaker."

"Secretary Massey, Mitch is here. Give us some good news."

"Sorry, Mr. President, I can't do that," Massey said.

The President's expression turned from sour to dour. "What do you mean?"

"After you gave us the green light, but before we could put our plan in motion, our team leader in Dallas went offline."

Massey's choice of words bewildered the President. "What do you mean by offline, Duane?"

"I mean we can't reach him and no one knows where he is," Massey said.

The President rolled his eyes in disbelief. "Are you telling me you've lost your key operative?"

Massey swallowed his pride and continued. "Soon after we lost contact, we tracked his car to the Texas State Office building in Dallas."

"Maybe he's coordinating with local resources," Elliott said. "That *was* part of your plan."

"I don't think so, Mr. President. Later on we tracked his vehicle to a rest stop just off I-10 near Abilene. When we sent a team to check it out, Walker was gone, and so was his equipment."

"What about a gang-related carjacking to get the guns?" Elliott asked.

"There's no way anyone could have known about the guns," Massey said. "They were hidden in a secret compartment. We have a team trying to find him, but as Convention hosts, the Texans aren't exactly cooperative."

Brady groped for a solution. "What about Granger? Could he help?"

"I don't think so," Massey said. "He's leading the very Convention that's trying to put us out of business."

"I'm counting on you to make sure that doesn't happen, Darryl," Elliott said. "Any more bad news?"

"I'm afraid so, sir," Massey said. "The local authorities in Madison have resumed the murder trial of our Special Operations Commander, Hank Applegate."

The anger in the President's voice crackled. "You assured me you'd take care of that, Duane."

"I was counting on assurances from the Justice Department," Massey said.

"Why didn't the Attorney General nix it?" Elliott asked.

"Oliver did send a letter asserting National Security, but the Georgians are about as cooperative as the Texans," Massey said. "The Georgia Attorney General sent a letter back stating we have no authority over a local murder case. And according to our attorneys here, he's correct.

To keep the prickly conversation from escalating, Brady interrupted. "According to White House Counsel, the trial is being heralded by the media as a prelude to the Convention, a states' rights victory over the authority of the federal government. The more we challenge local authorities for simply doing their job, the worse we look. I'm afraid we are gradually losing our case in the most important venue, the court of public opinion." Strong rumblings in his stomach interrupted his thought. "Excuse me," he said before rushing from the room.

"Those thirty-four governors showed more backbone than we expected," Massey said. "And public support for the Convention has been stronger than even they expected. The federal government cannot really function unless the people accept our legitimacy. Once it's challenged, the authority granted to the states by the Constitution fills the void."

Brady re-entered the room to hear President Elliott press Massey. "Are you a constitutional lawyer now, Duane?"

"No, sir. But I have several working for me, and they're not too confident right now," he replied.

"Two landslide elections give me all the confidence I need, and we control the entire federal government to get the job done," Elliott said.

Brady knew that was the problem. The President didn't seem to grasp that he was no longer really in charge. *There is a delicate tipping point where confidence becomes denial,* he thought.

Piqued by the look of concern on Brady's face, Elliott asked, "Any thoughts for Duane, Mitch?"

Brady masked the anxiety incinerating his insides. "Just keep us posted so we know what to expect, Mr. Secretary. And you might want to appoint a replacement for Walker so we can get things back on track."

"What if Walker is compromised?" Massey asked. "He could implicate all of us."

Deflecting the warning, the President said, "We'll deal with that later."

There might not be a later, Brady's instincts roared.

CHAPTER 10

—

Six hundred and fifty miles from the White House, Judge Johnson and Prosecutor Stone sat in the Crossroads Café—the "CC" as locals called it—over coffee, scrambled eggs, bacon, and grits. Despite the occasional disruption of freight trains rumbling by, the restaurant served as a favorite meeting spot for local politicians and businessmen. Today's meeting was spurred by Stone's trepidation over one of the most unique trials in American history.

"I'm not sure I can prosecute this case, Judge," Stone said.

Johnson mumbled through peppered grits dripping with butter. "Why not?"

Stone punctured an egg yolk with his fork. "You know I don't rattle easily, Judge. But I got a letter from the Justice Department threatening to send Federal Marshals after us for obstruction of justice if we proceed."

Johnson seined his steaming coffee through his bushy mustache. Leaning back in his chair, he fashioned a sardonic smirk. "Honestly, Fred, how much scarier are Marshals than the 82nd Airborne?"

Stone got the point. "So, do we just ignore them?"

"Surely you know from your fancy Columbia law degree that DOJ has no legal standing over a state felony. The Administration messed up sending the Army into Georgia, and they ended up with egg on their face. By the way, Fred, you have a smidgen on your chin."

Stone wiped the bright yellow yolk with a napkin.

With a dose of cynicism, Johnson added, "The Administration is trying to sweep this trial under the rug before the media picks up on the illegal role Elliott has in mind for Homeland Security." Each time the judge emphasized a point, he blasted particles of grits through his mustache. When he inadvertently picked up Stone's napkin to wipe his mouth, Stone casually signaled their waitress for a fresh one.

Their waitress had witnessed the entire episode and had already grabbed a replacement that she casually dropped into Stone's lap. "Here you go, honey. Hang onto this one."

Unabashed, Johnson continued. "You might have noticed, Fred, the Georgia Attorney General was copied on your letter. He called me this morning with assurance that we're on rock solid ground. He's already notified Washington that the trial will continue. And, Fred, the good citizens of Morgan County expect you to do your job."

"I'll do my best," Stone said.

Judge Johnson's courtroom was bursting at the seams by nine the next morning. Hank Applegate, the DHS Special Operations Commander captured by Ted Johnson's militiamen, sat in the defendant's chair flanked by his private attorney and one from the U.S. Attorney's office. His orange jumpsuit and standard issue tennis shoes projected the image of a common criminal. The bandages on his nose gave rise to speculation that he was not afforded the deference he was accustomed to. He had foolishly brandished his superior authority claim, but found his compliant side following a whack from the butt of Ted Johnson's Ka-Bar combat knife.

While rubbing his nose, vivid memories of that fateful night in the woods near Madison flooded back. Applegate had often boasted to DHS executives about the military prowess of his men, but that was before he had encountered veteran tunnel rats and Green Berets from the Vietnam War. The unexpected happened when he and his men deployed their M777 howitzers to inflict a demoralizing blow on the insurgent Georgians.

Applegate was bewildered when his guns fell silent one-by-one. Perched in his Humvee to escape the driving rain, he peered through the window at distorted images of his men being dragged into the woods. He focused intently to get a better view through the rain streaked glass. "What the—?" he gasped.

The door of the Humvee sprang open from his swift kick. When he leaned out, he was greeted by the cold driving rain and the razor-sharp blade of a Ka-Bar against his throat. The pounding of his heart drowned out the rain.

Ted Johnson's deep voice boomed, "One slight move, bud, and you'll be wearing this blade."

Unable to catch his breath, he slowly leaned back into the doorway. He scanned the camp through the open door like a cornered cat. None of his men were at their posts. The howitzers stood silent, their hot barrels steaming from the relentless raindrops.

Avoiding any movements that might test fate, he stammered, "W-Who are you?"

"I'm just a local farmer," Johnson said. His breath reeked of beef jerky and stale coffee. "Stay calm and you won't have to join your friends over there fertilizing kudzu."

Mindful of the warning, Applegate slid out of the Humvee with the knife pressed against his jugular. To his horror, he felt warm blood trickling down his neck into his shirt. For the first time in his fantasy-ridden career, he feared for his life.

"Easy there, partner, you've already got a little nick" Johnson warned. "Now if you'll walk to our campfire under that tarp, we'll have a little pow-wow."

In the flickering firelight, he eyed the small squad of militiamen in camouflage clothing huddled around the fire drinking coffee. *Surely these old men had help from someone*, he reasoned. His underappreciation for combat-hardened veterans had cost him dearly.

While sizing him up, Ted noticed the name on his uniform. "We're riled by your presence here in Madison, Mr. Applegate, and we'd like you to explain why you are murdering innocent women and kids with those howitzers."

Now shaking from a combination of penetrating cold and fear, Applegate drew on his only defense. "If you look in my pocket you'll find a national security card that identifies me as a DHS combat soldier," he said. "It gives me immunity from lesser authorities."

"I don't care if you have a celebrity pass to Disney World," Johnson said. "You're going to be our guest tonight in the Morgan County jail. Not to digress, but my buddies and I know something about combat soldiers, and it takes more than a tactical uniform with a DHS patch to make the cut. Did you notice by chance that your men didn't fire a single shot while we overran your camp? I guess *their* immunity didn't work against us lesser authorities."

Applegate's grimace belied his abject humiliation.

CHAPTER 11

—

On the same day as Applegate's trial in Madison, delegates in Austin poured into the Convention with high expectations. Texas Governor and Convention Chairman Clay Granger stepped onto the stage to make history. With one swing of the gavel, he set a non-violent revolution into motion. Like the beginning of liturgy at St. Peter's Basilica, a sudden hush fell over the crowd.

"Welcome, Convention delegates and guests," he began. "Under the authority of Article V of the United States Constitution and the affirmation of thirty-four State Legislatures, I hereby call this Constitutional Convention to order. I am honored to guide these proceedings based on a process outlined by your Drafting Committee, made up of Governors Timothy Kelley of Indiana, Andrew Spivey of Georgia, Eleanor Pearson of Arizona, Thomas Young of Pennsylvania, and Phil McKinney of North Carolina, plus their respective state attorneys general.

"Seldom since the original Convention in 1787 has a more solemn and profound responsibility fallen on the shoulders of so few patriots. Everyone here shares an overwhelming sense of duty in this time of national crisis."

The crowd remained dead silent.

"Today we face a peril never anticipated by the founding fathers. America is being undermined from within. It is obvious to all of us assembled here that we simply were not prepared to repel an insurgent political philosophy intent on destroying our most fundamental principles. It is up to you as delegates to protect this country from any further wounds inflicted by those who under the fog of ideological delusion swore upon the Bible to promote and protect the Constitution, but chose another course."

Granger perused the crowd. Everyone was spellbound. "I therefore bestow upon each of you, as delegates of this Constitutional Convention, the authority to right this floundering ship. Ladies and Gentlemen, please raise your right hand and repeat after me."

Seventeen-hundred delegates from across America obliged.

"I, repeat your name, as a lawfully appointed delegate of the people…" With each word, the response from the delegates grew louder and stronger until Granger's voice was completely drowned out. The walls reverberated from the collective voice. Driven by the passion and energy swirling around them, the delegates resurrected the spirit of the founding fathers. The great American experiment breathed new life, inspired by the determination of the patriots represented in the great hall.

"…hereby pledge loyalty and allegiance to the United States of America, and do solemnly swear to accept, protect, and restore the principles upon which the country was founded during the Constitutional Convention of 1787. I also resolve to restore confidence in the governance of the United States by holding responsible those who intentionally degraded the original principles upon which the country was built, so help me God."

The hall erupted in a rapture of howls, cheers, and high-fives. Some delegates threw their hats into the air while others simply looked on. A few cried tears of joy as emotions swelled over. Real power would finally be restored to the people.

Wham, wham, wham. Granger pounded his gavel to restore order. The delegates quieted and took their seats.

Tim Kelley, Indiana Governor and Chairman of the Drafting Committee, sat motionless, head in hands.

"What's wrong, Governor?" an Indiana delegate asked.

"Nothing," he murmured. "I'm just so relieved that we'll be able to pass on to our children and grandchildren the same freedom and opportunity we enjoyed." His serious tone defined the moment. "It's been a long, hard struggle, and we need to make sure we don't blow this opportunity."

"I have to admit, Governor, I wasn't sure we'd be able to build a powerful enough coalition to accomplish this," the delegate said. "And now that the hunt is over, we have the tiger by the tail."

"Right after Madison it looked like the whole county was unraveling," Kelley said. "If we hadn't been able to pull this off, or if the President had declared martial law as some expected, we would've been thrown into civil unrest for sure."

Just then, Luke Harper of the Television News Network, otherwise known as TNN, interrupted the emotionally charged moment. "Excuse me, Governor, could I have a word?"

Kelley put on a happy face, then said to the Indiana delegate, "Catch you later."

Turning to the reporter, he beamed. "Welcome to history in the making, Mr. Harper. I saw you interviewing Governor Granger earlier this morning."

"I'd like to interview you as well," Luke said. "Do you mind if I record it?"

"Not at all," Kelley replied. "I'm all for getting the facts straight."

Mickey Short, Luke's cameraman, raised his equipment and nodded.

"How would you describe your feelings right now?" Luke asked.

"I feel a profound sense of relief, but an equal sense of responsibility to get this right. Our citizens have been treated like pawns by an imperial president who doesn't share their values or the values of our founders."

Luke glanced at his cameraman. "Did you get that, Mickey?"

"Loud and clear," Mickey said.

Luke turned back to Kelley. "Please continue, Governor."

Kelley outlined his belief that positive reform was under way.

Mickey varied his shots to correspond with the newsworthy sound bites.

"Today's proceeding is the first step to get America back on the right track," Kelley said.

Luke reviewed a list of questions he had made for himself. "And when will you address the body on behalf of the Drafting Committee?"

"I'm scheduled in about an hour," Kelley replied. "So I have to run."

"Good luck, Governor, and thank you," Luke said.

Luke and Mickey knew their interview would be the lead story for the evening news. Both were experiencing something more dramatic than anything else in their careers. As the two dashed toward the press room, Luke yelled out. "Get it to the studio, Mickey. This is a warm-up for the main event."

CHAPTER 12

—

On the other side of the Convention hall, Commander Perez retrieved his buzzing cell phone. The strained voice of his detention center supervisor rang out. "You need to get over here right away, Commander! We just pulled Carlos off Walker. He swore he's going to strangle the Gestapo parasite. Last thing we need is to have a federal agent murdered in our custody."

"Be right there," Perez said. "Keep them apart."

Chains connected to Carlos Sanchez's shackles rattled against eyebolts anchored in the concrete floor. Pent-up anger wracked his body, jerking the chains with each outburst. Bloodshot eyes glowed like embers in his beet-red face, stoked from his swearing tirade. Spittle clung to the stubble on his angular chin.

Perez wondered if the blood on one frayed cuff was his or Walker's. "Settle down, man," he said. "Here's a Coke to cool you off."

"They should have let me kill that snake," Sanchez said. "He's just like his buddies who dragged my kids off in the middle of the night."

Perez sat across from Sanchez, eying the bloodstain. "You didn't mess Walker up, did you? We need to squeeze him for information."

"No worry, compadre," Sanchez said. "He's already been singing like a canary. I guess he thought we'd be amigos if he spilled his guts to us."

"Enjoy your Coke and tell me his story," Perez said.

Sanchez licked some soda dribbling down the can. A deep, raspy breath helped him relax.

Perez handed some paper napkins across the table.

Sanchez wiped his trembling mouth and then his brow. "I'm okay now," he said. "That hombre rubs me the wrong way."

"Tell me everything," Perez said. "The details are important."

Carlos leaned back in his chair, and for the next hour recounted how Walker and a thousand other agents were assembling in Dallas for a raid on the Convention. They expected to be backed up by various police agencies nationalized under an obscure provision of the Patriot Act. The combined forces would arrest the delegates as domestic terrorists. Without delegates, the Convention would crumble.

"I'm no military man," Sanchez said. "But it sounds like they're preparing for another Madison. This Walker twerp thinks he's Pancho Villa. He bragged how heavy armament was coming in on a secret government train. Why do these agents need heavy military equipment? They're not the Army."

"We've been wondering the same thing," Perez said. "No guarantees, Carlos, but I'll talk to the DA about how much you've helped. And thank Ricardo for us. By the way, we've moved Walker to another location for further questioning."

Sanchez downed his last swig of Coke and crushed the can in his gnarled hand. "Let us know if we can help with that, compadre."

While Perez briefed Meeks on the DHS plot, his phone buzzed. "Gotta go, George. Another call."

He hit flash and answered, "Perez here."

"It's Taylor, sir. I'm in the parking lot of the compound Walker told Carlos about. It's a secluded area behind the Waco Gulch National Park. If I didn't know better, I'd think it's a prison rather than a disaster relief center. It's crawling with activity inside, so I'd say they're up to something big. Hold on a sec, Commander. A security guard's coming."

"Don't give us away, Taylor," Perez said.

"Don't worry, Commander. Stay on the line." Taylor placed his still-connected phone face-up in the passenger seat.

The guard walked up and motioned for Taylor to lower his window. "Hi, Officer. Got a problem?"

"Just running a plate on a vehicle we've been watching for drug activity," Taylor said.

The guard shook his head. "There must be a mistake. The owners of these vehicles have been cleared by Homeland Security."

"I thought this was a FEMA center," Taylor said. "Why would DHS clear them?"

The guard shifted his weight. "Sorry, that's not my department."

Taylor upped the ante. "I'm just doing my job. If you have a problem with that, I'll talk to your supervisor."

"We don't need to go there, as long as you stay in the parking lot," the guard said. "This is a secure facility with restricted access." Satisfied that his warning was adequate, the guard walked back toward the gate with his assault rifle slung over his shoulder.

Excuse me if my badge doesn't give me access to your secure facility, Taylor thought. *Maybe next time I'll have a warrant.* He picked up the cell phone, keeping a sharp eye on the guard. "Commander, you still there?"

"Yep, I heard that line of smoke," Perez said. "Can you get some photos of the place without arousing suspicion?"

"I've had my dashcam running the entire time. I'll circle the parking lot to get more shots."

"Good work, Taylor. Is Big Tess with you?"

"The Super sent her to the airport to check on those commandos coming from D.C. She's not exactly inconspicuous on a stakeout, but she's tenacious."

Perez chuckled. "My sympathies to anyone who tangles with her. Our friend Walker learned that too late. By the way, can you send your dashcam images to Dell Smith in our intelligence unit when you get back?"

"Consider it done, Commander."

"I've got another call, Taylor. Keep me posted."

Superintendent Meeks was breathing heavily into the phone when Perez answered. "What's cooking, George?"

"Hi Dale. Just got a call from one of our officers in Austin. There's an unregistered train on a spur just off the Austin to Waco line. The yard detective said when he pressed the operators for transit orders, several federal agents showed up and started throwing their weight around."

"Any more of your officers in the area?" Perez asked.

"We have a radar unit close by that we could divert over there."

Perez weighed the importance of the train. "According to Walker, that train's transporting heavy arms for their raid. We might have to commandeer the whole kit-n-caboodle before all of this is over."

"We can do that," Meeks said.

Perez interjected, "When your guys reach that detective, ask him if he can tie the train up if needed."

"I know this guy, Commander. He's a retired State Patrolman. If it can be done, he can do it," Meeks said.

"Perfect. And tell him to play it safe."

"This guy's an Irishman from the old head knocking days, Commander. I'm more concerned about *him* taking out the federal agents than the other way around."

A few minutes later, Granger was going over some notes with the Drafting Committee when Perez burst in. "You look stressed," Granger said.

Perez paused to catch his breath. "I have reason to be, sir. Could we talk privately?"

"Go ahead. These folks need to know what I know."

"Yesterday the State Patrol arrested a guy on the interstate with a trunk full of automatic weapons. He later told his cellmates that DHS is preparing to raid the Convention. Their agents are flying into Dallas as we speak, while heavy equipment is being shipped in by train. We're intercepting both."

Granger's face turned red. "First the U.S. Army and now DHS? What is the President thinking?"

"The only thing I know for sure is we can't have another Madison," Perez said. "As we sit here, this Convention is more secure than Fort Knox. With or without armored personnel carriers, DHS is not going to penetrate our perimeter. I can keep the Convention safe, Governor, but it will be at a heavy cost to both sides."

Eleanor Pearson, the popular Governor of Arizona, listened intently.

Granger turned to her, anxious and angry. "What do you think, Eleanor?"

Pearson bit her lip momentarily. "I think we should expose this reckless plot to the public and let President Elliott face some more ferocious public outrage. Let's give Luke Harper the scoop of his career."

Granger seemed to relax a bit. He gave Eleanor a smile and a wink. "I like the way you think, Eleanor. Will you take the lead on this?"

She smiled back with confidence. "I'll do my best."

"Dale, would you work with Eleanor to milk Walker's story?"

"Absolutely," Perez said.

"I suspect Luke Harper will want to interview Walker and his two cell mates," Pearson said. Can you arrange that, Dale?"

"I can, but are you sure Harper wants to deal with these guys?" Perez asked. "Even though Carlos and Ricardo helped us with Walker, they are generally suspicious of people outside their small circle. That makes them tricky to deal with."

"Honestly, Dale. If Harper can handle the hooligans in the

Administration, he shouldn't have much trouble with a couple of street criminals," Pearson said. "Give me a few minutes with him and we'll be ready."

L uke Harper relaxed in the press gallery. He was washing down a chocolate bar with diet soda when Pearson walked up. Aware of the Governor's interest in health and nutrition, he reacted with contrition. "Hello, Governor. Guess I'm busted."

Pearson chuckled. "So you've discovered the John Connelly diet." Connelly, a former Texas Governor, was known for snacking on high-calorie candy bars and washing them down with diet colas. "I've learned over the years that it's less painful to watch what I eat than to replace my entire wardrobe," she said.

He wrapped up his half-eaten candy bar and stuffed it in his pocket. "I'm guessing you didn't come over to sell me on good nutrition."

"No, I came over here to give you a story."

"Oh, yeah? This Convention is the mother lode of stories."

"Not like this one," she said. "How would you like to report on a conspiracy?"

He licked melted chocolate from his fingers. "Some people say that's what I'm doing covering the Convention."

"Only the bad guys," she said. "I've seen your coverage, Luke, and I sense empathy for the cause."

"Don't let that get back to Carter Haynes or I'll be reporting on Yeti sightings in Nepal. Seriously, what is this conspiracy you're talking about?" he asked, drying his fingers on his pants.

"The Rangers are holding a federal official named Walker who confessed to a DHS plan to raid this Convention and round up the delegates. He admitted that the President personally ordered the raid."

"That's a smoking gun if there ever was one," Luke said. "Didn't they learn anything from Madison?"

"I don't have all the answers," she said, "but I can hook you up with this Walker guy who might."

"Why me? There's a horde of reporters here."

"We believe that even though you're with a biased organization, you strive to be fair and accurate."

The compliment spurred his imagination. He wondered how things might have been different if he had gone to work for a firm like Pearson's instead of going to work for TNN. His original perception of cable news as a glamorous and rewarding career had changed. Every day his superiors questioned his commitment to objectivity and fair play. Working for Carter Haynes was part of the problem, but being in a generally biased cable news environment was at the heart of his difficulty. He derived some satisfaction from slipping good stories past Haynes and the other producers.

Luke turned his focus back to Pearson who was busy people watching. "When can I see Walker?"

"I like your enthusiasm," she said.

"I'll owe you one, Governor," he said.

"All you'll owe me, Luke, is a good report on this malicious, reckless plan. The success of the Convention could depend on it."

Luke chuckled, then looked away. "Thanks for not putting any pressure on me."

"You've already proven you can handle it," she said.

With the Governor's unconditional vote of confidence, Luke felt a wave of reassurance. His vibrating phone showed Carter Haynes on the caller ID. "Excuse me a minute, Governor. I have to take this."

"Sure," she said.

"Hello, Carter. No, I can't get you the follow up with Granger this afternoon. Something's come up. Of course I'll tell Mickey to run it by you before I feed it to the studio." He winked at Pearson and ended the call.

Pearson's finger tapped her chin. "I can't give you this exclusive if it's going to be deep-sixed at the studio."

"Let me deal with that, Governor," he quipped. "My cameraman, Mickey, has my back."

Perez escorted Luke and Mickey through the large tiled lobby of Ranger Headquarters on Guadeloupe Street in Austin. Mickey raised his camera to capture Luke strolling past a photo of Frank A. Hamer, the legendary Ranger who ended Bonnie and Clyde's murderous rampage on May 23, 1934.

An eerie feeling gripped Mickey as the trio proceeded through the lobby and down a long hallway, passing through several security doors with electronic locks. Mickey flinched with each click. Perez directed them to a vacant interview room where they went to work setting up their camera and lights. Both felt uneasy when Perez left the room and the door slammed shut.

Mickey stopped fidgeting with his camera. "How important is this, Luke?"

Luke stopped writing notes. "Pearson thinks it's as important as the Madison story."

"If Walker makes Elliott look bad, how are we going to get the story past Carter?" Mickey asked.

Luke patted Mickey on the shoulder. "I assured Governor Pearson you're a wizard at slipping stories through."

Mickey peered up at his towering colleague. "Thanks for putting me on the spot, pal. You know Carter's onto all my tricks." He continued stringing a yellow extension cord across the room and plugged it into a wall socket. The room lit up like a shooting star.

Luke lit up as well with a sudden stroke of brilliance. "Maybe Nicole can help us with some sleight of hand."

Mickey nodded as he checked his camera. "We definitely need to get this stuff on the air. Those quotes from Kelley are pure gold."

Just then the door clicked and Perez led a grumbling Carlos Sanchez into the room. To Mickey he looked like one of the banditos from an old B western.

Before introductions could be made, Sanchez launched into his street persona. "Do either of you gringos have a smoke?"

There you go, a line right out of the movies, Mickey thought. "Not this gringo," he blurted. "I'm allergic to smoke and cancer."

"Sorry, Mr. Sanchez, neither of us smokes," Luke said while shooting Mickey an angry glance.

Sanchez peered from under his bushy eyebrows. "I can remember a lot better with a smoke to calm my nerves. I've had a tough day."

Perez hit a buzzer on the wall, causing Mickey to jump. Sanchez didn't flinch. When a guard poked his head in the door, Perez asked, "Do you have a smoke, Martin?"

The guard pulled a pack of cigarettes from his pocket and handed it to Perez. In one motion, Perez grabbed the pack and flipped it to Sanchez who reached out and deflected it to the table.

"I owe you a pack, Martin," Perez said.

"Forget it, Commander. I've been trying to quit. That's why the pack isn't opened. My compliments, Carlos."

Perez launched into introductions as Carlos bummed a light from Martin. "This is Luke Harper from TNN and his cameraman Mickey Short."

"I know who he is, compadre. I seen him on TV. What do these gringos want from me? I already tol' you all I know."

"We want to make you a TV personality, Carlos," Luke said. "Since you heard Walker's story firsthand, you have more credibility than anybody else."

Carlos perked up and shouted, "Bravo, bravo. Carlos Alameda Sanchez has more credibility than Dale Perez, legendary Commander of the Texas Rangers. Olé."

Perez leaned against the wall smiling, content to let Carlos bask in the spotlight.

"Parts of this interview will make the evening news, Mr. Sanchez," Luke said. "Avoid anything you don't want your mother or children to hear."

Sanchez picked a speck of tobacco from his tongue and flicked it to the floor. "For your information, Gringo, my mother never left Mexico, and my kids were taken when ICE raided my home last week."

Luke looked into Sanchez's sad, dark eyes. "I'm sorry about that."

"Are you, Gringo?" he asked. "What have you ever done to fight your Gestapo federal police?"

Luke crafted a lie to appease Sanchez. "This is my first attempt, so I would appreciate it if you'd help me make it good."

Sanchez puffed on his gratis cigarette, then nodded. "Si, Amigo. Can do."

Perez opened the session by explaining how Walker ended up in a cell with Sanchez and Rodriguez. Sanchez picked up by repeating the plan Duane Walker had outlined in detail during their twelve hours together. By the time Luke finished his follow up questions, Sanchez was down to a couple of smokes.

Luke had one more question to wrap up the interview. "Do you believe Walker, Carlos?"

"I tol' him I would strangle him if he fed me a pack of lies."

Luke's response was automatic. "I understand you tried to kill him anyway."

Sanchez sneered. "I just scared him a little. I don't like the guy. Besides, he was due some payback for my kids."

Sanchez ended with a stark warning. "Listen, Gringo. I come from Mexico where the people have no protection from a corrupt and oppressive government. If things don't change here, the same people who kicked my door down and dropped shells on those kids in Madison will take more liberties away."

Luke leaned over the table, eyeball-to-eyeball with the prisoner. "That's a dark prediction, Mr. Sanchez."

"I'm no expert on anything, Mr. Reporter. But I know human nature from years on the street. I can tell you this president is high on power. He doesn't care any more about the common people than a cartel boss cares about the kids they hook on poisonous drugs."

Mickey was relieved when Luke signaled an end to the interview. "Thank you, Mr. Sanchez. You've shown a lot of courage stepping forward on this."

"What are they going to do? Raid my home, take my kids, or throw me in jail?" Smoke curled from Carlos's flared nostrils and trailed through his bushy eyebrows.

"Come on, Carlos. Let's see if we can find you some more smokes," Perez said, leading him out of the room.

"That's a wrap, Mickey," Luke said. "Did you get everything?"

Mickey looked up from the cord he was coiling up. "I did, but how do we validate his story?"

"Perez says our interview with this Walker guy will confirm—" Before Luke could finish, the lock clicked. "That was fast!" he said as Perez led Walker in by his shackles.

"Sit down," Perez growled, nudging Walker toward a chair in front of the camera.

"I don't want any part of this charade!" Walker shouted, spraying saliva.

"You don't have any choice," Perez said. "You can talk to these guys or return to Carlos and Ricardo. Both watched Mickey wipe his equipment with a towel.

"I'm a federal agent, and I demand to talk to the United States Attorney in this District," Walker blurted, dribbling saliva down his chin.

"You can make all the demands you want, Mr. Walker," Perez said. "But as long as you're in my custody, I decide who you see and who you don't. Understood?"

"You're the one who doesn't have a choice!" Walker said, while rubbing his throbbing neck. "You're bound to observe my National Security Card or face dire consequences."

Perez bristled. "We don't respond well to threats here in Texas, Mr. Walker. You might recall a fellow named Generalissimo Antonio Lopez De Santa Anna who threatened us back in 1836. Things didn't end well for him, and unless you start cooperating, this won't end well for you. On the other hand, we could return you to Carlos and Ricardo, so you can boast some more about how tough you and your agents are."

Clearly rattled, Walker wiped his chin on his sleeve. "OK, Perez, point made." He rubbed his sore neck again. "But I'm sworn to secrecy, so I can't tell you anything."

"You also swore to uphold the Constitution, and we all know how that went. Plus, you spilled your guts to Carlos just hours ago, so there goes your pledge of secrecy. Besides, Carlos has already outlined everything you told him about your plan to raid the Convention. Before we get bogged down any more, this is Luke Harper from TNN and his cameraman Mickey Short. They have a couple of questions for you."

Mickey started recording when Luke signaled he was ready. "Mr. Walker, Carlos described in great detail how President Elliott ordered DHS to raid the Convention and intern the delegates in Camp Bravo-6 near Waco. Can you confirm such a plan?"

Walker looked at Luke as if he were a mangy dog. "I'm only willing to confirm that I'm a federal official carrying out my sworn duties. I don't have anything else to say to a treasonous news reporter."

Bam! Perez slapped the button on the wall, bringing a guard into the interrogation room. "Take him back to his original cell."

Terror danced in Walker's eyes. "Wait a minute! I need to talk to an attorney," he gasped.

"We can probably have one here in a couple of hours, while you relax with Carlos and Ricardo," Perez said.

Walker feared that the next meeting with Carlos would be his last. Pillory was an easy choice over strangulation. Settling back in his chair, he began blabbing. "There are traitors attempting to roll back the rightful authority of the federal government under the guise of a Constitutional Convention. In the eyes of President Elliott and DHS, the delegates are domestic terrorists who need to be held accountable for treason."

Mickey adjusted the audio to make sure he was capturing every caustic word.

Luke rose from his chair. "You do realize that these so-called terrorists are supported by Article V of the Constitution and the vast majority of Americans?"

Intimidated by Luke's size, Walker stammered. "I-I-I w-would remind you that President Elliott was elected by a vast majority of Americans."

Luke sat back down to put him at ease. "True," he said. "But that was before he ignored the law and murdered thirty innocent civilians in Madison. Why should conventioneers be held accountable for carrying out the will of the public, while the President isn't held accountable for corruption and murder?"

"That's not for me to say, nor for you," Walker insisted.

"What recourse then, does the citizenry have against a sitting president who is corrupt and dangerous?"

"That's your take on the President," Walker said.

"Don't you think the murder of innocent civilians is a legitimate reason to resist the President? And now he's ordered a direct attack on a lawful Convention where more lives will be lost."

"I can understand why political opponents would object to those actions, Mr. Harper, and it's unfortunate that so many people have suffered during this difficult time. But the President is obliged to protect the country against terrorists, foreign and domestic."

"Tell that to the mothers of the innocent children murdered in Madison," Luke said. "But what we really need is for you to confirm what you confessed to Carlos. Did President Elliott order you to raid this Convention and incarcerate its delegates?"

Perez saw the need to loosen up his prisoner. *Wham!* His hand slapped the wall near the guard call button.

Walker's eyes shot to Perez's hand. "The President has said repeatedly that he will do what's necessary to preserve the integrity of the presidency. To him the Constitutional Convention delegates are nothing more than traitors."

Luke surrendered to Walker's recalcitrance. "That's good enough for me, Mickey."

"I'm afraid that's as close to a confession as you're going to get from this bureaucrat," Perez said. He returned Walker to his new holding cell as Luke and Mickey packed their gear.

On the drive back to the Hampton Inn on San Jacinto near the Convention Center, Luke dialed Nicole Marcel at TNN.

Nicole suppressed her excitement over hearing from Luke. "Hi there," she said. "How goes it in the fast lane?"

"We're holding it between the yellow lines, but I need help," Luke said. "Do you have any contacts in Madison?"

"I covered the trial of the DHS agent," she said.

"Have you interviewed him yet?" Luke asked.

"Yep. His name is Hank Applegate. He talked to me off the record right before his trial. He was extremely guarded and I didn't get much."

"We have our own DHS prisoner down here, who says the President intends to raid the Convention and arrest its delegates for treason. We're trying to validate his story, which I admit was obtained under duress."

Nicole hesitated briefly. "Has the President gone totally insane?"

"There's a real fine line between desperation and insanity," Luke said.

"I see in my notes that Applegate said the Convention wouldn't be a problem much longer. He alluded to a lot of men with heavy equipment and big guns. I'm no military expert, Luke, but the way he talked reminded me of the World War II movies my dad used to watch."

"Did he give you any specifics?" Luke asked. "I need some confirmation."

She made a rustling noise. "Let me boot my notebook," she said. "Here it is. He made a reference to someone named Walker dealing with five companies of weekend warriors in Austin, and the conventioneers being brought to justice in Waco. Whatever all of that means."

Luke gave Mickey a confident smile. "That's it, Nicole," he said. "There's no reason for him to mention Waco or to know the number of guardsmen in Austin unless he knew about Walker's plan."

"I have one more thing, Luke," she said. "He boasted that all of this would be over soon and he would be on his way back to Washington along with his colleagues in Dallas."

"He had to be referring to the special ops agents who are amassing in Dallas for the raid," Luke said with excitement. "One more favor, Nicole. Could you get my video to Blake Snyder, the new producer of *TNN Breaking News* without going through Carter?"

There was a brief pause. "I probably could, but it would cost me my job," she said.

"Just tell Snyder you can give him a story that will make his career, as long as he doesn't disclose the source," Luke said. "I've had drinks with him and he seems real hungry for recognition."

Reconnecting with Luke brought out her rebellious spirit. "Okay, I'll give it a shot," she said.

"Thanks, Nicole, you're the best," Luke said. "Mickey will get the story to you within the hour. Bye, gorgeous."

Though they both had their hands full, she yearned to chat longer. *Maybe later*, she thought. "Bye, Luke."

By late afternoon, Luke's shocking report was broadcast nationwide. Hours after the initial broadcast, the BBC and Al Jazeera repeated the story around the clock, making it the dominant headline in international news. While Luke received accolades for his report, it sparked condemnation from the American people and the international community. No amount of spin could repel the backlash. The Elliott administration was stunned by Walker's betrayal, but the worst was yet to come.

Back at Camp Bravo-6, Lonnie Bell had just returned to his office from back-to-back meetings. His cellphone, mistakenly left on his desk, showed several urgent messages. Before he could check them a guard stuck his head in the open office door. "Excuse me, sir. A Ranger named Perez is here to see you. He says it's urgent and he has a search warrant."

Bell feared the visit was no more coincidental than Walker's disappearance and his backed-up messages. Even his worst suspicions didn't prepare him for what came next. "Please bring him in."

Perez entered, his chiseled features expressionless. "My name is Dale Perez. I'm the Commander of the Texas Rangers in Austin."

"Your reputation precedes you, Commander. Why are you here?"

"I think you might know," Perez said. "Regardless, I have a warrant for your arrest on charges of conspiracy to commit criminal trespass, felony breaking and entering, and kidnapping."

Bell's stomach flip-flopped. His mind jumped to his wife. *How would she deal with this? If I go to prison, how will she take care of herself? Why did I go along with this crazy plan?*

Desperate to retain his composure, he cleared his throat, then lashed out in futility. "Commander Perez, as you know, I'm a federal agent, and everything I do is protected under federal sovereignty."

Perez stared Bell down, stone-faced and deliberate. "I disagree, Mr. Bell. When someone commits a felony in Texas, I get called to bring them in. You can save your pleas of federal immunity for the magistrate in Austin."

Bell surrendered to his fate. "Do I get a chance to discuss this with my people or call my wife?"

Perez felt a brief twinge of empathy. "Your key people are already being rounded up. We'll assign all of you to the same cellblock so you can talk all you want. You can make a call after you're processed in. By the way, before you face the magistrate, you might want to see this." Perez picked up the remote control and tuned Bell's widescreen TV to TNN.

Luke Harper's interviews with Sanchez and Walker flashed across the screen. The TNN report constituted an irrefutable confession.

Bell fell back into his chair, stunned by his colleague's betrayal. He recalled his orientation when Justin Brook, head of the Civil Unrest and Domestic Terrorism Unit for Homeland Security, boasted that command and control wouldn't be a problem on this mission. His worst nightmare had come to pass. "What are the American people going to think?" he murmured.

"They are going to think correctly that this federal government has gone off the rails. And they are forever going to identify you and Duane Walker with one of the most egregious government boondoggles in history."

In his last official act, Bell showed a vestige of leadership. "What will happen to my people?" He glanced away from Perez, determined not to show his surging anxiety.

"Like you, key people will appear before a magistrate tomorrow and be formally charged with conspiracy under Texas law. Rank and file employees who have nothing to do with planning or policy will be sent home. Once everyone is cleared, our contractor will shut down this facility. But right now we need to clear out so our crime scene investigators can do their work."

With a nod from Perez, another Ranger placed Bell in handcuffs. "This way, sir," the Ranger said, leading Bell toward a van just outside the gate.

Several investigators carrying containers marked "Criminal Evidence" scurried past them as they exited the lobby.

Lord, I hope they don't find my safe, Bell worried. *Who would have expected that our raid would be preempted by one of us?*

John Moran, Bell's deputy, was escorted to another van. *What's Moran saying to that agent who's taking notes?* Bell wondered.

While the Rangers were sweeping up at Camp Bravo-6, Superintendent Meek's officers, accompanied by the Dallas Police Department and officers from several surrounding counties, were apprehending DHS agents at the Dallas Airport. With the tactical precision of SEAL Team Six, other officers confiscated the federal vehicles and all their weapons.

The Dallas County detention center was soon full, so overflow prisoners were taken to Fort Worth, Arlington, Irvine, and Waco for processing. Every single agent claimed immunity from local jurisdiction. All received the same response. "Tell the magistrate in the morning."

One thousand national security cards were collected and stored in the evidence locker.

When one of the agents got overbearing with Officer Grissom, she told him he was lucky Judge Roy Bean, the infamous hanging judge, was no longer on the bench. "Bean would have strung you up just for your lousy attitude," she said.

"I'm from Delaware. I've never heard of Roy Bean," the agent said.

"That figures," she replied.

CHAPTER 13

—

Inspired by implausible arrogance and misplaced faith in deals, President Elliott rattled the wrong cage after being briefed on the counter-raid in Texas. He would find Texas Governor Clay Granger to be a formidable adversary.

"Clay, this is Jerome Elliott."

"Hello, Mr. President," Granger replied solemnly.

"I understand you have some federal agents under arrest down there," Elliott said.

"That's right. Texas law enforcement officers have them in custody," Granger said.

"Clay, I don't know what provoked your officers, but I can assure you those agents are there to secure the border."

"Please, Mr. President, spare yourself the indignity of further lies about your failed scheme. Duane Walker's confession confirmed DHS's plot to raid the Convention and detain the delegates. That has nothing to do with border security."

Elliott sucked up his pride and reached out to Granger. "What can we do to defuse this situation and cancel your Convention? I'm open to any ideas."

"I can't think of a thing, short of you resigning," Granger said.

Elliott strained to control himself. "Can't we strike a deal to get both of us out of this mess?"

"Honestly, Mr. President, I wouldn't consider a populist movement to correct federal overreach a mess." Seizing the upper hand, Granger pressed forward. "You, sir, were elected on a campaign of 'Progressive Change.' Instead of correcting existing problems, you implemented a radical agenda that undermined the very foundation of this country. You blew a historic opportunity. I can assure you, we won't make the same mistake."

Elliott cursed under his breath.

"I can assure *you* of another thing," Granger said. "The public will not allow you to continue to chip away at liberty and prosperity earned through tremendous sacrifice. If you don't like what this country stands for and don't believe in the Constitution, you shouldn't have sworn before God and three hundred million Americans to preserve and protect it."

"I'm not accustomed to being preached to, Governor."

Granger ignored the diversionary tactic. "At some point down the road, you will have to face your Maker for breaking your pledge to Him, but now you are going to have to face the American people. You seem to have forgotten, or have chosen to ignore, that we're a country of laws. And not even the President of the United States is above them. The people are the ultimate authority here, not the federal government."

"How can you call the Convention lawful when you're espousing insurrection? Your Convention is made up of people largely from the South who hate me because I'm a minority."

"Mr. President, once again you are resorting to the race card to cover your failures. You think anyone who opposes you hates you because that's what you were taught in Havana. They indoctrinated you to oppose those who do not accept your ideology. Most faiths and philosophies are fundamentally different. We Christians, for example, are taught to hate the sin, but love the sinner."

"I'm not feeling much love from the Convention," Elliott said.

Granger felt his patience waning. "As far as treason is concerned, we're simply exercising our right to object to an unconstitutional overreach by the federal government in the same way George Washington objected to the oppressive rule of King George. I suppose if Washington were part of our Convention you would consider him a traitor, too?"

"One could certainly make that argument," the President said, stumbling into quicksand.

Granger seized the moment. "I'm really sorry to hear you say that, Mr. President. I'm confident the majority of Americans would not feel good about you insinuating that the father of our country was a traitor."

"What do the majority of Americans have to do with this conversation, Governor?"

"This conversation is all about the American people, Mr. President. And they will have a chance to weigh in on your radical opinion of the Father of our Country, because Luke Harper from TNN is recording everything, including this conversation."

"Hold on a minute, Clay. You entrapped me into saying something I didn't mean." The President sunk further.

"Excuse me for my bluntness, Mr. President, but as we have already witnessed, you're perfectly capable of stepping in it without any entrapment from anyone. It's unfortunate that your political advisers were able to convince you that opposition to your policies can be cleared up with the proper messaging. You've heard the old saying 'You can put lipstick on a pig, but it's still a pig.'"

Elliott winced at Granger's indelicate reference.

"The truth is, you are quickly losing the support of your staunchest political allies, including those you've enlisted through favoritism and pandering. Apparently, Mr. President, you don't buy into the immortal words of President John F. Kennedy who said, 'Ask not what your county can do for you. Ask what you can do for your country.'"

"I think we're through here, Governor," Elliott said.

"For now, maybe, but as soon as this Convention is over, I'm convinced we'll be talking again," Granger said. "In the meantime, on behalf of thirty-four governors and the majority of the states, I ask that you exercise restraint in dealing with this Convention."

Elliott pivoted from coercion to charm. "And I have a request for you, Clay. Would you assure me that the recording of this conversation will not be exposed?"

"I'm sorry, Mr. President. If we chose to walk away from full transparency, we would lose our moral authority to represent the people, as you have. Besides, the decision on what to do with this conversation is Luke Harper's alone."

"You know it's politically imprudent to divulge private conversations among chiefs of state," Elliott argued.

"I can see why you feel that way," Granger said. "But when the character and the policies of the President are in question, the people deserve full disclosure."

"You are throwing me under the bus, Governor?"

"Your staff and political handlers have been doing that for six years. And you, in turn, have been throwing the American people under the bus. Now, thanks to the Convention, the people will be driving the bus. Goodbye, Mr. President."

Elliott turned off his speakerphone and slammed his open hand on his desk. "Do you believe that, Mitch? That SOB tricked me into implying that George Washington was a traitor."

"I've warned you over and over not to ad lib, Mr. President," Brady said.

"I was just having a casual conversation!" Elliott said.

"Nothing the President says during a crisis is casual, sir," Brady said.

"What do we do now? How do we keep this dike from springing any more leaks?" Elliott asked.

"I'm afraid the dike is likely to fail," Brady said. "Friends and critics agree the raids are clear examples of the Administration's lawlessness and incompetence. By the way, the Attorney General wants to meet with you today or tomorrow to discuss all of this."

The President folded his arms. "Is he wavering?"

Brady answered reluctantly, "I think so."

"How is the rest of the Cabinet holding up?" Elliott asked.

Brady chose his words carefully. "Based on the chatter I'm hearing, they desperately need reassurance. Some have considered jumping ship."

"Let's schedule a cabinet meeting for tomorrow afternoon."

"How are you going to reassure them?" Brady asked.

"I'm counting on you to come up with something, Mitch. Meantime, ask the AG if he can have dinner with me tonight."

"Yes, Mr. President."

Brady retreated to his office, ill and dejected. Slumping onto his sofa, he popped two more antacids. To his regret, they offered no relief.

CHAPTER 14

—

Attorney General Dennis Oliver approached the security checkpoint at the east entrance to the White House with dread. It was up to him to convince President Elliott that the groundswell of opposition represented a clear and imminent threat to his administration.

In his own expression of concern, Danny Whittaker, the young Secret Service officer manning the east entrance, asked the AG when the bleeding would stop. "I saw the report on TNN this afternoon. I can't believe the President called George Washington a traitor."

Oliver hesitated as he slipped his security badge into his pocket. "Remember what Will Rogers once said, Son. 'Believe nothing you hear, and only half of what you see'. Who's most likely to tell the truth, the President of the United States or a southern governor at a traitor's conference?"

"Excuse me, sir, but my father served under Granger in Viet Nam. Dad believes he's a patriotic American, a true war hero."

"Maybe so back then," Oliver said. "Now he's a political opponent and that makes him our enemy."

Oliver's venomous words hung in the air like a bad odor. How could the AG characterize a patriotic American as an enemy just because he holds a different political viewpoint? For the first time, Whittaker faced a conflict between what he knew to be true and right, and his pledge of loyalty. He simply could not shake the AG's hateful, divisive words.

During his next break Danny called his friend, Bruce Connor, the officer in charge of the President's personal security detail. "Hey, Bruce, this is Danny. Can I buy you a cup?"

"I'm due," Bruce said. "Meet me at The Perk in five."

Danny carried two decafs to Bruce, already seated on a stool near the front window.

"Here you go, Bruce, black with two sugars, just the way you like it."

Bruce looked tired and ragged out. "I need a shot of whiskey, but this will do for now. The press is all over us and the President's been real cranky. What's up?"

With no one sitting nearby, Danny felt free to talk. "I'm beginning to wonder which will happen first, the Convention or impeachment. And what will happen to us? Do we stand by the President, or stand down?"

"I don't know, Danny Boy," Bruce said. "I do know we took a pledge to protect him and I don't remember anything about conditions or qualifiers."

Outside the window, pedestrians streamed by, seemingly oblivious to the crisis two blocks down Pennsylvania Avenue. Danny wondered how they would react if they knew what he knew. "I just talked to the AG when he signed in to see the President. He referred to Governor Granger and the other Convention delegates as traitors. That's just not true, man."

"How can you be so sure?" Bruce asked.

Danny stood his ground. "My dad was the crew chief on Granger's C-123 in Viet Nam. He told me how on one mission, their plane was shot full of holes. Even with a round in his leg, Granger wrestled the crippled plane back to base. President Nixon presented him with the Congressional Medal of Honor for saving all of those lives."

Bruce nodded respectfully. "Sounds like he deserved it, but what's that got to do with us?"

"How can President Elliott label a Medal of Honor recipient a traitor?" Danny asked. "I don't mind telling you, pal, I'm having a hard time wrapping my brain around this."

Bruce wiped his mouth with a napkin, then checked his watch. "I know, Danny Boy. Me too. Truth is, others on our detail have raised the same concerns."

Danny surveyed the pedestrians passing by the window. He was envious of their detachment. "I was wondering. As head of the detail, could you go to someone for guidance?"

"Like who?" Bruce asked. "Our Director is a close friend of POTUS, and Chief of Staff Brady is fiercely loyal." Another sip of coffee triggered a different tack. "Why don't you ask your dad to call Granger and see if he can help us?"

"Are you kidding?" Danny scoffed. "If the President considers Granger an enemy, how would he view us for seeking advice from him?"

"Good point, but how would he know?" Bruce asked.

"He wouldn't as long as we hold our cards close to our vest,"

Danny answered.

"So, you'll call your dad after work?" Bruce asked.

"Okay, but don't breathe a word to anyone," Danny said.

Bruce flashed an okay sign. "Not to worry." He pitched his cup in the trash on their way out the door.

The late-night drive to his apartment gave Danny Whittaker time to plan his strategy. How would he convince his dad that things were reaching the breaking point? Would he have to?

Kurt Whittaker, a South Carolina State Patrolman and longtime friend to Governor Granger, had just pulled into his driveway after a long shift. He reached under papers on the passenger seat to recover his ringing phone. "Hello."

"Hi, Pop," Danny said cheerfully. Talking to his dad was always uplifting to him.

"Hello, Son. How are you holding up? It must be stressful right now."

"You've got that right," Danny said. "It's hard to keep a good attitude these days. The President has aged twenty years in the past two months, and he's cranky most days."

"Is there anything your mom or I can do to help?" Whittaker asked. "Mom just baked a batch of your favorite chocolate chip cookies. We could send you some."

"That sounds great," Danny said. "But I have a different request. Have you kept up with Governor Granger in Texas?"

"It so happens I'm flying there tonight to help with Convention security," he said. "It just came up, so I haven't had time to tell you."

"Does it concern you that the administration considers the convention-eers traitors?" Danny asked.

"Let me tell you something, Son. I'd trust Granger with my life. He's the most honorable man I've ever met. As for the President, most of the people I know wouldn't spit in his ear if his brain was on fire."

"Tell me, Pops. How do you really feel about the President?"

They shared a hearty laugh before Danny's dad turned serious. "I think the man is terribly misguided," he said. "Elliott mesmerized the electorate during two well-orchestrated political campaigns, and now the American people are paying the price for their naiveté. I remember a quote from college that read, 'How fortunate for governments that men do not think.' The American people still have a chance to pull their heads out of the sand and learn from Adolf Hitler's cynical observation."

"We're in a real pickle, Dad," Danny said. "We've sworn to protect the President and we're willing to take a bullet to honor that pledge. But we don't know how to remain loyal if he loses his legal authority or begins to act irrationally. Our training and procedures simply don't cover those contingencies."

"Sorry, Danny. I don't know what to tell you. Folks like me and Governor Granger break out in a sweat at night knowing that a narcissistic President holds the codes to the nuclear arsenal."

The younger Whittaker pulled the conversation back on track. "Some of us were hoping you'd talk to Granger for his advice."

"As soon as I get to Austin tonight I'll do just that and get back to you."

"Thanks, Pops, you're the best."

"I know, Son. That's where *you* get it."

"You sound just like Mom."

Both chuckled before signing off.

CHAPTER 15

—

Alone in the White House dining room, Dennis Oliver rehearsed his foreboding message for the President. Though normally youthful and energetic, the Attorney General looked haggard and tired. Dark circles under his eyes and his irritated expression were carryovers from several sleepless nights. He slumped in his chair, knowing that the President wasn't going to like what he was about to hear.

"Thanks for joining me, Dennis," Elliott said, smiling broadly. "How's the family?"

"My wife has some health issues, but we're dealing with them," Oliver murmured, his voice trailing off to a whisper. His spirit was broken, but his need to purge was strong.

Elliott continued to engage in small talk to ease the tension. "How's the coffee tonight? I need a boost."

"You might need something stronger when you hear what I have to say," Oliver said.

The tension spiked.

Elliott sipped his coffee, then picked at his salad as if he were searching for a special hidden morsel. He finally broke the awkward silence. "It's been a brutal week, Dennis, so lay it on me as gently as you can."

"I can't find a way to sugarcoat my regret for giving you questionable legal advice."

Confusion swept over the President. "You're one of the administration's staunchest defenders, Dennis. There is no way to trace our problems to your advice."

"I disagree, Mr. President. Though no single misstep has been fatal, but our collective positions have raised questions about our willingness to uphold the Constitution and the rule of law. Those questions are eroding the political and moral legitimacy of the administration."

Elliott loosened his tie. "For example?"

"We shouldn't have let Massey's people go rogue in Madison," Oliver said. "Those civilian deaths are inexcusable."

A chill swept over the room from the silence that followed.

"Hold on a minute, Dennis," the President said. "I understand what you're saying, but I'm not sure what it means. I'm still the lawfully elected President. No one can question that."

Oliver put his fork down and lifted his coffee cup. "That's true, as long as two things don't happen." He took a sip. "First, there is growing bipartisan support for your impeachment. Polls now show the majority of Americans believe you cannot be trusted and do not really care about the public." Oliver paused, allowing his point to sink in. "I received a call from the Minority Leader who said an impeachment bill is imminent."

"You're our top lawyer," Elliott said. "How do we fight it?"

"I'm afraid there's nothing we can do except counter their arguments during the trial in the Senate."

With another surge of detachment, Elliott boasted, "President Lockhart prevailed, and so will we."

"There are certain realities we need to face," Oliver said. "Several cases pending before the Supreme Court could play into the proceedings in Congress. For example, our reliance on the Patriot Act to trump Posse Comitatus for the raid on the Convention is being contested. The Court will rule that delegates at a legally called Constitutional Convention are not domestic terrorists. I expect to lose that case by a unanimous decision."

President Elliott pursed his lips in defiance. "But you assured me we were covered on that."

"The problem is, sir, the Court might not agree with our interpretation of either the law or the material facts. If the Court rules as expected, we could be charged in the deaths and injuries suffered by both soldiers and civilians in Madison. Aside from the criminal charges, civil penalties could be massive."

Elliott detected fear in Oliver's eyes. "How can we counteract all of this?"

"We need to lay low," Oliver said. "Anything that looks like lobbying or coercion will play into the opposition's hands."

Despite the distasteful conversation, Elliott dug into a generous slice of apple pie 'a la mode. "Are you a gambling man, Dennis?"

"Based on what I'm hearing from Congress, Mr. President, all bets point to you being impeached."

Elliott pushed the rest of his pie away. "It sounds like I should just finish my coffee and go upstairs to pack."

"We drastically underestimated the importance of tradition and principles to the American people. The use of force against the Convention was viewed as a direct attack on the principle of law and order."

"Are you saying you were wrong when you supported me on that issue?"

"I'm saying it's much more difficult to make a call before you know how it'll turn out."

"Tell me something I don't know," Elliott sneered.

Dejected and tired, Oliver turned to the server. "I could use some coffee spiked with Baileys."

"Coming right up, sir."

Oliver watched the server depart, then turned back to the President. "I fear we're at greater risk from the Convention than from impeachment. The proposed articles of impeachment seek redress for the mismanagement of government programs or departments. There are numerous charges, but they are limited in scope. The outcome of the Convention is likely to include criminal prosecution through a special prosecutor."

The President's brow furrowed over squinting eyes. "Why didn't we figure this out before now, Dennis?"

Oliver found courage with the help of his spiked coffee. "That's my fault, Mr. President. For the past six years you have relied on my office to provide legal cover for key initiatives. As long as the public and the media were firmly behind your Presidency, we were okay."

"I agree," Elliott interjected. "I sense a *however*."

"As public support waned, your policies and our legal interpretations came under closer scrutiny. On close legal calls, when I was giving you the green light, I should have been urging caution." With his liquid courage suddenly failing, he resorted to deflecting blame. "Leaders of your policy team let you down as well when they failed to anticipate the unintended consequences of our more aggressive actions."

Oliver glanced at the President who sat motionless, absorbed in his reality check. Oliver sipped his fortified coffee before resuming. "I understand why you are wondering how we can defend ourselves. I regret there are few options at this point, and they're all lousy. Oliver then lobbed a bombshell. "Since I cannot help you going forward, I am no longer useful to the Administration. Mr. President, it has been an honor to serve you, but I am obliged to resign as Attorney General."

Elliott turned to the server. "Maybe I need a spiked coffee, too. But I'll take mine with cognac."

"Right away, sir," the server said.

Elliott turned back to face Oliver. "Now hold on, Dennis. I need loyal advisers now more than ever. How would it look if my Attorney General left during a major legal crisis?"

Unwilling to state the obvious, Oliver only sighed.

Elliott switched topics. "What can you tell me about the Convention at this point?"

"Almost nothing, I'm afraid," Oliver admitted. "There's a cop named Perez in charge of security, and he has the place locked down tighter than Area 51. According to the FBI, we simply aren't going to be able to get in. They've denied all of our requests for admission. As a matter of fact, they booted two private investigators who were trying to get information for us."

Oliver savored more coffee. "Governor Kelley and the other members of their so-called Drafting Committee are formidable adversaries. As Indiana's Governor, he successfully defended several precedent-setting constitutional issues before the Supreme Court. The other members of the committee are equally talented, so unfortunately we are not up against a bunch of hacks."

"Do you mean like us, Dennis?" Elliott asked with a sneer.

Oliver straightened in his chair. "No, sir. I wasn't implying that at all."

"Well, I'm beginning to wonder," Elliott moaned. "When I got dressed down by Governor Granger yesterday, he made it clear I'm not exactly the poster boy for good government."

"Do you remember that TNN reporter named Luke Harper?" Oliver asked.

Elliott glared. "He's the journalist who interviewed Walker and quoted my statement about George Washington out of context."

"Right. He's TNN's lead for the Convention. As soon as anything important develops, he has a story on it. I'm afraid he's our best source for information."

"So, here I sit, the most powerful person on the planet, and I'm getting information on the Convention the same way the janitor at Starbucks does?"

"That's about it, Mr. President."

"How did we come to this, Dennis?"

Oliver temporarily defied his elitism. "Well, sir, the people in Austin might say we've risen to the lofty stature of the common man. If we had viewed ourselves that way sooner, we might not be in this predicament." Turning to the server, he made his last pronouncement of the evening. "Another cup, please. And make it a double this time."

Elliott raised his cup to his deflated friend. "We've been friends a long time, Dennis. Please stick with me as long as you can."

Oliver raised his cup in a dubious gesture.

CHAPTER 16

—

The Convention hall was charged with excitement when Kurt Whittaker walked in for the first time. He agreed to serve as a security consultant to his old friend from Viet Nam. A tightly knit cluster of delegates near the stage meant he had likely found Granger. "Is Governor Clay Granger around here?" he yelled.

"Hello, Kurt," Granger said, craning his neck around his colleagues. "Good to see you when you're not knee-high in a rice paddy."

The others parted to allow this important new guest to approach. They had seldom seen Granger address a friend with so much joy.

"Thanks," Kurt replied. "Good to see you, too. You're quite the celebrity now, the star of the Convention."

Granger shook his head. "Not hardly. That gentleman getting ready to go on stage is the real star. He's Timothy Kelley, Governor of Indiana, and the real brains behind this operation. He and his committee of like-minded governors have drawn up a platform that will get our government back to solving problems instead of creating them."

Dale Perez approached the pair. "Is this our new security consultant from South Carolina?" He asked, grasping Kurt's outstretched hand. "Welcome to the party."

"Glad to be here, Commander. Congrats on the way you handled the DHS incident."

Perez smiled. "Thanks, Kurt. When you're ready, I'll show you around. We can use your expertise in facility security."

"A minute with the Governor and I'll be right with you," Kurt said.

"Take your time," Perez said. "I'll be in my office near the main entrance."

Whittaker sensed that he and the Commander would make a good team. "Governor, I apologize for jumping right into business, but could I have your advice on something critically important? It involves family."

"Fire away, Sarge—I mean, Kurt." *Old habits formed under fire are the hardest to break,* he thought.

"As you know, Danny serves on the President's personal Secret Service detail," Kurt said. "Last night he called to ask what he and his team members should do if it becomes clear that the President's going down. When I told him I wasn't sure, he asked if I could get your advice."

Granger's eyes twinkled while his face relaxed. "I'm flattered Danny Boy values my opinion. I'm sure Elliott would curse him for reaching out to me. That aside, I'd be happy to offer my thoughts."

Granger loosened his tie and moved closer to his old friend. "In a nutshell, I'd advise him to do his job as if everything were normal. We're dealing partly with the man himself; his ideology, his political orientation, and his proficiency as the CEO of the federal government. But we're also dealing with the Office of the President. We can criticize the man, but we should always revere the office."

"That makes a lot of sense," Kurt said.

Granger chuckled at the weakness of the analogy he was about to make, but proceeded anyway. "It's sort of like we used to say in Nam: 'It's not much of a war, but it's the only one we've got.' This Presidency is the same. The man might be flawed, but he's still our President. None of what I'm saying suggests we should stick our heads in the sand and let him defile the institution of the Presidency, because even though he occupies the office, it belongs to the people."

An aide signaled that the meeting was about to start. Granger acknowledged the notice, then wrapped up his advice. "Elliott views himself as an imperial president, but in my opinion he has done more to weaken the office than any of his predecessors. I still would advise your son to carry out his oath to the letter and protect the President to the best of his ability."

Inspired by Granger's advice, Kurt said, "Thank you, Governor. I hope I can be as clear when I pass this on to Danny later tonight."

"You can, Kurt. And thanks for watching my back again."

On his momentous first day, Kurt Whittaker witnessed Tim Kelley in action. Kelley was wearing his lucky tweed jacket, a purchase made during a trip to London for an international law seminar at Oxford University. He wore the jacket during the most important events in his life. It was clearly warranted today.

Whittaker and Granger watched from the sidelines as Kelley approached the microphone. "Ladies and Gentleman, my name is Timothy Kelley. I am the Governor of Indiana and chairman of your Resolution Drafting Committee. Together, we're facing a watershed moment in the life of the Republic. President Elliott was swept to power at a time when change was clearly needed. He was elected twice on campaigns promising not only to correct problems, but also to restore hope. So, where are we today compared to the time we were promised improvements in government? Here are the miserable facts:"

One: The Federal Reserve is pumping $85 billion per week into the Treasury to prop up deficit spending by the federal government. For political purposes, they call it quantitative easing.

Two: Millions of Americans are unemployed or underemployed. We have the lowest labor participation rate since the Great Depression.

Three: Companies are fleeing this country to be free of excessive regulations and taxation.

Four: Forty million Americans are now on Food Stamps. According to the nonpartisan Congressional Research Service, we spend $956 billion annually on welfare at a cost of $8,776 a year per taxpayer. This is a 32 percent increase since 2008.

Five: The President spent a trillion dollars on infrastructure improvement that resulted in no sustained increase in employment.

Six: The National Debt is now twenty trillion dollars and expected to grow to twenty-two trillion in the next two years.

Seven: Home foreclosures continue to rise while the home ownership rate decreases.

Eight: The President has capitulated eleven million square miles of legacy lands, the entirety of Yellowstone National Park, to the Chinese government in lieu of debt repayment.

Nine: Our country has lost its AAA credit rating.

Ten: President Elliott has been sanctioned by the United Nations and eleven European countries for spying on world leaders through the National Security Agency.

Eleven: The President picks and chooses which laws he will enforce based on political expediency.

Twelve: The President instructed his Secretary of State to sign a small arms treaty with the United Nations in direct violation of the Second Amendment of the United States Constitution.

Thirteen: The President ordered federal forces to attack and kill innocent citizens in Madison, Georgia in violation of all moral principles and the Posse Comitatus Act.

Fourteen: The federal government has consistently sued states for passing immigration and voter registration laws designed to protect law-abiding citizens.

Fifteen: The President failed to protect the United States borders by employing a policy of 'catch and release' of illegal aliens, including dangerous felons.

Sixteen: The President has placed the country in danger by substantially increasing immigration from dangerous parts of the world without proper vetting.

Seventeen: The President has bypassed the Congress to impose burdensome regulations on the power industry, which are expected to cost billions of dollars and innumerable jobs.

Eighteen: United States foreign policy is in disarray as we abandon our allies and embolden our enemies.

Nineteen: The Veterans Administration is in shambles at a time when record numbers of veterans are dependent on it for medical care.

Twenty: The President has allowed the politicizing of government agencies to reward supporters and punish political opposition.

Twenty-one: The number of scandals under this Administration are too numerous to list.

"Ladies and Gentlemen, this is a country I no longer recognize. We're weaker now than we were a decade ago, and the majority of Americans fear their own government more than Russia or China. At the same time, foreign adversaries continue to challenge our military, viewing our President as weak and ineffective.

"Private businesses are being prosecuted for doing exactly what the federal government does. For example, the federal government fined Express Commercial Bank seventeen billion dollars for lying about the quality of mortgage-backed securities. During the same period, the Administration lied about the real impact of a government shutdown, misrepresented the Yellowstone land deal, and lied about several government scandals. Unlike the bank, no one in the government was held accountable.

"Elections won through deceit and sleight of hand do not represent a referendum. This Convention was established to get our country back on course. With help from Almighty God, we will accomplish that goal. This afternoon your Drafting Committee will submit a series of reforms called Articles of Resolution. It will be up to you to accept or reject those resolutions."

Realizing this was only the backdrop for the grand finale, the delegates showed their approval with a steady round of applause. With the gauntlet laid, Kelley nodded politely and walked backstage where Granger and the other members of the Drafting Committee were smiling with approval.

Granger complimented Kelley then moved to the next step. "Now that Tim has outlined the problems, it's time to sell workable solutions."

CHAPTER 17

—

With the Convention underway, news broadcasts headlined the trial in Madison, Georgia, the DHS/FEMA trials in Texas, the impeachment hearings in Congress, and now the Convention. Battered by a perfect storm, Elliott's cabinet hemorrhaged with the resignation of Attorney General Oliver, the Chairman of Economic Advisors who resigned "to pursue other interests," and the Secretary of Health and Human Services who was asked to resign due to mismanagement.

News outlets described the personnel changes in devastating language. One broadcaster infuriated the President with his opening headline: "Appointees are scurrying for cover to avoid being identified with a lawless and failed administration."

Kurt Whittaker ended his first day in Austin by jotting down some notes, underlining Granger's key points. He grabbed a cold drink and dialed his son, Danny. "How was your day, Danny?"

"We're hanging in there, Dad. Are you in Austin?"

"I am, and I've talked to Granger who made some sound suggestions that I'd like to share with you." Whittaker scanned his notes and relayed Governor Granger's advice. "The takeaway is that presidents vary in skill and popularity, but the office remains indispensable. The institution must be protected if the Republic is to survive. In that light, you owe it to the American people to protect both to the best of your ability."

"Thanks, Dad. I'll pass the advice on to my team members," Danny said.

"It's important that you do. But let your old dad throw out a caveat."

"What's that?" Danny asked.

Expecting the Convention or impeachment proceedings to be a game changer, Whittaker added, "If Elliott is found to be unfit for office by another legitimate authority, you and your buddies will have to call an audible."

"Come on, Dad," Danny said. "You make it sound like we're the New England Patriots and I'm Tom Brady."

"I'm just saying that if things continue to unravel, you might have to make a spontaneous decision. We're both trained to deal with extraordinary circumstances. When the time comes, you'll know what to do."

"I sure hope so," Danny said. "If I don't, I'll be calling."

"Good luck, Danny Boy. Maybe when all of this blows over you can visit me in Austin. We could go to San Antonio and take in the Alamo. There's a lot to see here."

"I'd like that," Danny said.

Whittaker set his phone down, more conscious than ever that the Convention was for Danny's future and the future of Danny's children. He was now part of something much greater than himself: a movement to protect all American families.

While the Convention moved forward, Judge Johnson's trial of Hank Applegate, the DHS Special Operations Commander captured in Madison, took a disastrous turn for the Elliott Administration.

Prosecutor Stone pressed hard for the name of the person or persons who ordered DHS to shell Madison's civilians. "Mr. Applegate, it is essential for members of this community to find out who's ultimately responsible for those deaths. They demand full accountability for that cowardly and heinous act."

Applegate squirmed while perspiration glistened on his forehead. His cheek twitched and his eyes darted from one juror to another.

Stone turned to face the jury as he laid his carefully worded trap. "I'd like you to answer this next question carefully, Mr. Applegate. Did you take it upon yourself to fire those howitzers into Madison, or were you under orders from someone higher up?"

Sweltering under the white-hot focus of the court, Applegate stuttered, then faltered. The prospect of stumbling into this minefield alone terrified him. Reaching for a tissue, he patted his brow without answering.

Johnson's stern warning reverberated like a thunderbolt. "This court expects an answer, Mr. Applegate."

The defendant swallowed before finding a shallow voice. It cracked from the dreadful truth. "When Secretary Massey directed me to lead this mission, I asked him what was expected. He instructed me to do everything necessary to neutralize resistance."

The brutal admission cast a pall over the courtroom. Spectators looked at each other as if Charles Manson had just confessed.

Stone continued tightening the noose. "Did you fully understand his instructions?"

Applegate gulped a drink of water while scanning the jury. He avoided direct eye contact with Stone. "I asked the Secretary point blank if he was ordering me to fire on civilians."

The audience erupted. A reporter prematurely darted toward the door. The raucous chatter was silenced with a swift response.

Wham! Wham! The Judge's gavel brought a hush to the crowd. "This court will remain in order," he bellowed. "Please continue, Mr. Prosecutor."

Stone hovered over the jury to deliver the coup d' grace. "And what was Secretary Massey's reply, Mr. Applegate?"

Sweating profusely with his face glowing beet-red, he stammered, "M-M-M-Massey stressed that the White House was worried the military wouldn't use force against civilians." He paused. "Neither he nor the President fully appreciate the military's Rules of Engagement."

Stone glared at Applegate, his eyes boring through him. "I need to be perfectly clear on this important point. Did Secretary Massey state implicitly that your job was to guarantee the success of the mission unhampered by the military's rules of engagement?"

"Yes, sir, that's exactly what he said."

The raw implication of Applegate's testimony again disrupted the courtroom, sending anxious reporters scurrying for the door. The father of Heath Andrews, the young clerk injured in the chocolate shop, jumped to his feet with his fists clenched. "You need to fry like my boy, you cowardly SOB!" Andrews grabbed Applegate by the shirt before anyone could stop him. With rage in his eyes, he clawed at the defendant like a rabid beast. Hampered by haste and anger, his ham sized fist barely missed the defendant's nose. Another swing was blocked by Bailiff Parker who wrestled Andrews to the floor. Parker's wire-rimmed spectacles hung on one ear with his labored breath fogging the lenses.

Despite his sympathy for the Andrews family, Johnson lowered the boom again. *Wham! Wham!* "Bailiff Parker, remove Mr. Andrews from my courtroom until he settles down. I won't tolerate any more outbursts. And Andrews, make arrangements to replace the bailiff's glasses or I'll hold you in contempt of court."

"Yes, Your Honor," Andrews mumbled as Parker escorted him from the courtroom.

While Applegate guzzled more water, Prosecutor Stone took his usual stance in front of the jury.

"Is the defendant prepared to continue?" Judge Johnson asked.

"If you can guarantee my safety, Your Honor," he replied.

"All I can guarantee is a fair trial," Johnson said. And if you're found guilty, I can also guarantee the appropriate punishment prescribed by law. "Please continue, Mr. Stone."

"Back to your previous statement, Mr. Applegate," Stone said. "Are you telling this court that the President deployed these non-military troops to circumvent the Posse Comitatus law and the military's rules of engagement?"

Applegate squirmed in his seat. "Yes," he mumbled.

"Would you instruct the defendant to speak up, Your Honor?" Stone asked.

"I said yes," Applegate bellowed, his blotchy cheeks twitching.

Stone placed his thumbs in his suspenders, leaning toward Applegate. "Does that mean what we witnessed in Madison was the deployment of a Gestapo-type police force that carried out the whims of this President without regard to legality or any other constraints?"

"Yes, God, yes," the defendant wailed in resignation.

Stone relaxed his locked jaw. "It sounds like you are telling us that the trail of guilt in this case leads directly to 1600 Pennsylvania Avenue in Washington, DC."

Applegate placed his head in his hands. "Guess so," he whispered.

"Mr. Applegate," the judge warned.

"God help me, yes," he wailed.

Stone turned to face the bench before lobbing a bombshell. "Your Honor, horrific acts of this type are typically handled by the International Criminal Court where those who commit crimes against humanity are tried, then hanged. Saddam Hussein is a recent case."

As Stone emphasized his point, Applegate's face turned ashen. His shackles jangled as he tugged frantically to loosen his collar.

Following Stone's remarks, Phil Owens, Applegate's DOJ attorney, invoked federal immunity as a basis for dismissal. "You can't do this to a federal official," he said.

Wham! Wham! Judge Johnson's gavel struck again like thunder. Owens froze while the courtroom went dead silent. "Sir, we have long passed the point of your argument. I urge you to adopt a defense based on material facts, not the immunity of the federal government, a claim that does not impress this court."

A spontaneous applause from the courtroom and the jury brought another swift rebuke from the Judge. "Ladies and Gentlemen, you will maintain proper decorum in my courtroom. We will have a brief recess. Counselors, please join me in my chambers."

The judge departed, followed closely by opposing counsel.

"Take a seat, gentlemen," he said, closing the heavy door with a firm click. "Before this trial began I received a letter from the United Nations in New York City indicating they intend to investigate the civilian deaths in Madison as international human rights violations. The letter from the Secretary General states that they intend to seek testimony from Mr. Applegate and others during their investigation. That could include some of us."

Owens asked to see the letter. Pondering the implications of yet another investigation of the administration, his smugness faded.

Stone broke the awkward silence. "How are you going to handle this, Judge?"

With full conviction, Johnson answered. "My position is this, gentlemen. If the United Nations has a beef with the federal government, they need to talk to the President. This is not a war crimes trial, it's a murder trial. As long as I am the Superior Court Judge, I have jurisdiction over murder trials. The United Nations does not."

The Judge's comment provided a brief ray of hope for the beleaguered Owens. It dissipated with the next declaration from the iron fisted Judge. "This trial will continue, and the guilty parties will be brought to justice in accordance with the laws of the sovereign state of Georgia. If and when the United Nations asks us to cooperate, we'll work out the appropriate arrangement. It's clear from Mr. Applegate's testimony that others outside our jurisdiction are complicit in the Madison murders. If the United Nations can play a role in addressing that broader issue, I support them."

The judge's thinking reflected prophetic precision and clarity. Within an hour the trial resumed, and shortly thereafter the jury returned a verdict. By evening, the airwaves were full of news flashes that DHS official Hank Applegate was found guilty of multiple counts of first-degree murder.

He was quickly sentenced, then remanded to the Georgia Department of Corrections, where at the appropriate time he would be put to death by lethal injection.

Attorney Phil Owens reported back to the Department of Justice that in this extraordinary showdown, justice had prevailed despite strenuous objections from the federal government.

CHAPTER 18

—

The following morning, President Elliott skirted his family to prepare for another round of setbacks. While juggling coffee with a stack of newspapers containing virulent headlines, he summoned his Chief of Staff. "Morning, Mitch. Join me in the bunker."

Brady braced himself and walked into the Oval Office. "Good morning, sir. How are we doing today?"

"Worse than lousy, Mitch. Have you heard about the verdict in Georgia and the letter from the United Nations?"

Brady grasped the top of a high-backed chair to brace himself. "I have, Mr. President, and it's going to be hard to outrun the stink from all of this. Applegate's testimony plays into the argument that we're blind to the law. The UN's human rights investigation will further erode public opinion, while empowering our opponents."

The President's strained expression made him look older than his years. "This streak of bad luck is getting under my skin. Why is everyone turning against us?"

If I have to explain that to you, Mr. President, we probably should be impeached, Brady thought. "As a constitutional lawyer you should understand their concern, even if you don't agree with it."

Elliott sidestepped the real issue. "I don't see it that way, Mitch. We won re-election by a wide margin, which means we get to call the tune."

"We do have wide latitude, sir, but that doesn't mean we're above the law," Brady said, sounding like a reformed man.

Elliott recoiled from the dramatic insinuation. "That's a bit disingenuous coming from someone who's been egging me on all along."

"I know, Mr. President, but the political landscape is always changing, and we need to adapt. I'm afraid we dropped the ball in gauging the public's appetite for certain types of change."

"With so many things going wrong, I need assurance that my team is solidly on board. Is there anything you want to tell me before we get mired down any further?"

Brady's skin crawled. He knew better than most that unquestionable loyalty was sacrosanct to Elliott. "What do you mean, sir?"

"I heard some scuttlebutt that you contacted Granger about immunity from prosecution. I don't believe you would betray me, but I need to hear it directly from you."

Determined to repair the emerging crack in their bond, Brady said, "Actually, sir, I approached him about immunity for all of us, including you."

Mad enough to spit, Elliott lashed out. "Wait a minute, Mitch. You asked a mere governor for dispensation for the President of the United States?"

"You need to be clear on an important reality, sir. Granger could emerge from the Convention with enough clout to bring your entire administration down and hold you personally accountable for every-thing you've done as president. I would say he is anything but a mere governor, as you describe him."

With a look of consternation, Elliott relented. "How can that be?"

Elliott's ignorance of constitutional history astounded Brady. Other presidents were inspired by America's rich past; this one was not.

"Mr. President, I'm sure you learned in law school that the Constitutional Convention in 1787 limited the authority of the federal government while safeguarding the authority of the states. The founders didn't intend for the President to have imperial powers. In fact, they overtly expressed fear that a strong federal government could overstep its bounds and hold the states and the public in bondage the way Great Britain had done."

"Wait a minute, Mitch. You think the public blames me for the growing power of the federal government?"

"That's not what I'm saying, sir. The public knows it's expanded over several administrations, but they believe your aggressive agenda crossed the line by ignoring legitimate restraints on your office."

Elliott revealed his emerging insecurity. "How do you know so much about what the opposition is thinking?"

"I've been discussing Luke Harper's news coverage with some Justice Department attorneys. They're convinced the Convention has strong legal standing to bring this administration down."

Elliott resorted to sarcasm. "It sounds like you have everything figured out."

Brady flirted with insubordination. "Everything except how to avoid impeachment or prosecution. The opposition, and a growing number of supporters, fear that you consider yourself an imperial president without regard for the Constitution or the law. The very idea smacks of nobility and privilege instead of service to the American people."

Brady's unfettered candor brought a swift response. "Those people are fools if they think the country can improve without change."

"That might be true, sir. But even a fool knows that change isn't always good," Brady said, pushing his boundaries further.

Resting his hand on a priceless Remington sculpture, Elliott said, "Don't they see the improvements we've made since our predecessors left office?"

"What they see, sir, is you've been in office for nearly two terms now," Brady said. "The economy is yours, the international standing of America is yours, and the mistakes of the administration are yours. Every time you blame your predecessor for current problems you look weak, unaccountable, and cowardly." The words tumbled out before he thought them through.

Elliott simply winced from the stinging assessment. "Are we really doing that well?"

"The painful truth is, Mr. President, you need to take ownership of your presidency, irrespective of praise or criticism," Brady continued. "The honeymoon you enjoyed during the first term has long expired, and your predecessor is now ancient history."

CHAPTER 19

—

While Washington stewed in its own turmoil, Patrick Graham, former Commander of the 82nd Airborne, relaxed on the screened porch of his comfortable home in the small fishing village of Oriental, North Carolina. Most days since his retirement, he could be found sitting on the porch enjoying sweet tea and one of his prized Montecristo cigars. Within eyeshot of the porch, shrimp boats sporting names like *Captain Blarney* and *Sweet Caroline* slowly traversed the Neuse River with their nets dragging the tannin-colored water for nature's bounty.

"The Sheriff," a tenacious mockingbird named by Graham's wife, interrupted the Norman Rockwell setting. With the ferocity of a velociraptor, he patrolled the lush greenery for interloping bluebirds and cardinals. These aerial displays, plus the harmony of other songbirds, provided non-stop entertainment for the Grahams.

Fortunately for the general, the homestead had been inherited by his wife at the time of his precipitous fall from grace. Though it provided a comfortable setting for the general, he struggled to enjoy the prosaic routine. Harriers, Ospreys, and F-35 Strike Fighters, following the river to outlying bombing ranges and landing fields, were constant reminders of his previous calling. And even though he was no longer responsible, he worried constantly about the soldiers who had been captured in Madison.

Still highly respected by members of the military community, he received a steady stream of invitations to speak during ceremonies at Fort Bragg, Camp Lejeune, Cherry Point, and Seymour Johnson AFB. In each instance he respectfully declined, avoiding all reminders of his painful departure.

Mrs. Graham stepped onto the porch carrying the telephone. "Honey, Tennessee Governor Simpson is calling from the Convention. He seems anxious to chat."

Mesmerized from watching The Sheriff chase other birds, he answered in a soft voice uncharacteristic of his alpha personality, "Graham here."

"Hello, General. I understand you are enjoying a nice breeze on your screened porch," Simpson said.

"It's just another day wasting away in paradise," Graham said. "I'm watching a shrimp boat catch my dinner from the Neuse River."

"Sounds like early retirement isn't so bad," Simpson said.

"You know the old saying, Governor: 'You can take the soldier out of the Army, but you can't take the Army out of the soldier.' I'm well-rested and well-fed for sure, but professional soldiers aren't wired to sit on a porch drinking tea."

"What if I told you we'd like to pull you back into active service?" Simpson asked.

Graham shifted his considerable weight, causing his Adirondack chair to creak. "I'd say you have my undivided attention," he said. "But who is 'we', and how could that happen? I'm convinced the President hasn't forgiven me for failing to shut down your Austin Tea Party." A hearty chuckle forced twin plumes of cigar smoke from the general's nostrils.

"By 'we', I mean the Convention," Simpson said. "The 'how' is more complicated, but there are some determined people working on that. In very short order we expect resolutions to be adopted that will dramatically reform the federal government."

Graham's lack of response spurred Simpson onward. "To someone outside the Convention, what I'm saying might sound unlikely. But as someone who has been involved in the entire process, I can tell you with certainty that it's going to happen. When all of this comes down, would you be interested in helping us rebuild the military?"

Graham straightened in his chair, causing another creak. "What's the job, Governor?"

"Something similar to or higher than your previous one," Simpson said.

"Can I think about it for a moment, and how do I sign up?" Graham answered.

"We'll take that as an affirmative," Simpson said. "I'll report back that we can count on your help. Obviously, this subject is sensitive, so please keep it between us."

"Scout's honor," Graham said.

"We'll be in touch, General. Thanks for keeping the faith," Simpson said.

"I never doubted the country, Governor. It sounds like we've relocated our compass and will be making adjustments to the course."

"Just as sure as the sun rises over shrimp boats on the mighty Neuse River tomorrow morning, General," Simpson replied.

"Excuse me, Governor. Is there any way you and Governor Granger can help my guys who got arrested in Madison?"

"That's a bit dicey," Simpson said.

"I'm sure, but those guys were just carrying out what they thought were legitimate orders," Graham stressed.

"I doubt they were under orders to fire at innocent civilians," Simpson said.

"You're right, Governor," Graham said. "I'm not sure you know what it's like in the fog of combat. When things get chaotic, soldiers, especially inexperienced ones, sometimes make mistakes."

"I can assure you that my two tours as a jarhead in Viet Nam are imbedded in my memory. I know exactly what you're talking about. War, by its very nature, is chaos."

"Oorah!" Graham called the Marine salute out of respect for the Corps.

"Semper Fi!" Simpson responded. "No promises, but I'll talk to Granger for you. Goodbye, General."

"I'm eternally grateful, Governor. Goodbye."

The Sheriff fluttered in panic as Graham jumped to his feet and bounded through the sliding door. "General Patrick Graham reporting for duty, ma'am," he said, standing statuesque with a gallant salute.

"At ease, soldier. What's this all about?" Mrs. Graham asked with amusement.

"It looks like I'm not washed up after all. Not sure, but I think I just got drafted! Don't press my uniforms yet. There seem to be some details to work out, like putting my old nemesis, President Elliott, out to pasture."

The two returned to their porch to enjoy the picture-perfect morning. As they critiqued the chaotic repertoire of the birds, Mrs. Graham noted a resurgent spirit in her previously broken husband.

"Look at that foolish bird," Graham said, pointing to The Sheriff frantically patrolling the yard. "He thinks he's in charge of everything."

"Maybe I should have named him 'The General'," Mrs. Graham said with a proud wink.

CHAPTER 20

—

The Northern Cheyenne Indian Reservation sat cradled between the Custer National Forest and the Little Bighorn National Monument in southern Montana. Though separated from Washington by two thousand miles, Indian Country and the white man's world were about to collide at the hands of their great white father.

Avonaco Ma'tano sat in his truck at the minimart enjoying elk jerky and beer while scanning the majestic Pryor Mountains reaching toward Montana's endless sky. There had to be a way to report his discovery without getting into trouble for trespassing on restricted land. He had hunted the Absaroka Mountains of Yellowstone his entire life until the government ceded it to the Chinese in exchange for forgiving debt. The new owners immediately posted warnings to stay out, warnings that violated thousands of years of tribal hunting rights.

Three years earlier he was dragged into court in the town of Red Lodge for bagging an out-of-season moose in the Absaroka Mountains. Lucky for him, the presiding judge was Skip Alexander, an avid hunter and strong proponent of Native American rights. Avonaco walked away with a warning and a fine, but no confiscation of his rifle or truck. *Maybe I'll get off easy again,* he thought, washing down the last morsel of jerky.

During the twenty-minute drive to Lame Deer, the seat of the Cheyenne Nation, he mustered the courage to face Tribal Police Chief, Platte Driscoll. This would be his first encounter with his ex-wife's father since his painful divorce. He parked in front of the weathered prefab building that served as the police station. *Should I stay or should I go? Maybe the Chief still blames me for the breakup.* He glanced at the building and caught the Chief watching him through his office window. "He knows I'm here; I might as well face the music," he mumbled.

A deputy sitting at a reception desk teased him. "Hey, Lean Bear. I see you're still driving that junky pickup. Is that a new Honda CR250 in the bed?"

Accustomed to harmless ribbing from his ex-father-in-law's men, he didn't take offense. "Right, Brother," he said. "That's my new tracking bike. I could either buy a better truck and walk the trails or keep my old truck and buy the bike. By the way, I like my given name. Lean Bear just doesn't feel right."

The deputy turned from the window to lighten the interchange. "Sure, Avonaco. At least if the truck breaks down again, you can ride the bike home."

Their brief laughter eased his nervousness. "I noticed the Chief is in. I need to see him."

"I'll check," the deputy said. "Chief, your ex-son-in-law is here to see you." He rolled his eyes in response to what must have been a snide response. "Go on in, but walk softly. He's grumpy today."

"When isn't he?" Avonaco asked. His nod signaled that he knew better than most.

Driscoll didn't look up or offer a greeting. "Take a seat, Son," he said with a habitual reference. "Have you talked to Waynoka lately?"

Avonaco bit his lip and glanced at the floor. "She's wrapped up in her studies in Bozeman. She doesn't want to hear from me."

The Chief looked up, noting the pain in Avonaco's dark eyes. "I wouldn't be so sure. When she was home last weekend, she asked about you. Maybe you should give her a call. But I know you didn't come here to cover that ground." The chief knew it would take something important to bring Avonaco in.

"I don't know how to tell you this, Chief, 'cause I'm banned from the mountains for the moose incident."

"I remember," Driscoll said. "It kept us in meat all winter."

"I was riding the trails on the northern slope of the Absarokas early this morning to do some tracking," he said. "I swear I wasn't poaching. Several miles in I heard noise in the valley. It sounded like heavy equipment with diesel engines."

Driscoll looked up with laser-like attention. "Go on, Son."

"I thought it was Chinese logging trucks or earthmovers. When I rode down I saw tanks, armored personnel carriers, artillery, and all kinds of war materials. The place was crawling with soldiers carrying AK-47s, so I cleared out and came straight here."

"*Maxhevéesevohtse ooahé'e,*" the chief mumbled "never" in his native language.

Avonaco stepped up to the chief's desk. "I know it sounds squirrely, but I'm telling you exactly what I saw."

"I'm not doubting you," Driscoll said. "It's just that our highest government leaders promised that the land would only be used for energy exploration and forestry."

Avonaco couldn't hold back his disdain for the federal government. "How many times has Washington lied to our people?"

"The count's rising," Driscoll said. "Thanks for the information. I'll get on it. Don't forget to call Waynoka."

Relieved to have the news off his chest, but unsure about calling his ex-wife, Avonaco hustled from the station.

Driscoll dispatched deputies to post warnings at the barber shop, the general store, the casino, and Chief Dull Knife College, all distribution points for important tribal news. Meanwhile, he phoned Tribal Council members to schedule an emergency meeting, a rare occurrence on the reservation.

Later that evening, Driscoll arrived at the administration building to brief the Tribal Council on Avonaco's discovery. The headquarters resembled a hunting lodge more than an office. Its rough-hewn walls were adorned with colorful Cheyenne artifacts, buffalo and elk trophies, and treaty documents dating back to the early 1800s. A framed copy of the 1868 Laramie Treaty served as a source of pride for the Sioux and Cheyenne since it ended the Northern Plains Indian Wars on Chief Red Cloud's terms.

Seasoned firewood and a potbellied stove occupied one corner of the room. Council members wearing ornaments befitting their status huddled around a table on the opposite end. Above the table hung an exotic elk antler light fixture, a gift from the Billings Hunter's Association in appreciation for licenses sold to them to hunt bison and elk on tribal land. Unlike the Council members, Driscoll wore a cowboy hat and a Springfield semi-automatic on his hip, non-tribal attire that distinguished him as the police chief.

White Owl, one of the tribe's elders, spoke first. "We can't just sit by as if nothing is wrong. If true, this is a violation of Indian Country sovereignty."

Danny Half Moon pounded his fist on the table. "Foreign soldiers so close to the reservation are a threat to our homes and families."

Even though most council members shared Avonaco's distrust of the federal government, they conceded that some emergencies couldn't be handled solely by the Tribe. "Shouldn't we notify the authorities in Billings?" White Owl asked reluctantly.

Another council member avoided Driscoll's steely gaze to raise his skepticism. "What if Avonaco is mistaken? Peyote and beer messes with the mind."

Driscoll sat forward, squinting with intensity. "What could he have mistaken for tanks and artillery?"

The skeptical councilman held his ground, still avoiding Driscoll's stare. "I'd feel better if we verified what's going on down there."

"We could send a scouting party back to photograph the evidence," White Owl said.

"We should send our best scouts," Danny Half Moon said.

"Everyone knows Avonaco is the best and Will Black Wolf Lowry is next," White Owl said.

Lowry, the tribe's wildlife agent who managed the elk and bison herds to earn lucrative hunting fees, was also an accomplished photographer. He once recorded a grizzly chasing an elk nearly three miles down a river valley. That rare video dispelled the popular myth that grizzlies can't run long distances. In that case, the elk was able to jump a steep riverbank, an escape that had more to do with the elk's luck and agility than the grizzly's shortcomings as a distance runner.

After a lively discussion, a unanimous vote by the Council cleared the way for the two scouts to gather evidence that would support Avonaco's claim.

Just before sunrise the duo towed their trail bikes deep into the bowels of the Absaroka Mountains. With great care to avoid detection, they wound their way to within a mile of partially-constructed bunkers. After hiding their bikes in heavy brush, they walked the remaining distance. Markings left by Avonaco on the first sighting led them to a rock ledge behind a stand of tall pine trees. Using stealth learned from their forefathers, they worked their way to within yards of the construction site.

They carefully surveyed the scene below. Eleven medium-sized tanks, five armored personnel carriers, four artillery pieces, and several stacks of wooden crates full of small arms and ammunition occupied partially-constructed concrete hangars. The red star prominently displayed on the armament, and a Chinese flag at the highest point of the compound, left little doubt that a Chinese military base had been built within the confines of the continental United States.

Chinese sentries were posted beyond earshot, but Avonaco still whispered, "How could this happen so close to us? This makes the Little Bighorn look like a Boy Scout gathering."

Placing his fingers on his mouth to signal silence, Lowry pointed to another sentry approaching just below them.

Moving to a location with an unobstructed view, Lowry videoed the entire valley. He caught ongoing construction of bunkers and hangars, as well as the assembly of military communications equipment. Meantime, Avonaco inventoried each category of heavy armament. They moved back into heavy brush each time the sentry approached, then re-emerged when he had passed. Cheyenne warriors had employed this tactic successfully for millennia against tribal enemies.

Their surveillance completed, they carefully picked their way back to the rocky ledge, again employing their consummate stalking skills to remain undetected. Safely outside the range of the sentries, Lowry checked the camera to make sure his video was good. "Man, this is going to create a firestorm when we get back," he said. The two fired up their bikes and retreated to the northern valley, where they loaded the truck to return to Lame Deer.

A nxiety mounted inside the tribal police station where Driscoll and the elders watched Chinese soldiers fortifying their position. "It doesn't take a white man to figure out they aren't there for trees or oil," White Owl said.

"We can't let them complete that base, regardless of what the federal government thinks," Driscoll said.

"How can one person, even if he is President, have the right to give sovereign land to another country, especially an old enemy?" White Owl asked.

"Many of our brave Tsitsistas brothers and neighboring warriors were lost fighting them in Korea. My wife's uncle was killed at Inchon in 1950," Danny Half Moon said. His voice boomed with anger. "And now the President has allowed them to bring their soldiers close to the rest of my family."

After another hour of berating the federal government, the Council cleared Driscoll to contact Congressman J.J. Thompson and fill him in on their discovery. "Maybe Congress can do something to stop this," Driscoll said.

From the outset, J.J. Thompson, Montana's only congressman and a strong proponent of Native American rights, had objected to Elliott's deal with the Chinese. Already in Billings for the weekend, he agreed to meet the Chief at The Griz Café, a popular breakfast house at the Billings Stockyard frequented by local politicians and law enforcement officers.

Thompson spied Driscoll and Avonaco as they entered the restaurant. "Hello, Chief!" he yelled across the room.

All eyes turned toward the two Cheyenne as they approached Thompson. "Hello, Congressman," Driscoll said. "You know my ex-son-in-law, Avonaco."

Thompson stopped spreading butter on his toast. "I feel for you, Son, losing your beautiful wife. Most of us expected the Chief to hang your hide out to dry for breaking his little girl's heart."

Avonaco warriored up. "It wasn't like that at all."

Driscoll chimed in to rescue him. "It's a complicated, boring story. Waynoka is doing fine at MSU. I'll tell her you asked about her."

Sensing their urgency, Thompson changed the subject. "I'm sure you two didn't drive from Lame Deer just for breakfast. No one can top those flatbread and egg tacos in the college cafeteria."

"We wouldn't bother you, but this is important," Avonaco said.

"Important doesn't quite describe the video we'd like to show you," Driscoll said. The laptop he pulled from the leather saddlebag looked out of place in the Chief's large weathered hands. When he had trouble bringing up the video, Avonaco scooted closer to give him a hand.

"If this damned thing had a trigger I could use it," the Chief said.

"I don't think they could customize one like that even for you, Chief," Thompson said with a grin. He adjusted the screen to eliminate glare from the sunlight streaming through the restaurant window. Moments into the video, the Congressman's expression hardened. "Where was this filmed? It looks like Yellowstone, but it can't be."

"You're dead on, sir. It's the Absarokas," Avonaco said.

"I can't believe this!" Thompson said.

"Saw it with my own eyes," Avonaco said. "I was there when Will Lowry recorded this. The park has been turned into a military garrison crawling with Chinese troops."

The Congressman's uncontrollable outburst quieted the entire restaurant. "President Elliott has really crossed the line this time. It's one thing to mismanage the government. It's quite another to jeopardize our security." Thompson paused and lowered his voice. "Did the Chinese see you record this?"

Avonaco sat back and folded his arms, clearly offended. "Remember, we're Cheyenne. Nobody saw us, and we left no tracks."

"I need a copy of this," Thompson said.

Avonaco pulled a flash drive from his pocket. "We made one for you."

"Chief, I suggest you issue an emergency order for all tribal members to stay out of Yellowstone," Thompson said. "Could you warn Chief Spotted Horse, since the Crow Reservation borders the park?"

"We've already put the word out to our people," Driscoll said. "I'll drive to Hardin from here and warn Spotted Horse. What about Red Lodge and Cook City? They're within shouting distance of the Chinese."

"I'll have my people warn them," Thompson said. "I'm afraid hunters tracking in the Absaroka's might encounter Chinese sentries who may be instructed to shoot first and ask questions later."

"Most hunters aren't tracking this time of the year," Avonaco said.

"Nobody but poachers," Driscoll said with a wink to his former son-in-law.

Driscoll and Avonaco headed to Hardin to brief Spotted Horse while Thompson drove to his office in the Federal Building in downtown Billings to call the White House. He stopped in the men's room where he splashed water on his face to get his anger under control. While walking down the hall to his office he dialed the personal number for President Elliott's Chief of Staff.

"Hello, Brady here."

"Hello, Mitch. J.J. Thompson."

"Something darned important must be in the works for Montana's third senator to be calling during constituent time," Brady said.

Thompson fired back. "It's more than important, Mitch. I need to see the President right away."

"Assuming you're in Montana, that's not going to be easy," Brady said.

"I've booked a flight to DC. I'll be there by five," Thompson said.

"What's going on, Congressman?" Brady asked, dreading more trouble.

Thompson hesitated to maintain his self-control, then chose his words carefully. "The Chinese have moved military armor into Yellowstone. Tanks, artillery, and who knows what else are already in position. They're in the process of building bunkers for choppers or planes."

"Come on, J.J.," Brady scoffed. "Who spiked your coffee this morning?"

Brady's cavalier attitude provoked the Congressman to draw a line in the sand. "I have irrefutable evidence, Mitch. Either I sit down with the President tonight or I go straight to TNN."

Brady had argued privately with the President against the deal. He couldn't tell Thompson, but he had been worried at the time that the Chinese might exploit the deal to advance their agenda. Thompson had convinced him that his fears were well-founded. "Don't get hysterical on me, J.J."

"Hysterical? Thompson blurted. "I'm livid. I warned you about trusting the Chinese. You people have dyslexia when it comes to foreign policy. You trust the bad actors and distrust our allies."

However distasteful, Brady had sworn to support the President. "I know you objected to the deal, J.J., but the Chinese were demanding payment and we didn't have a choice."

"The President had several choices, and you know it," Thompson said. "He didn't have to deplete the Treasury like a drunken sailor and promote programs we clearly couldn't afford."

"I'm not going to re-plow that old ground with you, Congressman. I'll contact the President and set the dinner up for six o'clock."

"Make it seven so I have time to pick up the Speaker."

"That's not going to fly, J.J.," Brady insisted. "With impeachment in motion, the President won't sit down with him."

"He doesn't have a choice," Thompson said. "You people are going to have to put the country before politics for a change."

Brady signed off with Thompson and begrudgingly dialed the President's direct number. "Hello, Mr. President, Sorry to bother you while you're unwinding."

"No bother, Mitch. We were just heading to the 19th hole for a cold drink."

"You might want to hold off on that, sir. We have another crisis that needs your full attention. Congressman Thompson from Montana just called to say he has evidence that the Chinese have moved military armament into Yellowstone. If you don't meet with him and the Speaker for dinner tonight, he's going straight to TNN."

Elliott cursed this new setback. "The last thing we need is for Harper to blast us again during prime time."

"I agree, Mr. President. But, I understood our deal with Liu Sheng was endorsed in Beijing."

"They must have started moving that armament in as soon as they took possession of the park. That could have been their plan from the beginning."

"And we fell for it," Brady said, embarrassed by the development. "How do you suppose they're smuggling it in?"

"They must be paying the longshoremen to look the other way while they smuggle it through the Los Angeles Port."

"They still have to get it past Homeland Security," Brady said.

Elliott paused for a rare confession. "You know we had to cut way back on their inspectors to fund the special ops units. The right-wingers are going to go ballistic over this."

"They're already on the warpath, Mr. President. Besides, I think you are underestimating how the rest of the country will react. No one is going to feel good about a Chinese military base in the heartland."

"We'll deal with that later," the President said. "Set up the dinner and make sure there's plenty of our finest Merlot on hand to soften up the Speaker."

"Right away, sir," Brady said. *How will the President talk his way out of this one? How could any explanation pass muster, given Thompson's long-standing opposition to the deal and the eminent danger posed by Chinese encroachment?*

At 7:00 p.m. the President's negligence would provide further impetus for impeachment.

CHAPTER 21

—

The political world recognized Clyde Dobbins as a shrewd career politician with a keen mind and a fondness for Merlot wine. Empowered by overwhelming victories in the off-year elections and egged on by his caucus, the Speaker of the House of Representatives routinely challenged President Elliott on spending and the deficit. The tension between the two reached critical mass when Dobbins supported a House bill to impeach the President.

Differences aside, Elliott was determined to charm his way through the Yellowstone crisis. Despite his shortcomings as a chief executive, he was a consummate panderer and deal maker. He was counting on those attributes to carry the evening.

A White House butler escorted Thompson and Dobbins through the White House vestibule into the state dining room. Elliott flashed a contrived grin as if he were posing for a photo. He graciously shook hands, but avoided direct eye contact with Dobbins. "Mr. Speaker, Congressman Thompson," he said. "How is everyone tonight?"

"We're concerned for our country," Dobbins said. "And to be blunt, we can't fathom how we got into this mess."

The President's grin faded as he tried to ignore the comment. Pivoting to the role of imperial host, he pointed to chairs around the dinner table. "Please take a seat. Mitch, you sit next to the Speaker. Would anyone like something to drink before dinner?" The waiters perked up on cue, holding bottles of fine French Merlot in their white gloves. As if choreographed on Broadway, they held the bottles slanted with their prominent labels showing in full view.

Both guests avoided the snare.

"I'd like black coffee, please," Thompson said.

"Same here," the Speaker said.

With no alcohol to pacify his opponents, Elliott whispered beneath his breath, "It's going to be a long evening." Anxious to put the meeting behind him, he began. "I've asked the Secretaries of Defense, Interior, and Homeland Security to join us. I hope you don't mind."

"Good idea," Dobbins said. "They need to weigh in."

With perfect timing, Secretaries Harrison, Massey, and Ramirez, were escorted into the room. "Please have a seat, gentlemen," Elliott said. "You all know Speaker Dobbins, Congressman Thompson, and of course Mitch Brady. Thank you for coming over on such short notice."

"At your service, Mr. President," Harrison said. He and the others reached across the table to shake hands.

Turning to Thompson, Elliott sneered with his usual arrogance. "I understand you have a little movie for us tonight, Congressman. I hope it's suitable for mealtime." The President flashed his irritating Cheshire grin.

Thompson responded swiftly to Elliott's veiled mockery. "Mr. President, the Speaker and I consider our video to be unsuitable at any time, which is precisely why we're here tonight."

The rebuke chilled the room like an arctic blast.

Thompson signaled a staffer to start the video on a screen in the front of the room. Everyone's attention was drawn to a large valley surrounded by sheer mountain cliffs and stands of colossal pine trees. Nestled in the middle, newly-constructed concrete bunkers were occupied by green and brown camouflaged military equipment. A large red star painted on each vehicle stood in sharp contrast to the sights usually seen in American national parks.

As the image scrolled across the screen, a Chinese flag waving conspicuously from the highest point captured everyone's attention. The sight brought an instant reaction from Secretary of Defense Harrison: "Oh, my God!"

Thompson was more direct. "Gentlemen, tanks and artillery just don't belong in Yellowstone."

A tank came into view, its turret rotating. The movement stopped with the gun pointing directly at the viewers, a coincidental but symbolic gesture to everyone.

Duane Massey, Secretary of Homeland Security, leaned forward in his chair. He strained to see around the President who was sitting in front, partially blocking everyone's view. Frustrated, he rose and walked around the President. "I simply can't believe what I'm seeing," he said. "How did you get this video, J.J., when the White House and the intelligence community didn't know anything about the buildup?"

The President shifted nervously in his chair, wondering who dropped the ball this time.

"A hunter from the Cheyenne Reservation stumbled across the site while tracking elk," Thompson said, turning to the President who continued to avoid eye contact. "The next day, he and a friend went back to take this video, in case certain parties disputed their claim." He walked around the table to hand everyone a sheet of paper. "Here Mr. President, I have one for you, too. As you will note, the written inventory of their equipment is extensive. What you saw was not intended to be a minor outpost."

Harrison and Massey cringed like they had been gut-punched. "It's clear they aren't logging or looking for energy with this equipment," Massey said.

Unable to contain his anger any longer, Dobbins struck out. "Can you explain this blatant violation of our security, Mr. President? After all, you're the one who brought the Chinese to American soil."

The President answered in humiliation and confusion. "I don't know what went wrong. Our deal was made in good faith." The President sounded pathetically naïve to everyone in the room, including his own cabinet members.

"Mr. President, you trusted a foreign government that has consistently hacked into our most secret servers while practicing commercial espionage on a grand scale," Thompson said. "It's obvious that your trust was misguided and misplaced."

"That's the way I see it, too," Secretary Harrison said.

The open allegations of his misjudgment incensed the President.

But Thompson and Dobbins were just getting started. "This so-called deal sounds like a treaty," Dobbins said. "I don't recall you sending it to the Senate for confirmation."

Elliott eventually found his voice. "You're right, Mr. Speaker. It wouldn't have a snowball's chance in hell of getting through the opposition-controlled Senate."

Dobbins strained to control his rising anger. "The Constitution is clear on that issue. It doesn't say you are only required to submit those agreements you expect to be confirmed. You can't ignore the Constitution to avoid questions or opposition."

Brady tried to rescue the embattled President. "Technically, this was not an agreement. It was more like a real estate transaction with stipulations."

Dobbins struck again like a coiled rattlesnake. "And what, Mr. Brady, gives the White House the authority to sell public land to a foreign government?"

Squirming in his seat, Brady turned to the President, who again went on the offensive. "I realize you are a man of rules and regulations, Mr. Speaker, but I am a politician who won the presidency by a landslide. I have a mandate to conduct the people's business, and that's what I did."

Dobbins turned to the President. "Your office isn't authorized to transfer legacy lands to a foreign country."

Reaching for straws, Elliott argued. "Listen Clyde, the Small Business Administration, The Federal Deposit Insurance Corporation, Fannie Mae, and Freddie Mac all sell government owned land."

"As a lawyer I would expect you to understand that their statutory authority limits them to selling property pledged to the government as collateral on a loan," Dobbins said. "They can't and don't sell legacy lands held in public trust. Only Congress can authorize that."

With a confused look, Elliott responded. "That may be in a perfect world, but I didn't have a choice. The Chinese government threatened to suspend future bond purchases if we didn't redeem ones that were already matured. Since we didn't have the money in the Treasury, we offered the land instead. If they had suspended their purchases, we could no longer pay the government's bills. Don't you see that I had no choice?"

"Of course they agreed to the land," Thompson boomed. "It was a fool's bargain."

Elliott fumed from the Congressman's dress down in front of his cabinet members.

Speaker Dobbins doubled down. "You could have heeded the warnings against deficit spending. Instead, you promoted unsustainable budgets that required us to borrow forty cents of every dollar spent. And the Chinese were happy to oblige."

Elliott trumped his old adversary. "*I* was elected to run this government, not *you*."

The cagey speaker shot back. "Everyone at this table wishes you would do just that. You can start out by telling us how you're going to deal with this clear and present danger to our national security."

Once again, the President attempted to deflect responsibility. "What do you gentlemen suggest?"

Secretary of Defense Harrison stated the obvious. "We cannot allow a hostile military base on United States soil. It could be used as a platform for weapon deployment, as a center for intelligence gathering, and as a staging point to destabilize the country."

Massey agreed. "That base gives them a strategic advantage to recruit home-grown terrorists and spy on our defenses."

With an eyebrow raised, Dobbins intervened. "So I take it neither of you gentlemen were consulted on this magnificent deal."

Harrison risked further ire from the President. "I would have strongly objected."

With a cautious glance toward the President, Massey concurred. "Ditto that."

Stung by the harsh criticism, Elliott strolled over to the projector and hit the power switch. Directing his counter-attack at Dobbins, he said, "My administration is not run like your caucus, where everyone gets a vote. I saw a need and I took care of it."

"You made a unilateral decision with dangerous consequences, Mr. President," Dobbins said. "You should have sought advice from those with more expertise. What about you, Secretary Ramirez? Did Interior weigh in on giving away our oldest national park to an adversary?"

Conspicuously quiet up to that point, Ramirez glanced furtively at the President. Exhaling with resignation, he said, "When my Solicitor learned about the transaction, he resigned in protest. He took the position that in addition to being unwise, the transaction was clearly illegal."

The President objected. "And that protest was duly factored into decisions by the Attorney General and White House Counsel, both of whom cleared the deal."

"These are the same legal advisers who rubber-stamped the raids on Madison and Austin," Thompson pointed out. "And how did that advice serve you, Mr. President?"

Exercising uncharacteristic restraint, Elliott let the jab pass.

"By the way," Thompson asked, "exactly how was the land transferred from an administrative standpoint?"

"It was simple," Brady said. "The lawyers at Treasury drew up a contract, and as soon as Liu Sheng signed it, the Secretary issued a general warranty deed."

Thompson saw another opening. "As you know, Mitch, I'm an attorney by trade. I learned early in law school that anyone can issue a warranty deed, but it's only valid if it's signed by someone with proper authority. That's why a man cannot sell property if the deed is in his wife's name."

Elliott bellowed. "We're not talking about the common person here. These are cabinet level officials appointed by the highest office in the land."

"That's one of the great things about this country, Mr. President. You are subject to the law just like the common person. Your legal authority to sign documents on behalf of the United States stems from authorizing statutes. Your executive authority is also limited by those statutes. That's the law."

In desperation, Elliott reached for another flimsy straw. "I will instruct the Attorney General to give you a letter citing Treasury's authority to sign that deed."

Thompson jumped out ahead of the President. "It won't make any difference," he said. "That deed is worthless to me, to the folks in Austin, to the media, and to the American people. From a legal standpoint, your Chinese friends are squatting on American soil and need to be evicted."

"That's the way I see it," Dobbins said.

Interior's Ramirez raised a crucial point. "What makes you think the Chinese troops are going to oblige us? They have orders with tanks and artillery to back them up."

"That's the President's problem," Dobbins said. "As he reminded us tonight, he was elected in a landslide to run the country. It appears he's created a landslide of his own. A come-to-Jesus meeting with Liu Sheng seems to be in order. I'd recommend you have it before the Chinese garrison becomes fully operational."

While walking to his car, Massey pulled Dobbins aside. "Clyde, could you give me a hand with the trial in Texas?"

Dobbins looked Massey square in the eye. "Sending a bunch of armed agents down to raid the Convention was foolhardy. What were you thinking, Duane? You get black jump suits and guns and you think you're Rambo."

"Lighten up, Clyde. I know it was ill-advised, but the President is paranoid about the Convention. The 82nd's failure made him more so."

"And you had to show him you could succeed where Harrison failed," Dobbins said. "You'll have plenty of chances to outshine Harrison while the two of you spend the rest of your careers testifying before our committees. If you thought the plan was ill-advised, why didn't you just stand up to him like you did tonight?"

"You saw what he's like," Massey said. "He thinks he's Napoleon. It's astonishing how little he knows about the Constitution and the inner workings of the government. He thinks he can run the government by the seat of his pants."

"What are you leading up to?" Dobbins asked.

"I need your help. Will you call Granger and ask for leniency for my agents?"

"If I call Granger, it will be to plead for Congress. He's convinced we share responsibility for the country's failures. Based on what I heard here tonight, I tend to agree with him."

"Believe me, Clyde, I've learned my lesson," Massey said.

"As an aside, Duane, if the Convention goes after Elliott, you and the other Cabinet members won't be immune from personal responsibility. If I were you, I'd hire a good lawyer."

"Thanks for the vote of confidence, Mr. Speaker."

"Your team needs redemption, not endorsements," Dobbins said.

Back in their car, Thompson turned to Dobbins. "Is this nightmare for real?"

Dobbins twisted to get comfortable, then rubbed both sides of his forehead. "Way too real. These guys are out of control. And what about Elliott keeping his key advisers in the dark?"

Pulling the seat belt across his chest, Thompson focused on the future. "I notice you didn't mention impeachment."

"I didn't think it was the right place or the right time. I didn't want to speak up and lead the bill's sponsors to think I was coaching the President."

"A lot of people would have warned the President out of professional courtesy," Thompson said.

"You mean politician to politician?" Dobbins asked. "How do you think that kind of courtesy would go over with the American people right now, J.J.? They're hungry for accountability, not political correctness."

"Point taken," Thompson said. Are you really going to make the call for Massey? Granger might hand you your head."

Dobbins adjusted his seat belt. "I've been friends with Granger a long time. I hope he takes that into consideration. Besides, I'm sure his primary motive is to fix things around here."

"Fixing things is a tall order, Clyde."

"That's the truth," Dobbins said. "Based on what we learned tonight, I don't see how things could be more broken."

Back in the White House, Elliott continued to mull the crisis with his Chief of Staff.

Brady wracked his brain for answers while Elliott paced the floor munching on a carrot. "Okay, Mitch. Here's what we'll do. We'll get Treasury to sell a hundred billion to the Fed, take half of the money to redeem the original bonds from the Chinese. In exchange, they tear up the deed and vacate Yellowstone. We end up with an additional fifty billion to finance the cost overruns on the Renewable Energy Act and other programs. No harm, no foul."

"I just hope our friends in the House view it that way," Brady said. "There's no telling how Liu Sheng's people will react."

As if Brady hadn't even spoken, Elliott said, "Find out how long it will take Treasury to get the money from the Fed. We need to get things rolling before the media gets wind of this mess."

CHAPTER 22

—

While the Convention moved forward, the seeds of impeachment were taking root in the U.S. House of Representatives. The White House fielded awkward inquiries about the botched raids in Madison and Austin. Judge Johnson had already tried and sentenced DHS's Hank Applegate. Plea deals with the 82nd Airborne soldiers captured in Madison were opposed by a group of vocal residents. Meantime, Judge Johnson's counterpart in Texas was preparing to try the DHS and FEMA conspirators rounded up in Waco and Dallas. As the Chinese say, the Administration was dying from a thousand cuts.

Undeterred, President Elliott chose to fight on. He would appeal to opposition governors, despite the smackdown from Governor Granger. "Hello Governor Spivey, how are things in the Peach State?"

"Very well, Mr. President. What can I do for you today?"

"As you know, we are currently putting together the fiscal budget, and we need to know if you want any earmarks for Georgia. We were thinking about an addition to the Savannah Nuclear Site to spur employment, or some renovation work at Dobbins Air Base. Senator Sandoval tells us you're facing a primary opponent this cycle and might need some help."

"Thanks for the offer, Mr. President. I'm not accustomed to help from the opposition party. You might remind the good Senator that my approval rating is solid at seventy percent and the people in Georgia expect me to eliminate pork barrel waste, not accept it as a political bribe."

Two governors, two rebukes. Still undeterred, Elliott chose a more direct approach. "Andy, why don't you pardon Hank Applegate? He's just a pawn in our political tussle."

"I agree, he's not the issue," Spivey said. "And I can understand why you would want to get him back in Washington where he can be muffled. His conviction has already galvanized tremendous support for the Convention. The death of those thirty innocent citizens showed exactly why your administration needs to be reined in."

"Let's cut to the chase, Spivey. What can I offer you in exchange for Applegate's pardon?"

Governor Spivey seized his opportunity. "I'll take a one-for-one deal. You resign, and I'll issue the pardon."

"Curse you, Andy!" Elliott snapped. "I'll have you busted for obstruction of justice and breach of national security!"

"Thank you for another golden quote for Luke Harper, Mr. President."

"W-What do you mean?" Elliott sputtered.

"NSA doesn't have a monopoly on recording conversations these days," Spivey said. "Would you like to add any more ungrounded threats for the evening news?"

Click. Dial tone.

Out-maneuvered and rejected, Elliott shuffled to his couch. The power he had fought so hard to win was steadily slipping away. As he surveyed the most prestigious office on the planet, he realized for the first time that he might have to give it up. How would he change the world without the bully pulpit? The "Anointed One" was clinging to a narrow ledge with no safety line in sight. Below him lay a dangerous craggy precipice.

In Madison, Sergeant Dawson and Private Helms sat cross legged and shackled in a secure conference room. Dumbfounded by their predicament, Helms buckled. "What are they going to do to us, Sarge?"

"Stay strong, soldier," Dawson said. "According to our public defender, Prosecutor Stone has offered a minimum sentence in exchange for a guilty plea. I don't know how much negotiating room we have, but we need to either represent ourselves or leave things to our appointed lawyer."

Helms stopped biting his fingernails. "We don't know anything about negotiating legal stuff. If we mess up we could end up in prison for a long time."

"We've already messed up," Dawson said. "Now we need to negotiate our punishment."

"I can't go to jail, Sarge. My folks back in Virginia would be ruined. My dad's a small-town mayor and mom's a school teacher."

"Better prepare yourself, private," Dawson said. "We're likely to face time; it's just a matter of how much."

Helms's nails were already chewed to the quick. He lowered his head into his hands and said, "God, help us. Will we get kicked out of the Army, Sarge?"

Dawson saw irony in his question. "The Army doesn't want convicted felons."

"So we get double punishment for following orders?" Helms whined.

Dawson tried to reassure the young private. "We would have been all right if Ingram hadn't gone rogue on us. I tried to warn Baker, but he has bars, and I only have stripes."

"Maybe you should tell Stone about that when you negotiate our plea deal. It might make a difference."

"The Captain wouldn't be happy about me negotiating instead of him. I don't want to upstage a superior, but we need to cover our own butts."

Helms resumed nibbling on a jagged nail. "I don't care if he likes it or not, Sarge. I trust you more than him."

When a guard walked by to check on them, Dawson reached out. "We'll talk to Stone."

"Are you boys sure you want to deal with me instead of going through your attorney?" Stone asked as he stepped into the room ten minutes later.

"Yessir, we've talked it over and we're ready," Helms said, still nibbling.

"And you, Sergeant?"

"I'm with Helms," Dawson said. "But first I'd like to mention something that hasn't come out so far. Before we left on our recon mission, I expressed concern to Baker about Ingram's fitness for duty. He kept saying irrational things on the ride from Bragg."

Stone focused his attention. "What kind of things?"

"Threats to deal with civilians who are disloyal to the President. Stuff like that."

"And what was Baker's response?" Stone asked.

Dawson's answer was brief and contrite. "I don't want to appear disloyal, sir, but he basically told me to stick to my knitting and let him worry about the men."

"I witnessed his arrogance," Stone said. "If he corroborates your story, I'll consider it a mitigating factor in your plea deal."

"What does that mean?" Helms asked.

"I'll explain later," Dawson said.

Helms interpreted Dawson's grin to be a positive sign.

"Thank you, gentlemen. You've done the wise thing," Stone said. "I'll draw up our agreement and submit it to your attorney." He paused at the door. "And gentlemen, I'll do what I can within the law to help you."

Helms looked odd biting his fingernails while smiling.

Based on Baker's corroboration and evidence showing that Ingram was the only one who fired his weapon, charges were dropped against Dawson and Helms. Ingram was found to be mentally incompetent to stand trial and was remanded to the Georgia State Hospital in Rome, Georgia, where he continued to recover from his leg wound. Captain Baker, the one who shouldered responsibility for the mission, was sentenced to one year in the Georgia State Penitentiary in Augusta. As part of the deal, all three gave affidavits describing their roles in the raid. During his trial, Baker condemned Dawson and Helms for selling out. In private, however, he complained that he wasn't offered the same deal.

Ted Johnson showed empathy when he was asked to endorse the plea deal. "Those boys have suffered enough," he said. "Even good soldiers make mistakes in combat. I don't think we have to worry about them making the same mistake again."

That evening at dinner, Ted Johnson concluded to his father that the most divisive president in history had finally found a way to bring the country together. "President Elliott has defiled nearly everything about America that makes it great: its traditions, its principles, and its people."

During grace that evening, Judge Johnson prayed, "Lord, as another sad day for America comes to a close, please deliver our country and its citizens from this political quagmire."

"Amen to that," Ted sighed. "Let's eat."

CHAPTER 23

—

Benjamin Radcliff was legendary throughout Texas legal circles as the "go-to guy" on the most difficult legal cases. Universally respected, especially by those who faced him in the courtroom, he routinely out-lawyered his most seasoned adversaries. In *Texas v Duane Walker*, an angry public expected him to mount an aggressive prosecution. After reviewing the case, he asked for an audience with Marion Warner, Senior Judge of the Superior Court. Due to the unprecedented nature of the case, Warner agreed to depart from the court's usual protocol.

Despite the sweltering afternoon, Radcliff walked the four blocks from his office to the courthouse. Halfway there he paused to remove his jacket and felt perspiration wicking through his starched shirt. *Why didn't I just take a cab?* he thought. A glance in a storefront window showed prominent wet streaks on his back and under his arms. Two more tortuous blocks led to the courthouse cantina where he deposited a handful of sweaty change into a vending machine. While the ice-cold drink quenched his 100 degree thirst, a newsman approached with a cameraman in tow.

"Mr. Prosecutor, I'm Luke Harper with TNN. Could I have a moment?"

"Sorry, Mr. Harper. I'm in a miserable mood and late for an appointment."

Luke moved closer, ignoring the prosecutor's brush-off. "Do you have jurisdiction over federal officials who are carrying out orders from their superiors?"

Some of Radcliff's irritation was neutralized by the soothing air conditioning and another refreshing swig of soda. "It's not defensible to break the law because your boss told you to," he said. "No employer anywhere has the legal authority or the right to tell an employee to commit multiple felonies."

"Does it make any difference if the employer is the President of the United States, and he claims immunity under the Patriot Act?"

"Let me be clear, Mr. Harper. Serious crimes were committed here, and the good citizens of Texas expect me to execute my responsibility as a prosecutor. No one, not even the President of the United States, is above Texas law."

While Radcliff downed another long drink, Mickey motioned for Luke to keep going.

Luke's own parched throat made talking difficult. He'd get a cold drink after he forced the Prosecutor's hand. "What will you accomplish by prosecuting them for something that didn't happen?"

Radcliff paused to roll the cold can on his forehead. The relief brought a brief smile. "Congratulations, Harper," he said. "You just stumbled onto the key issue in this case. Now if you'll excuse me, I have an appointment."

"Thank you, Mr. Prosecutor," Luke said as Radcliff walked away. "Get that, Mickey?"

"Every spoken word," Mickey said. "Just as important, I got the hint that a deal might be struck. There's gonna be a good follow-up to this piece."

"Absolutely," Luke said.

On the elevator to the Judge Warner's chambers, Radcliff mentally rehearsed his pitch. He hoped his unconventional idea would fly with the judge.

Warner draped his black robe, a symbol of judicial authority, on a rack just as Radcliff entered. "Hello, Ben. How are you this afternoon?"

"I'm soaked from walking over in this heat and irritated from being accosted by Luke Harper in the cantina. During our brief discussion he asked the question I would like to talk to you about."

The judge loosened his tie, then took a seat behind his cluttered desk. "And what's that?"

"You and I both know I can't charge these DHS agents with any weapons violations, since Congress gave them special dispensation to carry firearms. They didn't really injure anyone or damage any property, thanks to Perez's quick action. I can use Walker's confession to make a slam dunk case for conspiracy, but even if the months of work and millions of dollars spent result in a conviction, what do we accomplish? I'm certain the federal government will appeal to avoid an untenable precedent."

"I see your point, Ben, but we can't just turn them loose. Imagine what could have happened if they'd gotten to Austin with all those guns."

The judge had given him a perfect opening. "Why don't we see if these guys know anything that could help advance the Convention in exchange for their release? A plea deal is the only thing that makes sense at this point."

Warner pushed up his drooping reading glasses and scratched his nose. "That's an interesting idea. I can move the court date back to give you more time to try it."

"Thanks, Judge."

Radcliff left Johnson's chambers with an alternative to fighting the feds in court, a costly and risky proposition under the best of circumstances. His first move was to squeeze his DHS captives for information. He called his old friend and ally, Commander Perez, for help. "Hello Dale, Ben Radcliff."

"Howdy, Ben. How is your case against our DHS friends coming along?"

"Actually, that's why I called. I'm considering a plea deal, but it only makes sense if I can get something of value in return. I think there is a good chance these guys have information that could advance the Convention."

"Granger should weigh in on that," Perez said. "I have a regularly scheduled meeting with him at two tomorrow. Can you be there?"

"You bet," Radcliff said. "See you then. And thanks."

"I'll go ahead and let him know you're coming," Perez said.

The following afternoon, Granger was chatting with Kelley when the prosecutor arrived. "Welcome, Ben," Granger said. "This is Governor Timothy Kelley from Indiana. He's the chairman of our Drafting Committee. He also happens to be a gifted constitutional lawyer."

Radcliff took a seat next to Kelley and shook his hand. "It's good to meet you, sir. Your brief on the Anderson Trucking Company case was brilliant. I have a full plate with DHS, but it's nothing compared to what you're dealing with here at the Convention."

"We all have different cards to play, Mr. Radcliff," Kelley said. "Those of us who are believers take solace in the knowledge that God has a master plan and we're simply following it."

Radcliff wiped perspiration from his forehead with a hanky. "While I could always use some spiritual inspiration, I'm here today to discuss legal strategy. As you know, we've charged the DHS and FEMA agents with conspiracy. If we get a conviction, they will undoubtedly appeal. We'll drown in unending litigation."

Kelley nodded in agreement.

Radcliff resumed with a bit of intrigue. "I'm convinced there is a way to turn this to our advantage. Most of these guys are foot soldiers and were just following orders, but they're smart enough to be concerned about their personal culpability. I'm betting some of them have information more incriminating than the raid, possibly something involving the President. Would incriminating information be helpful to you in your work here?"

Kelley's eyes lit up. "Go on."

"Their two leaders, Walker and Bell, aren't accustomed to confrontation," Radcliff said. "Both have been bureaucrats their entire careers, so I suspect they've been sheltered from accountability. The prospect of severe punishment can be a scary thing when you've never encountered it before."

"Any information proving that the White House has intentionally violated or intends to violate the law would be a windfall," Kelley said. "The public needs to be clear that this administration places their power above the rights of the people. Plus, the people have a right to know the true character of the officials who are running their country."

"I think we can paint a picture," Radcliff said. "But they're not going to be comfortable ratting out their superiors."

Kelley placed his hand on the prosecutor's shoulder. "An old mentor of mine once said, 'If bulls didn't have horns, everyone would be a matador.' You've already done the heavy lifting. The rest is just follow-through."

"Hope you're right, Governor."

"Good luck, Ben," Granger said.

CHAPTER 24

———

Lonnie Bell was the first target of Radcliff's interrogation. He pondered his uncertain future while he languished in jail. His descent from a respected public servant to a prisoner charged with conspiracy fueled contempt for himself and his colleagues. Going along to get ahead had cost him his freedom, possibly his career, and worst of all, his self-respect.

He promised himself that he was going to make things right if it was the last thing he did. But redemption would come at a cost—a cost far greater than he imagined.

Armed with incomparable interrogation skills, Radcliff walked in like a predator stalking prey. Before he even started, Bell looked defeated. He was slumped over a table, shackled, unshaven, and disheartened. Dressed in an orange jumpsuit with the words "Ranger Detention Center" imprinted on the back, he was indistinguishable from the drug dealers, rapists, and murderers incarcerated there.

From his seat opposite the prisoner, Radcliff sized him up. *This guy's already broken*, he thought. "Hello, Mr. Bell. My name is Benjamin Radcliff and I'm the local prosecutor. I have a copy of your waiver to counsel for this little chat. Is there anything you need like medical attention, a cigarette, or a cold drink?" He paused for a response.

Bell simply raised his head and gazed at Radcliff with sullen, empty eyes, but no response.

Radcliff's formidable interrogation skills had developed over time from dealing with hardened criminals. *Maybe if I reason with this guy, he'll open up.* "You're in a world of trouble, Mr. Bell," he began. "It's not for doing your job, but for doing it illegally. You can argue that the Convention delegates are violating the law by opposing the federal government, but civil disobedience isn't against the law in this state or any other state. Besides, the right to hold a Constitutional Convention is expressly allowed by the Constitution itself. So what do you have to say for yourself?"

Radcliff had heard every excuse known to man, and he wondered which one he was going to hear now. But Bell surprised him.

"I don't have any excuse, Mr. Radcliff," he said. "My bosses have a way of justifying everything based on the sovereignty of the federal government and the mandate Elliott received in the election. They were very convincing at first, but I'm beginning to see now how they're wrong."

Radcliff relaxed with the easy headway he was making. "Do you think the electorate would have voted for this president if they knew he was going to shell their towns? Can you understand why people aren't likely to sympathize with you?"

Raising his hands in submission, Bell's shackles rattled as if he were in a medieval dungeon. "Enough, Mr. Radcliff. I get it loud and clear. I'd give anything if I could undo the whole fiasco, but I can't. The best I can do is take a different path forward."

Radcliff sprang on the opening. "I may be able to help you with that."

As Radcliff outlined his plea deal, Bell weighed his own redemption against loyalty to the people who had coaxed him to betray everything that's important to him.

"Mr. Bell, the public deserves to know how far this president will go to accomplish his political agenda. Need time to think it over?"

"No, I'm in," he said. "I want to right this wrong, and if exposing the administration is what it takes, I'm ready."

Radcliff was relieved by his partial victory. "You've made a wise decision, Mr. Bell. I'll get someone to take your statement while I draw up our plea agreement."

"Thank you, Mr. Radcliff; you've given me a way to redeem myself."

Bell's statement was a devastating blow to President Elliott. It outlined billions of dollars transferred from various appropriations to the construction of projects like the secret FEMA detention centers. Camp Bravo-6 in Waco, one of several camps throughout FEMA's ten regions, was typical of "black projects" hidden from Congressional oversight and public scrutiny. Bell described a secret plan to round up local political leaders during civil unrest, leaving total control to the federal government. The plan included the forced confiscation of legally owned firearms and the suspension of habeas corpus. At the end of his interrogation, Bell provided the combination to his safe in Waco where Radcliff could recover top secret documents on FEMA's black projects.

Stunned by the scope of the abuses, Radcliff appealed to Bell's insight. "You seem like a reasonable man, despite your involvement in this mess. How do you suppose the White House convinced so many people to go along with such insanity?"

Bell bowed his head in shame and said, "You have to understand, Mr. Radcliff. President Elliott values loyalty above everything else. He does not like confrontation or drama. Subordinates know these things about him and understand they must either fall in line or go elsewhere. I regret that many of us placed career advancement above our sworn pledge to serve the public."

O nce Lonnie Bell's interrogation was over, Radcliff turned his attention to Duane Walker, Regional Director for DHS.

Shackled to anchors in the floor, and clouded by a sense of self-importance, Walker felt empowered by the extraordinary measures taken to restrain him. During simulated special operations training only the most dangerous combatants were secured this way. And even though his nose had been broken during his struggle with Grissom, he detected the pungent scent of an industrial disinfectant. "*Achoo, aaaaachooo.* Damn, that hurt," he yelled in agony. His tear-filled eyes fell on a guard near the door who was unarmed except for hands the size of Christmas turkeys and a muscle-bound body that tested the limits of his bullet-proof vest bulging under his uniform. *It would take a death wish to challenge that Titan.*

Like Bell, Walker had willingly signed a waiver to legal counsel so he could plead his case directly to Radcliff. He was confident he could handle a backwater prosecutor. Unfortunately for him, he was not in the same league as Benjamin Radcliff.

While Walker adjusted his shackles, Radcliff entered with two cups of coffee. "I realize you might like your coffee with cream and sugar, but you'll need it strong and black today."

The prisoner lied to advance his illusion of control. "Black is just how I like it," he said. His contempt for Radcliff was as strong as the coffee.

Since Walker had already confessed, Radcliff would need something compelling to seal any deal with him. Even with Bell's documents in hand, simple corroboration wouldn't be enough.

An awkward pause for a sip of coffee allowed the men to size each other up.

Radcliff walked to a switch on the wall to activate a tape recorder. "Have you given any thought to your predicament?" he asked.

Walker's mouth curled on both ends in a recalcitrant smirk. "The best laid plans sometimes go awry. It's that simple."

"Maybe your plan didn't work because it was a stupid idea," Radcliff countered. "As a prosecutor I see a lot of stupid ideas go down in flames."

Walker couldn't contain his pomposity. "DHS has the entire federal government behind it. We hire the best people, and they receive the best training available."

"I understand what you are trying to say, Mr. Walker. But your high praise simply doesn't hold water. The federal government that you praise so highly can't deliver the mail efficiently, can't operate on a budget, and can't keep its own agents from murdering innocent citizens."

Walker deflected. "What does that have to do with me?"

"You need to accept the fact that there is a common thread of ineptitude and mismanagement throughout those failures. I don't believe the fall of Rome was inevitable, and I certainly don't believe the problems with this country are a matter of bad luck. The public deserves accountability for corrupt leadership, which is why we're here today."

Walker didn't like the implication that he and his colleagues were incompetent. He was even more incensed over the insinuation that they were corrupt.

Then Radcliff made his offer. "You will be prosecuted for violating several Texas laws, unless you give me something of value in exchange for leniency."

"What do you expect me to barter?" he asked. "You already have my national security card and my guns."

Radcliff assumed he was cracking a bad joke. "Any information the public can use to protect itself from additional oppression by this administration will do. You and I will never agree on issues of propriety, but if you give me something useful today, I'll drop your charges and see that Perez sets you free. Otherwise, you'll be remanded to the Texas criminal justice system where you'll encounter some of the most vicious human beings on earth. Your former cell mates, Carlos and Ricardo, are angels compared to most of our felons. With your credentials, you'd be a walking target."

Beads of perspiration glistened on Walker's forehead. "I feel like I'm being coerced."

"If you don't want to accept what I'm offering, that's up to you," Radcliff said. "You can take your chances in court with a jury made up of your peers—or maybe I should say our peers." Radcliff turned to the mammoth guard next to the door. "Take this prisoner back to his holding cell and give him an hour to make up his mind."

The shackles rattled from Walker's squirming. "Just a minute, Radcliff. Let me pull my thoughts together so I get this right."

Radcliff reached across the table to adjust the microphone mounted there. "Take your time," he said. "We want you to get it right, too. If the federal government challenges your statement, this recording will back it up. And your waiver of right to counsel will allow us to use it."

CHAPTER 25

—

The prospect of ratting out the President of the United States terrified Walker. His trembling lips leaked coffee that streamed down his chin before puddling on the table. His shackles rattled as he wiped his chin on his shirtsleeve. "What I'm about to tell you will guarantee me a spot at the top of the President's enemies list. You don't know how ruthless the federal government can be."

"The slaughter of those kids in Madison gave everyone a clue," Radcliff said.

Pandora's Box was about to open. "You don't know the worst of it," Walker said.

"I'm listening."

"Do you remember reading about the death of Anwar al-Awlaki and Samir Khan from a drone strike in Yemen?"

Radcliff stopped taking notes and looked up. "It was all over the news."

Walker picked his next words with great care. "Did you know both were American citizens?"

"I'll take your word for it," Radcliff said. "So what?"

"Why do you think two American citizens were targeted instead of foreign terrorists?" Walker asked.

"I assume the government of Yemen had something to do with it."

With the detachment of a park tour guide, Walker continued. "I'm afraid it was more deliberate than that, Mr. Prosecutor. There are two parts to this administration's radical departure from the War on Terrorism. The first involves the issuance of a top secret executive order authorizing the use of deadly force against any terrorist, foreign or domestic."

"Go on," Radcliff urged.

"Initially, the administration feared backlash from civil rights groups if the target was a United States citizen," Walker continued. "They artfully defused that problem by targeting two of the most feared and despised terrorists known. Their strategy worked. The public and the media hailed the assassinations as a heroic feat. The fact that they were American citizens went nearly unnoticed."

"You mentioned two parts, Mr. Walker," Radcliff said.

"The lack of condemnation emboldened the President to expand his secret anti-terrorism program. An enemies list was assembled to identify terrorists who would be targeted under the program. Several names on that list have now been scratched off as a result of successful strikes."

Radcliff frowned. "I view that as a success. I don't see the connection."

Walker hesitated to hype up the drama of the moment. "The rest of the story gets sticky," he said.

"I'm in the sticky business," Radcliff assured him.

"When Elliott's approval rating suffered a precipitous dive two years ago, he blamed a political conspiracy against his administration," Walker said.

Radcliff nodded. "I remember that."

"The President's response to the perceived conspiracy was swift and visceral," Walker continued. "In a shroud of secrecy, he ordered the Secretary of the Department of Homeland Security to assemble a domestic enemies list made up of anyone in opposition to his presidency. That list became an addendum to Executive Order 14900, interpreted by DHS as authorizing deadly force against those listed as domestic terrorists."

There was a long awkward pause while Walker basked in a moment of self-importance. Radcliff sat paralyzed, overcome with horror and disbelief. His cigarette dropped from his fingers. He simply couldn't fathom what he was hearing.

Walker straightened in his seat, waiting for a response.

Radcliff sipped more coffee to recover. "Let me be clear about this, Mr. Walker. Are you telling me the Department of Homeland Security had direct approval from the President of the United States to eliminate delegates at the Convention if they resisted during the planned raid?" *Please tell me I'm wrong*, he prayed to himself.

"That's exactly what I'm telling you, Mr. Radcliff. But the secret authorization went much further than that. DHS construed the order as authorization to eliminate political opponents in the event of a financial collapse, a nationwide cyber-attack, a catastrophic natural disaster, or any crisis cited by the President."

Radcliff tried to take notes, but only scribbles came out. He struggled to digest what he was hearing, but couldn't seem to process the inconceivable story. "So President Elliott authorized assassinations of opportunity as well as assassinations for national security?" Again, he prayed he was wrong.

"That's one way to phrase it," Walker said.

"Am I to assume that you and your men were prepared to carry out Executive Order 14900?" Radcliff asked.

"Agents of DHS are loyal," Walker said. "Need I say more?"

Walker slumped in his chair, relieved to have the weight of the secret lifted. At the same time, he realized his reputation, his career, and perhaps his President had been sacrificed in exchange for his freedom. In a rare lightbulb moment, he understood the motivation of the patriots fighting for liberty in Austin.

Radcliff warily closed his notebook and flipped off the microphone, dispirited by Walker's secrets. "Mr. Walker, what you just told me is beyond any rational person's comprehension." He leaned back in his chair, pulled a pack of cigarettes from his jacket, and handed one to Walker. Both lit up, sending dual streams of smoke spiraling upward. "For the purpose of discussion, let me ask you something," Radcliff said. "Given the barbaric nature of the plan you just outlined, what sets President Elliott apart from Robert Mugabe, Joseph Stalin, or a common Mafioso kingpin?"

Walker's shackles rattled again as he tapped his cigarette in the ashtray. He let out a slow, deep breath. "President Elliott has the backing of a huge electoral referendum. Like it or not, 'might makes right' in situations like this."

"Not so," Radcliff bellowed, scattering ashes from his waving hand. "Jerome Elliott is the president of all the people, both supporters and dissenters. People who disagree with his policies are still legitimate Americans, not enemies. He swore a solemn oath as a condition of office, to support and defend the Constitution, and to protect *all* of the American people. He has broken that solemn oath while dragging the Constitution through the mud. And now, with God's help and yours, he will be held accountable."

Walker shifted in his seat, finally realizing the gravity of his confession. Perspiration trickled down his temples.

Radcliff had one more itch to scratch. "Did you read in the papers that the United Nations has opened an investigation of human rights violations as a result of the civilian deaths in Madison?"

Walker took the last drag on his cigarette, then snuffed it out. He turned his head to avoid blowing the smoke toward Radcliff. "I didn't need to," he said. "A friend and colleague of mine, Hank Applegate, was tried and convicted by local authorities in Madison. He told me he's been threatened with another trial at the International Criminal Court."

"How do you think the United Nations would view what you just told me?" Radcliff asked.

"They would undoubtedly consider President Elliott a violator of human rights along with the other rogue leaders of the world. The rub is, the United Nations has no authority in this country."

"To the contrary, Mr. Walker," Radcliff said. "The United States and all other member nations agreed to certain conditions when they joined the UN. Under that agreement, they have as much authority to investigate war crimes here as in Syria or the Sudan."

Walker shuddered at the thought of being on the International Criminal Court's radar. He had viewed secret footage of Saddam Hussein's hanging.

"One final question," Radcliff said. "Can you provide me with any documentation verifying what you just disclosed?"

Thinking he had nothing more to lose, Walker surrendered his most valuable secret. "As a matter of fact, I have a copy of Executive Order 14900 in my safe in Dallas," he said.

Radcliff's mouth fell open and his breath escaped him. He never dreamed this kind of evidence would fall into his lap. "Would it be possible to get my hands on those documents? Your full cooperation will make it easier to free you."

Walker recovered some of his previous arrogance with a warning. "I can give you the combination, but that won't get you past our iron-clad security."

Radcliff took another puff and exhaled, glaring at Walker's ghostly figure through the smoke. "I think we've already proven we shouldn't be underestimated, Mr. Walker. By the way, how do you feel about going down in history as the man who brought down a sitting American president?"

All the light left Walker's eyes. "Like a walking dead man," he stammered. His expression went totally blank. "Now, I have a question for you, Mr. Radcliff. Is there any way you can protect me once the White House gets wind of my confession and sends the Grim Reaper my way?"

"We don't have anything like the federal witness protection program," Radcliff said. "But the Rangers can protect you as they would any prisoner or key witness."

"And my family?"

Radcliff straightened from a pang of compassion. "I think we can arrange that."

Walker showed his first sign of humanity. "That, sir, is a great relief."

Radcliff pondered his next steps. Within minutes of leaving Walker, he called to brief Judge Warner. "Judge, are you sitting down? You're not going to believe what I'm about to tell you."

"Fire away, Ben," Warner said. "There isn't much that will surprise this old war horse anymore."

Radcliff outlined Walker's disclosure in great detail, emphasizing that he and the Judge were probably on the President's domestic enemies list. There was a brief pause on the line.

"What has this country come to?" Warner gasped. "What's next?"

"I'll need a search warrant to get my hands on the evidence in Walker's safe. We should share it with Granger and his delegates."

The judge grappled with their options. "Shouldn't we give copies to the appropriate committees in Congress? I understand they're moving forward with impeachment."

"That's a good idea, Judge. Maybe we should share it with both. I even wonder if we should give it to the media."

"I'd rather keep this in official channels, and let the journalists get their information from other sources."

"Okay, but right now I need that search warrant," Radcliff said.

Within hours, a joint strike force made up of Texas Rangers, Texas State Patrolmen, Dallas County Sheriff's deputies, and Dallas Municipal Police descended on the DHS office in the basement of the Earle Cabell Federal Building in Dallas. To kick off the search, State Patrol Officers Lance Taylor and Tess Grissom flashed their badges while breezing past the security checkpoint.

"How's that for restricted access?" Taylor asked, recalling the guard's comment outside the Waco FEMA camp. They marched straight to the office lobby and advised the receptionist they had a warrant to search the premises.

"Can you do that?" she gasped. "This is a federal office, you know."

"It could become a crime scene if you don't comply with that warrant,"

Grissom said. "She's a prissy little thing, isn't she, Taylor?"

Within seconds, Rob Holton, Duane Walker's former deputy and now acting director, entered the lobby from a hidden door behind the receptionist. He scanned the search warrant. "What is this all about, officers?"

"It's all in that paper," Grissom said. She and Taylor pushed past him on their way through the hidden door to his office.

"You have no authority here," Holton said. He awkwardly signaled two security guards posted near the elevator.

Grissom stopped and turned to face him. "Take a peek out that window. Our SWAT team says we have all the authority we need, plus the firepower to back it up. And before you start your yarn about how we have no authority over federal officials, you might want to know that your boss is in a holding cell in Austin. Unless you want to join him, you'd better stand down and let us do our job."

By the time Holton dialed his headquarters in Washington, Taylor was spinning the knobs on Duane Walker's safe. Once inside, he located a bright red envelope marked *Top Secret*. Verifying that it contained Executive Order 14900, he stuffed it inside his protective vest and turned to Grissom. "We're out of here, Partner."

Hustling out of the lobby, they brushed by a shaken Holton. "The Department will mail you a receipt for these documents," Grissom said with a wink.

Escorted through the main entrance by members of their SWAT team, Taylor pulled out his cell phone and dialed Prosecutor Radcliff. "We have your package, sir. We'll have it in your hands in a tad over three hours."

"Did they offer any resistance?" Radcliff asked.

"Once Big Tess challenged their acting director with a good look at our SWAT team, they stood down. When we left, their acting office head was on hold because his headquarters couldn't find anyone who could deal with our warrant. Meantime, we found the documents and boogied."

"Good work, Taylor," Radcliff said. "Compliments to your team. That document is too valuable to risk. On your way here, swing by the Dallas State Patrol barracks and make a couple of copies. Stash one copy with the barracks commander and the other in your ticket book. Bring the original to me."

"We'll do that," Taylor said. "Superintendent Meeks instructed the SWAT team to escort us to Austin in case of any interference."

Radcliff dialed Perez to give him the good news. "Hello, Dale, this is Ben."

"I've already heard about your hit and run," Perez said. "The feds are howling like scalded dogs. I told them you work for the people and I couldn't interference with your orders."

"Great line. Are you scheduled for your two o'clock appointment with Governor Granger today?"

"I am. Come on over."

"I think our news will make Granger's hair stand on end."

The Convention was abuzz when Radcliff arrived sharply at two. After the usual greetings, he handed Granger a copy of the documents from Walker's safe.

As Granger scanned Executive Order 14900, his neck and face flushed brilliant red. "This makes Watergate look like a board game," he said. "No one this unprincipled should have access to our nuclear arsenal. We need to move quickly." He frantically motioned for an aide standing next to the stage. "Could you ask Governor Kelley and the other members of the Drafting Committee to join us?"

"Right away, sir," the aide said.

In short order, Granger was explaining to his colleagues how Walker had confessed to the existence of a top secret executive order authorizing the use of deadly force against opposition political leaders.

The governors stared in disbelief.

Governor Pearson was the first to speak up. "We always questioned the President's scruples, but now we know he's a raving madman as well."

Granger feared further retaliation against the Convention. "I'm afraid he'll become more desperate once we take final action. No telling what he'll do then."

Pennsylvania's Governor Young stepped forward. "Can we neutralize the threat quickly?"

Kelley stood tall and ashen-faced. "In light of this information, we don't have much choice. We should proceed as planned and incorporate this latest information into our recommendations to the delegates. We can rely on Perez to keep us safe while we proceed. Once the press reports on this there'll be another firestorm greater than the Madison backlash."

Granger added his own prediction. "This development will likely light a fire under the United Nations investigation as well."

Kelley stepped over to Granger. "I think as Convention Chairman, you should call Speaker Dobbins and brief him."

"I second that motion," Pearson said.

Spurred by a consensus, Granger walked back to his office to make the all-important call.

Dobbins's staff transferred the call. "Hello Clay, how are you and your band of reformers doing today?"

"We're up to our necks in God's work, Mr. Speaker. We've uncovered something that's too hot for us to handle by ourselves."

"I can't imagine that since you've dealt with everything else. But I can hear the urgency in your voice, so lay it out for me."

"During our interrogation of Duane Walker, we learned that President Elliott has issued an executive order authorizing the use of deadly force by DHS during periods of civil unrest," Granger said. "Their orders are to take out people on a list at the President's discretion."

"Hold on, Clay," Dobbins said. "Are you saying the President has an assassination list of American citizens?"

"That's right, Mr. Speaker. It's called the 'Domestic Terrorist List.' It's made up of bona fide terrorists as well as the President's political opponents. It gets even better. Not only do we have a signed confession from Walker, we recovered a copy of the secret executive order from his safe."

"Sounds like a smoking gun!" Dobbins gasped.

"Right again, Mr. Speaker. It's the most compelling evidence yet that Elliott is not only unlawful, but is morally and psychologically unstable. We're concerned that if he gets more desperate, he might resort to something worse than Madison."

"I share your concern, Governor," Dobbins said. "If I could have a copy of those documents, I'll share them with the House Committee considering impeachment."

"We'll get them to you as soon as possible, Granger said. "You might want to move quickly if you're interested in redemption for this Congress."

"There are several of my own caucus members who feel like we're part of the problem, Governor, and they're not all Libertarians or Freedom Party members. According to some of our more outspoken members, the entire federal government should be indicted."

"Have you been spying on our deliberations, Mr. Speaker?" Granger asked.

"That's not funny, Governor."

The Drafting Committee assembled in a conference room to review their draft Articles of Resolution. Granger interrupted to brief them on his conversation with Dobbins.

"What was his reaction?" Pearson asked.

"He was appalled, but not particularly surprised. Naturally, he asked for copies of the documents so he could pass them on to the committee working on impeachment. I suggested that he and his colleagues move quickly, since Congress is partially responsible for the country's miseries."

"Do you think he has any idea how serious we are about Congressional reform?" Pennsylvania's Young asked.

"I doubt it," Granger said. "He shares the view that accountability for politicians comes from the ballot box."

Young had just reviewed the draft Articles of Resolution and offered a prediction. "The Speaker and his colleagues might be in for a big surprise."

Pearson stood up to stress a gnawing concern. "We need to get this Convention moving before the President tries to trip us up again."

"We're prepared to make our recommendations to the delegates on Wednesday," Kelley said.

Pearson was pacing the floor with her arms folded. "Are you sure we can pull everything together by then?"

Granger glanced around the table to survey everyone's reaction. "I don't think we have a choice."

"Then let's pull out our quills and get back to work," Kelley said.

CHAPTER 26

—

Kelley returned to the stage on Wednesday morning as scheduled. The auditorium was overflowing with delegates yearning for closure and journalists searching for a blockbuster story. Two infiltrators had been detained earlier in the day by astute screeners who questioned their credentials. When their delegate identification numbers were found to be duplicates, Perez charged them with trespassing and ejected them from the building. The incursion was another sign of the administration's growing desperation.

Tim Kelley was destined to go down in history as a leader of the most comprehensive reform movement since Reconstruction. Unlike then, this movement sought to change the very Constitution that served as the Republic's guiding beacon since 1787.

Kelley knew the proposed reforms had to satisfy the founders' intent as outlined in the Federalist Papers. Any change that weakened that foundation would be a permanent setback. This historic opportunity would be lost unless they got the formula exactly right.

Just before Granger introduced him to the delegates, Kelley closed his eyes and prayed. "Lord, I come to you today, a simple man facing a complex task. I ask that you bestow wisdom, courage, and clarity on me, and I pray for divine guidance in making these recommendations to the people. I ask all of these things in the name of the Savior, Jesus Christ. Amen."

Granger waited out of respect before proceeding. "Ladies and Gentlemen, it gives me great pleasure to introduce the Honorable Timothy Kelley, Governor of Indiana."

Kelley walked to the microphone and nodded to Granger, who briskly shook his hand.

The delegates broke into thunderous applause, accompanied by intermittent whistling and cheering. Within minutes the sergeant-at-arms had restored order.

"Thank you for your enthusiastic welcome," Kelley said. "Thank you."

As the delegates settled down and returned to their seats, Kelley paused to stress the gravity of the moment. Raising his hand and striking the pose of a country preacher, he spoke clearly and forcefully. "Fellow delegates and patriots, I am honored to represent you during this dark hour in our Republic's history."

He paused again as the crowd erupted with shouts of support. Once the outbreak subsided, he continued. "America is a great experiment for humanity, an experiment in the promotion of human freedom and dignity. A government of the people, by the people, and for the people means just that. The government works for us, and its leaders should be undeniably attuned to what we expect. There is no place for an elitist attitude that government is the oracle of wisdom."

More applause accentuated the sentiment.

Kelley raised both hands. "And delegates, let me remind you. You pay for this government, you elect its officials, and you empower it. In every respect this is your government and it's your responsibility to make sure it is performing up to your expectations."

More rousing applause.

"Your Drafting Committee is now prepared to propose Articles of Resolution to help you reform your dysfunctional federal government. We have heard your concerns and have incorporated your input. The Honorable Eleanor Pearson, Governor of Arizona and primary author of the proposed reforms, will present them to you. Governor Pearson."

Charged with exhilaration, she closed her notebook and approached the podium. "Ladies and gentlemen, Governor Kelley has just set the tone for us. I couldn't paint a clearer picture. So without further delay, here is the official platform of this Convention as proposed by your Drafting Committee." She read the resolutions word for word from her notebook.

Articles of Resolution

Whereas President Elliott is the most divisive president in history; and

Whereas President Elliott is the most corrupt president in history; and

Whereas President Elliott placed winning at politics above honesty, integrity, and fair play; and

Whereas President Elliott desecrated America's heritage and history by supporting foreign political groups who consider the American people corrupt colonialists; and

Whereas President Elliott promised the most transparent administration in history, but instead used intimidation, coercion, and violence to cover up numerous scandals and suppress whistleblowers in violation of federal law; and

Whereas President Elliott announced that he would use the vast power and resources of the presidency and the federal government to punish political opponents and reward political allies in violation of federal law; and

Whereas President Elliott brought felons, tax evaders, avowed Communists and poorly prepared managers into key posts in the federal government; and

Whereas President Elliott utilized the Department of Homeland Security to assemble and maintain an enemies list of United States citizens and authorized their assassination; and

Whereas President Elliott's administration consistently supported anti-American groups such as the Muslim Brotherhood, the Libyan Resistance Movement, and the People's Syrian Free Army thereby undermining the national security of the United States; and

Whereas President Elliott refused to demonstrate any leadership or willingness to work with Congress to avoid default; and

Whereas President Elliott has continued unsustainable fiscal policies that resulted in default; and

Whereas, the country's debt has risen to an unsustainable level under President Elliott's tenure; and

Whereas the credit rating of the United States has been downgraded as a result of President Elliott's lack of fiscal restraint and effective fiscal policy; and

Whereas President Elliott transferred legacy public lands and public energy assets to the People's Republic of China in lieu of debt repayment without proper authority; and

Whereas President Elliott issued numerous executive orders to circumvent the authority of Congress; and

Whereas President Elliott ordered a violent attack on of Madison, Georgia resulting in the deaths of thirty innocent civilians including eleven children; and

Whereas, some members of Congress are complicit in the failures of the federal government due to their lack of oversight; and

Whereas Jerome Powers Elliott has failed to faithfully execute his sworn duties and responsibilities as President of the United States of America,

Let it be known that, under the authority of Article V of the Constitution, this Convention hereby offers the following Articles of Resolution.

Pearson outlined a comprehensive series of reforms including term limits on members of Congress, mandatory passage of an annual federal budget, limitations on and an annual audit of the Federal Reserve Bank, and prohibitions against any laws that exempt or show preference to members of Congress. In addition, interpretations of the Commerce Clause and the President's appointment and Executive Order authority were clarified.

Pearson raised her hand the way Kelley had to emphasize the next point. "We are recommending two independent offices to insure implementation of our resolutions while ensuring public parity with the powerful federal government. A Statutory and Regulatory Review Commission will implement Tort Reform, lobbying reform, campaign finance reform, correct bias in the media, and regulate the movement of federal employees between the public and private sectors. The Commission will appoint a People's Judge Advocate, a permanent special prosecutor, to investigate abuses by the President, other government officials, and members of Congress. The Advocate would be empowered to hold government officials to the same legal standards as regular citizens."

By the time Eleanor Pearson finished, the delegates were spellbound by the breadth and depth of the recommendations. Even Luke Harper was stunned by the prospect of this body bringing the powerful federal government to its knees. As Luke panned the delegates, he noticed that some were writing notes, some were simply staring at Eleanor Pearson in awe, while others were smiling and nodding in agreement. Within a few moments, a delegate from New Hampshire rose and began singing the National Anthem. Other delegates joined in, echoing the emotional chorus through the hall. "Then conquer we must, when our cause it is just, And this be our motto: 'In God is our trust.' And the Star-Spangled Banner in triumph shall wave, O'er the land of the free and the home of the brave."

With the final chorus fading through the corridors, Pearson expected the crowd to settle down and accept her charge. Instead, the crowd spontaneously shouted, "USA, USA, USA, USA." Another young delegate grabbed a large American flag from a pedestal and began waving it in front of the packed hall. Pandemonium swept the event as people realized their worst nightmare was finally coming to an end. In spite of the risk, in spite of the violence and coercion, the people were taking their government back from the Washington-centered politicians and special interests who had risen to power through misinformation, pandering, and outside influence. The effort to change America from a "shining light on the hill" to a European-type nanny state had failed. President Elliott's narcissism had blinded him to the real strength and resolve of the American people.

"Ladies and gentlemen, please," Pearson shouted. "Please be seated, folks. Delegates, we need your attention, please!"

The sergeant-at-arms struck the gavel several times to bring the hall to order.

As the energy level ratcheted down, Pearson continued. "Ladies and gentlemen, we have only begun our task here. The most crucial step is for each state delegation to discuss and evaluate our recommendations."

She paused for a drink of water before concluding her charge to the delegates. "Your Drafting Committee asks that you consider every aspect of these historic changes. Sort out any and all questions you have about them. Weigh the political, legal, social, and other ramifications of what we have asked you to consider. Remember while you carry out your deliberations that we are the United States of America, not the Washington Establishment of America."

Staffers spread out in the auditorium to distribute written copies of the Resolutions to the delegates and reporters. Several approached Pearson, Kelley, and Granger to obtain their autographs on the historic document.

Pearson's legs were rubbery as she walked the short distance from the podium to the assembly area behind the stage. Tim Kelley took her arm to steady her.

"Superb, Eleanor," he said. "How does it feel to walk in John Adams's footsteps?"

"It feels like forging history is darned hard work, and a little scary to boot," she said. "I was worried about the long pause at the end."

"That New Hampshire delegate seemed to know exactly how to seal the deal," Kelley said.

"Wasn't that great?" Pearson asked. "You didn't plant him, did you?"

Kelley smiled. "No. I just hope Luke Harper's crew recorded it."

"I agree," she said. "Why don't you ask him? He's standing right below the podium."

As Kelley walked up to Luke, Granger approached Pearson with his hand out and a smile of satisfaction on his face. "You sure have the gift, Eleanor. I've never seen the President charm a crowd the way you just did."

"I wouldn't be much of a public relations person if I couldn't sell an idea," she said.

"It was more than an idea," Granger said. "You just sold the greatest shift in public policy since the New Deal."

"I wouldn't pop the Champagne cork yet," she said. "We still have the formality of a vote on Friday."

Just below the stage, Luke watched Mickey fiddle with his equipment. "Please tell me you got all of that," Luke said. "Some moments demand a larger audience, and this is one of them."

"I got it all, including that little happy dance by the delegate with the flag. I'm not sure how the sound will come out, though. The decibels were so high my meter pegged through the entire chorus."

"That's okay," Luke said. "As long as our viewers get a sense of the enthusiasm."

"I don't really understand a lot of this stuff," Mickey said, "but I don't think I'd want to be in the President's shoes right now."

CHAPTER 27

—

Mitch Brady sat motionless except for his finger's errant tapping on the coffee table.

The mood in the reception room just off the Oval Office was dampened by Luke Harper's coverage of the Convention's progress. Brady let out an "Oh, damn," as Luke listed each proposed reform.

Elliott strolled in and joined Brady on the couch. He watched with his arms crossed and his jaw set in opposition to what he was hearing. "Look at that bunch," he sneered. "They're all angry old white people."

Brady nodded his head, even though he knew better. Just five minutes before, TNN had reported that the delegates represented roughly the same demographic, age, and racial makeup as the country.

"What's the story on this Eleanor Pearson, Mitch?" Elliott asked. "I don't recall any dealings with her."

"Remember the day you campaigned in Phoenix?" Brady asked. "Pearson was on TV discussing a new Hispanic jobs program in fluent Spanish. We had to bus students from the University and members of the local unions to fill the hall."

The President looked up as if he were drawing from a long-lost memory. "Oh, I recall. That was the day the student challenged me on my failure to implement immigration reform."

Mitch laid his pencil on the table. "That girl was on the student council at a local university. She eventually endorsed Governor Pearson and worked on her campaign. When our state chairman asked her why she supported Pearson, she said she liked Pearson's policies more than ours."

"I didn't expect such a strong opposition state to go our way," Elliott said.

"Sorry, Mr. President," Brady said. "But I think we need to face some things we've been sidestepping."

The President punched the mute button and slid back in the couch. "If you have something to say, Mitch, spit it out."

Brady stood facing Elliott with his hands in his pockets. His pained expression provided some warning of what he had to say. "I'm certain there are major changes coming, and they're not what we campaigned for."

"Our agenda has never been easy," the President said. "But we still have some fight left."

Brady's concern edged him forward. "The impeachment proceedings are picking up bipartisan support in the House, and the Convention is going to make changes to the Constitution that might remove your immunity from prosecution."

The President remained combative. "There's no law against being too progressive for the flat earth crowd."

Brady issued the ultimate reality check. "No, sir. But there's the problem with Executive Order 14900. I warned Massey to pick reliable people, but instead he picked Walker." Mitch wasn't prepared for Elliott's response.

"There is no way they can prove I agreed with DHS's interpretation of that executive order," Elliott said.

Brady's warning signals blared since he was the only one in position to speak for the President. "You know Truman's most famous quote?" Brady asked.

"That baloney about 'The buck stops here?'" Elliott scoffed.

"Yes, sir." Brady said.

"I'm not taking the rap for everything that goes wrong in the federal government!" Elliott said.

Brady shuddered to think the President might deflect blame to his subordinates. "That's what being the top dog means, Mr. President," he said. "A demand for accountability is brewing, and in the real world heads roll when things go terribly wrong."

"People in that world don't face the same level of responsibility I do," Elliott said. "As large as the government is, there are going to be mistakes, plain and simple."

Brady was appalled by the President's cowardice.

Elliott stood and turned his back to Brady. "I shouldn't bear the blame for my cabinet members' mistakes."

"Our public might disagree," Brady said. "The proceeding we just watched doesn't represent some radical fringe that's out of touch with the public. It *is* the public. I get an earful every day from staunch supporters who've lost confidence in our leadership. Worst of all, Mr. President, the military and the intelligence community are hunkered down in anticipation of your removal from office."

Elliott worried that his Chief of Staff might be weakening. "We'll replace them with team players we can count on," he said.

"No one wants to be part of an administration in crisis, sir." *The President really doesn't understand why the cabinet members are so concerned,* he thought.

Elliott's face lit up with an idea. "What if we go on the offensive with a series of speeches across the country?"

"I don't think it will make any difference," Brady said. "I'm afraid we're beyond the tipping point."

"You make it sound like our demise is imminent, Mitch," Elliott said.

"Sorry, Mr. President. I'm simply delivering the facts, however thorny. I have to tell you the truth when no one else will."

"I prefer ideas on how to deal with all of this," Elliott countered.

"As unpalatable as it sounds, sir, I think we need to prepare for the unthinkable. If we cooperate with both the House and the Convention, maybe they'll cut us some slack out of respect for your office."

"Before we do anything, I need to discuss this with a couple of other people," Elliott said.

Brady sighed. "That's fine, sir, because my magic hat is fresh out of lucky rabbits."

"I'll get back to you by the end of tomorrow, Mitch, and we can decide how to proceed."

"Have you seen enough TV?" Brady asked.

"Enough for a lifetime," the President said, pitching the remote on the couch. The walk up the stairs to his residence was brutally lonely.

CHAPTER 28

—

Attorney General Oliver sat at home enjoying popcorn and some rare TV time with his wife. Both enjoyed classic movies like tonight's choice, *Casablanca*. Mrs. Oliver cringed when the phone rang. "Please don't let them tie you up all night, Dennis."

With a labored smile he handed her the popcorn bowl. Then, recognizing the President's number on caller ID, he answered, "Good evening, Mr. President."

"Hello, Dennis. Sorry for calling so late. How are you and Doris tonight?"

"We were just enjoying an old movie on TV," Oliver said. "When we first turned it on, we were greeted with Luke Harper's latest report. It looks like a worst-case scenario from the Convention."

"That's why I'm calling, Dennis," Elliott said. "I need your assessment and some advice on how to proceed."

"I can tell you straight up, Mr. President, Oliver said. "Between the Convention, the impeachment proceedings, and the new United Nations human rights investigation, we are going to be totally consumed defending ourselves."

Doris sat patiently on the couch with the movie on pause, motioning for him to be brief.

"How serious is the United Nations witch hunt?" Elliott asked.

"They're convinced serious violations occurred in your administration, or they wouldn't be investigating."

Elliott winced from his choice of words. "Isn't this *our* administration?" he asked.

"Do you remember what Harry—?"

Elliott interrupted. "I don't get it. When I first got into politics, Harry Truman was just a Missouri hayseed. Now all of a sudden, he's more quotable than Ronald Reagan."

"Truman was a president of the common man," Oliver said. "He knew what the people were thinking, and he expressed it in some of his populist quotes. The one that applies here is relevant because people want you to be held accountable."

"I am accountable at the ballot box," Elliott insisted. "And during two elections I received strong endorsements."

"I believe those endorsements will be challenged, Mr. President," Oliver said.

"Could you have breakfast with me in the morning, so we can discuss this further?" Elliott asked. "I'm too tired and frustrated tonight. And you need to get back to Doris."

"I'll be there, but I need to give you fair warning," Oliver said. "She's on my back to resign and get as far away from all of this as possible." He glanced at his wife who flashed him a wide smile.

The President sidestepped the warning. "There'll be hot coffee for you at seven-thirty."

"See you then, sir."

"Good night, Dennis."

The next morning, Attorney General Oliver prepared for his dreaded meeting with the President. For several weeks he had been suffering in silence over his complicity in the administration's failures. During the forty-five-minute drive from his upscale home in Adams Morgan to the White House, he wracked his brain for new ideas to salvage the Elliott presidency. A splitting headache signaled his inability to overcome the ugly truth.

He greeted the President's personal secretary in the reception area just outside the Oval Office. "Good morning, Mary. Do you have a couple of aspirins, by chance?"

She rummaged through her desk drawer, then handed him a small sealed packet. "I'm worried," she said. "So many people have turned against the President."

"I know," he mumbled while reading the aspirin label. "Keep in mind we've stepped on a few toes to force change. Some of those toes belonged to powerful people who don't want progressive government."

She lacked her usual cheery demeanor. "But, Mr. Oliver, even our staunchest allies are abandoning him."

"You've heard the old saying, 'you can't be all things to all people,'" he said. "In retrospect, we overcommitted, and when we couldn't deliver, disappointment turned to opposition. Washington is all about *what have you done for me lately?*"

"It's sad to see him look so defeated," she said. "We're all hearing scary rumors about impeachment and criminal indictments. Is any of that possible?"

Oliver resorted to his usual political correctness. "I'm afraid we made some tactical mistakes that could pose problems for us."

"You mean like targeting innocent citizens for assassination?" she asked bluntly.

Oliver looked stunned. "Is that one of the rumors you're hearing, Mary?"

"It's one of the things Luke Harper reported from the Convention last night," she said.

"I'm afraid a trusted DHS operative threw the President under the bus on that one," he said.

"You can go on in now, Mr. Oliver. He's ready for you."

"Good morning, sir," Oliver said, entering the President's dining room.

"Hi, Dennis. How would you like your coffee this morning?" Elliott asked, feigning high spirits.

"Strong and clairvoyant," Oliver said. "I was up most of the night trying to figure out how I could give you sound advice this morning."

"From the look of your eyes, you came up short."

"That's about it," he said. "Does Mitch have any ideas?" he asked while washing Mary's aspirins down with steaming coffee.

Elliott smirked. "He tells me his magic hat is all out of lucky rabbits."

"That's bad news," Oliver said. "According to scuttlebutt, he's been polling the Cabinet and staff. I understand the Joint Chiefs told him to count them out of any further military options. That civil trial in Georgia really spooked them. Facing a hostile soldier toting a rocket-propelled grenade goes with the territory, but they don't want any part of a judge who can put them away in a dingy prison."

"We've been through a lot together, Dennis," Elliott said. "I really need your help here."

Oliver grasped the opportunity to keep his promise to his wife. "Sorry, sir. I'm going to withhold any advice, since I won't be here to help you follow it."

Elliott's stomach jumped into his throat. "You can't bail on me now."

"I don't have a choice, sir. My family means more to me than anything in this world. As you know, Doris suffers from erratic beating of the heart, atrial fibrillation they labeled it. When a friend called to tell her what might come out of the Convention, she went into AFIB and was in the hospital for three days. The doctor said she was a few heartbeats away from a debilitating stroke."

"Sorry, Dennis. Is there anything I can do to help?"

"There is, Mr. President. You can accept my resignation and allow me to get Doris out of this Washington pressure cooker."

"I don't see how I can do that, since you were a party to our decision making."

Sensing the same deflection of responsibility Brady had feared, Oliver resorted to some deflection of his own. "I realize that, sir. But you also had access to the White House counsel as well as other advisors. Besides, you taught constitutional law and should know the legal issues as well as I do."

"That's baloney, Dennis, and you know it," Elliott sneered. "I've never practiced law in my life. I've always been in politics."

"Sorry, sir, but you are the president, so you are ultimately responsible for your administration."

"You mean like *the buck stops here*?" Elliott asked with sarcasm.

"Exactly," Oliver said. He made a concerted effort to reinforce his point to the President. "No one forced you to follow the advice you were given. In most cases you were looking for cover for a position you had already chosen. You made that perfectly clear to all of us."

"That's ancient history, Dennis. Things are going to get real testy around here in short order, and I need your help fighting off the wolves."

"If I were a betting man, sir, I would put my money on the wolves," Oliver said. "You boasted that you were going to fundamentally change this nation. What you failed to recognize is the vast majority believe the country's underlying principles are what make it great."

Uneasy about rebuking the President, Oliver proceeded with the painful truth. "You promised to bring people together during your campaigns, then you demonized Wall Street, insurance companies, big banks, and others. People viewed your identity politics as hypocrisy. When TNN exposed various scandals, people began questioning your honesty and leadership."

"I thought you were on our side!" Elliott snapped.

"One hundred percent, sir. That's why I feel compelled to tell you the truth, no matter how much it stings."

"It probably won't surprise you to hear that Mitch said exactly the same things last night."

"I'm happy other advisers are finally talking straight to you," Oliver said. "But I fear it's too late."

"One more thing before I go, Mr. President. A friend who happens to be a magazine columnist told me the Convention is going to set up a Statutory and Regulatory Review Commission. That commission is going to appoint a guy named Jack Tanner to head up a permanent special prosecutor's office. If he uncovers your orders to DHS, he'll surely indict you."

"Can they do that?" Elliott asked.

"They can, and they will," Oliver said. "This guy Tanner makes a junk-yard dog look like a sleeping gerbil. As an independent prosecutor, he's a nightmare. And that, Mr. President, is another reason my eyes are so blood-shot this morning. If the Articles of Resolution pass at the Convention, Tanner will have plenty of authority, plus enough evidence, to indict all of us. With that unfortunate assessment, I thank you for breakfast, I thank you for the trust you placed in me, and I bid you farewell and good luck."

"Are you really going to walk away, just like that?" Elliott asked.

"Just like that, sir. If I were in your shoes, I would begin preparing for a cataclysmic firestorm. And, by the way, you're going to need a much better lawyer than I am. Goodbye, Mr. President."

As the attorney general hurried out, Elliott felt a resurgence of the betrayal he suffered as a child. A few years after his father had been killed, his mother moved away, leaving him to be raised by his mother's brother in a border town in Mexico. His childhood abandonment created a void no amount of power or prestige could fill.

Mitch Brady opened the door leading from the Oval Office. The sight of President Elliott seated alone mumbling to himself drew him in. "Do you mind if I join you for coffee, sir?"

"Please do, Mitch," Elliott said. "You need to restrain me from slitting my wrists with a butter knife."

"Beg your pardon, sir?" Mitch asked with alarm.

Elliott leaned back with his fingers intertwined behind his head. "Oliver just resigned after telling me that a special prosecutor named Jack Tanner wants my head in a basket."

"I've been checking up on him," Brady said. "From everything I've learned, he's as smart and as hard driving as they come."

"I was hoping to hear that he's a bumbling hack," Elliott said.

For the first time, Brady saw desperation in a man who had previously seemed infallible. With a sip of coffee and a surge of determination, the President pulled himself out of his personal pity party. "While you're negotiating immunity with Granger, and Dennis is jumping ship, I have a country to run."

"We need to fix our messaging, Mr. President," Brady said. "The discord being spread by some of our spokespersons is not helping with either the media or the public."

"Can't we just require everyone to use our talking points?"

Brady gave the President a reassuring nod. "We've already ordered radio silence within the government and the White House. Most of the ill will is being generated by outside organizations that have their own agendas."

"All of that political stuff is interesting, Mitch, but I'm not running again. Could we focus on how to survive the rest of my term?"

Driven by self-preservation, Brady said, "I've talked to dozens of our people who believe some contrition on your part is in order. A handful of cabinet members think you should sit down with Granger and Dobbins to reason with them."

Elliott shook his head in disbelief. "What do our well-intentioned but naive conciliators recommend I say to people who happen to be on an assassination list that I approved? Granger and Dobbins probably confiscated a copy of Executive Order 14900 from Walker's safe. We're in a quagmire, and the harder we paddle, the deeper we sink. I still can't fathom how we ended up here when we had everything going for us." He kicked his trash can then slumped in his desk chair.

Brady said. "Dennis shared his thoughts with me after he resigned, then suggested I hire the best criminal lawyer I can find."

Elliott glared from behind his desk. "By the way, Mitch, we don't do contrition, we do progressive reform."

"That slogan worked in the campaign, Mr. President, but it didn't work running the government."

CHAPTER 29

—

Percy Leach worked for the British Foreign Ministry before becoming chief investigator for the International Criminal Court of the United Nations. With a PhD in forensic science from Cambridge and six years of experience in the forensic lab at New Scotland Yard, he was eminently qualified. His reputation as a shrewd investigative forensic scientist earned him the most dangerous assignments in Sudan, Somalia, and Syria.

With the physique of an athlete and an appetite for custom-made suits, he resembled a polished diplomat more than a detective. His upcoming assignment would serve as the pinnacle of his long, distinguished career.

Leach sat hunched over his computer to finalize a report on his most recent investigation. When his concentration was broken by the muted ring of his desk phone, he lifted the receiver, clamping it between his shoulder and chin. "Leach here," he answered in a monotone.

"Mr. Sukarno would like to see you right away, Mr. Leach," the secretary said.

"I'll be right up," he replied.

A call from the Secretary General's office meant that another extraordinary case was coming his way. He cradled the receiver then saved the draft on his computer. Sliding back in his chair for a moment, he mentally prepared himself for another grueling assignment. *Which exotic location am I off to now?* he wondered. *Hot and cold running water, recognizable food, and sanitary bathroom facilities would be nice for a change.* Anticipating another third-world assignment, he reached into his desk drawer for his shot record. A quick review showed he was good to go anywhere except jungle locations with dengue fever. A quick stop at the UN dispensary for that inoculation would clear him to travel anywhere. He couldn't remember if dengue fever was the shot that burned on the way in and made his arm sore for a week. That would explain why he hadn't kept it current.

The elevator dinged on the top floor where he was greeted by Secretary

General Yandi Sukarno's secretary, a middle-aged woman from Indonesia. "Thanks for coming up so quickly, Mr. Leach. I know he's anxious to see you. Go on in."

"Good morning, Percy," Sukarno said.

"Good morning, sir," Leach replied with anticipation. He dreaded another high-profile case from the Secretary General.

Sukarno's Indonesian features were more strained than usual as he prepared Leach for his next assignment. "I realize you just returned from a strenuous investigation, Percy, but I have a priority request that must be addressed. The High Commissioner for Human Rights was horrified by the attack on Madison, Georgia and reports of President Elliott's so-called hit list. She has submitted an urgent request that you be assigned to investigate those violations."

"It's nice to be needed, sir, but I haven't had a good night's sleep in weeks," Leach said.

"I realize that, and I am truly sorry, but this could be the most consequential investigation we will ever do," Sukarno said. "That's why we need the best, and that's you."

A surge of adrenaline temporarily blocked Leach's exhaustion.

"As usual, you are authorized whatever resources you need, including international subpoena powers," Sukarno said. "INTERPOL has pledged their full cooperation. And on a personal note, you are reminded of the sensitivity of the case as well as the extraordinary danger. Concern is mounting in diplomatic circles that President Elliott is a tyrant masquerading as a polished world leader. I know you're up for retirement in a few years and I don't want anything to get in the way of that."

"Four years, two months, and eight days, in case you want to mark your calendar," Leach said, wondering if he would make it until then.

Sukarno chuckled, despite the gravity of this new assignment.

Both men knew it was no joke. Even though Leach routinely confronted dictators, warlords, and corrupt government officials, none wielded the clandestine capabilities of a United States president. True to his reputation, he accepted the assignment and bid the Secretary General farewell.

Choosing to stalk his prey near its lair, Leach booked the next flight to Washington, DC. After checking into his room at the Excelsior, he settled in the lounge with a latte and blueberry scone. He had decided during his flight to Washington that this investigation called for the special assistance of Manny Romano, by far the best freelance investigator he knew. He dialed Romano's private number. "Hello, Manny, Leach here. Are you in-country?"

"Hi there, Governor. Just got back from Vienna yesterday. They still serve your favorite dish at the Bavaria Grande, by the way."

Romano routinely addressed Leach as 'Governor,' partly out of respect, but more to poke fun at Leach's British persona. On their first assignment together, they were like day and night. Leach was subdued and methodical, while Romano was spontaneous and emotional. When Romano got overly excited, Leach would say to him in typical British style, "Calm down, Mate, and carry on."

Soon, they developed a rhythm that was complementary and effective. A healthy chemistry developed as Leach ribbed Romano over his tendency to fly off the handle while Romano questioned how Leach could function in such a subdued state.

"We've got an important job if you're available," Leach said.

"For you, Governor, I'm always available. What's the job?"

"Are you holding anything? I don't want you to fly off the handle and spill something," Leach said.

"Lay it on me," Romano said, "I'm braced."

"We've been assigned to investigate human rights abuses by the Elliott administration," Leach said.

A long pause ensued. "Are you kidding?" Romano gasped, using one of the phrases he had adopted from his American friends. "This is the World Cup of human rights investigations. I read about the attack on Madison in the *Financial Times* on the flight back to New York."

"You're dead right, Manny," Leach said. "Madison is the epicenter of our investigation. It's about a hundred kilometers east of Atlanta. I'd like you to fly there to depose General Martinez and Governor Spivey. Their dossiers are being sent to you. Follow your formidable Italian nose to sniff out the facts. By the way, I can offer your usual fee plus expenses and hazardous duty pay, if that's acceptable."

"I can be in Atlanta in a couple of days," Romano said.

"Excellent," Leach replied. "I've already deposited a generous advance into your account."

Romano chuckled. "You wouldn't take me for granted, would you, Governor?"

"Wouldn't think of it," Leach said. "But I know how you can't resist a good hunt."

"Speaking of hunting, I picked up on your slippery reference to hazardous duty pay," Romano said.

"That was the Secretary General's idea based on President Elliott's hostility toward his own countrymen," Leach explained. "You can imagine how he'll react when he learns a couple of blokes from the United Nations are investigating him. Feel free to carry your popgun in case you end up down some dark alley."

"I'll have you know a Beretta is not a popgun. It's a finely designed and constructed firearm. It's a far sight better than that prissy Walther they issued you at the Ministry."

"Here we go again," Leach lamented. "I apologize, Manny."

"No problem," Romano said. "We can't all be Italian."

"I have a custom-tailored Italian suit, if that counts for anything?"

Romano tried to appease his friend. "You could be mistaken for an Italian in that suit as long as you don't say anything. By the way, I know we've just begun this case, but who do you think the keys are at this point?"

"That's something I've been wondering since I left the office," Leach said. "The local government people in Georgia and Texas are the ones who dug up the most damaging information from officials they captured in the field. Then there's this guy Jack Tanner who's been appointed to conduct his own investigation into criminal behavior."

"Perhaps we can join forces with him at the appropriate time," Romano said.

"I'm certain some ringers will fall out of the sky as soon as they feel threatened by our snooping," Leach said. "The administration has already suffered a number of what they call whistleblowers. I'm hoping someone will provide important clues to our investigation. Good luck Manny. Stay on your toes."

"Same to you, Governor."

Leach settled into his wing-backed chair, stowed his phone, and reached for his latte. Out of the corner of his eye he caught someone walking toward him toting a microphone.

"Excuse me, Mr. Leach. My name is Luke Harper. I have some

questions about your work here."

"Hello, Mr. Harper. Nice to meet a real journalist for a change, but I don't do interviews about my work, especially in the midst of an investigation."

True to form, Luke ignored the brushoff and continued his questioning. "So it's true, you're investigating the incidents in Madison and Austin on behalf of the United Nations?"

"You'll need to take that up with either the Secretary General's Office or the High Commissioner for Human Rights."

"I've already contacted both offices, and they would only confirm that you work for them. They wouldn't elaborate."

"I can tell from your previous work that you get it, to use an American expression. Surely you appreciate the need for prudence when one is attempting to uncover information that others want to conceal."

"Yes, sir. I think you just described what I'm experiencing at this very moment. I was hoping we could join forces in our quest for the truth."

"I'm sorry, Chap, but my rules are not negotiable. You will know what I know when my final report is released. In the meantime, anything I might say is just speculation or hearsay, not what you would call prime material for a story of such importance."

"I see your point, Mr. Leach. Here's my card. Feel free to call if I can assist you in any way."

"I appreciate your determination," Leach said, placing the card in his pocket. "You might make a fine detective if this reporter gig doesn't work out."

"Appreciate the compliment," Luke said. "I'm sure we'll meet again."

"No doubt, Mr. Harper. Good day."

CHAPTER 30

—

Determined to take on his adversaries, President Elliott instructed his secretary to ring Yandi Sukarno, Secretary General of the United Nations. The overly confident President assumed that generous financial support for the UN from the U.S. would give him some leverage. Once again, he was about to confront his dwindling influence.

"Sukarno is on your line," the secretary said.

"Hello, sir. How are you this morning?" Elliott asked.

"I'm fine, Mr. President. I assume you are calling about our investigation."

"That's exactly why I'm calling. What makes you think you have the right to investigate my administration?"

"Because your predecessors agreed to it when they signed the United Nations membership agreement," Sukarno said. "Not only is it our right, it is our sworn duty."

"This is no third-world republic you're dealing with," Elliott sneered. "We have a festering insurrection in the works, and I have the responsibility to protect the United States against domestic terrorists as well as foreign ones."

Sukarno resented the negative inference to developing countries since he came from one. "Believe me, I understand that responsibility, but I do not see what that has to do with murdering innocent civilians."

"We were in the midst of a pitched battle against the insurrectionists. Unfortunately my subordinates inflicted some collateral damage."

Sukarno knew the reference to collateral damage was used freely by murderous tyrants. "Maybe that's the way you see the death of those thirty civilians, but to the rest of the civilized world and the Human Rights Division of the UN, it's a crime against humanity. A government's execution of innocent civilians in your country is no more justifiable than the same insane act in the Sudan, in Syria, or in Iraq."

"Excuse me, sir," Elliott said. "Are you implying people in my administration are insane?"

Sukarno's tone became stern. "Please be clear, Mr. President. Our investigations are not based on implication. We have reason to believe, based on recent news reports, that you personally authorized the use of deadly force against political opponents. Bona fide documents exist that prove your motives and your personal approval of such heinous acts. This body is bound by its Charter to investigate, expose, and do what we can to prevent such inhumane acts."

"That sounds like a threat," Elliott said.

"The International Criminal Court was established to protect human rights from tyrants who occasionally rise to power. That's no threat. That's reality."

The Secretary General paused to give Elliott a chance to respond.

The prospect of charges by the International War Tribunal momentarily paralyzed the President.

Sukarno picked up the slack. "I regret to say this, but it is becoming clearer to the American public as well as the international community that there is something dreadfully wrong with your approach to government. We all need a United States that is stable, strong, and credible to provide balance and order in an otherwise disorderly world."

"What I need, Mr. Secretary General, is for people to mind their own business and let me do my job," Elliott said.

"That's the problem, Mr. President," Sukarno said. "You don't seem to be clear on the best way to do your job. Be clear on this. The United Nations will carry out its responsibility. And if any harm comes to our investigators or anyone else associated with the investigation, our members will hold you personally responsible. Goodbye, sir!"

Elliott dropped the phone and slumped in his desk chair with his head in his hands. For the first time, he realized that his job was in jeopardy, and he might be held criminally liable for his actions. CIA video of the grisly execution of Saddam Hussein had terrified him. There was absolutely nothing he feared more than death by hanging.

When Brady entered the Oval Office, the President appeared shaken. "I take it your call to Sukarno didn't go well."

"That's an understatement," Elliott said. "I don't see any way to stop their investigation short of nuking the United Nations."

Brady recoiled. "I would advise you to refrain from making comments like that, sir. It's time to exercise caution in everything we do and say. With so many investigations going on we need to assume the walls have eyes and ears. The CIA and FBI notified me an hour ago that they have launched their own investigations into the raids in Madison and Austin."

Elliott growled. "How can they do that without my approval?"

"When people feel threatened, they revert to the rule book to make sure they can defend themselves and their organizations," Brady said. "Now that some of our cabinet appointees are gone, the bureaucrats are running things. They are naturally risk averse, and most have built careers based on an age-old Washington adage, 'Cover your backside.'"

"Who is the Acting Attorney General?" Elliott asked.

"We temporarily appointed an Assistant AG who was acceptable to the Speaker and the Majority Leader," Brady said.

Elliott's eyes flashed with anger. "Are we allowing opposition leaders in Congress to staff our administration now?"

"We need all of the support we can get, Mr. President. There is no need to add fuel to flames that are already consuming us."

"I see your point, but I still don't like it."

"If it makes you feel any better, sir, he's totally apolitical," Brady said. "He probably won't help us, but he won't hurt us either."

"Do you have anything else for me?" Elliott asked.

"I learned this morning that the General Accountability Office has an army of accountants camped out at DHS headquarters," Brady said. "They're reviewing the transfer of funds from border control and port inspections to special ops and the construction of FEMA detention camps. White House counsel tells me intentional misappropriation of funds is an impeachable offense."

Elliott glanced at the ceiling as if looking for divine intervention. "Great. When is this onslaught going to end, Mitch?" Under growing pressure, the rock of the administration was cracking.

"I don't expect any relief until these investigations lead somewhere," Brady said. "To be brutally honest, Mr. President, I can't imagine a favorable outcome from any of them."

Brady's cold dose of reality temporarily averted Elliott's emotional meltdown. "How would you rank the risk from each threat?" he asked.

"I'd say the Convention has the most clout at this point. It's likely to push Tanner to indict us. I would say impeachment is less risky only because

Congress has such low credibility and can barely get out of its own way."

Elliott ignored his queasy stomach and made a circular motion for Brady to continue.

"One caveat, sir, would be this new investigation by the General Accountability Office. They have the highest credibility of any federal organization. If they prove we intentionally misappropriated funds at DHS, it could be the fatal blow."

Despite Elliott's emotional melt-down, Brady mentioned one more warning. "The United Nations investigation is truly a wild card," he said. "To my understanding, we've never been investigated since joining. According to my information, Percy Leach is a British version of Jack Tanner. He's a junkyard dog with the demeanor of a high-level diplomat. Like the GAO, his reputation is beyond reproach, and his findings could go to the International Criminal Court for the worst of all outcomes."

The President hesitated briefly, then exploded. "Is there any way to stop these witch hunts?" His stomach was now turning flip flops.

"One thing I learned a long time ago, and unfortunately forgot for a while," Brady said, "is when you find yourself in a deep hole, the first thing you do is stop digging. We are in such a deep hole, the walls are caving in around us."

"Maybe you can be more direct, Mitch," Elliott pleaded.

"You need to chill out, Mr. President," Brady said. "Put your agenda aside and take your medicine."

"You're saying I should give up?" Elliott asked.

"Not it at all," Brady said. "I'm saying you need to face certain realities. Our political support has dissipated. Our momentum for major reform is dead. We're facing universal opposition for our actions in Madison and Austin. And DHS's interpretation of Executive Order 14900 is indefensible."

Brady's pessimistic assessment rocked the previously impervious President, but he wasn't finished. "Perhaps the most consequential question is whether we will be charged with felony murder in the U.S. or at the International Criminal Court. Do you understand what I'm saying, Mr. President?"

"It sounds like this nightmare pertains to someone else," Elliott said.

"Well, sir, you need to discard those rose-colored glasses and get prepared for the perfect storm," Brady warned. "If nothing else, think of your family, especially your kids."

Elliott's silence was unnerving.

Brady added, "I called the attorneys who represented former President Lockhart during his impeachment. They're the best in the country and they're willing to represent you. I recommend you take them up on their offer sooner rather than later."

Elliott resorted to sarcasm, sprinkled with reality. "Thanks for your rosy assessment, Mitch. Clear the decks for the rest of the day so I can talk to my family."

CHAPTER 31

—

Like a marathon runner facing the last brutal hill before the finish line, Elliott labored up the staircase to the First Family's residence. Laboring with each step, he approached his most ardent and most vulnerable allies. The prospect of admitting his role in the deaths of children the same age as his daughters sent spasms through his insides. Guilt, shame, and cowardice chipped away until his will faltered.

"I really can't do this tonight," he mumbled while retreating downstairs to seek refuge in the Oval Office. *There must be some way to escape this nightmare,* he thought, as he collapsed into his desk chair. He retrieved a bottle of thirty-year-old Scotch, a gift from one of his largest campaign contributors, from his bottom desk drawer. While relishing a sip of single malt, he worried about how his wife would react to the truth. *What is the truth?* He really didn't know anymore.

Bolstered by scotch-induced courage, he trudged up the staircase to face Kianna. Through the dimly-lit bedroom, he could see her graceful outline on the piano bench in their cozy sitting area. She was surrounded by family photos, fresh cut flowers, and their girls' play things, cherished possessions that made this historic place a home. His silhouette cast a distorted shadow over the piano as he stood in the doorway. His confession would test their relationship like a broken vow.

Kianna gazed at her husband cowering in the doorway. She lost track of how much wine she had consumed to soften her anger, but it wasn't enough. Her petite body trembled from the storm of emotions churning within. She tilted her head, bringing her deep penetrating eyes in line with his. "I want to hear it all, Jerome," she said. "And I want to hear it now."

The figure in the doorway moved closer, then gently pulled her to her feet. He held her tightly in an attempt to soothe her. "Now, now, Kianna. I'll explain everything."

They nestled on the piano bench like a duet performing a musical tragedy. Kianna listened intently while Jerome recited the points outlined earlier by Brady and Oliver.

Through her wine-enhanced paranoia, she listened to her husband's convoluted excuses. When he characterized his opposition as politically and racially motivated, she lashed out with uncharacteristic fury. "What does politics have to do with the murder of innocent children?"

She had called Jerome out on one of two indefensible mistakes. Her unvarnished question was a harbinger of more to come. She blasted him with the most inconceivable question of all. "How would you feel if another president murdered our girls?" She pierced his heart as only a mother and wife can do, forcing him to face his own inhumanity.

The light in his eyes dimmed, then died. "How could you ask that, Kianna?"

"It's a reasonable question, Jerome," she said. "How could you disregard the safety of those innocent children you swore to protect? Then you authorized deadly force against your political opponents. What were you thinking?"

She wept in despair, crushed by her husband's wanton disregard for innocent children. She raised her head, glaring with empty eyes. "I now understand why the public is so outraged."

The rebuke from his most ardent supporter made Jerome realize that he had poisoned everything. Daniel's chastisement reopened deep wounds from his childhood. Defeated and demoralized, he rose, kissed his wife on the cheek, and whispered, "I'm sorry." He retreated to the loneliness of their bedroom, hoping to put sleep between himself and his self-induced misery.

CHAPTER 32

—

Far removed from the crisis engulfing the White House, Manny Romano pursued his investigation with vigor. In accordance with Leach's instructions he obtained depositions from Ted Johnson, Judge Johnson, Prosecutor Stone, and others during his initial visit to Madison. His next step was to obtain case records from the prosecution of Hank Applegate to corroborate his depositions. The Morgan County Clerk of Court let him know, in no uncertain terms, that he was not entitled to court documents under their strict privacy rules.

"We can't let any Tom, Dick, or Harry with a good cause come in here and rifle through our records," she said.

"Excuse me, but I am hardly any Tom, Dick, or Harry. I'm a commissioned officer of the United Nations on a sanctioned investigation. I can obtain an international subpoena if that would make you feel better. I can hardly do my job without essential evidence."

"Sorry, Mr. Romano," she said. "I don't make the rules, I just follow them. You need clearance from the sheriff, the Morgan County prosecutor, the Superior Court, or a recognized state authority to get access to my documents." Her sleepy eyes showed no sympathy.

"Which official of those you just named carries the most clout?" he asked.

"Depends on your point of view," she said. "Around here we consider the sheriff to have the most clout since he's the highest elected official in the county, plus he has a badge and a gun."

"I have a badge and a gun, but it doesn't seem to give me any clout at all," Romano replied.

"If that's so, I hope you checked them in the security screening area," she warned. "It's against the law to carry a firearm in this courthouse. How would it look if a commissioned officer of the United Nations got thrown in jail during the course of a sanctioned investigation?" she mocked. With an officious smirk, she pointed to a large graphic sign showing a circle with a line through it overlapping a firearm.

Romano tried in vain to appease the stubborn clerk. "I also have a permit sanctioned by the United States government to carry my firearm."

"I understand how people like to feel special," she said. "But even our FBI agents have to check their firearms. The only exceptions are local law enforcement officers who are testifying on a case, and bailiffs who are required to be armed while on duty."

Accepting the heavy-handed ruling, Romano backed off. "In that case, you'll have to excuse me, Madam."

Backing slowly down the hallway, he approached a guard near the security checkpoint. "Pardon me," he said. "I didn't know I'm supposed to check my firearm. When I showed my credentials, they waved me on through."

"And why are you carrying a firearm in this building?" the guard asked.

He anticipated the question and was already displaying his badge. "As a United Nations investigator, I carry out dangerous assignments where self-defense is essential," he said.

"You're a long way from New York," the guard said. "What's the nature of your business here?"

"I'm investigating the massacre of innocent civilians by your federal government," he explained.

The inquisitive guard yelled to another uniformed officer sitting at a desk off to the side. "Hey Cap, can you come over here a minute?"

Captain Anderson walked up, eyeing the Beretta on the counter. "What's up?"

"This is Mr. Manny Romano," the guard said. "According to his I.D., he's a special investigator for the United Nations in New York City. He's here to investigate the civilian deaths during the attack."

"Please excuse our caution, Mr. Romano," Anderson said. "As far as I know, we've never received such a distinguished visitor before. It falls outside our security protocol."

"I've never been asked to check my firearm during the course of an official investigation before," Manny said. "That falls outside my protocol, too."

Anderson flashed the other guard a sheepish grin. "I think we can overlook our rule in your case," he said. "What can we do for you today?"

Romano relaxed a bit. "Maybe I could buy you a cup of coffee. My story will take a while."

"There's a coffee shop in the basement," Anderson said, motioning toward the stairs.

Romano stowed his Beretta, while hustling to keep up with Anderson's long stride.

Over a cup of coffee that could not be made palatable with any amount of cream or sugar, Romano outlined his investigation to Captain Steve Anderson, head of security for the Morgan County Superior Court.

"I never dreamed the United Nations would investigate an American president," Anderson commented.

"None have been as ruthless as this one," Romano said.

Anderson gazed into the distance as he remembered the horrible scene. "You don't have to tell me. My nephew was critically injured when a shell hit his chocolate shop downtown. He suffered third degree burns and will have some permanent scarring on his neck and hands, not to mention the expected mental and emotional scars. Thank God he's alive."

"Sorry," Romano said. "I consider my investigation to be for your nephew and the relatives of other innocent civilians that were killed or injured."

"Appreciate that," Anderson said. "But you need to understand that we are a country of laws and regulations. Some of the strictest ones are designed to safeguard privacy. Law enforcement officers are trained to deal with them. In this instance, the best way to get case records is through a court order from a judge."

Romano tried his coffee again and spit it back into his cup.

Anderson continued as if he hadn't noticed. "Our local judge, named Johnson, is a tough old bird, but he gets it, and he's a fair man. There's a good chance he'll work with you on your investigation. If you need an intro, just mention my name. He's known me since he caught his son Ted and me lifting firecrackers from his gun cabinet back in the fifth grade."

Romano snickered at the thought of a future law enforcement officer stealing fireworks from a judge. "Thank you, Captain," he said.

"Thank you for the coffee," Anderson said.

Romano hesitated. "About this coffee. Does it always taste like this?"

Anderson let out a hearty laugh. "No, it's usually worse. That's why we call it mud around here."

"A perfect description," Romano said. He laughed as he tossed his full cup in the trash bin.

E arly the next morning, Romano entered the Morgan County Courthouse on his way to see Judge Johnson. As he approached the metal detector, he pulled his Beretta from its holster and extended it butt-first to the guard.

"Do all of your colleagues carry these puny .380s?" the guard asked.

"I'll have you know this is a finely crafted firearm," Romano replied.

"I'll give you that. It's as cute as my missus. We cotton to .40s and .45s around here. It's just plain silly to have to shoot more than once."

Is every American related to John Wayne somehow, Romano wondered good-naturedly as he stowed his Beretta. After clearing the metal detector he noticed Captain Anderson at his desk, chuckling in response to the comical exchange.

As Romano lifted his cup of gourmet coffee, Anderson flashed him a wide grin. "Break a leg, Manny."

The secretary escorted Romano into the judge's chambers where Johnson sat behind his huge desk, his spectacles dangling on his nose. Cluttered with bulging case files, the desk reminded Manny of his own back in New York.

"Don't forget, Judge, you're in court in forty-five minutes," the secretary said before drawing the door behind her.

"Hello, Mr. Romano," Johnson said, peering over his spectacles. "I've been expecting you. Our attorney general has been in touch with your office in New York. He talked to a colleague of yours. Percy Leach was his name, I think."

"Mr. Leach is my partner on this investigation," Romano said.

Johnson twirled to retrieve a sealed envelope from his credenza. "I'm going to grease the skids on your investigation today. This envelope contains a letter from Governor Spivey appointing you as an Adjunct Investigator for the Georgia Bureau of Investigation. It will open all of the necessary doors for you, including full access to official court records." He pitched the envelope across his desk to Romano.

"I'm grateful, Judge," Romano said. "I didn't expect this."

"The people of Madison went through something that no civilized folks should ever experience," Johnson said. "Innocent men, women, and children were murdered by a sanctimonious president in the name of national security. We want the world to know about his heinous crimes and to realize that the Convention in Austin is totally justified. Your investigation and the resulting report will reveal the truth to a skeptical world."

"Please know that all of us at the United Nations are saddened by your community's losses," Romano said. "Your court impressed a lot of people when you took on your federal government."

"My actions didn't take nearly as much courage as the actions of those at the Convention," Johnson said. "While I dealt with a few individuals, they reformed the entire federal government. Now if you'll excuse me, I have a case to prepare for. I assume you'll want to depose me at some point?"

"That's correct Judge," he said. "I need to get some of the other depositions out of the way, then we'll set something up."

"Works for me," Johnson mumbled. "Good day, Mr. Romano, and good luck."

The authentic Italian restaurant just off the square was an unexpected surprise. Romano downed a caprese salad and a helping of linguine marinara. He was humbled when the couple who owned the restaurant told him they were trained chefs from Croatia. *Leach isn't the only one with an overblown appreciation for all things Italian*, he thought!

After the meal, he returned to the clerk's office where he proudly presented his new credentials.

The clerk tried to ignore the overpowering scent of garlic. "This will open doors for you that even the mayor can't enter," she remarked.

"Will it get me a good cup of coffee in the basement café?" he quipped.

"There are some things even the Governor can't do!" she said.

Romano spent the rest of the week obtaining depositions and reviewing the prosecutor's extensive notes on the Applegate case. On the fourth day he was going over depositions in his motel room when he received a call from headquarters.

"Hello Mr. Romano. This is Ingrid in the mail room. You've received a certified package from Mexico, and it's marked urgent. Do you want me to open it?"

Romano's imagination shifted into overdrive. "That won't be necessary, Ingrid," he said. "Please overnight it to me here in Georgia."

"Give me your address and I'll get it in the mail this afternoon," she said.

As Romano reeled off the address, he speculated about the mysterious package. Several news outlets were aggressively reporting on their unprecedented investigation. He recalled Leach's prediction that as the investigation progressed, persons with information would "fall out of the sky." The package proved it was no *Chicken Little* prediction.

CHAPTER 33

—

Romano recorded Ted Johnson's deposition in a conference room at the James Madison Hotel. It read like the script from an action hero movie. As Johnson recounted his hair-raising encounter with the DHS agents, there was an unexpected knock on the door. "Come in," Romano yelled before switching off his digital recorder.

The concierge stuck her head around the slightly opened door. "You have a certified package," she said. "I thought you might want to be interrupted."

"Thank you," he said, handing her a tip as she placed the package on the table. The package bulged under its URGENT markings, drawing immediate attention from Romano. He was reluctant to interrupt Johnson's entertaining deposition, but he knew the package could be crucial to his investigation. "Would you excuse me for a moment, Mr. Johnson?"

"No problem," Johnson said. He pulled out a cigarette and lit up, ignoring the "no smoking" sign.

Romano slipped his trusty Swiss Army knife along one end of the yellow envelope.

Johnson watched Romano scan the cover letter and slowly lean back in his chair. His eyes sparkled with intrigue.

"Is everything all right?" Johnson asked.

"Not quite sure," Romano said. "Would you mind if we took a thirty-minute break?"

"Not at all. I'll step out and get us some coffee," Johnson replied.

"Make mine a cold drink, if you don't mind," Romano said. He walked from the conference room to a private courtyard, where he sat on a stone bench to speed dial Percy Leach.

"Hello, Manny, how—"

"Leach, I have a surprise for you." Romano said.

"I like surprises," Leach answered.

"You are not going to believe what I'm holding," Romano said with excitement.

"Go on, old boy," Leach said. "You have my undivided attention."

"Headquarters just forwarded a package sent from Mexico," Romano said. "According to the cover letter, it's from a man named Victor Lopez who claims to be President Elliott's biological uncle. He says he raised Elliott until he became a teenager. There are all kinds of documents and photographs related to Elliott's family history."

Leach breathed heavily into the phone. "Anything confirming that Elliott was born in Mexico?" he asked.

"Not so far, but I haven't gone through most of the documents," Romano said. "Some seem to be personal letters are between Jerome Elliott and his mother. Others are between Elliott and a student at the University of Havana named Raoul Suarez. I can't tell how important they are, but I'm guessing there are some clues here." There was a long pause. "Are you still there, Governor?"

"Sorry, Manny," Leach said. "Just thinking. I realize it's already late, but wrap up whatever you're doing and book the next available flight back to New York. By the time you drive to Atlanta you'll have to book a red eye. Make copies of all the documents and put them in a rental locker at the airport. Bring the originals with you."

"I'll leave as soon as I tie up some loose ends here," Romano said.

"Text your flight information and I'll have someone pick you up at the airport," Leach said. "And Manny, watch your back. You're carrying some explosive information, and I'm sure we are on TSA's watch list. The FBI is probably tracking us as well."

"What are we going to do with all of this?" Romano asked.

"First, we need to decide if it's authentic. If it is, we'll go where the evidence leads us. Be careful, Mate."

"Ditto," Romano said. He then called his primary contact in the intelligence unit of the United Nations.

"What can I do for you today, Manny?"

"I need you to run INTERPOL profiles on some Mexican nationals," Romano said. "The first is Victor Vargas Lopez, originally from Veracruz, but now from Nuevo Laredo; his sister, Juliana Alameda Lopez, originally from Veracruz, disappeared while living in Pakistan; Maria Coronado Lopez, originally from Veracruz; Dr. Pablo Rodriguez Delgado, MD from Veracruz; and

Alexandra Delgado, Pablo's sister in Veracruz. I'll be in New York tomorrow to meet with Percy Leach and the Secretary General." He shamelessly invoked the Secretary General's name to get priority service. It never failed.

Romano returned to the conference room where Ted Johnson was patiently waiting. "I apologize for the interruption, Mr. Johnson, but something has come up. Could we postpone the remainder of your deposition?"

"Absolutely," Johnson said. "Give me a call when you're ready to pick up where we left off."

The next available flight from Atlanta to NYC departed at 5 a.m. the next morning. A one-hour layover in Philadelphia would delay his arrival until mid-morning. Meantime, he was able to get some restless sleep and pick up a few newspapers to keep him occupied on the flight.

The straight shot on I-20 from Madison to Hartsfield-Jackson International Airport was quick and easy. Though most chickens were still asleep, the county's busiest airport was already abuzz with activity. The expedited drop off of his rental car and expedited diplomatic security check put him in his assigned seat in record time.

Romano dropped his newspapers in the empty seat next to him. Before the plane was even airborne, his eyes scanned one of the papers for articles on Elliott's downfall. The headline by a prominent columnist reported that Speaker Dobbins had enough bipartisan support for impeachment. The same story criticized Elliott for threatening to withhold federal funds from those congressional districts of those who supported the bill.

A sidebar described how the General Accountability Office had uncovered blatant misuses of public funds in the President's green energy program. Grants to unprofitable companies were difficult to track due to poor recordkeeping. Funds to build detention centers and DHS's special operations teams represented billions in misappropriations. A second GAO team investigated the administration's transfer of Yellowstone National Park to China in lieu of debt repayment. They determined that Elliott lacked the authority to transfer any legacy land without approval from Congress, despite the Justice Department's contention to the contrary.

An article in a prominent international paper reported that Jack Tanner had already hired a team of astute Washington attorneys, a formidable cadre of former U.S. Attorneys and former deputy U.S. Attorneys. An "off the record" quote from one of them raised the specter of criminal indictments against Elliott for his approval of Executive Order 14900.

Romano's flight arrived at JFK International Airport just after morning rush hour. Dead on his feet from sleep deprivation, he staggered from his gate to baggage claim. A uniformed driver had already retrieved his luggage and was standing near the door leading to the diplomatic parking space just outside the terminal.

"May I help you with your briefcase?" the driver asked.

Romano instinctively tightened his grip on the case containing the evidence from Mexico. "Thank you. I've got it," he replied.

The driver ignored his curt tone, assuming correctly that his passenger was exhausted from his red eye flight. "This way," he said, leading to a gleaming black Town Car.

Drowsiness dogged Romano during the thirty-minute drive on I-495 through Queens and over the East River into Manhattan. A couple of times he dozed off just long enough to be jostled awake by a pothole in the roadway. Between lapses, he struggled to organize his thoughts for the briefing with Leach, the High Commissioner for Human Rights, and the Secretary General.

The public entrance to UN headquarters was crawling with journalists vying for the latest scoop. To avoid being hassled, Romano asked, "Could you take me around to the entrance through the parking garage?"

"Sure thing," the driver said. "That's where I always drop off the Secretary General."

"Are you his personal driver?" Romano asked.

"That's right," the driver answered.

"Man, I'm coming up in the world," Romano said.

"Stick with me, sir. I'll get you a direct ride up to his office on the executive elevator."

Romano pushed out his chest. "I could get used to this."

As soon as he stepped off the elevator, Romano was whisked through the waiting room to Sukarno's office overlooking the East River. The Secretary General, the High Commissioner, and Percy Leach were standing behind a massive hand-carved desk. Sukarno was pointing out the spot where Chesley "Sully" Sullenberger had been forced to land his crippled 737 airliner in the river right after takeoff due to a bird strike. The amazing feat was credited with saving 155 lives that fateful day on the 15th of January in 2009.

Sukarno was the first to notice Romano. "Hello, Manny. How was your flight?"

"I caught up on a lot of reading, but no sleep," he said. "Two interesting commentaries complained about how the President is being unfairly criticized by racists and partisan politicians."

Clara Baard, High Commissioner for Human Rights, was quick to respond. "And which category do the parents of the eleven murdered children fall into?"

"I don't know that, but we have some new information that might answer other key questions," he said.

Sukarno walked to a large conference table. "Step over here and spread everything out so we can all take a look."

While Romano organized everything on the table, Leach explained that document experts were standing by to review them for authenticity. As the four scrutinized the documents like curators reviewing valuable pieces of art, an air of awe and excitement swirled in the room.

Sukarno could hardly contain his curiosity. "Tell me, Manny, what do you suspect motivated Victor Lopez to send this information? And what is his relationship with Elliott?"

"According to his cover letter, he's Elliott's biological uncle," Romano explained. "The letter says that Lopez's favorite niece, a Maria Lopez, was one of the nurses killed when DHS shelled the hospital in Madison. It looks like he's exacting some revenge by helping us."

"That makes sense, but this case is still shrouded in mystery," Sukarno said.

"Perhaps we could untangle things quicker if Manny and I made a personal house call on Mr. Lopez and the others mentioned in these documents," Leach said.

"I think that's a grand idea," Commissioner Baard chimed in. "Even if our people can authenticate these documents, we need credible provenance."

"That's true," Sukarno said. "I like your idea too, Percy. When can you leave for Mexico?"

"As soon as I find some food that isn't fried," Romano said. "My Italian palate isn't suited for Southern cuisine. I did find an Italian restaurant owned by Croatians, if you can believe that!"

"You might want to eat all you can while you're here," Sukarno said. "Early in my career I was stationed in Mexico City. It seems the cooks in Georgia and Mexico share a profound appreciation for fried food. The Mexicans even fry their beans!"

CHAPTER 34

—

After a couple of days of rest, Romano and Leach flew to Laredo, Texas. Laredo, a dusty border town known for its connection to the Mexican drug trade, sat just across the border from its sister city, Nuevo Laredo, where Victor Lopez lived. In the interest of safety and convenience, they chose to stay on the United States side and drive to Nuevo Laredo to interview Lopez.

Romano had contacted Lopez before leaving New York to explain his interest in discussing the documents. Lopez reluctantly agreed to meet on the condition that he remain anonymous. "It's not President Elliott I fear," he said. "It's his allies in Mexico. As you know, it's illegal to own guns in my country, so the only people who are armed are the criminals, the drug dealers, and the corrupt policemen and military. Our government learned from Poncho Villa that an armed citizenry is a threat to a repressive government."

After renting a car at the airport they drove to the Rio Grande Plaza Hotel on Water Street in downtown Laredo. The motel overlooked the Rio Grande River and Nuevo Laredo on the Mexican side. Leach reserved rooms with a southern exposure so they could view scenic old Mexico. They checked in, then called Lopez to let him know they had arrived. He suggested they meet at noon the next day at a popular restaurant, La Unica De Nuevo Laredo, on San Bernardo Avenue. It was an easy drive from the border crossing.

For now, they settled in and began reviewing the documents one more time to make sure they hadn't missed anything. Once fully prepared, they ordered light sandwiches from room service to reserve their appetite for the Latin cuisine at La Unica. Leach went to bed early while Romano stayed up to watch a soccer match on Univision.

By eight the next morning the two had enjoyed breakfast and were prepared for their short road trip. Leach pulled out of the hotel parking garage and headed toward the Gateway to the Americas International

Bridge leading to Nuevo Laredo. He reached out and handed the attendant three American greenbacks. The steady stream of pedestrians walking toward the United States was several times the number of people going in the opposite direction.

As he cautiously drove across the Rio Grande River, or the Rio Bravo as it's called in Mexico, he thought about the relatively young history between the two countries compared to their counterparts in Europe. Like many Europeans, he grew up watching American westerns on TV. *What was it like being a high-spirited vaquero riding a silver-adorned saddle with a matching holster holding a Colt .45?* he wondered. The frivolous daydream was cut short by the labyrinth of exits and ramps leading into Mexico. With the help of a GPS, Romano directed him to the correct route.

Once in Nuevo Laredo he turned onto San Bernardo Avenue that led to a parking lot next to La Unica. "We have arrived, Manny," Leach said.

"I'm ready to meet our mystery informant." Manny said. He patted his ornate Italian leather briefcase. "I have everything we need, including some Pepto Bismol." Bringing it would prove to be insightful.

Remembering Sukarno's warning about Mexican food, Leach rubbed his stomach. "I hope there's enough for both of us."

The restaurant's exterior was typical of this part of the world. Earthtone-colored stucco provided a backdrop for bright green, red, and yellow contrasting trim. Romano and Leach watched the festive crowd from the portico. Everyone seemed to be laughing and enjoying themselves. Strings of fiery red peppers hung from ornate wrought iron dividers. Photos of handsome bull fighters and Flamenco dancers in spectacular costumes adorned the stucco walls.

"Welcome to Mexico," Leach heard above the noise as he strolled from the counter where he had gone to ask for a table.

The melodic Spanish voice rang out again. "Are you gentlemen here to see Victor Lopez?"

Leach turned to face a short, round man with wispy eyebrows wearing a dusty cowboy hat. He was vigorously shaking Manny's hand like he was shaking apples from a tree. Romano bobbed up and down, trying to stay balanced. "Welcome to Nuevo Laredo, Amigos," the man said with a broad toothy smile.

"Nice to make your acquaintance, Mr. Lopez. I'm Percy Leach."

"So formal, Mr. Leach," he said.

Romano recovered his equilibrium. "He can't really help it, Victor. The British stay on their toes in case the Queen is nearby."

"The closest thing you'll find to a queen around here, Mr. Leach, are the painted señoritas down on Prospect Street."

Lopez and Romano shared a hearty laugh while Leach remained stoic.

"There's an area in the back where we can talk," Lopez said. "Please, follow me."

Lopez rotated his rotund body to pass between two rows of tables.

Romano checked out the tantalizing dishes as they passed. His growling stomach caused Leach to chuckle.

"Looks like you're getting into a party mood, Governor," Romano said. "Places like this will do that to you."

"I just hope we can talk over your noisy stomach," Leach said.

Lopez stopped at a small alcove with a round table. "This is as private as it gets," he said. "Besides, no one gives two pesos about what we're here to discuss. We should order lunch first so Mr. Romano's stomach quiets down."

Leach scanned the menu's vast array of unfamiliar dishes. "What would you recommend, Victor?"

It was obvious from Lopez's rotund build that he knew a thing or two about food. "If you want, I'll just order for all of us," he said. He called to a pretty waitress with silky dark hair and deep brown eyes. "Senorita, a plate of flautas and tostadas with corn tortillas, por favor."

"Si, señor," she said, lingering briefly to write down the order. I'll bring chips and salsa to start out," she added.

"They only serve Coke and Fanta for drinks," Lopez said. "Which do you prefer?"

"Fanta for me," Romano said.

"Coke, please," Leach said.

Lopez turned back to the waitress who was eyeing Romano and Leach. "Dos Cokes, uno Fanta, por favor."

The waitress left to place their order.

"Don't mind the stares, Amigos," Lopez said. "She sees mostly locals and Texicans in here. We don't get many exotic Europeans in tailored suits."

"That's all right, Mate. We don't see exotic young señoritas in our work," Leach said.

Romano noticed that no one was paying any attention to them, except their waitress who set a large tray of colorful dishes in the middle of the table.

Lopez eagerly scooped up a tostada and covered it with rich red sauce that smelled of tomatoes and cilantro. "Help yourselves, Amigos," he said. "You'll just have to try things."

Feeling adventurous as well as hungry, Romano followed Lopez's lead by heaping sauce on a tostada. He rubbed his hands together in preparation for the feast.

"You might want to go easy on the sauce, Mr. Romano," Lopez warned. "It's strong for delicate palates."

"No worry, Victor," he replied with bravado. "We Italians love peppers."

"Si," Lopez replied, casting Leach a wink.

Both watched intently as Romano downed his tostada with gusto. Within seconds, beads of perspiration formed on his forehead while patches of red crept up his neck. Seconds later he gasped for air, his eyes darting from side to side in desperation.

"Señorita, another Fanta and a large glass of agua, por favor," Lopez said.

At first Leach was concerned with his partner's bizarre reaction. "How are you doing, Mate?" he said.

"This food is fantastic," Romano whispered, unable to catch his breath. He loosened his collar and licked the ice in his empty Fanta glass.

"You look like spontaneous combustion, Mate," Leach said, unable to suppress a chuckle.

The waitress appeared just in time with a large glass of ice water. "Gracias, Señorita," Romano said before chugging it.

"Maybe you should try one without the sauce," Leach said.

"How do they get so much fire in that stuff?" Romano croaked, still gasping for air.

"It's mainly puréed tomatoes and cilantro with a pinch of habanero and jalapeño peppers," Lopez said. "It's sort of a specialty on this side of the Rio Bravo."

"A *pinch* of peppers, you say?" Romano asked.

"Maybe more than a pinch." Lopez said. He chuckled, unable to contain his amusement with his adventurous and equally entertaining new friends.

Romano downed another Fanta. "Maybe if we proceed, I'll forget about my scorched insides." His voice remained raspy for the remainder of the discussion.

"Of course," Lopez said, casting another wink at Leach.

Romano loosened his collar some more. "We have a few questions about

Jerome Elliott's life that are crucial to our investigation." By now his squeaky voice was barely audible.

"Do you mind if we record your answers to make sure we get the facts right?" he whispered.

"Not as long as you honor your commitment to protect my identity," Lopez said.

Romano started to pick at a portion of flautas smothered in sauce, but decided against it.

"Let me take it from here, Manny, while you smolder," Leach said. He turned to Lopez. "Jerome's father is a mystery," he said. "Jerome's Texas birth certificate lists his father as deceased."

The joy drained from Lopez's jovial face. "My sister, Juliana, worked for a rancher in Laredo where she met Hector Santos, a petty criminal who'd been in scrapes on both sides of the border. He was a handsome, charming bad boy, the charismatic anti-establishment-type naïve young women often find attractive. As nature sometimes plays out, Juliana became pregnant. Hector abandoned her and their unborn child three months before he was killed during an attempted robbery."

"As you probably know, Victor, there is an unsubstantiated rumor that Jerome was born in Mexico," Leach said.

Victor paused to take another drink before continuing. "Juliana and Hector moved to Veracruz to live with Hector's parents when Juliana developed complications with her pregnancy. Right after Hector abandoned her, she moved back to Laredo where she could get government assistance and help from her former employer. She named the baby Jerome after her boss in Laredo who had been so kind to her."

"What you are telling us corroborates Jerome's Texas birth certificate," Leach said. "What became of Juliana?"

"As a bright student with good grades, she earned a scholarship to a small college in Laredo. She married a Pakistani student who insisted on moving back home when he finished his studies. At Juliana's request, Theresa and I agreed to raise Jerome in Veracruz where I was a headmaster. Jerome suffered from severe abandonment issues when Juliana moved without him."

Romano finally re-acquired his voice. "What were his greatest influences while he was growing up?" he asked.

Victor couldn't hide the pain exhumed by the question. "The answer is sad on so many levels," he said. "Jerome never gave up on the dream of reuniting with his mother. By the end of secondary school, with a small savings and money from me and my brother, he was able to visit her in Pakistan. It was a short visit and Jerome didn't feel comfortable there."

"That explains some of his insecurities," Romano squeaked. "But it doesn't explain how he developed his extreme political philosophy."

"I can explain that too," Lopez said. "Jerome shared his mother's intellect and excelled in the best schools in Pakistan. At the age of sixteen, he won an exchange fellowship to the University of Havana where he became friends with a communist activist named Raoul Bernardo Suarez. Raoul convinced him to study communist doctrine, a subject that sparked his personal interest in the Cuban revolution. Jerome fell under the spell of the same ideology that captivated Che Guevara and Fidel Castro."

Leach checked the recorder, interrupting with his own question. "Did you notice a marked difference when Jerome returned from Cuba?"

"Sí, sí," Lopez said. "While Jerome was there, Theresa and I moved to Nuevo Laredo to take another headmaster position. Theresa was stricken with cancer and died later that year. When Jerome came back for the funeral, he denounced Mexico for serving the rich while taxing the poor."

"How did he advance his education in the states?" Leach asked.

"Raoul had some mysterious friends that he and Jerome referred to as *comrades*," Lopez said. "They were able to pull strings to get Jerome into Rutgers University and then Yale Law School. While at Yale, he became involved in politics and began referring to America as an evil empire."

"It sounds like he lost interest in his mother at the university," Romano said.

Lopez sighed heavily. "By then his mother had disappeared in Pakistan," he said. "Her husband never explained what happened, and we never heard from him again. Everyone in our family had their own conspiracy theory. When I asked Jerome about his mother and stepfather, he simply stated, "Allah has a way of taking care of things."

Sensing Lopez's deep disappointment, Romano hesitated before asking the next question. "Sorry, Victor, but I have to ask. Did Jerome act any differently toward you after he entered the university?"

"During his last year at Yale, my niece Maria decided to immigrate to the states to study nursing, a lifelong dream. When I asked Jerome to help her obtain a student visa, he became enraged. He demanded that I never contact him about a family matter again. I was saddened that he seemed to be ashamed of his Mexican heritage. But that wasn't it at all."

"What happened then?" Romano asked.

"Jerome warned that if I didn't keep the family away from him, Maria's immigration would never go through. He said he knew some well-connected people who could block her visa and create problems for the rest of us. My brother and I sold our family land near Veracruz and used the money to hire an attorney who obtained the visa."

Romano stopped taking notes. "What was the most striking change in Jerome?"

"He and I were having coffee one morning when he started talking about how the Cuban Revolution was conducted from the inside. He boasted that the same strategy would work elsewhere."

"Your story is incredible, Victor," Romano said. "I realize we've dredged up some sad memories, but your information has given us valuable insight into Jerome's state of mind and motives."

"I'm still wondering about how Maria ended up in the middle of all this," Leach said.

"That's perhaps the saddest part," Lopez said. "The political unrest in the states didn't interest me until Maria completed her studies at the University of Georgia and got a job at DeKalb General Hospital in Atlanta. Two years ago, she and her husband moved to Madison, Georgia to take care of her husband's ailing mother. Shortly after that, Maria was hired by Morgan Memorial Hospital."

"This story is going down a dark path," Romano murmured. His eyes dropped with great sadness.

"Your suspicions are correct, Mr. Romano. Maria was one of the nurses killed when the government shelled the hospital."

"We're so sorry, Victor," Romano said. "During my investigation in Madison I witnessed the grief of victims who lost loved ones in that senseless attack."

"So that's your motive for doing this?" Leach asked.

"That's right, Amigos. It is one thing to know someone is a psychopath. It's something else when that psychopath causes the death of a loved one. Maria was like a daughter to me. She was a human treasure who was devoted to helping the sick and injured. Jerome needs to pay for depriving the world of her grace and love."

"Even with your first-hand knowledge, Victor, we expect President

Elliot's supporters to challenge the veracity of your story," Leach said. "We need substantiation to counteract any challenge. You mentioned the name of a doctor and his sister in Veracruz."

"Yes, that would be Doctor Delgado and his sister Alexandra. They were good friends with Juliana. Doctor Delgado treated her pregnancy when complications arose."

Romano gulped more water to extinguish his lingering burn. "Do you think we could reach them?" he asked.

"I'm afraid the doctor passed on a couple of years ago," Lopez said. "But I think his sister is still there. I have her address in my records. I can send it to you when I get home."

"That would be helpful," Romano said. "We're staying at the Rio Grande Plaza Hotel."

"Your story is truly historic," Leach added. "Again, we are saddened by the loss of your niece. To us this information is simply advisory, but to the Americans it could be more important than we know."

"And I apologize for doubting your warning about the pepper sauce." Romano said with a grin.

"Other than that, I hope you enjoyed our flautas and tostadas," Lopez said.

"There's no question about that," Leach said. "Goodbye, Victor. Godspeed."

"Buenos Diaz, Amigos," he replied. "Good luck with your investigation."

As they left the restaurant for the trip back to Laredo, both felt like they had made a new friend. The human tragedy Victor experienced at the hands of his nephew touched them. They chatted about the valuable leads he had provided as they crossed the Gateway of the Americas International Bridge back to Texas. They decided to continue on to Veracruz to interview Delgado. Meanwhile, Leach continued to rib Romano about his fiery red lips.

"At least I tried it!" Manny argued.

"We can't all be Italian," Leach said.

CHAPTER 35

—

Relaxing on his hotel balcony overlooking the Rio Bravo and Mexico beyond, Leach wondered what awaited them in Veracruz. Victor Lopez's reliance on hearsay and memories to explain Elliott's background left many questions open. Leach couldn't wait to find the answers.

Romano entered Alexandra Delgado's address into the rental car's GPS. Its readout showed that she lived near the Veracruz beach several hundred kilometers from the border. According to Lopez, she enjoyed a contented life in the hacienda she inherited from her brother. She kept busy tending flowers and fruit trees by day and knitting beautiful shawls by night.

Unlike Pablo, Alexandra was not well educated. She didn't understand why two important men from New York City wanted to see her. She routinely read the local newspaper and knew that some kind of political scandal was plaguing the Americans, but she wasn't particularly interested in knowing anything beyond that. Her life was insulated from such things. Or so she thought.

When Romano initially called her, his fluency in Italian with some knowledge of Spanish made it possible for them to converse. At first she was reluctant to meet with them. "I don't know how I can help you gentlemen," she said.

Romano hoped his Italian charm would appeal to her softer side. "Just thirty minutes of your time would make our work so much easier, Señora."

Delgado gave in. "Thirty minutes, but no more. I have important work to do in my garden."

"Gracias," Romano said. "We look forward to seeing you."

Originally planning to fly to Veracruz, they decided that a drive down the coast could be a pleasant road trip. After making reservations at the Emporio Plaza Veracruz, they packed for the long drive the next day.

They would drive down Highway 85, then follow the coastal route south through Monterrey, Ciudad, Victoria, and Tampico, some of the most scenic cities in the country.

That evening, after devouring a Texas-sized steak, Romano browsed the Plaza gift shop. A compact pocket camera he purchased could be a valuable asset on the trip. Back in his room he called their head of UN security to confirm his clearance to carry a firearm in Mexico. The disturbing reports about the kidnappings of foreigners for ransom led him to believe that his Beretta might be his second-best friend on this trip. The officer verified that Mexico had authorized them to be armed.

Brilliant sunshine and deep blue skies provided the perfect backdrop for their drive through Mexico's arid countryside. Unlike seedy border towns, the interior was rich in Spanish culture and architecture. Every now and then Romano urged Leach to pull over so he could take a photo of a statue or classic architecture. The city of Monterrey was especially picturesque with its palm-lined streets and beautifully landscaped parks. The Monterrey Mountains overshadowed sparkling skyscrapers and smaller Spanish-inspired buildings with colorful tiled roofs. Modern highways were designed to carry Monterrey's 1.2 million residents in and around Nuevo León state.

The two stopped for lunch at a sidewalk café just off the Santa Lucia Riverwalk near downtown Monterrey. Leach admonished Romano to avoid the various sauces displayed in their multi-colored decanters. Enamored with their beautiful surroundings, they took their time enjoying the steaming-hot fajitas and ice-cold Dos Equis. Unlike inflated New York prices, the two ample lunches cost less than twenty dollars.

Though refreshed and rejuvenated, their leisurely lunch delayed their arrival time. When Romano called the Emporio Plaza Veracruz motel for a late check-in, they were assured their room would be held. Romano snapped photos like a common tourist as they meandered along the Riverwalk, then strolled back to their car wondering if the remainder of their trip would be as pleasant.

Several hours later, they pulled into the Hotel parking lot in Veracruz. "I had a wonderful time, Governor," Romano said. "We'll probably never get the chance to do this again. How many investigations have you been on when you were able to enjoy three good meals in one day?"

"Usually, I'm lucky to get one bad meal," Leach said.

"This road trip should be a lesson for both of us," Romano said. "We need to slow down and smell the roses more often."

"Tell that to Sukarno," Leach said.

"I'll pass, Governor," he replied sheepishly.

They grabbed their bags and proceeded to the lobby. A local Mariachi band serenaded the bustling guests. Both registered at the beautiful tiled counter, leaving wakeup calls for six the next morning. Fatigued from driving, Leach went straight to bed while Romano watched another soccer match.

Next morning's breakfast featured a variety of fresh melons, kiwi, and mangos. Traditional Mexican cheeses like manchego, cotija, and queso fresco complemented the fruit. Strong coffee and sweet pastries rounded out the menu. They discussed their upcoming interview with Alexandra Delgado while enjoying the cornucopia of Mexican specialties.

They grabbed a supersized cup of the robust coffee to go before jumping in their rental car for the drive to Delgado's hacienda. The route along the Gulf of Mexico passed through scenic coastal fishing villages filled with hand-painted wooden boats and nets hanging out to dry. The Gulf breeze lacked the strong salty smell so typical of Atlantic or Pacific breezes.

"Perhaps the Gulf isn't as salty as the other oceans of the world," Leach said.

"Or, perhaps Victor's habanero sauce permanently singed my nasal passages," Romano said.

The reminder brought a hearty laugh.

Leach slowly pulled up to Delgado's hacienda. A patch of bare ground served as a parking space. The cozy stucco house with a red tile roof was typical of others in the area with one notable exception. Beautiful flowers blazing with color basked in the sunshine over the entire landscape. Tiger lilies, hibiscus, and azaleas interspersed with ferns and cacti resembled an arboretum. Neatly-trimmed orange and lime trees laden with ripe juicy fruit lined the perimeter of the property.

A flock of colorful painted buntings chattered in harmony while feeding on slices of orange and pineapple hanging in the trees to keep them from sampling the ripening fruit. The birds swished to safety as Leach and Romano opened their car doors. A single straggler lingered for one more refrain, to the delight of both visitors. They approached a wrought-iron gate that led to an open garden landscaped with more manicured flowers and vegetables. Romano followed the painted stepping stones to a planter of habaneros gleaming green and red in the brilliant sunlight.

"I wouldn't touch those, Manny. They seem to have it in for you," Leach said.

"Agreed. These buggers scream danger," he said.

The door to the hacienda creaked opened and a grandmotherly lady wearing a loosely-knitted shawl greeted them. At first her strong Spanish accent was difficult for Romano to understand, but he quickly caught on to the nuances of her speech.

Romano grasped her small frail hand between his. "Buenos Diaz, Señora Delgado." Surprised by such an intimate greeting from a stranger, she blushed. "Buenos Diaz, Señor Romano."

"Do you speak English, Señora?" he asked.

Her round weathered face beamed with pride. "Why yes, I learned from my brother," she said.

Romano turned to face Leach standing in the shadow of the roof. "This is Señor Percy Leach, my partner."

Blocking the sun with her hand, she said, "Hello, Mr. Leach. Please come in out of this sun."

The entrance led to a comfortable sitting room just inside the door. The house was surprisingly cool with no apparent air conditioning. The Talavera tile, hand-painted in symmetrical designs of blue, green, orange, and brown, seemed to emit a chill. A lazy bamboo ceiling fan added a soothing breeze.

"Can I offer you gentlemen some lemonade?" she asked.

Romano licked his lips in anticipation. "Si, muchos gracias."

She poured two glasses of iced lemonade and handed one to each guest. Romano chugged the cool refreshment as if he had just tasted more habanera sauce.

She radiated with pride as she dried her hands on her floral apron. "This is made with lemons from my tree in the courtyard."

"It's absolutely delightful," Leach said. "So fresh and robust."

"I understand from our telephone conversation, Mr. Romano, that you are interested in information on Jerome Elliott and his family. That's President Elliott, am I correct?"

"Si, Señora."

"You are in luck," she said. "Doctor Delgado was a meticulous record keeper who never disposed of anything related to his work."

Leach glanced up from his notebook, his interest piqued.

Romano took another sip of lemonade, wondering what other refreshing surprises this visit would yield.

"I encouraged Pablo to throw out those old papers in our back bedroom. But he insisted that the Catholic Hospital had strict rules against destroying birth records. After we talked last night, Mr. Romano, I found a box with Jerome Elliott's name on it marked *IMPORTANTE* in bold letters."

Leach stroked his chin and shifted in his seat to release tension. Despite the comfortable temperature in the villa, his hands left perspiration stains on his notepad.

Noticing the growing impatience of her guests, Alexandra continued. "Pablo got medical training in North Carolina before doing baby practice. How do you say?"

"Obstetrics," Romano said.

"Oh yes," she said. "His time in the States sparked interest in politics."

Romano glanced at Leach, his eyes charged with excitement.

Neither imagined where the story was leading.

"More, Mr. Romano?" she asked, fixated on his empty glass.

Though charged with impatience, Romano remained courteous. "Yes, thank you."

She refreshed Romano's drink, then continued with her story. "When Jerome got into politics, Pablo saw a chance to learn from him." She paused to brush back long strands of granite-colored hair that had fallen onto her forehead. "He felt bad when Jerome insisted that he never contact him again."

Leach slid to the edge of his seat and interrupted her. "Mr. Lopez mentioned that letter, Señora Delgado. Is there any chance you still have it?"

Feeling more comfortable with her guests, she adjusted her shawl and said, "Why yes. Pablo kept everything. It's with the other documents I have for you. We'll get to that shortly."

Both men strained to remain patient. Leach doodled to relieve the tension while Romano shifted in his chair.

"Mr. Romano, please take another chair if that one is uncomfortable," she said.

"Sorry, Señora. I'm just antsy."

"Antsy?" she asked.

"Excited to see you," he replied.

Delgado wasn't quite sure what he meant, but she continued anyway. "Before Pablo had his last heart attack, Jerome was elected to the United States Congress. I remember Pablo saying if they knew what he knew, no one would vote for him."

Unable to contain his curiosity any longer, Romano cut to the chase. With his hands outstretched like a child begging for ice cream, he asked. "What other documents did Pablo keep in that special file on Jerome?"

Calm and demure, Delgado answered. "I'm going to let you see for yourself, Mr. Romano." She slowly rose, using her cane for stability, and shuffled to the back bedroom. Leach cast a supercharged glance at Romano, who was now squirming in his seat like a baby with a wet diaper.

She returned with a bulging cardboard file box that she gingerly placed on a small table next to Romano. The table creaked slightly from its weight.

Music to my ears, Romano thought.

"Please help yourself, Mr. Romano," she said. "Would either of you like more lemonade?"

She seemed a lot more interested in hospitality than the historic significance of the moment. It was a hallmark of her Spanish culture to honor guests. However, her guests were on a mission with their attention affixed on the alluring file box.

"No more lemonade for me, Señora," Leach said. "Thank you."

Mesmerized by the potential treasure trove of evidence, Romano didn't answer. With a conspicuous wink to Leach, he retrieved the box from the table and placed it in his lap. Its substantial weight promised volumes of evidence.

Rubbing his hands together as if he were ready to dive into a juicy steak, Romano lifted the lid. Underneath lay an array of black and white photographs portraying Juliana, Hector, Victor, and Jerome in different settings around Veracruz. Some shots were posed, others looked candid. Everyone seemed so happy despite the gravity of the problems they were facing.

Throwing a tail of her shawl over her shoulder, Señora Delgado reached down and picked up a photo of Juliana holding baby Jerome near the entrance to a church.

"I haven't seen this in many years," she said. She clasped the photo close to her heart then peered upward, as if speaking to God Himself. "Jerome was such a happy baby at first. His mother's abandonment was like a dagger through his little heart." Tears rolled from her clear grey eyes, prompting her to pull an embroidered handkerchief from her pocket to wipe them.

Still sniffling, she picked up a photo of Hector with what looked like a revolver tucked in his belt. "Hector's parents were lovely people, but he was a problem from an early age. We all warned Juliana, but she had her own reckless streak."

Digging through the box like a squirrel searching for acorns, Romano uncovered a tattered brown ledger near the bottom. "What do we have here?" he asked rhetorically.

Delgado gracefully dabbed her moistened eyes with an unsteady hand, then smoothed out her embroidered apron. "Pablo kept a ledger of all of his babies with their names, the parent's names, and certain medical information."

Leach arched his back to correct his slumping posture. "But why would it be in this box?" he asked. His eyes widened in anticipation.

Romano moved the box back to the table and placed the ledger in his lap. "Let's see if we can find out."

Leach sat motionless while his seldom-wrong instincts screamed that the register was an epic find.

Romano began his systematic inspection of each entry on the discolored pages. As he read, the ledger fell open to a small packet of papers tucked neatly in the crease. He dragged his finger down that page past several unfamiliar names, stopping three lines from the bottom. His eyes recognized what his brain could not absorb. There, in faded blue ink, written in hand with a fountain pen, was an entry listing Jerome Elliott, born to Juliana Lopez, father deceased. He stared at the entry, his eyes glued in place.

Manny's lack of movement seemed strange to Delgado. "Are you all right, Mr. Romano?" she asked.

He didn't budge. "Uno memento, por favor."

Surprised by Romano's stern response, Delgado slid back in her chair.

Romano couldn't break away from the bottom of the left page. He lifted his trembling hand and closed his eyes for a moment. *No need to rush beyond the finish line.* There was a profound discovery before him. How profound, he didn't know quite yet. "Governor, you're going to want to see this."

Leach had already pulled out his reading glasses. He focused on the entry at the bottom of the left page that had captivated Romano, then leaned toward his host, careful not to lose his place. "Señora Delgado, I'm confused, he said. "Victor Lopez told us Jerome was born in Laredo, where his mother sought help from her former employer. Presumably that's why he has a Texas birth certificate."

Delgado sat erect, waving her crooked index finger in the air. "No, no, Señor, she said. "Juliana had a difficult pregnancy and was under Pablo's care right up to Jerome's birth. Pablo definitely delivered him."

Her words struck the investigators like a lightning bolt. The world seemed to stop for them while they processed the truth.

Delgado refuted Lopez's historical account in greater detail, allowing Romano to inspect the packet of documents that had fallen from the ledger. His heart skipped a beat as he gazed at a letter from the Catholic Children's Hospital in Veracruz, congratulating Juliana Lopez on the birth of her son, Jerome, and listing charges for his delivery at the hospital. His heart skipped again at the sight of a cancelled check drawn against a bank in Laredo for payment signed by Juliana Lopez and dated two weeks after Jerome's birth.

Folded with the other documents was a government form from Tampico State. When questioned about the form, Delgado explained that physicians and midwives filed the form to request an official birth certificate. When sent to the State Health Department, a copy was kept in case the physician needed to follow up on one that failed to arrive. A copy of that form and a copy of the original birth certificate was tucked in the ledger for posterity.

Romano handed the documents to Leach, his hand still trembling from the magnitude of their discovery.

"You know what this means, Manny," Leach said. "As a naturalized Mexican citizen, Jerome Elliott was never eligible to be President of the United States. His entire tenure in office is as illegitimate as his birth. This is a game-changer for everybody, Partner."

Leach stared at the birth certificate as if he expected it to disappear. His heart pounded.

Romano turned to Delgado who was adjusting her scarf. "Señora Delgado, do you know how important these documents are?"

She smiled, her grey eyes sparkling. "I think so, Señor. I've never seen grown men get so excited about paper other than money."

Mindful of the need to verify the authenticity of the documents, Leach drew upon his consummate British courtesy. "Would you be willing to entrust us with these documents for a few days, Señora?"

Her resolute answer surprised both men. "Of course," she said. "I'm sure Pablo would want his papers to count for something. Excuse me while I assemble them for you." She disappeared into the back bedroom with the documents. Leach and Romano felt like they had won the lottery when she returned a few minutes later with a brown accordion file tied with a string. Alexandra struggled to carry the bulging file.

Let me help you, Señora," Romano said, reaching for the bundle. He embraced her frail, delicate hands, then placed a light kiss on her cheek. "We appreciate your help, Señora. We'll return these documents as soon as we complete our investigation."

Blushing slightly, she held herself steady with her intricately-carved cane. "It was a pleasure meeting you gentlemen," she said, her grey eyes still sparkling.

Romano checked his watch and smiled. The visit had lasted exactly thirty minutes. "You've been a wonderful hostess, Señora."

"And thank you for the world-class lemonade," Leach said, bowing slightly.

The blush in her cheeks blended perfectly with her beautiful knitted shawl as she nodded politely. "De nada," she said.

After escorting them through the wrought-iron gate to their rental car, Alexandra shuffled back to the hacienda's entryway, pausing to straighten an errant plant with her cane. She pivoted at the door to watch them leave.

Romano and Leach waved before they entered their car.

"I'm going to miss her, Governor," Romano said.

"I know, Mate. Me too."

As they rolled slowly westward, her diminutive silhouette faded into the distance. They probably would never see her again.

Leach peered sadly into his rearview mirror. "What a delightful, gracious woman."

"No question," Romano said. "A real desert rose."

The accordion file rested on the back seat like a bomb with the timer ticking. "I still don't believe how this investigation is coming together," Leach said. "It's almost as if things were destined to unfold this way."

"What makes you think they weren't?" Romano asked. "Never doubt the Great Plan."

During their thirty-minute drive back to the Emporio Plaza Veracruz, their conversation remained giddy with excitement over their indisputable evidence. Soon they settled into their usual animated banter about their game plan going forward. Pulling into the parking deck of the motel, Leach asked Romano to grab a bottle of wine and meet him in his room.

The peck on Leach's door was followed by an energized Manny Romano bursting in with his hand held high. "I found this nice bottle of Madeira, Governor."

Romano found a corkscrew left by a previous occupant and adroitly wound it home. The cork surrendered with a celebratory pop. Romano skillfully poured while the deep red wine swirled up to the rim.

As the second glass filled, Leach's phone buzzed. "Hello, Mr. Sukarno," he answered.

Romano stopped pouring and listened.

"Pardon me for interrupting Percy, but we have reason to exercise caution," Sukarno said.

Leach licked his lips at the sight of Romano tasting the wine.

Romano then took a large gulp just to tease him.

"I thought new restrictions would prevent the illegal eavesdropping on allies," Leach replied.

"I think that falls into the same category as, 'If you like your health plan, you can keep it,'" Sukarno said.

Both men chuckled.

Leach provided a veiled clue regarding the team's plans. "We were just reading a report on the complaints airlines receive from red-eye flights."

"Excellent," Sukarno said.

The line went dead.

Romano resumed pouring, then handed Leach a glass.

Leach clanked his glass against Romano's to celebrate their victory. "Bottoms up, Manny. We're flying to New York tonight."

Anxious to get their evidence back to New York as quickly as possible, Leach reserved seats on a late-night flight from Veracruz. Those seats were no problem, but only first class was available on the leg from Mexico City to Austin.

Romano sipped his wine as Leach sat glued to the phone waiting for the reservations clerk to confirm their flight. Five minutes passed, then ten.

"Sir, I have two reservations from Veracruz, Mexico to New York City, USA for Percy Leach and Manny Romano with the United Nations. Is that correct?"

A mental alert brought Leach out of his chair. "I didn't say I was with the United Nations."

"It's listed here in your file, sir. The names are Leach and Romano, aren't they?" Could you spell them for me, please?" She asked suddenly to cover her slip.

Leach didn't respond as he scribbled the flight information on a small pad then replaced the receiver in the cradle. He eyed Romano.

Romano drained his glass, then poured another. "What was the questioning all about?"

"It was almost as if she was checking our names against a list or something. She made sure she had our names exactly right and she knew who we work for."

Romano snickered. "That doesn't worry me as much as the prospect of the finance office taking the cost of first class out of our pay."

"When I explain to Sukarno that this was the only way to get back tonight, he'll gladly cover for us," Leach said. "Besides, you're a contractor, so you're perfectly safe."

"As long as you don't slap any deductions on me," Romano said.

"That call just doesn't sit right with me," Leach said. "Do me a favor, Manny and lock your briefcase when we get to the airport."

The two had a couple of hours before their flight to New York. They quickly checked out of the Emporio and cancelled their remaining reservations in Laredo. Based on their previous experience, both men had packed before the road trip.

Leach checked his watch. "We only have an hour left to get to the airport, so we need to get cracking."

"On it, Governor," Romano replied.

CHAPTER 36

—

Leach was relieved when their tickets clicked out of the kiosk. With boarding passes and credentials in hand they strolled toward the security checkpoint at the small Veracruz airport. A cigarette in one hand and coffee in the other, the Mexican security agent chatted with a gregarious female food vendor. He casually waved them through after a cursory glance at their diplomatic passports. Conscious of the prevalence of forged and stolen passports, Leach shuddered at the lax security.

Cramped space on the small airplane made them grateful for the quick hop from Veracruz. As soon as they reached cruising altitude they were dropping down to land. The Mexico City airport teemed with activity as they changed planes for their continuation to Dallas. As soon as they arrived, they stopped at a food court for coffee and a snack. They thought they were in the clear, but Texas proved to be more treacherous than Mexico.

Leach finished his snack, while Romano lingered. Last call for their flight blared over the loudspeaker. "Come on, Mate. We have five minutes to check in," Leach said.

Romano grabbed his briefcase and continued to eat on the run.

To their surprise, several TSA agents were waiting when they approached their gate.

The nervous ticket agent forced a smile while reviewing their boarding passes. "Mr. Leach, Mr. Romano, it will be just a moment before we can clear you for boarding."

A sense of dread rippled through Leach. He had been here before and it never ended pleasantly.

Romano checked his briefcase. He had locked it that morning when he attached the airline name tag. He leaned toward Leach and whispered, "What do you suppose is up, Governor?"

Fists clenched, Leach looked around, assessing the situation. He whispered back, "I don't know, Mate, but I don't like it."

An eerie tension hung over the adjoining gate area. Rows of seated passengers stared in their direction like zombies. Meanwhile, the agents faced the investigators with their hands behind their backs.

Romano felt like he was surrounded by robots.

Leach looked at the clerk with cold threatening eyes. "Is there a problem here?"

"Not unless you create one," the lead TSA agent interrupted. His accompanying nod was a signal for the other agents to encircle them.

Leach glared at the lead agent with his signature *don't mess with me* expression. "What can we do for you gentlemen? We've already cleared security."

Intimidated by the stare, the agent stepped backward before spouting a routine excuse. "We're conducting a spontaneous security check. You gentlemen need to come with us."

Leach flashed his credentials in the agent's face. "You would be wise to recognize our diplomatic immunity."

When Romano reached into his jacket pocket to retrieve his credentials, the closest agent noticed his Beretta and pounced. "He's armed," the agent shouted, lunging for the gun.

With the reflexes of a cat, Romano sidestepped the agent, leaving his left leg outstretched. The agent flailed his arms before executing a perfect face plant into the hard tile floor. Dazed from the impact, he stared up at Manny. Scarlet-colored blood gushed from a nasty laceration over his right eye. His asymmetrical face suggested that his nose was severely fractured as well. The other agents backed up in a defensive maneuver.

Startled by the altercation, passengers stampeded from the gate. Some dragged their carry-ons while others fled without them. All stooped low just in case someone started shooting. Small children, terrified by the pandemonium, cried out. A young girl, abandoned by her foolhardy parents, stood helplessly with her arms reaching out for help, tears streaming down her face.

With a solid grip on Romano's arm to stabilize him, Leach boomed above the malaise, "Settle down, Mates. We have special dispensation to carry firearms. It's authorized under our diplomatic status."

"Not since you attacked one of my men," the agent in charge barked. He reached over and pulled Romano's Beretta from its holster. Two others restrained Leach in order to remove his Walther.

"Let me assure you. If we had attacked you, there would be more of you bleeding right now," Leach yelled above the fracas.

"And we have a gate full of witnesses who can verify that you accosted us," Romano said.

The agent in charge smiled at his men. "We'll be sure to take their statements after we deal with you two. Now, if you'll follow me, we have some questions." Two agents helped their injured colleague in a different direction, presumably toward the dispensary.

Romano kept his fiery Italian temper in check as they were led down the hallway to an unmarked door. Sweeping a security card past a pad on the wall, the agent in charge pushed the door open to a large room full of uniformed guards scanning images from security cameras.

"Follow me, gentlemen," the agent said. He directed them into what looked like an interrogation room. "Make yourselves at home. I'll be back in a minute." He swept his card again and exited.

Romano paced the floor, checking the room for surveillance equipment. "What are we going to do now, Governor?"

"We're going to prevent these guys from shaking us down," Leach said. "Since we have no real leverage, we'll have to outwit them. Follow my lead. I have a plan."

After what seemed like an eternity, two entirely new agents entered the room and sat at the table. Standing erect in a corner, Leach calculated which of his two adversaries would be easiest to roll. The short timid one with wire-rimmed glasses, straggly mustache, and jowls probably was not in charge. His job was to take notes and back up his boss, the one with a square jaw and deep-set eyes. The boss's gnarled fingers and scarred hands were likely from a combat injury. He seemed to ignore his inconsequential partner as he prepared for the interrogation.

Leach approached the table from his corner, striking out first. "Are you gentlemen sure you want to violate diplomatic protocol? You need to know we are working directly for Secretary General Sukarno."

"That's impressive, Mr. Leach, but we don't really care who you work for," the leader said. "We have our own job to do." The second man nodded as if his concurrence was important.

The agent rocked back in his chair, hooking his thumbs in his belt. "We have reason to believe you are carrying contraband from Mexico. Did you visit Veracruz?"

"That's preposterous," Romano said. "We're on an official United Nations investigation. You can call our headquarters for verification."

"We have people checking that out now," the agent said. "We are also inspecting your checked luggage."

Leach nudged Romano's leg under the table. Romano reached down to retrieve his briefcase on the floor next to him, gripping the handle tightly.

Wary of Romano's movement and the defensive posture of both captives, the agent said, "We'll need to inspect your briefcase."

Leach bristled, casting the agent a steely glare. "It's not our intent to interfere with your official duties, but we can't let you do that. That briefcase contains critical evidence in an international criminal investigation."

The agent's assistant stopped writing and smirked. "It's not a request, gentlemen. Refusing to cooperate with an official inquiry is a federal offense. Unless you want to be arrested, I'd turn that briefcase over."

Leach's mouth curled with a subtle smile. "I have a suggestion for you, as well. Either bring me your supervisor or let me make a phone call, so INTERPOL can issue a warrant for your arrest for impeding a United Nations investigation."

Leach had called their bluff, leaving no other option but to stare at each other in a stalemate. Romano relaxed his grip to relieve the cramp in his hand. TSA's bluff had failed. The smaller agent doodled on his pad while his superior fumed from the counter-threat.

Leach was already one step ahead with a clever plan. In similar situations, he routinely outwitted his adversaries. These guys were hardly the sharpest knives in the drawer. And even though he and Manny had already missed their connection, no one was going to short-circuit their investigation.

The agent in charge thumbed his notebook for a few seconds, then broke the silence. "Under the Patriot Act, we're not subject to Miranda restrictions, nor are we required to allow phone calls."

"As I understand it, the Patriot Act only applies to issues of national security," Leach argued. "What does the transport of contraband have to do with that?"

The agent looked at his assistant for support. Failing any, he winged it. "Since you have no nexus with the United States, you are considered foreign persons of interest."

Sensing another bluff, Romano asked, "What do you mean by nexus?"

The agent relaxed under the delusion that he was gaining the advantage.

"That means an official connection with the government through citizenship or some other designation. Being an agent of the United Nations does not qualify, in our opinion."

To everyone's surprise, including Leach's, Romano reached into his pocket.

It was as if he had place a hand grenade on the table. The agents sprang into a defensive posture, backing away with guns drawn. Nearly toppling over in his chair, the assistant stuttered, "P-p-p-put your hands on the table, now!"

"Hold on," Romano said, amused by their clumsy reaction. "I have a document that might interest you. May I?"

The agent in charge rolled his eyes and exhaled, not expecting the document to be of any consequence. "You'd better not be wasting our time. Go ahead, slowly," he said.

All eyes were fixed on Romano as he pulled a folded document from his pocket in an overly animated fashion, then flipped it toward the agent in charge. "Maybe this will do," he said smugly.

The agent's expression hardened as he inspected Governor Spivey's signature on Manny Romano's appointment as an Adjunct Investigator for the Georgia Bureau of Investigation. He looked up from the document, locking eyes with Romano, then Leach. Rubbing his forehead, he said, "Excuse me a moment, gentlemen."

Minutes passed with Leach and Romano staring holes through the assistant agent, who continued to doodle in his notebook. The letter was a powerful trump card, and they knew it. Leach winked at Romano in recognition of his clever play.

The agent in charge reentered the room, his shoulders drooping and his eyes downcast. "You gentlemen are free to go," he muttered reluctantly. He walked around the table to grab the briefcase before Romano could react. "But this has to stay."

Romano sprang to his feet. The agent tumbled backward with the briefcase locked in his vice-like grip. Romano gripped it as well, pulling in the opposite direction in an awkward tug of war. Romano swore in Italian, drawing his clenched fist to end the struggle.

Caught totally off guard, the assistant joined the fray, but clumsily knocked his boss off balance even further. The agent in charge fell to the floor dragging Romano and the assistant with him.

Impressed by Romano's determination and agility, but more anxious to escape, Leach grabbed the briefcase handle with one hand and placed the other on Romano's back. "Let it go, Mate."

"But, Governor, it's irreplaceable!" Romano yelled, his Italian accent more pronounced.

The two agents lying on the floor with Romano smiled as if their adversaries were giving in. They rolled away from Romano with the agent in charge holding the briefcase. "If you two aren't out of my sight in two minutes, I'll arrest both of you for assaulting federal agents."

"Come on Manny, let's get out of here," Leach said. He pulled Romano from the floor.

"But—"

"No, buts, Mate, we're out of here," Leach said, shoving Romano toward the door.

On their way to the ticket counter to re-book their flight, Romano complained relentlessly about surrendering their prime evidence. "Our investigation is ruined," he cried. "I could have whipped both of those guys without breaking a sweat."

"You probably could," Leach argued, "and right now we'd be in a TSA holding cell instead of looking for the ticket counter."

"What are we going to tell Sukarno and Baard?"

Leach trudged through the concourse without answering. Romano dragged behind, stewing. Without warning, Leach paused in front of Romano, turned to face him, and gave his best Winston Churchill imitation. "Never, never, never give up, Manny. Last night while you were engrossed in football, I lifted the ledger from your briefcase and overnighted it to Sukarno. The other documents are safely tucked away in my money belt." He patted the bulge around his middle. "The only contraband they'll find in your briefcase is two very ripe avocados!"

Romano reached up and grabbed Leach by the cheeks, planting a big kiss on his forehead. "I knew you'd pull us through, Governor," he blurted. "You always do!"

Leach struggled free, glancing about to be sure no one of consequence, like the Queen, had witnessed Romano's kiss.

By the time Romano and Leach got back to their headquarters it was 5:30 a.m. Despite the early hour, Secretary General Sukarno and High Commissioner Baard had a steaming pot of coffee and a platter of pastries waiting.

"Good morning, Gentlemen," Sukarno said. "Welcome home."

Leach nodded with bloodshot eyes but high spirits. "Good morning, sir. We obtained the evidence we need." He poured himself and Romano a steaming cup of coffee.

Romano said, "Going to Mexico was a stroke of genius. It was the best lead we've had on an investigation in eons. We came back with conclusive proof that Elliott is a naturalized Mexican citizen."

There was a long pause as Sukarno walked behind his desk and peered out at the East River. Standing erect with his hands behind his back, he struck a familiar pose.

High Commissioner Baard responded first, "But I thought the President was born in Laredo, which would make him a naturalized American citizen. I've seen copies of his birth certificate signed by a Texas obstetrician."

"It's a forgery, plain and simple," Romano said. "We have the real one with indisputable supporting documentation."

"Manny's correct." Leach said. "We have the original supporting documentation plus the background explanation from the sister of the physician who delivered him. Just as compelling, we heard some helpful background from Victor Lopez, the uncle who raised him as a child. And their accounts are recorded."

As Leach removed the documents from his money belt and arranged them on the conference table next to the ledger, Sukarno and Baard gave each other reserved high fives.

Sukarno complimented his crack investigating team. "Is there anything you two cannot find?"

"A good night's sleep is about it," Romano said.

"Well, you certainly have earned that and much more. Your investigation proves how far Elliott will go to advance his own interests. He sacrificed his family and his heritage for a failed political career."

"He doesn't belong anywhere near America's nuclear arsenal," Baard said.

The three others agreed in unison.

"Why don't you fellows go down to the Lodge and get some sleep?"

Sukarno said. "We'll decide how to play our hand once you're rested up."

"I can't argue with the boss," Leach said.

"Me either," Romano said.

The exhausted investigators retreated to the temporary sleeping quarters in the basement, referred to by the staff as the Lodge, where they showered, then crashed.

Once Sukarno heard the elevator doors close, he turned to Baard. "Can you imagine the implications of their discovery? They've actually found the smoking gun that will remove a sitting American president from office."

"And thank God for that," Baard said. "No telling what kind of terror he could inflict during his last year in office."

For the rest of the day Sukarno and Baard discussed how they should issue their report. They also discussed what impact Elliott's removal might have on United States foreign policy. The final discussion focused on Vice President Andrew Simon's unsuitability to succeed Elliott. They both agreed that the United States Constitution dictates the order of succession, and they were bound to respect that.

After a couple of days of rest, Leach and Romano began the first draft of their report entitled *Human Rights Abuses by the Elliott Administration*. That title was appropriately amended to read *Human Rights Abuses by the Elliott Administration and other Matters* to include the country of origin information from Mexico. The report would conclude that President Elliott was ultimately responsible for the 220 civilian and military deaths suffered in the Madison attack. It also concluded that President Elliott approved Executive Order 14900 that DHS interpreted as authority to use deadly force against opposition political leaders.

The second section of the report highlighted the documents on President Elliott's country of origin, plus transcripts of the interviews with Victor Lopez and Alexandra Delgado. That section of the report ended with a nonbinding statement by the General Counsel of the United Nations that the election of Jerome Elliott, a Mexican national, violated Article II, Section 1 of the United States Constitution.

CHAPTER 37

—

While Leach and Romano wrapped up their report, Speaker Dobbins brought the bipartisan impeachment bill to the floor. Only a handful of House members voted against it. The overwhelming bipartisan vote for impeachment was a clear indication that Elliott must go.

Some constitutional philosophers argued that a protracted impeachment trial could cripple the government and disrupt markets. Of course, the presumption that President Elliott was eligible to be elected in the first place distorted their view. The United Nations report would challenge that presumption and eliminate all remnants of support for him.

Mitch Brady waited backstage in the auditorium of George Mason University. President Elliott was delivering an impassioned speech to restore support for his administration. Brady's observation was interrupted by his vibrating phone. When his caller ID showed the secret number for Brent McMahon, Director of the National Security Agency, he walked to a secluded corner and answered in a muffled tone, "Brady here."

"Hello, Mitch," McMahon said. "Thought you'd want to know that those two United Nations investigators have been in Mexico all week. They drove from Laredo, Texas to Nuevo Laredo, then to Veracruz. According to TSA, they took a red-eye back to New York. We intercepted a couple of cell conversations with a Mexican national in Nuevo Laredo and another in Veracruz."

"Have you listened to the conversations?" Brady asked.

"No, it'll take a while to isolate them and clean 'em up," McMahon said.

"Thanks for the tip," Brady said.

"Sure thing," McMahon said.

Brady mentioned the call to Elliott during the limo ride back to the White House. "Did he say Veracruz?" the President asked, clearly agitated.

"That's right, sir," Brady said.

"We need to figure out a way to stop those snooping foreigners," Elliott barked.

"What do you mean, Mr. President? Brady asked. "How do you expect us to stop them?"

"Pick them up as suspected terrorists," the President said. "Do whatever it takes to keep them from continuing their witch hunt."

Mitch tried his best to reason with the President. "We can't do that, sir," he insisted. "United Nations investigators have diplomatic immunity."

"Just do it, Mitch," the President said. "Now is not the time to question me."

"But, sir," Brady pleaded. "We have no authority to detain these guys. It would create an international incident."

Elliott flashed his dead serious glare. "I don't care what it creates," he said. "Just do what I say!"

As soon as the presidential limousine stopped at the entrance to the White House, Elliott dashed for the Oval Office while Brady hurried to the West Wing. In the relative comfort of his desk chair, he pondered the President's irrational behavior. The man had actually instructed him to violate international law, making him the scapegoat. His butt was already on the line for his role in the attempted raids on the Convention. He decided then and there that he could no longer stick his neck out for Elliott. He picked up his phone to take the first step to protect himself.

"Brent, it's Mitch again. This is extremely important. POTUS is going to call and instruct you to bring those recordings to the White House."

"He called two minutes ago." Brent said.

"We have the wrath of hell coming down on us from every possible angle," Brady said. "We can't afford any more slipups. Bring those recordings to me. Do not, I repeat, do not give them to the President."

"But, Mitch, he'll have my head on a platter," McMahon said.

"No, he won't. Remember who hired you," Brady said.

"You did," McMahon said.

"Do what I ask and let me deal with the rest," Brady said.

There was a brief pause. "Okay, as long as you have my back."

"I've got it," Brady said.

Neither man realized they were already on a slippery slope. And even the President of the United States could not save them from a long disastrous slide.

Early the next morning, Brent McMahon sat in the reception area of the West Wing fumbling with the flash drive in his pocket. The conversations on the drive had not been obtained through the legal FISA process, so he worried that he had broken the law. He knew that even though his actions were on behalf of the White House, he was the one on the hook. He had monitored the cell phones of key Convention delegates, and more recently Jack Tanner. Those taps revealed that Convention leaders intended to indict Jerome Elliott and other officials once Elliott was removed through impeachment. To everyone's surprise, the taps revealed a threat more ominous than impeachment.

"Mr. McMahon, you can go in now," Brady's secretary said.

Brady was sitting at his desk staring out the window, tapping a pencil on his desk. "Hello, Brent. Just wondering what you might have for me."

McMahon clicked the flash drive open as he approached Brady's computer. "Where's your USB port?"

Manny Romano's conversations with Victor Lopez and Alexandra Delgado intrigued Brady. "Why would they be interested in a physician's sister living in Veracruz?" he asked. "Did she make a reference to Jerome living in Veracruz?" *Surely he hadn't heard her correctly.*

McMahon shook his head as if to clear some cobwebs. "Maybe there is something to the birther rumors that circulated during the campaign."

"The President wouldn't blindside us like that," Brady said. "He couldn't keep such a volatile secret from the media."

"You're right, Mitch," McMahon said. "Secrets don't last long in this town. "Since Manning and Snowden blew the lid off of snooping, everyone in the know is a potential leaker."

Brady walked away from his desk shaking his head. "I think those investigators have been run around the flagpole and they just don't know it yet."

"You might be right," McMahon said. "But what if they're onto something?"

"In that case we're finished. Done. Over and out."

For the rest of the day Mitch was haunted by the possibility that the United Nations investigators had substantiated the birther rumors. At least the President would have a fighting chance at an impeachment trial. But there was absolutely no defense if his election violated the eligibility requirements of the Constitution. Brady knew he had to confront the President with the unthinkable. Once he did, there was no way to un-ring that bell.

Mustering all his courage, he snatched the flash drive and walked into the Oval Office where the President was chatting with his youngest daughter.

"If your security detail is okay with the field trip, I'm okay with it," Elliott told her.

Brady braced himself, knowing the President didn't like being disturbed when he was with his family. "Excuse me, sir. I have something urgent to discuss with you."

"Can't it wait a minute, Mitch? This is urgent, too."

"I think you need to hear what I have to say right now, sir," Brady insisted.

"If you put it that way, let me send my little girl on her way so we can take care of business," Elliott snarled. He said goodbye with a gentle kiss on her forehead. "See you later tonight, sweetie. Have fun."

"Thank you, Mr. President," Brady said.

As his daughter closed the door to the Oval Office, Elliott shot out at Brady. "What is so blasted important that I had to run my little girl off?" he asked.

Brady was determined to clear the air about the President's country of origin, information the President had been able to suppress for several years. "The NSA brought us some recordings between those two UN investigators and a couple of folks in Mexico."

"And?" the President asked.

"They make an unbelievable reference to Veracruz," Brady said.

Obviously uncomfortable with the subject, Elliott walked over to his computer. "Well, let's listen."

"I already have, sir. An unidentified woman in Veracruz makes a definite reference to you spending your early childhood there. I suspect you already know the two investigators were leaving Veracruz when TSA flagged their flight back to New York."

The President slumped into his chair with the resignation of a trapped animal. "I thought we could manage this," he murmured.

Brady realized his worst suspicions were true. "You wanted them detained to confiscate their evidence."

Elliott looked up with sleep-deprived eyes. "That's right, Mitch," he said. "I ordered NSA to monitor those two investigators because the CIA warned me when Leach and Romano get on a trail, they never stop. And they were on a dangerous trail."

"So you believe they found something significant in Mexico?" Brady asked.

"Something significant? Elliott snarled. "It's devastating."

"Are you saying you were in fact born in Mexico, sir?" Brady asked.

"I'm afraid so, Mitch. The campaign staff in Boston assured me none of this would ever surface. Their detectives assured us that everyone connected to me in Mexico was either dead or sworn to secrecy."

Brady was sickened by his sense of betrayal. "How could you do this to your supporters and your family?" he asked. "We all sacrificed so much based on our faith in you."

"Sorry," Elliott said. "I truly thought we could manage such a small technicality."

"Technicality!" Brady fired back. He couldn't contain his disappointment any longer. "You just confirmed our critics' claims that you're unfit to be President."

"But I was elected by the people and I deserve to be here."

"Not in the eyes of the Constitution, or in any sense of fair play," Brady said. He saw the President clearly for the first time.

"You're starting to sound just like those Freedom Caucus kooks," Elliott sneered.

"Hardball politics is one thing, but fraud is something else," Brady replied.

His doubts about the President had been growing for some time, but now he was sure. He could no longer support a man he did not trust or respect. "I can't be a part of this any longer, Mr. President," he said. "You'll have my resignation within the hour." He couldn't get out of Elliott's presence fast enough.

"A little problem arises and loyalty goes out the window," Elliott murmured. He remained in the Oval Office, wallowing in delusion and denial.

Later that afternoon the First Lady strolled into the West Wing to check on the President's schedule. "Hello Mary, is Mitch in?" she asked.

"Haven't you heard? Mary asked. "Mitch has resigned. He left this afternoon."

"Resigned?" she blurted, clasping her hand to her mouth. "When did this train wreck happen, and why?" Kianna's shoulders slumped as she looked to Mary for answers.

"Sorry, Ma'am," Mary said. "You'll have to ask the President."

"You bet I will," the First Lady said. Without asking if anyone was with him, she burst into the Oval Office. "Is your administration crumbling around us, Jerome?"

"Mitch and I had a disagreement over how things should be run around here," Elliott said. "It's better this way."

She bristled with anger. "How can that be? Your two strongest allies have resigned in the span of a week. I don't see how that can be good in the best of times."

"Now, now, Kianna," he said. "Don't get upset. Let me walk you upstairs. I have a lot to do this afternoon."

Irritated with the brushoff, the First Lady left the Oval Office with her husband. She pulled away violently when he tried to place his arm around her shoulder.

Mary overheard their conversation echoing down the staircase. She leaned toward her open office door, straining to hear.

"Jerome, is there anything you haven't told me about this stinking mess?" she asked.

"I have enemies out there trying to do me in, honey," he said. "Nothing more, nothing less."

The First Lady and Mary were skeptical of the President's lame explanation.

CHAPTER 38

——

Secretary General Sukarno summoned Leach and Romano to discuss how they should issue their report. With his investigators seated in front of his desk, he stood in his characteristic pose peering at Manhattan with his hands folded behind his back. "Gentlemen, we have a crucial decision to make. We hold some of the most explosive information in the world. What are we going to do with it?"

As he usually did in formal settings, Romano deferred to Leach with a nod.

"Well, sir, our usual strategy is to provide the information to the appropriate leader with a demand that they correct the abuse," Leach said. "Then, if they bury the information or refuse to act, we go to the membership and the press."

"That usually works, Percy," Sukarno said. "But based on my conversation with Elliott, he's not going to be receptive to our findings."

"With the outcome of the Constitutional Convention, power is now fragmented between Elliott, Speaker Clyde Dobbins, Governor Tim Kelley, and the newcomer, Jack Tanner," Leach said. "My suggestion, sir, would be to sit down with all of them, except Elliott, and share our findings."

"And then what?" Sukarno asked.

"Since the key issue is a constitutional one, I suspect they'll involve their Supreme Court," Leach said. "Hopefully, they'll get an order supporting his removal."

"I like your idea, Percy," Sukarno said. "What about you, Manny?"

"I agree with Percy, sir," he said. "Do we include the press?"

"I think we should let the Americans make that decision," Leach said.

"Then it's decided," Sukarno said. "I'll brief the Americans as soon as I can get a meeting scheduled. You two better stay in town in case they want to talk to you." He renewed his warning to his now-infamous investigators. "Keep in mind, desperate people sometimes take desperate measures. Once the President finds out what you've uncovered, you might become his worst enemies. I've already assigned extra security to both of you."

"That explains something," Romano said. "I caught a glimpse of Gunnar Hofmann tailing me around downtown yesterday. I was worried he was getting sweet on me or something."

In an unprecedented move, the Secretary General Sukarno contacted Speaker Dobbins, Tim Kelley, and Jack Tanner for a meeting in Washington. When asked what the meeting concerned, he alluded to information crucial to the operation of the United States government. Partly out of curiosity, but mostly out of respect for the Secretary General, each person accepted the invitation.

All three meetings were scheduled concurrently in the same place. On the appointed day and time, Jack took the metro to Farragut Station, then walked two blocks to the Army Navy Club on 17th Street in the heart of the District. He arrived at the front entrance just as Clyde Dobbins was getting out of a staffer's car.

"Hello Jack," Dobbins said. "I assume we're here for the same meeting."

"Mr. Speaker," Jack replied. "Glad you're here."

"Do you know what this is all about?" Dobbins asked. "I'm not exactly accustomed to being summoned by the Secretary General of the United Nations."

"I was hoping you could tell me," Jack said. "I suspect it's something darned important."

Dobbins watched a car approaching them.

Tim Kelley exited.

"Hello, Governor," Dobbins said. "Jack and I were just wondering about the purpose of our meeting."

Kelley glanced toward the entrance to the club. "It's strange to be invited to meet with a diplomat," he said.

Dobbins checked it out, too, anxious to get to the meeting. "You'd better get used to it, Tim. The Convention redefined a lot of roles. Like it or not, you're now a key diplomat."

Kelley smiled. "I was hoping to master my governor role before I took on anything else. Hello there, Jack. How's life on the big safari?"

Jack stepped closer to Kelley. "No more hectic than what you're dealing with," he said.

The three entered the main entrance and were escorted upstairs, past the library to a private meeting room where Secretary General Sukarno and two assistants were busy placing notebooks in front of seats marked with nameplates. He paused to greet his guests. "Good morning, gentlemen. Thank you for meeting me on such short notice."

Dobbins extended his hand. "We're happy to accommodate you, but as you can imagine we're all intrigued by the apparent urgency. Allow me to introduce Governor Tim Kelley, Chairman of our new Statutory and Regulatory Review Commission, and Mr. Jack Tanner, our new People's Judge Advocate. I'm Clyde Dobbins, Speaker of the House of Representatives."

Sukarno responded in effusive diplomatic language. "It's a pleasure to meet such courageous and distinguished leaders."

"Thank you, sir. The honor is ours," Kelley said.

Everyone shook hands and took a seat.

Sukarno kicked off the meeting by describing its purpose. "On the table, gentlemen, is a report representing the findings of a UN investigation into human rights violations by President Jerome Elliott's administration. In this case, the High Commissioner for Human Rights requested the investigation based on the events in Madison, Georgia and Austin, Texas. The members of the United Nations, including your country, have given us a mandate to investigate human rights violations anywhere in the world."

The three listened intently as the purpose of the meeting became clearer.

"As our investigation unfolded, the team came across information that superseded the human rights violations in terms of overall importance. Because of the explosive nature of this information, we decided to bring it directly to your attention. I could go into more detail, but I suggest you read the report, and we can discuss it afterwards. I'll excuse myself to tend to other matters. When you are ready, notify my aide here who'll retrieve me."

Dobbins picked up the report first. "I don't know about you guys, but my curiosity is getting the best of me." He immediately scanned the index and skipped directly to the second section, which covered the President's birth records.

His companions did the same.

"So the rumors were true," he murmured. "It's astounding what these guys dug up!"

"They actually found the smoking gun," Kelley said.

Stunned by the report's irrefutable evidence, the readers absorbed every detail. One by one they put the report down and eased back in their chairs.

Jack finally broke the silence. "How did he conceal this so long? I suppose we'd still be in the dark if Maria Lopez hadn't been killed in Madison. It's sad it took someone's death to expose the truth."

"Gentlemen, before the Secretary General comes back, we need to talk about what this means in terms of succession to the presidency," Kelley said. "It's clear to me we'll be able to convince the Supreme Court that Elliott's presidential bid was fraudulent."

"That's a great point, Tim," Jack said. "Since Vice President Simon was elected as part of the President's fraudulent ticket, I would think the Court would rule that his candidacy was fraudulent as well."

"That means, Mr. Speaker, you would ascend to the office instead of the Vice President," Kelley said. "I know how Jack and I feel about that, but I'm not sure about you."

Dobbins locked his fingers on top of the report. "If I can help eliminate some of the insanity in the federal government, you can count me in."

"The next logical step is to meet with the Chief Justice to get an order from the Court," Kelley said. "A supportive ruling from the highest court will allow us to clean house at 1600 Pennsylvania Avenue."

"It sounds like we have a plan," Jack said.

Dobbins turned to the aide standing at one end of the room. "Please retrieve the Secretary General."

The aide headed toward the door. "Right away," he said.

Sukarno could tell by the smiles around the table that everyone was pleased with the work of his team. "Gentlemen, do you have any questions?"

Jack spoke up. "Just one, Mr. Secretary General. How can we ever thank you and your investigators for what you've done for our country?"

"It's quite simple, Mr. Tanner. Remove your President from access to the U.S. nuclear arsenal, and resurrect the United States as the bastion of freedom, opportunity, and security for the world."

"With help from the men around this table, support from the American people, and the blessing of almighty God, you can count on it, sir," Kelley said

Everyone was preparing to leave the historic meeting when Jack Tanner made a special request. "I would like to meet with your investigators when it's convenient, sir."

"You have an open invitation to meet with them at the United Nations headquarters, Mr. Tanner, as long as you don't try to recruit them. Their contact information is in the back of the report."

"Thank you, sir," Jack replied. "We have talented investigators in this country, but yours are truly special. What do you intend to do with the report going forward?"

"Our responsibility has been met, Sukarno said. "The report will be filed in our archives. It's up to you and the American people to ensure that Elliott's human rights violations are never repeated."

"On behalf of a grateful nation, we thank you," Dobbins said.

They shook Sukarno's hand on the way out, happy to have such a valuable ally in their difficult quest.

CHAPTER 39

—

With Clyde Dobbins in line to become President, and the near certainty that Jack Tanner would indict President Elliott, Tim Kelley was chosen to present the United Nations report to Chief Justice Marshal Hall of the United States Supreme Court.

Hall struck Kelley as a caricature with his jet-black hair, dark suit, and polka-dot bow tie. Hall presumed Kelley asked for the meeting to discuss the relationship between the Court and the Federal Statutory and Regulatory Review Commission. These were unique times and though it was a radical departure from the Court's protocol, he was willing to meet informally with the highly respected constitutional lawyer. Hall expressed relief that exacerbating the country's polarization and eroding international confidence in America's leadership through an impeachment might be avoided. His greatest concern, he confided, was that Elliott would do something drastic to remain in power.

"It's essential that you agree to move quickly," Kelley said. "Elliott has already shown his tendency to strike out when he feels threatened. His reckless deployment of the 82nd Airborne caused two-hundred-and-twenty military and civilian deaths and numerous other casualties. No one knows what he's capable of, but we do know he has the launch codes for our nukes."

"I share your sense of urgency," Hall said. "But as a constitutional lawyer, you know I cannot issue an order on behalf of the Court without input from all the justices."

"How long will that take?" Kelley asked.

"I can't say for sure," Hall said. "It depends on everyone's schedule. Given the importance of the issue, I should be able to convince my colleagues to rule immediately even though we're out of session. Is there any way to remove the President pending our court order?"

"There'll be less backlash from the public if it's based on a Supreme Court ruling. Plus, support from the Court would facilitate the country's healing."

"Let me see if I can light a fire under my learned colleagues," Hall said. "I hope to have something to you by the end of tomorrow."

"There's one more issue," Kelley said. "Since Vice President Simon was elected on the same ticket, does that invalidate his position as Vice President?"

"That would certainly be my opinion," Hall said. "But I need my colleagues to weigh in on that as well, so we can include it in the Court's order."

"Thank you, sir. Meantime, we'll plan for the transition."

"Thank you for working to restore the integrity of the presidency," Hall said before closing the door.

G overnor Kelley received Hall's call the next day saying all the justices had reviewed the report and had committed to issue the Court's opinion by the end of the week, an unprecedented step by the Supreme Court. "I'll have our opinion delivered by courier to your office on K Street sometime Friday morning," he said.

"Thank you, sir."

When Kelley briefed Speaker Dobbins and Jack Tanner about the development, both expressed amazement that SCOTUS, the Supreme Court of the United States, could move so swiftly. A meeting was scheduled at the Capitol at seven that evening to formulate their transition plan.

T he trio gathered in a far corner of the Members Dining Room, one of the convenient restaurants in the Capitol Building. An especially cheerful attendant greeted them. "Good evening, Gentlemen."

"Tim, Jack, this is Arthur," Dobbins said. "He's been here since 1960, far longer than any member of Congress."

"That's right, Gentlemen. I'm sort of a fixture around here," Arthur said with pride. His traditional attendant's vest was decorated with buttons from every presidential campaign dating back to Dwight Eisenhower.

Tanner was the first to shake his hand. "We're happy to meet you, Arthur. Can you point out your favorite button?"

"People always ask me that on their first visit here," he said.

"And his answer is always the same," Dobbins said. "If the guests are Republican, he always points to his Ronald Reagan button. If he's serving

Democrats, he points to his JFK button."

"And what if he's serving a bipartisan group?" Kelley asked with a sly grin.

"I point to my AARP button," Arthur replied.

Tanner spoke up, "Have you ever thought of entering politics, Arthur?"

"No, sir. I don't have the patience for all of the shenanigans."

"What do you think about President Elliott?" Tanner asked.

"That's a loaded question, Mr. Tanner. I'm thinking he's in a heap of trouble with the three of you having dinner together."

Kelley interrupted to get everyone off the hook. "I think I'll have tonight's special, the lasagna."

"I'll have the same," Tanner said.

Dobbins held up three fingers. "Make it a trifecta."

Arthur flaunted his salesmanship. "We have excellent espresso if you want to go all Italian."

"Absolutely," said Kelley.

The others nodded in agreement.

"I have an order for three lasagnas and three espressos," Arthur said. "Our lasagna comes with buttered garlic bread." He departed with a crisp white towel folded across his right forearm.

Once Arthur was out of earshot, Tanner addressed the issue at hand. "If we could get the Secret Service to buy in, the eviction would be easier. We don't want them to think we're a physical threat to the President."

"But the Director is one of Elliott's closest friends," Dobbins said.

"Maybe we can get to his personal detail," Tanner suggested.

Kelley twirled his knife on the table. "I think I know a way. During the Convention, I met a South Carolina policeman named Kurt Whittaker whose son is a senior agent on the President's personal detail. Governor Granger and Kurt Whittaker are good friends. I'll call Whittaker and see if he can help."

"Perfect," Tanner said. "We'll need the element of surprise for this to go down smoothly. If Whittaker's son is willing to help, we can serve the Court's order and get Elliott out of the line of authority before he realizes what's happening. Whittaker can line up Blair House as temporary accommodations until the Elliott family decides what to do."

"I like your plan, Jack," Dobbins said. "We can't subject either the President or his family to any indignity. Americans are a sympathetic lot, and I'm sure they will feel sorry for the First Family, even if they support their removal."

"Good point, Clyde," Kelley said.

Tanner agreed.

"Seems we have another trifecta," Dobbins said. "The eviction needs to be quick and non-confrontational."

The conversation shifted to sports when Arthur and another attendant approached with plates of steaming lasagna. While the three enjoyed dinner, House Minority Leader Janet Monroe approached Dobbins. "Hello, Clyde. The special looks yummy today."

"I can recommend the espresso as well, if you can tolerate caffeine this late," he said.

She moved closer, placing her hand on Dobbins's shoulder. "I was wondering if my caucus will get a chance to see the rewrite of the impeachment bill before it comes up for a vote."

He slowly placed his fork on his plate then swept a glance at his colleagues. "Madam Minority Leader, what happened to your philosophy that we need to pass these bills to find out what's in them?"

"Everybody knows that statement was taken out of context," she snapped.

"The fact is, you were videotaped saying those exact words," Dobbins said.

Red-faced and flustered, Monroe mumbled something unintelligible before stomping off to her table.

Kelley bumped Tanner's knee under the table. "Well done, Clyde."

Tanner bumped back. "That's a good warm-up for things to come. And if that puts her back on her heels, wait until she finds out what we have in store for her pal, Jerome Elliott."

The following day Kelley called Granger's office to obtain Kurt Whittaker's personal telephone number. He dialed, then cleared his throat on the first ring.

"Hello Mr. Whittaker, this is Governor Kelley. We worked together briefly at the Convention in Austin."

"I remember," Whittaker said. "How's the new commission coming?"

"I'm happy to report we're already making remarkable progress. I'd like to talk to you about our next step, but I'd prefer it to be face-to-face."

"We're in luck, Governor," Whittaker said. "I'm in DC for a state police association conference. Could you join me for dinner tonight at Potomac Grill in Old Towne, say eight?"

"That's perfect, Kurt. They serve wonderful soft-shell crab. See you then."

Over dinner Kelley outlined the findings of the United Nations investigation and described the action he expected from the Supreme Court.

"It sounds like we've all been given a wonderful gift," Whittaker said.

"We have, but we need to avoid an ugly confrontation when we deliver the Supreme Court order. We'll need help from his Secret Service detail to get the Elliott family out of the White House without incident."

Whittaker nodded in agreement. "They have already anticipated this development, but they expected impeachment to be the trigger. In fact, my son called during the Convention to ask what they should do in case of a legitimate challenge to the President's authority."

"We don't want him to do anything dangerous out of desperation," Kelley said. "Once we get the order from the Court we'll need to move immediately."

"Absolutely," Whittaker said. "What if I set up a meeting between you, my son, and the leader of the detail, who happens to be one of my son's best friends?"

"That's a generous offer, Kurt, but there are so many moving parts it would be better if I organized the meeting. You could help by endorsing our legitimacy if your son questions it. I'm wondering if we should meet with them before or after the Court issues its order."

Whittaker offered a salient point. "It seems a ruling from the Supreme Court would remove all uncertainty."

"But I don't expect to get it for a couple of days," Kelley said.

"I'm just a police officer, Governor. But if a little more patience would make it easier for the detail to cooperate with you, why not wait?"

"Excellent point," Kelley said. "I won't contact your son until I get the order and we're ready to move."

"Good luck, Governor. The country weighs in the balance."

CHAPTER 40

—

The bicycle courier's spandex clothing gleamed in the sunlight. His flame-emblazoned helmet, sports shoes, and fanny pack were typical of Washington's famed daredevils. He had delivered important packages to every office in the capital, but this one was different. The dispatcher had instructed him to go straight to the Hightower Office Building on K Street downtown. He was ordered to keep the package in sight at all times and to refrain from discussing it. Never in his years as a senior courier had any instructions been so strict.

The terraced landing to the Hightower Office Building was crowded with reporters and technicians carrying news cameras.

"What's all the excitement about?" the courier asked.

"This is the office of Tim Kelley, the new chairman of the Statutory and Regulatory Review Commission," the reporter said. "He's going to be implementing the reforms passed by the Convention. This is the biggest news story in this town since the impeachment of President Lockhart."

"Big deal," the courier sneered. "I thought Bono or somebody important was here." Bono, philanthropist and leader of the famous Irish band U2, was known to frequent Washington, DC to drum up support for his anti-AIDS initiative in Africa.

The courier entered the lobby and handed the package to the guard. "Kelley is the only person who can sign for this. Strict orders."

The guard grabbed the package and tucked it under his arm.

The courier watched nervously as the guard picked up the phone on his desk.

"Security here," the guard said. "We have a delivery in the lobby that only Governor Kelley can sign for."

"He's expecting it," the receptionist said. "He'll be right down."

"Yes, ma'am," the guard replied, realizing the package was something special.

The guard sized up the courier. "You must be more important than you look. The Governor himself is coming down."

Still straddling his bike, the lanky courier pulled out a cigarette. His Humphrey Bogart imitation was priceless. "I might seem like a peon to you, but I know people in this town." The cigarette wagged up and down with each word.

The guard pointed to a large "No Smoking" sign on the wall. "I don't care who you know. If you light that smoke, you're outta here."

"No need to get pushy," the courier said. His handlebars swung sideways when he let go to maneuver the cigarette back into its package.

The guard watched in amazement as he crammed the package and lighter into his bulging fanny pack.

Just as the guard was about to thank him for not smoking, the elevator dinged and Kelley stepped into the lobby. He'd been anticipating this day, or a day like today, for a long time.

"Hello, Governor," the guard said. "We have an important package for you."

Kelley scribbled his illegible signature on the receipt. "Gentlemen, this could conceivably be the single most important package delivered in the world this century."

The guard and the courier gaped as if Lady Gaga had just waltzed in.

To the courier, the ten-dollar tip Kelley slapped into his outstretched hand seemed short given the importance of the delivery. But government officials who face tight restrictions on paying tips with precious tax dollars were often tight-fisted.

"Thanks," the courier said, shoving the ten into his pack. He adroitly dodged pedestrians, mostly reporters, as he worked his way through the entryway to the street.

Kelley watched him bob and weave through cars while picking up speed like a runaway horse on a tear.

As the elevator rang off the floors between the lobby and his office, Kelley fumbled with the flap on the envelope. By the time he arrived at his office, it was completely open. Settling into his desk chair, he tipped it open end down, allowing the multi-page document to slide into view.

The cover letter was addressed to: The Honorable Timothy Kelley,

Chairman, Federal Statutory and Regulatory Commission. It was signed by Marshal Hall, Chief Justice of the United States Supreme Court. The letter read: After careful consideration of the documents and other evidence provided in the *United Nations Investigation of Human Rights Violations and Other Matters,* this Court is of the opinion that Jerome Elliott, a natural-born-citizen of the Republic of Mexico, is ineligible to hold the office of President under Article II, section 1, of the United States Constitution. In addition, it is the unanimous opinion of this Court that since Vice President Benjamin Simon was elected as part of an ineligible ticket, he is ineligible to hold the office of Vice President. In accordance with the Constitution, the Speaker of the House of Representatives is next in line of ascendancy to the office of President of the United States. The Court's complete legal analysis is attached.

Elated with the Supreme Court's findings, Kelley laid the precious documents on his desk and nearly floated to his credenza. He poured a celebratory glass of his lucky charm, Bushmill Irish whiskey. He returned to his desk and buzzed his secretary.

"What can I do for you, Governor?" she asked.

"Could you get Speaker Dobbins on the phone, please?"

In a few seconds, the call was put through. "The eagle has landed," Kelley told him.

"With both feet?" Dobbins asked.

"Ears and all," Kelley replied, taking a sip of Irish. "We can discuss this in more detail later."

Both men drew great satisfaction from the knowledge that those monitoring Dobbin's line wouldn't have a clue.

Tanner had asked Kelley to call on his personal cell phone, since it had been encrypted with security software so good that even the National Security Agency couldn't intercept his calls. Kelley had the same software on his phone. "Jack, Kelley here. Where are you?"

"At my daughter's championship softball game," Tanner said. "Should be back in my office in an hour if you need me."

"Just calling to let you know we got everything we wanted from the Court," Kelley said. "I've already notified the Speaker."

"Hot dang," Tanner said. "When do we move forward?"

"We need to make sure the Secret Service detail stands down. Can you meet with a couple of them tonight at 9:00 p.m. in my office?"

Tanner's voice raised an octave. "Are you kidding? I wouldn't miss it for anything."

"I'll set it up," Kelley replied.

He took another sip, and dialed Arsenal Security, a private firm he trusted implicitly, and asked them to plant an agent at the coffee shop around the corner from the White House. He texted a photo of Danny Whittaker on his encrypted phone. "Let me know when he shows up for a break. I can be there in five minutes."

Ninety minutes later the agent called Kelley. "He just met a girl here for a cup of coffee, and from the looks of things, he'll be here for a while."

"I'll be back shortly," Kelley told his secretary on his way out. "Tell my driver to pick me up at the curb."

Within five minutes, Kelley entered the coffee shop and picked out Danny Whittaker wrapping up the conversation with his friend.

"Bye, Danny. I'll see you Saturday night," she said, walking away.

While Whittaker waved to his friend, Kelley approached from behind. He recoiled when Kelley faced him. "Danny Whittaker, I'm Timothy Kelley. I'm a friend of your dad's and Governor Granger's. Can we chat for a moment?"

"Excuse me, Mr. Kelley, but you startled me. I know exactly who you are, so I'm not sure it's a good idea to be talking to you."

"It's crucial that you and Bruce Connor meet me in my office tonight at 9:00 p.m."

"Can you tell me what this concerns?"

"Not here. If you have reservations, call your father."

"What does my dad have to do with this?"

"He knows how important it is for us to talk," Kelley said.

"Excuse me a minute," Whittaker said. He turned toward the counter. "I'll be right back."

With assurance from his father, Danny returned to Kelley. His relaxed expression was a welcome sign.

All I know about your, Governor Kelley, is your reputation for opposing President Elliott. Despite all the complications that represents for me, my dad encouraged me to cooperate with you. Based on his trust, I'll bring Connor to your office this evening at nine.

"Thank you, son. You won't regret this decision."

Kelley returned to his office and called Granger's encrypted phone to brief him on the development.

"So this self-inflicted nightmare is about to end," Granger said with a deep sigh.

"Thanks in major part to your hard work with the Convention," Kelley said.

"What are your plans when this is over, Tim?" he asked. "You know Dobbins is going to ask you to help in the new administration."

"I made a commitment to implement the reforms of the Convention," Kelley said.

"That's what I expected," Granger said. "But Clyde is going to need a crack Attorney General to help him sort things out."

"We can cross that bridge later," Kelley said. "Right now I'm focused on pulling the transition off."

Finished with Granger, Kelley called his contact at Arsenal Security Company. "Can you guys do a spontaneous sweep of my office? I have a critical meeting tonight and I don't want anyone snooping. Seven will be perfect since we're meeting at nine."

At seven o'clock the head of Arsenal Security walked into Kelley's office suite carrying cases of electronic equipment. "Time to exterminate," he said. Holding up an instrument, he added, "This device will jam their signal while I search for bugs. He flipped a switch and made a couple of adjustments. "Keep everyone out of your private office until I give the all clear."

In less than fifteen minutes he walked out of the office with his hand outstretched. "It's definitely a hot zone," he said. "We found these little beauties, one on your phone, the other in the base of your lamp."

Kelley stepped forward to check them out. "What can you tell about them?" he asked, peering intently.

"They're top shelf," the agent said. "No question, they were planted by the CIA, the FBI, or the NSA. No one else has access to these babies. They have the greatest range and longest battery life in the industry. I'd say somebody high on the food chain wants to know who you're talking to and what you are saying."

Kelley swallowed hard, knowing that his confidential conversations earlier in the day could have compromised their plan. "Do you know how long they've been there?"

The specialist noted the concern on Kelley's face and knew something unusual was in the works. "When we conducted our scheduled sweep two days ago, everything was clean. I just tested the batteries on these bugs and they're still at 100%. In my opinion, they were planted in the last hour or two."

"That's impossible," Kelley said. "I was in the office all day except for a quick trip to the coffee shop an hour ago."

"Bingo. That was their window of opportunity," the agent said.

Kelley approached his secretary. "Was anyone in the office while I was out?"

"It's funny you ask, Governor. A building inspector came in to do a routine inspection of your fire escape as soon as you stepped out. He had a badge and paperwork, but he was dressed like an insurance agent."

"Did anyone go in with him?"

"No," she said. "He said he had inspected the office many times and knew where everything was."

"Of course," the security agent said. "We'll send someone over tomorrow to give your office staff some security training."

Kelley still looked concerned. "Could you check my safe for tampering?"

"We installed that safe right after you were appointed," the agent said. "Nobody's going to crack it in less than a couple of hours, and even then they'd make a racket. But I'll check it anyway to put your mind at ease." Now he was certain something big was up.

"Appreciate it," Kelley said.

Assured that his safe had not been tampered with, Kelley relaxed. "I'm just relieved they didn't pick up my conversations earlier in the day. That would have been catastrophic!"

"I'm going outside to find their recon team," the agent said. "They're usually close by in an unmarked or commercial van. They're no doubt wondering why their transmitters went dead when we pulled the batteries."

Five minutes later he returned smiling. When he noticed a van parked a block away in front of a fire hydrant he called the DC police and stuck around to see the feds get a parking ticket and an order to leave.

"Serves them right," Kelley said. "I hope they get points on their license and a bump in their insurance rate."

At nine sharp Kelley greeted Danny Whittaker and Bruce Connor, then introduced them to Jack Tanner. All accepted a glass of his prized Irish whiskey.

"I have a feeling we're going to need this before the night is over," Whittaker said when he accepted his glass.

Connor was as jumpy as a grasshopper at a robin's convention. "I don't mind telling you gentlemen, I'm not comfortable meeting with the President's political enemies."

"Settle down, man," Whittaker said. "This is not about the President anymore, it's about the country."

Tanner was struck by how young the two agents looked. He tried to shake the image of children guarding the most important person on the planet.

"Gentlemen, I know this meeting is highly unusual and I can understand your discomfort in being here," Kelley said. "But I can assure you what we're doing is completely legal and can in no way be held against you."

In an attempt to calm Connor's nervousness, Tanner spoke up. "Tim Kelley is a federal official with unique responsibility. He is also one of the top constitutional lawyers in the country. He is honest to a fault and would never ask you or anyone else to do anything illegal."

"Sometimes what is proper and appropriate is more important than what's legal," Connor said.

Tanner agreed. "But in this case you'll have to decide for yourself what is proper and appropriate. We think you'll agree that President Elliott's actions don't meet either test. But we didn't ask you to come here to discuss technicalities."

"Why did you bring us here, Mr. Tanner?" Connor asked.

"The Supreme Court has concluded that President Elliott was never eligible to be President of the United States," he replied. "The Court has ruled that his entire political campaign was fraudulent."

Connor sat with his arms crossed, clearly unconvinced. "The President insists that you people hate him because he's a minority."

"The only thing we care about here is his eligibility to be President. According to the Constitution and a ruling from the U.S. Supreme Court, he isn't."

Kelley handed both men a copy of the epic ruling. "Review these documents and everything will be clearer."

Agent Connor read and then addressed his partner. "Do you see what I see, Danny Boy?"

"What I see is President Elliott lied about being an American citizen," Whittaker replied.

Tanner walked in front of the two agents. "Gentlemen, Jerome Elliott is an illegitimate president, and he has not been rational when exercising the power of the office. We're obligated to make sure he doesn't murder any more American citizens. In addition, we need to make sure he doesn't have access to our nuclear arsenal, which could expose the world to catastrophic consequences."

Kelley cast his version of Tanner's steely glare. "The Supreme Court ruling is President Elliott's eviction notice and we are going to execute it. But we need to be sure you don't confuse our action as an assault on a legitimate sitting president."

Connor looked confused. "Are you asking us to stand down when you evict him from the White House?"

"Let me state it another way, Agent Connor," Kelley said. "We're asking you to assist us in correcting a violation of the Constitution in accordance with an order from the highest court in the land."

Tanner added, "We're asking you to let us into the White House so we can formally serve this notice. We'll need some female agents to escort the Elliott family to Blair House until they can get resettled."

Connor looked at Whittaker. "Do you have any objections, Danny?"

"We don't seem to have a choice."

Connor's next question was music to Kelley and Tanner. "How do we proceed?"

"First, we need to know the President's schedule," Tanner said.

Connor pulled out his smart phone. "He's in the Oval Office in the morning and has a meeting at NSA after lunch."

"The NSA meeting was probably called to talk about what we're up to," Kelley said. "We just need to pick a time tomorrow morning to meet you at the entrance to the West Wing."

"He'll go over his schedule at nine in the morning," Connor said.

"Who will be with him?" Tanner asked.

"His Acting Chief of Staff," Connor said.

Kelley raised his hand. "Perfect. Let's do it then."

"Okay with me," Tanner said.

"It works for me," Connor said. "Do you have any objections, Danny?"

"I'm good."

"We want to make this as non-confrontational as possible," Tanner said. "Your cooperation will ensure that no one intervenes on the President's behalf."

"We'll do everything we can to make it go smoothly," Connor said. "Right, Danny?"

"Right, Bruce."

Tanner gave Kelley a nod. "Thank you, gentlemen. You're showing a lot of courage."

The two young agents drained their glasses, shook hands with Kelley and Tanner, then left.

"I think we're all set, Jack," Kelley said.

"Yes, and it went better than I expected. "What about Vice President Simon?"

"We'll let Dobbins deal with him, once he's in the driver's seat."

Before leaving for home, Kelley called the Chief Justice to brief him on the eviction plan. The Chief Justice agreed to be at the White House at nine-thirty the following morning to swear in the next President of the United States of America.

CHAPTER 41

—

At nine the following morning, Kelley and Tanner met Whittaker and Connor at the Pennsylvania Avenue entrance to the White House. Tanner greeted the agents as he walked briskly through the security check point. "Good morning, gentlemen. Are you ready to make history?"

Connor looked stressed but determined. "Good morning, Mr. Tanner. We just want to get this over. I've instructed the detail to follow my lead this morning. They know something is going to happen, they just don't know what. But don't worry; they'll follow my orders."

"They'll get the picture shortly," Tanner said.

The men hurried to the reception room just off the Oval Office.

"Can I help you gentlemen?" Mary asked. "I don't see an appointment."

Agent Connor brushed by her without hesitating. "They're with me, Mary. We need to see the President."

"I'm sorry, but he's tied..." Before she could finish, all four had barged into the Oval Office, unannounced.

President Elliott and Leslie Hart, his Acting Chief of Staff, were bent over his desk checking the schedule on a computer screen. The commotion of the men entering startled the President, who turned away from the screen. "Connor, what's the meaning of this?"

He then noticed Kelley and Tanner standing behind the agents. "What are those traitors doing in my office?" he yelled, his anger igniting. "Get them out of here!"

Agent Connor signaled his men, then nodded to Kelley and Tanner. "Sorry, sir. I can't do that."

"What do you mean?" the President snapped. "I'm ordering you to clear this room. It's not a request, Connor." He walked around and hit the panic button under the lip of his desk.

Connor wasn't quite sure how to address Elliott now. "I've disabled the alarm, sir. No one is coming. You need to hear these men out."

Kelley stepped in front of Connor and walked toward the President. "I have an order from the Supreme Court you need to review right now, sir."

Acting Chief of Staff Hart backed away, not knowing what to do.

The fact that no one was addressing him as president put Elliott on the defensive. "Listen, Kelley, you might feel high and mighty now that you have that People's Commission behind you, but I'm still the president."

"Not anymore," Kelley said, standing firm. "We have a copy of your Mexican birth certificate and statements attesting to your country of origin. Article II, section 1 of the Constitution is clear. A Mexican citizen cannot be President of the United States."

Acting Chief of Staff Hart approached Kelley and stammered. "What are you talking about?"

Kelley placed a copy of the Supreme Court's order in her hand. She immediately began reading the cover letter from the Chief Justice.

"Mr. President, you do need to look at this," she said, placing the documents against his arm.

Elliott grabbed the order and threw it on the floor. The pages drifted onto the Presidential Seal like an omen. "That doesn't mean a thing," Elliott said. "I don't care who your sham order is from. I was elected by a landslide, and I'm staying. I don't care what the Court or anyone else says." He walked behind the President's desk in a show of defiance.

"I'm sorry, sir, but you need to vacate this office right now," Connor said. He motioned to two Secret Service agents in the back of the room who walked up and took Elliott's arms to escort him to the exit. Elliott reached for the panic button again while swearing and threatening the agents. "I'll have all of you crucified, including you, Kelley," he swore.

"Now that you're a private citizen, you could end up in jail for threatening others," Tanner said with a less than subtle hint.

"Damn you, Tanner," he yelled. "I'll deal with you and Kelley later!"

His arms pinned behind his back, the agents pulled him from behind the desk and proceeded to the exit. They would remain with him at Blair House to prevent him from calling on help that would disrupt the transition. The former President's swearing tirade would last long after he had been delivered to Blair House, exposing his former agents to despicable behavior from the man they had once served so loyally.

Acting Chief of Staff Hart stood crippled by disbelief. "What should I do?"

"You need to go back to your office," Kelley said. "Elliott's replacement will decide who serves as chief of staff. In the interim, you will likely be kept on to help with the transition. And Ms. Hart, don't do anything foolish to disrupt this lawful transition."

"Yes, sir," she said meekly.

For a brief moment, Governor Tim Kelley held the reins of power to the entire U.S. government.

Connor instructed an agent to accompany Hart back to her office to ensure her compliance with Kelley's instructions.

A female agent escorted Mary, the former president's secretary, into the Oval Office to neutralize her. "What on earth is going on, Connor?" she shrieked before slumping into a chair, frightened and confused.

Connor briefed Mary while two female agents went up to the residence to escort the First Lady down. Within minutes she burst into the Oval Office demanding an explanation. "Where is the President? She asked. What's going on here?"

"He's no longer the President, Mrs. Elliott, and you are no longer the First Lady," Connor said. "We'll escort you to Blair House where you can stay with Mr. Elliott until you decide what to do."

She instantly latched onto his odd reference to "Mr. Elliott." Cowering like a frightened animal, she asked, "What are you telling me, Connor? Has there been a coup or something?"

Tim Kelley stepped forward. "The Supreme Court has ruled that your husband is a citizen of Mexico and as such is ineligible to be president."

"And who are you?" she asked, recognizing his face from the news, but not remembering his name.

"That's not important," Kelley said. "But it is important that you read these documents." He handed her a copy of the ruling.

She lowered herself onto a couch and began reading. As a layperson she didn't understand the legal technicalities, but she was bright enough to grasp the gist of the Court's conclusion.

The former First Lady looked pathetic while learning the truth about her husband. "My children are ruined," she cried out. "Their father isn't even an American. What else has he lied to us about?"

"I'm really sorry, Ma'am," Connor said. "You need to gather your things and join Mr. Elliott at Blair House."

"I don't want to be with that lying, murderous man another minute," she shrieked. With teary eyes she asked about her daughters.

"The girls will be brought to Blair House after school," Connor said. "We've already made arrangements. Don't worry, ma'am, they'll be taken care of."

Shuffling into the reception area, she hesitated next to Speaker Dobbins who was standing by Mary's desk holding a worn Bible. Placing a trembling hand on the Bible, she whispered, "Please pray for us, Mr. Speaker."

"Sorry for your grief, Mrs. Elliott. I've been praying for your family for a long time."

Within minutes, the Chief Justice had sworn Speaker Clyde Dobbins in as the President of the United States. "Good luck, Mr. President. Please get this house in order."

"I will do my best," Dobbins promised.

"Jerome Elliott is all yours, Jack," Kelley said.

"We start building our case tomorrow," Tanner replied.

Dobbins caught Kelley mouthing something from across the room. "Congratulations, Mr. President."

"Thank you, Tim," Dobbins replied. "I'm going to need a lot of help. I hope I can count on you and Jack."

"As long as we're able."

Dobbins wasted no time recruiting Norman Sheets, his Chief of Staff from the House, to help with the transition.

Sheets had been a loyal staffer with strong management and administrative skills. Due to the urgency of the situation, he quickly disengaged from the House to assume his new duties.

"Norman, get Vice President Simon on the phone for me," Dobbins instructed. "We need to help him transition out as soon as possible. I don't want anyone on board who's not 100% with us."

With support from the Supreme Court, Warren Price, the senior senator from Iowa and President Pro-Tempore of the Senate, became Vice President to ensure an unbroken line of succession. In accordance with their respective rules, the leadership of the House and the Senate, in conjunction with the affected states, selected replacements for Speaker Dobbins and Senator Price.

Dobbins quickly called a joint meeting with the cabinet and the White

House staff to brief them on the transition and to announce new lines of authority. Afterward, the press office issued an announcement to inform the media and the public on what had transpired. A presidential press conference was scheduled for the next day to answer questions.

Dobbins and Sheets worked tirelessly to build a competent White House staff. The President immediately fired all the special counselors and czars Elliott had brought into office. The Cabinet members had already been put on notice that their qualifications would be reviewed before any changes were made. Dobbins was appalled to learn how many appointees in the administration were poorly qualified, or in some cases had no relevant experience at all.

Brent McMahon's replacement at the National Security Agency was ordered to clear all phone and computer taps through the Foreign Intelligence Surveillance Act, or FISA process.

Next, Dobbins cleaned house at the IRS department responsible for approving nonprofit status for organizations. He soon learned that corruption had spread throughout the agency. A task force was set up to weed out all affected employees.

The Secretary of Health and Human Services had already resigned at Elliott's insistence, but all of those below the Secretary level who botched the rollout of the Affordable Health Care Act were fired as well.

Career employees who played a role in any of Jerome Elliott's illegal actions were suspended and sent home, pending a personnel review. The Office of Personnel Management was ordered to institute a hiring freeze to prevent Elliott's political appointees from burrowing into the career service. A panel was set up to review all hires in the last 90 days.

General Martinez was appointed Chairman of the Joint Chiefs of Staff, and General Graham was appointed Chief of Staff of the Army.

In another critical sector, the Federal Reserve chairman resigned voluntarily. He insisted that the Fed could not function with complete transparency and oversight, or interference as he referred to it, by Congress. He was quickly replaced with the well-respected banker who had been criticized by the Elliott administration for his refusal to accept funds under the controversial Troubled Asset Relief Program, also known as TARP.

The new chairman was welcomed by Congress and quickly confirmed by the Senate. He promptly contracted with one of the nationwide accounting firms to conduct the first annual audit of the Bank. He revised Bank policy to allow interest rates to reach market levels, thereby eliminating the unlegislated subsidy to the large money center banks. He halted the huge monthly purchase of Treasury bonds conducted to enable uncontrolled spending by the federal government.

On a totally different front, Dobbins suspended several executive orders and unilateral regulations pending a full review by Congress. In a meeting with leaders of the House and Senate, he asked members to draft a balanced budget based on the common ground between all parties. Within weeks, the first balanced budget in decades was overwhelmingly passed by Congress, with strong bipartisan support.

Dobbins's new Secretary of State met with China's Ambassador, Liu Sheng, to negotiate the return of Yellowstone National Park. As an inducement to avoid a confrontation, Congress appropriated funds to repay the Chinese twice the amount of the original interest. After much wrangling, the Chinese agreed, handing President Dobbins his first victory in international affairs.

Within days the Chinese vacated the park, clearing the way for a military inspection team to verify that offensive military construction was underway. They reported the Chinese were building a missile defense system as well as hangars for military aircraft. China's ambitious plans for an American military base evaporated.

Finally, Dobbins suspended all foreign aid either in the form of weapons, medicine, or money to anti-American regimes and freedom fighters. This included the many Arab Spring organizations in Egypt, Syria, and Lebanon with known ties to ISIS, Al Qaeda, Boko Haram, Hamas, and Hezbollah.

Dobbins set up an interagency group to work with Governor Kelley's commission on a comprehensive review of all executive orders. Executive Order 14900 was immediately rescinded and the enemies list was destroyed.

The Federal Statutory and Regulatory Commission forged ahead with media reform. Hearings were held on all existing media outlets. Each received a chance to comply with the new Constitutional requirement for fair and unbiased reporting. Two major news organizations, the American News System and the Sphinx News Network, voluntarily endorsed the Journalism Tenets.

Several outlets refused and threatened lawsuits. The commission wasn't intimidated, knowing that the Convention resolutions trumped other statutes. Outlets refusing to comply with the *Tenets* would be required to cover the cost of litigation without the benefit of revenue. Their license to broadcast the news would be revoked, or in the case of cable news outlets, the license they now needed to cover the news would not be issued. The "Fifth Branch of Government" was yanked out by its roots.

CHAPTER 42

—

For the first time since his meteoric rise to power, Jerome Elliott was no longer the "anointed one." In fact, without either citizenship or a visa, he faced life after the presidency as an undocumented alien. The likely prospect of criminal indictments compounded tensions within his family and raised the specter of huge legal expenses. Concerned about their ability to prevail in court, his legal team issued a formal request to Jack Tanner for leniency. Tanner's response was harsh and visceral. "The relatives of the thirty civilians and the nearly one hundred and seventy young soldiers who were killed in Madison deserve more consideration than our unrepentant former president."

While Jerome faced indictment, Kianna and the girls faced constant disgrace. They couldn't watch TV or read a newspaper without suffering additional indignation. Seeing no other choice, the former First Lady pulled her children out of school and moved them back to Illinois. Boston news outlets reported that she purchased a home even though her husband already owned one there. Elliott watchers mourned the fracture of what had previously been viewed as a model First Family.

Jerome complained bitterly to anyone who would listen. His wife got the worst of it. "How could the people turn someone like Jack Tanner loose on their president?"

"If you had acted more responsibly instead of considering everyone either a friend or an enemy based on their political persuasion, they probably wouldn't have," Kianna said.

His wife's raw honesty further irritated the former president. "First Dennis, then Mitch, and now you."

Kianna stood her ground with eyes blazing. "Grow up, Jerome. You surrounded yourself with spineless people who told you what you wanted to hear. You brought in counselors who did everything except provide sound advice. And where did all that loyalty lead? It enabled your worst behavior and convinced you that you know what's best for everyone else. It's time to accept the fact that America did just fine before you came along, and it will do fine without your divine guidance. You messed up big-time, Jerome. Face it and deal with it!"

The United States was moving forward, and so was former President Elliott. He accepted his wife's harsh advice and abandoned his legal defenses. As his driver exited the Potomac River Parkway onto G Street toward Foggy Bottom and then north toward George Washington University, memories of his days as president flooded back. He had traveled these same roads hundreds of times, accompanied by a full complement of staffers and Secret Service agents. Today he was alone and on the run.

The Lincoln Town Car provided by his legal firm could not match the comfort or amenities of the presidential limousine. On the advice of his attorneys, he was traveling to the Mexican embassy to get a passport from his native country. Ironically, the former president now had to obtain his passport with the same Mexican birth certificate that precipitated his downfall. He cursed the United Nations for the millionth time. His lawyers had already filed all the necessary paperwork on his behalf, so he only had to sign for and claim the document. In another twist of irony, he would sign for the passport with the same pen he had used to sign Executive Order 14900.

Elliott spoke his native language for the first time in many years when he was handed his new passport. "Gracias," he said.

He was fleeing the country he had once ruled. The ultimate irony, however, and the one that weighed most heavily on him, was the enormous secret he was taking with him.

CHAPTER 43

—

Anticipation gripped Sam Buchannan's new reporter, Nicole Marcel, as her taxi approached the ornate marble building on Constitution Avenue that served as the United States District Courthouse. She gazed at the passing hallmarks of government—a government embroiled in transition.

The ocean of news trucks clogging the streets around central Washington, DC signaled an epic event. The work of the Constitutional Convention, called by a majority of states to reign in a corrupt federal government, was finished. The country's attention now focused on Jack Tanner, The People's Judge Advocate, a permanent special prosecutor empowered by the Convention to try federal officials for illegal conduct. For the first time in history, the American people could hold their president and other political officials accountable in a court of law, in the same way the government holds every citizen accountable. Today the country would have its day in court. Would it emerge with renewed confidence in the future, or continue its freefall into political mayhem?

Still a few blocks from the courthouse, Nicole wiggled to get comfortable in the sagging back seat. The aging cab lurched from one pothole to the next, rattling with each impact. Its worn suspension did little to soften the ride. The antiseptic smell of a cheap air freshener added to her discomfort. A couple of sneezes prompted her to crack the window, being careful not to disturb her picture-perfect French braid. It was styled to project a professional image following hints from colleagues that her striking good looks were often a distraction. With her long wavy hair, exotic emerald eyes, and sculpted physique, she was Salacia in a sea of media personalities.

Her sneezes caught the attention of the cabbie, who craned his neck to check out her curves in his rearview mirror. Her skirt crept up slightly, exposing her long lithe legs, pumping for leverage against the stubborn window crank. The cabby's dark eyes filled the mirror like two chunks of coal, darting between the stop-and-go traffic and the captivating image behind him. Her magnetism was irresistible.

"Hello, Ms. Blackburn," the cabbie said, recognizing his favorite news personality. "You are even lovelier in person than on TV. Everyone is looking forward to your coverage this evening." His gaze followed every move as she slid over behind the passenger seat for better eye contact.

Though slightly unkempt, the driver struck her as kind and non-threatening. A foreign accent complemented his perfect English. A few more gyrations and the window was up to shut out the noise. While she nonchalantly straightened her skirt, her eyes cast an enchanting spell in the mirror. "Thank you," she said, flashing her award-winning smile. "This is my first assignment since moving to the American News Service from TNN, so naturally I'm a bit nervous. By the way, my name is Marcel now, not Blackburn."

Prompted by a twinge of embarrassment, the cabbie apologized for his gaff. "Sorry, I didn't know," he said, still mesmerized. "As for being nervous, there's no need. Your previous reports on the Elliot administration were masterpieces."

"You're too kind," she said with a slight blush that highlighted her fair complexion. She slumped back in the sagging seat with her head tilted toward the window, gazing beyond the granite and limestone buildings. Her cabbie wasn't the only one with high expectations. She sighed heavily, knowing the eyes of the world would be following her coverage of this important event. The daunting pressure to come up with another masterpiece weighed heavily on her. She knew all too well that there is no resting on laurels in the TV news business. With millions of dollars in advertising revenue at stake, ratings were her master.

Only one other reporter could match her ratings. Thanks to his own scoops on corruption in the Elliott administration, Luke Harper had scored unprecedented ratings for TNN's political bureau. Now that he was gone, her only competition was her own expectations. And that was a much higher bar.

The cabbie hoped he'd been able to reassure her. Like the rest of her faithful viewers, he had followed her steady rise in the cutthroat arena of television journalism. At an age when most reporters were still understudies, Nicole had been recruited by TNN from a big three network affiliate in Indianapolis. There she enjoyed wide popularity as an aggressive, yet personable, investigative reporter. Her celebrity status blossomed at TNN, earning her a weekend co-anchor chair with Bob Blackburn, a veteran newsman ten years her senior.

Bob became hopelessly smitten with his popular, attractive new co-chair. Following a whirlwind courtship, he proposed over a candlelight dinner at De Lafayette, a popular Cajun and Creole restaurant. Romantic lighting and Middle Eastern music provided a mystical setting in Le Marque, a dining room set aside for celebrity patrons like Nicole and Bob.

The hostess led them to a semi-private table far in the back. Fresh cut roses and aromatic candles in elegant sterling holders graced their table.

"This is gorgeous," Nicole swooned from her seat facing Bob.

"Nothing is more gorgeous than the honored guest at this table," Bob said, throwing a kiss.

A sampling of jambalaya and crawfish étouffée with a bottle of 1999 Château Lafite Rothschild was served. "Save some room for dessert," Bob said. "Some of my relatives in Baton Rouge eat dessert first because life is so unpredictable."

"I don't think anything can top the main course," Nicole said. But she was mistaken.

Bob had gone all out on the menu. The waiters brought a platter covered with beignets, pralines, and smooth banana pudding. The selection was topped off with a steaming hot carafe of chicory coffee with whipped cream and fresh honey.

Nicole had gotten a hint of what it's like to be Cajun. "You're going to have to roll me out of here, Bob."

While she munched on a praline, he lowered himself onto one knee next to the linen-covered table, caressing the piece de resistance in his pocket. At a cost of his entire annual bonus, only Nicole's effusive charm matched the grandeur of the one-carat mine-cut diamond in a vintage platinum setting. Bob blinked nervously while his heart raced. He didn't want to ruin what had so far been a perfect evening. Droplets of perspiration from his right hand seeped into the fine linen tablecloth. Without arousing suspicion, he pulled his napkin over the unsightly wet spot. Like an animated Statue of Liberty, he thrust the dazzling ring upward toward her. "Nicole, will you marry me?"

Twinkling in the candlelight, the large diamond commanded everyone's attention.

Nicole's arm dropped onto the table, crushing her half-eaten praline. Her eyes darted around the spellbound crowd before locking on Bob's outstretched hand. Teetering off guard, she hesitated while the brilliant diamond worked its magic. Despite her misgivings about Bob's flirtatious personality and his free-wheeling outlook on the world, the diamond cast a one-carat spell. Before she had thought it through, she accepted Bob's theatrical proposal to the rousing approval of the crowd. "Yes, I'll marry you," she said.

Accepting the answer as an unmitigated yes, Bob sprang up, nearly upsetting the table. "Dom Perignon for everyone," he shouted to seal the deal. Le Marque erupted into a lively round of applause.

Shortly after their wedding, the newlyweds were summoned to Carter Haynes's office. Their rough-hewn, overbearing news chief stood to motion toward two chairs. With a strained expression, he cut to the chase. "I'm afraid we have to make some assignment changes."

The two glanced at each other, anxious about what was coming. Nicole nudged Bob for reassurance, but only got a shrug.

Haynes held up a memo with bold TNN letterhead. "The company's Vice President for Administration has pointed out that we are violating the company's policy against married employees working together. When you signed your contracts, you accepted company policy and I'm expected to enforce it." A copy of the exact wording of the prohibition lay on Haynes's desk. He chose not to read it.

"But weekend ratings have never been higher," Bob said. "We turned that dead time slot into a plum for the company."

"That's why we're keeping you on the anchor desk and replacing Nicole with Victoria Moretti from the morning cooking show. She's attractive and smart. We're hoping the formula that worked with you and Nicole will work with you and Victoria."

Choosing to ignore Haynes's unfortunate choice of words, Nicole leaned forward with laser-like focus. "And me?"

Haynes sat back in his chair with his arms folded, hoping to avoid an outright row. "We're moving you to the political beat where we can capitalize on your proven investigative skills."

"Will she be working with Harper?" Bob asked. Though elated to keep his prime assignment, he wasn't happy about Nicole working with TNN's dashing political superstar. Luke Harper's maverick streak drove conformists like

Bob crazy. He felt threatened by Harper in the same way two alpha males are naturally wary of each other.

"I wish we had other options," Haynes said. "But the decision has already been made upstairs."

With their celebrity egos bruised and Bob becoming wary of the plan, the duo stormed out of Haynes's office. Bob shuffled along with his hands in his pockets, head bowed. "How do you feel about this?" he asked. "I'm ticked."

"I need time to sort it out," she said, suppressing her intrigue over the prospect of teaming with Luke. "We can discuss it later."

Secure in the solitude of her private office, Nicole embraced her true feelings about working with a brilliant journalist like Luke Harper. Unlike Bob, Luke's aggressive style could push her hard enough to help her grow. A little competition might be exciting. With no time like the present to coronate their new partnership, she checked her directory and dialed his number. "Hello, Luke. This is your new partner."

"Nicole? Sounds like you just got a big promotion."

"The jury's still out on that," she said. "Nevertheless, I look forward to working with you."

"Same here. And don't take the change too hard. I've been moved dozens of times. I have to admit though, I've never been replaced by a cook."

Nicole tried to forget that she lost her anchor seat to Victoria Moretti, host of the morning cooking show. She winced from the jab. "I've been warned not to expect any coddling from you."

"Good journalism always trumps good behavior," he said.

"Your brash style obviously works with your viewers." *Is there really room in this new partnership for the two of us, plus his ego? She wondered.*

Over time, Luke's charm cast a spell on Nicole, too. Daily exposure to his populist ideals convinced her that the news is much bigger than those who make it, and even greater than those inflated egos who report it. Their collaboration on controversial and often un-cleared stories earned them reputations as rogue reporters, often placing them on shaky footing with management. Their blockbuster reports exposing the sinister side of the Elliott administration earned them a cult-like viewer following, but branded them inconvenient superstars at TNN.

In an effort to pull the irreverent pair into line, Haynes began giving

Nicole remote assignments. At first he sent her on domestic stories, then diverted her to international politics. Her frequent absence enabled Bob to revert to his wild ways, leading to hints from Nicole's friends that he was getting too cozy with his new co-anchor. Realizing that she should have heeded her initial misgivings, Nicole hired a private investigator who confirmed that Bob was, in fact, having an affair with Victoria Moretti. Infuriated by his betrayal, she immediately filed for divorce and reacquired her maiden name, Nicole Marcel. Determined to put the dismal episode behind her, she pursued her career with renewed vigor, setting herself up as an integral player in one of the most important episodes in the country's history.

Soon after her divorce, Nicole received an unexpected call from WJXT news, TNN's staunchest competitor. Their fair and balanced news coverage consistently beat TNN in the Nielsen ratings during primetime programming.

"Ms. Blackburn, my name is Sam Buchannan. I'm the president of WJXT. Do you have a moment to chat?"

She took a quick sip of coffee to recover from her surprise. "My name is Nicole Marcel now, Mr. Buchannan. What can I do for you?"

"I apologize for being so presumptuous, Ms. Marcel, but would it be convenient for you to have coffee with me this morning? You'll want to hear what I have to say."

Intrigued by the prospect of meeting a renowned media icon and curious about why a competitor wanted to talk, she agreed. "I do have time and I'd love to have coffee with you."

"I have a car waiting for you outside your building. The driver will bring you to my office."

"Presumptuous maybe, Mr. Buchannan, but you don't waste time for sure."

"I didn't get where I am by being timid," he said. "And I don't think you did either. Thank you for agreeing to meet on such short notice."

Within twenty minutes, she was pushing a button in the elevator of WJXT's ultra-modern office building. A monument of glass and marble, the building screamed "important business takes place here."

Catching her reflection in the polished chrome elevator door, she pulled out her ever-present Chanel compact. In one sweeping motion she checked her hair, then her makeup. A couple of adjustments to her mascara with a fingertip moistened on her tongue, she snapped the lid shut just as the dinging elevator arrived at the top floor. As soon as the door slid open, she was greeted by Buchannan's secretary who unceremoniously ushered her into his office.

Her eyes gravitated to the framed awards and photos of Buchannan shaking hands with various dignitaries. Prominently placed on one wall behind a large wooden desk was a photo of Buchannan and President Ronald Reagan. Walking closer to the photo, she was able to make out the inscription that read, "Sam, Keep the Faith. Ronnie."

"Please have a seat over here, Ms. Marcel," Buchannan said. Nicole took a seat in the comfy-looking sitting area with Corinthian-covered furniture and a rustic hatch cover coffee table. "Even these tired old eyes see why everyone is so taken with you."

Accustomed to compliments about her appearance, she let the remark slide. The equally pleasing aromas of expensive leather and freshly brewed coffee tantalized her nostrils.

With the finesse of a veteran host, Buchannan poured steaming coffee into a white china cup displaying a WJXT logo. "Luke tells me you like your coffee with cream and sugar."

His deep brawny voice jarred her from her aroma induced trance. Wrapping her long graceful fingers around the cup, she said, "So you know Luke Harper?"

"Know him?" he scoffed. "I practically raised him in this business. Luke came to work for me when he was a young pup straight out of Syracuse. He stayed for eight good years until Carter Haynes lured him away with an outrageous signing bonus and a fairy tale about unfettered journalistic freedom at TNN."

She raised a perfectly plucked eyebrow. "Sounds familiar. I swallowed the same bogus pitch."

Buchannan's hearty chuckle reminded her of her beloved grandfather. As a child she would spend hours on Grandpa Marcel's lap listening to him reminisce about the old country. With a pair of suspenders to hold his baggy pants over his generous belly, a mop of wispy white hair, and a kind round face, Buchannan would have passed for nearly anyone's grandfather. She would soon learn, however, that his disheveled appearance belied his razor-sharp wit and considerable influence.

"I'm thinking you didn't bring me here to talk about Luke Harper's career." She said, pausing with regret over her unbridled impatience.

Buchannan paused, too, sizing up his precocious young guest. "No, I didn't, and I apologize for delving into the past. I thought it might give you comfort knowing that Luke and I are friends."

"That's insightful, Mr. Buchannan. Anyone who's a friend of Luke's is okay with me. But I'm surprised he never mentioned you in that way." Her reply suggested that she might view Luke as more than a mere co-worker.

Buchannan glossed over the subtle inference. "Well, it's sad to say, but there's a degree of guilt by association in this business. Journalists are group thinkers; they generally follow the pack. We are considered outsiders here at WJXT because we don't tow the consonant line. Luke probably feared he'd be held back if Carter Haynes knew he was still friendly with the likes of me. 'Loose lips sink ships,' a widely used Navy slogan during World War II, is one of the first things I taught him about this business."

She leaned forward to add some cream to her coffee, her bright eyes sparkling. "That's not really how I think of Luke. Loose in some ways, maybe, but certainly not loose-lipped."

Buchannan nodded. "Anyway, I need to get to the reason for bringing you here. As you know, this country is going through a tumultuous period. We have a president who won two elections quite simply because his campaign put out an unprecedented amount of misinformation. The campaign was consciously aided by a celebrity-worshipping and biased media."

"Yes, I know that," she said.

"This president does not view America as a great country, he does not share the same patriotic feelings as most Americans, and he does not believe in capitalism. He paused to catch his breath and take a sip of coffee. *Hope I'm not laying it on too thick,* he thought. "Please bear with me, Ms. Marcel. I'm getting to my point."

She couldn't resist interrupting. "Excuse me, Mr. Buchannan. I agree with what you've said so far. But how does all of that relate to the reason I'm here?"

Without acknowledging the question, he pushed on. "Things started unraveling for the president this past year. Taking his lead from a banana republic playbook, he set out to break the back of his opposition. When the military failed to shut the Convention down, he deployed a Gestapo-type police force to round up the delegates and intern them in federal camps. He callously approved a hit list of political opponents, then authorized the use of deadly force to neutralize them. Several expert psychiatrists now characterize him as a pathological narcissist who will preserve his power at any cost.

She caught herself unconsciously tapping her foot. Placing her cup on the table, she apologized. "Sorry. Too much caffeine this morning."

To her relief, Buchannan barely noticed and continued unfazed. "So here we sit, Ms. Marcel. After six long years under this corrupt president, the people have revolted. While the Constitutional Convention weighed the best course of action to counteract our plight, the House of Representatives introduced articles of impeachment to remove Elliott from office. Despite plummeting public support, media outlets continued to defend the administration."

Buchannan's monologue outlined what she already knew. Nevertheless, she humored him, sitting attentively, nodding her head now and then to signal her agreement.

The long exposé ended with some prophecy. "The Constitutional Convention is bringing drastic changes to the federal government. More relevant to you and me are the sweeping changes coming for the news business. Cable and broadcast outlets, as well as the print media, are in for a rude awakening."

Her foot no longer tapping, Nicole sat spellbound by the dramatic build up. She wasn't fully prepared for the denouement.

"I don't think all of the details have been worked out yet," he said. "But the new Statutory and Regulatory Review Commission, set up by the Convention to reform the government, is implementing new media guidelines called the Journalism Tenets. Those guidelines will replace the abandoned Fairness Doctrine to prevent bias in the media."

With the drama of the moment rising, Nicole leaned closer to hear his stunning climax. "I have it on irrefutable authority that a new national news organization will be formed and I will be appointed to lead it. I'd like you to join me as my senior White House correspondent."

Nicole sat dumbstruck. *Did he just offer me a prime position in his new organization?* She groped for the appropriate response, but everything that came to her mind seemed inadequate. Though her career had already exceeded her wildest dreams, this step would place her among the crème de la crème in the industry.

Buchannan tempted her with flattery. "Luke praised your reporting on the President's plan to raid the Convention. This country needs more objectivity and integrity in the news business. That won't happen unless we give a platform to principled journalists like yourself, while sending the news charlatans and propagandists into other lines of business."

"Apparently those charlatans and propagandists have labeled you an insurrectionist," she said. "What drove you to such odds with the industry?"

"It's a pretty involved story. Are you sure you want to hear it?"

"I'm in the story business, Mr. Buchannan. Please continue."

"It all started when Texas Governor Clay Granger invited me to address the Constitutional Convention on ethics in the media," Buchannan said. "At the time, I wondered what an old newsman with high blood pressure could contribute to the monumental task facing the delegates."

"Out of all the media people, why you?" she asked.

Buchannan's face brightened. "Granger knew that as a graduate student at the Marquette University School of Journalism, I had researched the so-called Fairness Doctrine, which was designed to keep news fair and unbiased. Concluding that the doctrine had not been either fair or effective, I wrote my thesis on an alternative, called the Journalism Tenets. It outlined a series of reforms to correct bias in news reporting. When I became the president of WJXT, I implemented the *Tenets*, a move widely credited with making us the premier news source in Washington, DC. We're known best for our unprecedented accuracy in reporting. Governor Granger noted our success and wondered if the delegates at the Convention would be interested in applying the *Tenets* universally."

"How did you get from there to here?" she asked.

"It's a long story, but if you're up for it, I'd be happy to tell you," Buchannan said.

"Absolutely," Nicole replied. "If I learned anything at all from Luke Harper, it's the value of a good story." Nicole sat back in her seat and relaxed.

"I first met Jack Tanner at Texas Governor Clay Granger's sprawling ranch near Temple, Texas. Clay and I were enjoying a cool drink by the pool when Jack arrived. The most notable thing about him, other than his infectious smile, was the aura that he knew something important that no one else did. I remember he exuded a rare combination of humility and confidence. And that grip was like a vice.

"When Jack suggested we dispense with formalities, I knew we were going to be good friends. In retrospect, it was the beginning of one of the most consequential alliances in modern politics.

"Early in the meeting we got a glimpse of Tanner's character. When Clay asked him if he liked bourbon, he set off a round of chuckles when he answered, 'Only Monday through Sunday.'

"Clay and I were caught off guard when Tanner asked us why we invited him. When I asked him if he had been briefed on the Convention, he explained that he understood a People's Commission was being considered. Other than that, he said he had been overseas and out of touch.

"Clay and I proceeded to fill him in on our progress at the Convention and the administration's response. We explained that at first the government wasn't too concerned because they thought we were only going to come up with an amendment or two. When they realized our intent to severely reign in the government's authority, they pushed back hard."

"How?" Nicole asked.

"They elevated arm twisting and coercion to a whole new level. The thirty-four states that supported the Convention were threatened with a cut off of federal funds. Homeland Security began intimidating the most outspoken governors. We had some tense stare downs between DHS agents and State Police security details. Ironically, on July 3rd, the day before Independence Day, the President warned all thirty-four governors that he would oppose the Convention at all cost."

"I'm guessing a direct threat from Washington didn't sit well with the governors," Nicole said.

"You bet. The threat roared through statehouses like a polar vortex," Buchannan continued. "Each opposition governor blocked the President's attempt to mobilize their Guard units, fearing that such a move would render them virtually defenseless. All the adjutants, except one, pledged allegiance to their governor. At his governor's urging, that recalcitrant commander retired and was promptly replaced. Those Guard companies were essential for Convention security in and around Austin."

"How did Tanner react to your briefing?" Nicole asked, mentally building another masterpiece.

"We knew from his demeanor that he had a clear picture. He asked where things stood presently. Clay explained how bacon and eggs fit into breakfast."

Nicole sensed something special was coming. "How do they?"

"Well, the pig and the chicken both have an important stake in the meal, but only the pig is fully committed. We were committed like the pig, with no turning back!"

CHAPTER 44

Reflections of her conversation with Buchannan months earlier brought Nicole great pride in being the lead political reporter for the new American News Service. Now covering the epic Tanner Hearing, she would get this story exactly right, proving to herself and to Buchannan that his faith in her was completely justified.

Nicole's focus returned to the hearing as the cab made its last turn from Magnolia onto Constitution Avenue. She pulled out her compact. Her makeup was subtle, yet expertly applied, based on years serving as a canvas for network makeup artists. With her customary good luck wink, she snapped it shut and pulled out a crumpled ten dollar bill.

"That will be seventeen dollars," the cabbie said. Before she could object, he defended the charge. "I know it sounds high, Ms. Marcel, but gas was five dollars a gallon this morning. If I don't make two hundred dollars on fares today, I'll be out of business. I have a wife and five kids to look after."

Bolstered by an American News Service expense account, she handed him a twenty, then gingerly stepped onto the curb a block from the courthouse.

"Bless you Ms. Marcel. Good luck with your story," he yelled, speeding away to search for his next fare. One last look in the rearview brought a smile.

Rows of extended satellite dishes, resembling a field of enormous robotic sunflowers, lined both sides of the street. They all pointed skyward toward the orbiting TransCom VI satellite to upload breaking news to their respective studios. Miles of cables led from the tangled maze to the courthouse steps.

Nicole picked her way through the maze, taking care to avoid eye contact with former colleagues passing by, most of whom coveted her new position. Few were there in any official capacity, having lost their press credentials when the Journalism Tenets were enacted. They were relying on the insistence of their political handlers that the new Statutory and Regulatory Review Commission, commonly referred to as the People's Commission, would not dare arrest a journalist for doing his or her job.

But Nicole knew differently. Bob Blackburn, her ex-husband and current TNN anchor, had been arrested a few days earlier for characterizing the Tanner Hearing as a witch hunt without proper justification or authority. Bob had called her from jail, begging her to ask Buchannan to lobby for his release. She'd adamantly refused, fearing such a blatant request would raise questions about her commitment to journalistic reform, while risking her relationship with her new boss. Besides, she still owed Bob for cheating on her while she was on assignment in Argentina.

She neared the courthouse annex, a large auditorium set up like a theater for public hearings and other events. Tanner's staff had chosen this facility because of its unusual capacity. Two reporters could be heard chatting a few steps away. "She was Buchannan's first hire at ANS. What makes her so special, other than the obvious?"

Shaking the discomfort of being in the spotlight before the show had even started, she forced a detached smile and pulled a bottle of water from her briefcase. A few refreshing sips calmed her nerves, allowing her thoughts to drift. *Who was this mysterious man upon whom the Convention had bestowed so much power?* Buchannan had glossed over Tanner's background. *What qualifies him to pass judgment on the most powerful politicians in America, including the president?*

She cleared the top step, conscious that her tailored Anne Klein suit and new Ralph Lauren heels made a profound fashion statement. She paused to relieve pressure on blisters created by her new heels. While reaching for the railing, she flinched from a hand on her shoulder.

"Hi there, Nicole. Are you here for ANS, or are you freelancing?"

The smell of menthol cigarettes and the sarcastic tone of Carter Haynes, her former boss at TNN, rankled her. He was the last person she wanted to bump into on this important first assignment with ANS. Already irritated from her blisters, she turned to face him.

Clenching a cigarette in his nicotine-stained teeth, Haynes took a deep drag, causing the ash to flare, crackle, and simmer. "How did you get hired so fast, when the rest of us can't even get an interview?" Smoke spiraled into his reddened eyes as he spoke. He blinked, then turned his head sideways to avoid further stinging.

Nicole took a step backward, beyond the range of the smoke. "Buchannan hired me about the time you were threatening to fire me."

"Why would that old news hound want a young reporter to cover such an important event?"

She snatched the golden opportunity to take issue with her old boss. "Because I'm accurate, unbiased, reliable, and I've never made public excuses for the administration's failures. Tell me, Carter. When was the last time you did a totally objective political report?"

His eyes narrowed. "You know that's not the job of a cable news commentator. Besides, it's a lot more invigorating to embrace the news than to report it." He snickered and flicked his cigarette into the air.

Nicole stiffened as ashes drifted slowly toward her expensive shoes. "Maybe the next time I see you, you can tell me how invigorating it is to embrace your status as another unemployed, biased cable news commentator. Meantime, I have a deadline to meet."

Shaking the humiliation of being dressed down by a former subordinate, he lit another cigarette. The chrome flask in his hip pocket would soothe his bruised ego before he shuffled off to his seat in the spectator section of the courtroom annex.

Nicole's reserved seat, on the other hand, was strategically placed just below the podium in the front row. The gold American News Service logo emblazoned on the back symbolized the elite status of its occupant. As she approached the front of the room, her phone buzzed.

A strong, deep voice boomed. "Hi, gorgeous. Check out the balcony."

Glancing up, she caught Luke Harper's mop of curly brown hair towering above everyone else.

He waved his long muscular arms, then placed his phone to his ear. "Does anyone here hail from Mount Airy?" From the time they met, he kidded her about being a hayseed. She never minded though, since both shared the benefits of growing up in small town rural America, where dedication to faith, family, and country were still core values.

"You're not looking for another favor, are you?" she asked.

He scanned the seats that were quickly filling. "Heck no. My pass for special favors expired when Carter fired me."

The chance encounter had sent her spirits soaring. She took a quick sip from her water bottle.

With a few long strides, Luke vaulted down the stairs toward her, his deep blue eyes and Robert Redford smile illuminating the room. His pleated corduroy pants, loose vest, and vintage fedora projected an image of a college student more than the country's best-known ex-journalist. Reaching her in the front of the room, he wrapped his long arms around her for a bear hug. She felt the need for another dose of water, but couldn't get to it.

"Make my day, Nicole. Flash one of your million-dollar, prime-time smiles."

She wiggled slightly, feigning an effort to get free. Luke's presence defined the moment. Engulfed in his warm embrace, her thoughts drifted out of bounds.

With blind exuberance, Luke ventured there, too. "What in the world possessed you to waste these hugs on that loser Bob Blackburn? By the way, how is old Bob?"

She turned her head and looked away. "He's ancient history, Luke. Let's not go there."

Spurred by her obvious embarrassment, he changed the subject. He had already opened a still-painful wound. "Did you know I'm partially responsible for your job at ANS?"

Her eyes ignited with natural playfulness. "I know you're totally responsible for getting a lot of people, including Carter, fired at TNN. That soundbite of President Elliott calling George Washington a traitor was awesome. How do you get that stuff?"

"Like Casey Stengel once said, 'I'd rather be lucky than good.' And having a little moxie helps."

"I'm thinking humility is not required," she said. "Why don't you join us at ANS? Like everyone else, Buchannan was impressed with your work at the Convention. He might even get you a chair with our ANS logo on the back." She sat down, crossed her legs, and pulled her Anne Klein skirt up slightly to add some extra appeal.

Basking in her not-so-subtle gesture, he said, "Now that's how to dress up a chair."

Noticing that Luke was not the only one enjoying her pose, she rose and echoed her plea. "Come on, Luke. Don't you want to work with me again? Give Sam a call. I know he'd love to hear from you."

Picking up on her flirtation, he gently grasped her hand. "I'll admit, it's tempting now that you're single. But people like Carter keep warning me about going to the dark side. They say ANS is more interested in anti-government activism than journalism.'"

"That's a clear case of the pot calling the kettle black," she said. "I'll take Carter's rebuke as a badge of honor." Though she secretly wanted to spend more time visiting, duty called. "Sorry, but I have to get ready. When will I see you again?"

"Actually, I have a security job that will keep me close by. It pays fairly well, and I have a lot of flexibility."

She smiled broadly, her exotic eyes fixed on Luke. "Flexibility is right up your alley, Luke. It's clear your new employer didn't talk to Carter, who would've warned them to keep you on a short leash."

He absorbed the jab with good humor, accepting that his own behavior had rubbed off on his ex-partner. "My new boss only cares that I'm on time every day. I guess I'll see your bright sunny smile for the duration. By the way, how long do you think the hearing will take?"

She glanced at the stage to check for any sign of activity. A couple of aides milling around with last-minute arrangements gave her some breathing room. "Buchannan told me to be available for the entire week."

Casting his eyes downward, he shuffled his left shoe. "I've heard Tanner won't last that long."

"Don't say things like that," she snapped. "Tensions are high enough without people spreading inflammatory gossip."

He recoiled slightly. "I'm just repeating talk on the street."

"It's still rubbish," she said. "I'm surprised you even listen to your informers, since you can't use what they give you."

"If nothing else, their stuff is entertaining," he said. "Besides, after what's happened, their conspiracy theories are no longer stranger than reality."

Still conflicted, she mimed the time-out signal. "Please, Luke, I have to go." Her dreamy gaze said otherwise.

Tearing himself away, he sauntered back toward the balcony, casting a departing wink over his shoulder.

She settled gracefully into her seat, removing one shoe, then the other. She regretted the decision to break them in on this assignment. Rubbing her tender heels didn't help much.

An eerie tension permeated the room like a dense moist fog. *Is this how it felt at Nuremburg?* she wondered. The thought of Hermann Göring and Rudolph Hess testifying on the inhumanities of the Third Reich sent chills down her spine. The unsettling thought was pre-empted when an impish bald aide in an ill-fitted suit approached the podium. His pudgy index finger tapped the mike. *Thump, thump, thump.* The gesture quieted the crowd, drawing everyone's attention to the front of the room. An antiquated air conditioning system emitted a rhythmic hum as it struggled to neutralize the heat from the overflow crowd.

Nicole booted up her tablet and typed "Show Time."

Backstage, Jack Tanner carefully reviewed his cryptic notes. His challenge was to strike the right balance between holding offenders accountable while assuring the public that the United States was once again a country of laws instead of political ideology run amuck.

There simply was no easy path to carry out the work of the People's Judge Advocate. The awesome responsibility weighed heavily on him. At the same time, his new role struck fear in the hearts of government officials who had abused their power and were expecting impunity. Members of the Elliott administration's inner circle now faced judgement, just like Göring and Hess.

Tanner stood erect and headed for the stage.

CHAPTER 45

——

Nicole's patience was nearly exhausted after waiting two hours for the hearing to begin. Luke Harper had brought her a vegetarian wrap and a bottle of juice for a snack. The two reminisced about the old days at TNN while waiting for the big moment. A few minutes after Luke left to resume his security duties, the bald staffer returned to the mike to do another sound check. "Testing, testing, testing, one, two, three, four. Can you hear me in the back?"

"You're good. Get on with it," Luke yelled from the balcony.

As laughter erupted, the staffer clumsily clawed his retreat through a break in the curtain.

Seconds later Tanner strolled onto the stage accompanied by Texas Governor Clay Granger. Thunderous applause greeted the pair. Now one of the most recognizable men in the world, Granger was generally considered a leading candidate, along with President Dobbins, in the upcoming presidential race. Both were wildly popular.

Granger took the microphone while Tanner scanned the crowd. "Thank you, thank you. Please be seated. Thanks again," he said. Cameras flashed as people slowly returned to their seats.

"Thank you, everyone. My name is Clay Granger. I am the Governor of Texas and past chairman of the Constitutional Convention. My purpose here today is not to rehash the Convention's outcome, but to introduce one of its unsung heroes."

The crowd resumed its spontaneous applause as photographers jockeyed for position below the stage.

"As you know, Mr. Tanner will report to you on the findings of the Office of the People's Judge Advocate. His focus is on the abuses of The Elliott administration. What you don't know is Mr. Tanner was instrumental in the investigation leading up to Elliott's removal. He was present at the White House when the removal took place. So, without further delay, it gives me great pleasure to introduce Mr. Jack Tanner, the People's Judge Advocate."

As Granger backed away from the podium and Tanner approached the mike, the hall again erupted into thunderous applause. The courtroom lit up with flashing cameras and flashing smiles. Expectations were cosmic.

"Thank you, Governor Granger. Thank you," Tanner said. He motioned for the crowd to be seated. "I want to start today by recognizing Clay Granger as a true national treasure. Through his organization, America Strong, he worked with each of the thirty-four Convention states to introduce Title V authorization bills in their respective legislatures. Without that courageous first step, there would have been no Constitutional Convention and we would not be here today."

Another crescendo swept through the crowd, drawing Granger back to the podium where he shook Tanner's hand.

Granger returned backstage as Tanner stood tall and confident to begin his report. "The formidable task before the Office of the People's Judge Advocate was clearly outlined in the Convention's *Articles of Resolution*. We were charged by the Convention to identify criminal offenses by the Elliott administration, identify those responsible, and recommend the appropriate punishment. My office has assembled some of the best investigators and attorneys available. That team has analyzed every shred of evidence to make an airtight case for the people. I am happy to report to you today that we have concluded our task and are prepared to report on our findings."

After a brief pause for water, he continued. His hand shook slightly under the tremendous weight of his responsibility.

"My office is only authorized to handle criminal violations. The Congress is responsible for investigating issues of malfeasance and mismanagement. I understand the articles of impeachment passed by the House addressed those issues. The Senate was prepared to hold its impeachment trial when the Supreme Court's removal order pre-empted their action."

There was a brief pause in anticipation of Tanner's ultimate findings. The moment of truth had arrived. Nicole sat patiently, her hands prepared to type word-for-word into her tablet.

"In the case of Jerome Elliott, our office found that the former President personally deployed Department of Homeland Security agents to Madison, Georgia, where thirty civilians, including eleven children, were murdered. In addition, he personally ordered the attack on the Georgia National Guard, resulting in the death of seventy guardsmen and one-hundred-and-twenty United States Army soldiers. The encounter also resulted in numerous other casualties on both sides, as well as millions of dollars in property damage. Finally, we found that former President Elliott signed Executive Order 14900 interpreted by DHS to allow the use of deadly force against political opponents.

"We found other actions we consider to be reprehensible, but the above are the most criminal. Based on these findings, all of which are backed up by sworn affidavits and other ironclad evidence, the Office of the People's Judge Advocate has issued a warrant for the arrest of former President Jerome Elliott on charges of manslaughter and conspiracy to commit murder."

A hush fell over the crowd like a gentle spring rain. Attendees looked at each other in disbelief. Some reporters scrambled out to get the announcement on the air. Nicole stopped her feverish typing and turned toward the balcony where Luke listened intently.

Tanner sipped water before resuming his unprecedented report. "We just learned that the warrant for the former President's arrest cannot be served. As we were wrapping up our investigation, he obtained a Mexican passport and on Friday morning crossed over into Mexico on his way to his birthplace in Veracruz."

The unexpected development stirred the crowd as attendees discussed the ramifications.

"Please, please, let me finish," Tanner pleaded. "Companion warrants have been issued for the arrest of former Chief of Staff Mitchell Brady, former Attorney General Dennis Oliver, former Secretary of the Department of Homeland Security Duane Massey, former Secretary of Defense Alex Harrison, and former Chairman of the Joint Chiefs of Staff Bill Ziegler. In a separate action, warrants were issued for Dorothy Caldwell, Secretary of Health and Human Services and several of her subordinates for violating federal contracting laws and regulations in the implementation of the Affordable Health Care Act.

"Brent McMahon, head of the National Security Agency, has been arrested for numerous violations related to the Federal Information Security Act, also known as FISA. All parties at the Internal Revenue Service, both employed and retired, and other agencies who targeted political opponents of the former President, have been indicted. Several members of the former President's White House staff and former Secretary of the Treasury Walter Emerson have been arrested for illegally transferring legacy public lands, specifically Yellowstone National Park, to the Chinese in exchange for absolving United States debt."

Tanner paused for another drink of water. He adjusted his notes and prepared to resume his statement. TV cameramen hustled to make minor adjustments and jockey for a better angle. Reporters who began their commentary at the back of the room were warned not to interrupt the proceeding. As soon as the room settled down, Tanner resumed.

"Those who committed serious abuses under past administrations are not immune from accountability. Additional warrants have been issued for those in the Justice Department who were responsible for the Fast and Furious scandal, or who attempted to cover up evidence. The former Secretary of State and several subordinates have been indicted for manslaughter, gross negligence, and perjury for lying to Congress during oversight hearings."

He paused with an aside to the audience. "By the way, President Dobbins has assured my office that a strong warning has been sent to our adversaries. Any unprovoked aggression against American assets will be met with the full force of our military. Our UN ambassador has notified Iran that any ships that harass our navy will be blown out of the water. The USS *Nimitz*, carrying a full contingent of F-18 Super Hornets and Apache gunships, has been re-routed to the Persian Gulf to keep the Straits of Hormuz open. The United States will no longer be attacked or provoked without devastating consequences."

The crowd applauded for a full minute before the gavel brought everyone to order.

"President Dobbins announced in his news conference that there will never again be unheeded pleas for help by Americans under attack. Al Jazeera immediately reported from Al Qaeda that Dobbins, like Elliott, was too weak to honor such a guarantee. They are mistaken. The President has already instructed General Martinez to use everything in our conventional arsenal to repel such attacks in the future. That order has gone out to all our military bases around the globe. Anyone who threatens U.S. military assets will be aggressively repelled. Just days ago, two Iranian attack boats learned this new policy the hard way as they sunk in the Persian Gulf."

Tanner continued, "There will be critics who claim my office is engaging in a witch hunt as political retribution. Nothing could be more misleading or inconsistent with the facts. The clarion call for former President

Elliott and his followers to be held accountable came from the people. We intend to respond to the people's charge, and will issue additional warrants as required."

Nicole documented every detail.

Tanner was prepared to wrap up the hearing with questions from the floor when a lively discussion distracted him. In one corner of the stage, Tim Kelley and Clay Granger were engaged in an animated discussion. Tanner could tell from the expression on Kelley's face that all was not well.

"Excuse me for a moment, folks," he said. He walked to the corner to see what was going on.

"We need to regroup," Kelley said. "Something's wrong."

Tanner's heart raced at the thought they had somehow messed up. "It's kind of late in the game for that," he whispered.

The more Kelley hesitated, the redder Granger's face became. "Come on Tim, you're killing us here."

Kelley placed his hands on each man's shoulder.

The restless crowd noticed the parlay.

"I just got off the phone with President Dobbins," Kelley said. "He informed me that former Secretary of Defense Harrison and former NSA Director McMahon have joined Elliott in Mexico. Duane Massey was picked up on his way to seek asylum in France."

"What the heck's going on?" Granger mumbled.

"That's not all," Kelley said. "The President has uncovered evidence that things aren't exactly the way they seem and Elliott might have had ulterior motives for his actions. He couldn't say more because information from the intelligence community is sketchy. They did confirm, though, that something extraordinary is happening."

Tanner gave Kelley his now-famous steely-eyed glare. "Are you saying there's something going on that even the President doesn't know about?"

"That's the way it looks. I don't think we can ignore his concern," Kelley said.

"There's no way I can retract what I've already reported here today," Tanner said. "I don't like the way this is going down."

"I don't like it either, Jack," Kelley said. "But we need to remain steady. We're on solid ground with what we've put out so far. There's no question Elliott needed to be removed. But if there are mitigating circumstances for his other actions, we need to know about them."

Tanner glanced out at the increasingly suspicious audience. "Are you suggesting my warrants might be unjustified?"

"We know the former President abused his authority, but it's possible his motives weren't self-driven," Kelley said. "I can't think of a case where that would mitigate his charges, but stranger things have happened."

Tanner nodded toward the crowd. "So, what do we do now?"

The crowd noticed the gesture and started buzzing. Nicole turned to look at Luke. He was already moving toward her.

Kelley glanced at Granger for reassurance. "I suggest we end the hearing until we sort everything out. You're on the tail end anyway."

"I was going to open the floor to questions, then end it," Tanner said.

Kelley nodded. "I think that's okay. Maybe for the time being we should refer to Elliott as a person of interest instead of a fugitive. That gives us some wiggle room until everything is clearer."

"We can do that for semantics, since it wouldn't squash my warrant," Tanner said.

"Is there some way you can slip that reference in?" Granger asked. His expression showed obvious concern.

"With luck, a questioner will give me an opening," Tanner said.

"Give it a whirl, Jack," Kelley said. "We could always pull the warrant later if necessary."

Tanner took a deep breath and wiped his forehead with a tissue before returning to the podium. "I apologize for the delay, folks. As you can imagine, ongoing investigations are constantly evolving."

Nicole noted a distinct change in Tanner's demeanor. She cast Luke, who was now crouched beside her, an inquisitive look.

Luke's instincts cried out. "There's something wrong," he whispered.

"I realize most of you have been here for a long time," Tanner said. "Nevertheless, I want to give you the information you need. We'll devote the rest of this hearing to questions."

Nicole was the first person to step up to one of the microphones strategically placed near the stage. "Mr. Tanner, where is the former First Lady, and what will happen to her?"

Tanner scanned his notes. "Thank you for reminding me of that, Ms. Marcel. Unfortunately we haven't been able to obtain a statement from Mrs. Elliott because her whereabouts are unknown. She was in Boston for a while, but disappeared before we could depose her. Unlike her husband, she and her two daughters are naturalized citizens. Any attempt to join her husband in Mexico would require a passport from the United States, which she has, and a visa from Mexico which she has not obtained." Tanner glanced at Kelley who flashed the okay sign.

"As far as your second question, there is no evidence the former First Lady was complicit in any of her husband's questionable activity."

"Did you catch that, Nicole?" Luke asked. "He said questionable instead of criminal."

"As a matter of fact, we have credible evidence that she was consciously kept in the dark," Tanner continued. "Witnesses say she was outraged when she learned that her husband had jeopardized their family. We will keep everyone posted as more information develops."

Another reporter walked up to a microphone on the opposite side of the room. "Several of us are wondering what will happen to Elliott if he tries to reenter the States."

"That's a good question," Tanner said. "As a fug—, excuse me, person of interest, Mr. Elliott is on every law enforcement and border entry watch list. As soon as his passport is used to reenter the country, the attending authority will hold him until a United States Marshal can take custody. For all intents and purposes, Jerome Elliott is an exile."

"Now he's a person of interest," Luke whispered. His investigative juices were surging.

The questioner remained at the microphone. "A follow-up question, please. Why is former President Elliott a person of interest instead of a fugitive from justice?"

Tanner shifted nervously. "In the interest of transparency, this is a complex investigation that changes from moment to moment. We hope to provide the answer to your question very soon."

Nicole looked down with another confused expression, but Luke had already crept back to the balcony.

After several minutes of enthusiastic questions, and an assurance that the ANS cameraman had a wrap on the story, Nicole stowed her notebook and strolled toward the exit. She had all she needed for the evening news, except answers about Kianna Elliott's whereabouts. Another masterpiece in the works? Maybe.

As she passed under the balcony where Luke was manning his security post, she yelled, "Goodbye, Luke!"

Leaning over the railing, he threw her a kiss. "Bye, gorgeous. I'll call," he yelled back.

"Can't wait," echoed back as Nicole disappeared under the balcony.

The lead for her historic broadcast later that evening was "Government of the people, by the people, and for the people was restored at a federal courthouse in Washington, DC today, but pressing questions remain."

ABOUT THE AUTHOR

—

Gary A. Keel's upbringing in Hope, Indiana, revolved around family, the Moravian Church, and sports. His father, an Eisenhower Republican and decorated World War II veteran, exposed him to politics through hunting trips with local politicians, and discussions during poker games at the local American Legion Hall. His mother, a Great Society/War on Poverty Democrat, exposed him to pressing social issues by taking him on trips into the back woods to introduce the rural poor to social welfare programs.

He enlisted in the military, spending a year in Vietnam where many childhood ideals were challenged. A degree in political science and a graduate degree in Public Administration from Indiana University led to his career with the federal government, where he moved up the hierarchy to executive level positions. He was appointed by Ronald Reagan to a task force designed to set up Inspector Generals throughout the government. When George W. Bush was elected, he was appointed to a political position where he gained an intricate understanding of government.

Milestones in his career included talking to Secretary of State Colin Powell the morning of his infamous WMD speech at the UN, and a discussion with Bono about his philanthropic projects in Africa. He worked with special assistants to Leonid Brezhnev and Nobel Prize winner Lech Walesa on business development programs in Russia and Poland. His work on economic development projects around the world included a geothermal plant in India, sanitary wells in Kenya, and entry-level housing development in South Africa. When NAFTA was adopted, he worked with maquiladoras in Mexico.

The above provided a backdrop for his novel *Executive Order 14900* and its sequels, which together form the compelling *Strife in America* series.

CPSIA information can be obtained
at www.ICGtesting.com
Printed in the USA
FFHW020616060619
52853152-58415FF